PRAISE FOR LEE CHILD'S EXPLOSIVE
NEW YORK TIMES
BESTSELLER

ONE SHOT

"CHILD HAS A GIFT FOR THROWING YOU A CURVE JUST WHEN YOU'VE SEEN IT ALL."
—*Rocky Mountain News*

"*One Shot* is filled with the kind of pulse-pounding action and thrills Child writes with the skill of a master. **REACHER, ONE OF THE MOST POPULAR CHARACTERS IN CONTEMPORARY THRILLERS, IS THE PERFECT HERO** for the action movie audience—loved by women, feared by men and respected by all."
—*Chicago Sun-Times*

"THERE WILL BE PLENTY OF HOT THRILLERS THIS SUMMER . . . BUT ONE OF THE BEST IS SURE TO BE LEE CHILD'S NINTH JACK REACHER NOVEL. *ONE SHOT* IS PURE ADRENALINE, from its well-constructed setup to its explosive, unforgettable finale."　　—*Miami Herald*

"A thrill a minute." —*People* (Best Beach Reads)

"COMPELLING, FURIOUSLY PACED ESCAPIST FICTION that doesn't stint on deduction."
—*Los Angeles Times*

"Thriller lovers can't go wrong." —*Denver Post*

"A vintage double play for author and leading man."
—*Publishers Weekly*

"Opens with a big bang. More accurately six . . . *ONE SHOT* IS APTLY TITLED, FOR IT IS INDEED A ONE SHOT READ."

—*Crimespree Magazine*

"*ONE SHOT* IS WITHOUT QUESTION LEE CHILD'S BEST OUTING WITH PROTAGONIST JACK REACHER IN SEVERAL YEARS. From the opening sniper sequence to the final surprising disclosures about the bad guys, this one crackles with excitement. *One Shot* is a heavily layered story, and Reacher has a lot of digging to do to find the rather surprising truth."

—*St. Petersburg Times*

"If you are looking for a new series, this is one of the best in the thriller genre."

—*Salt Lake Tribune*

"Unraveling and retangling violent narratives is the author's specialty. . . . Reacher—smart, rootless, and brave—will not only get his man but make him suffer."

—*New Yorker*

LEE CHILD
PERSUADER
A JACK REACHER NOVEL

A DELL BOOK

PERSUADER
A Dell Book

PUBLISHING HISTORY
Delacorte Press hardcover edition published May 2003
Dell mass market edition published April 2004
Dell mass market reissue / August 2008

Published by
Bantam Dell
A Division of Random House, Inc.
New York, New York

This is a work of fiction. Names, characters, places, and incidents either are
the product of the author's imagination or are used fictitiously. Any
resemblance to actual persons, living or dead, events, or locales
is entirely coincidental.

Library of Congress Catalog Card Number: 2002034965

Dell is a registered trademark of Random House, Inc.,
and the colophon is a trademark of Random House, Inc.

ISBN: 978-0-440-24505-6

Printed in the United States of America

www.bantamdell..com

OPM   10   9   8   7   6   5   4   3   2

FOR JANE

AND THE SHORE BIRDS

CHAPTER **1**

THE COP CLIMBED OUT OF HIS CAR EXACTLY
four minutes before he got shot. He moved like he knew
his fate in advance. He pushed the door against the resistance of a stiff hinge and swiveled slowly on the worn
vinyl seat and planted both feet flat on the road. Then he
grasped the door frame with both hands and heaved himself up and out. He stood in the cold clear air for a second
and then turned and pushed the door shut again behind
him. Held still for a second longer. Then he stepped forward and leaned against the side of the hood up near the
headlight.

The car was a seven-year-old Chevy Caprice. It was
black and had no police markings. But it had three radio
antennas and plain chrome hubs. Most cops you talk to
swear the Caprice is the best police vehicle ever built.
This guy looked like he agreed with them. He looked like
a veteran plain-clothes detective with the whole of the
motor pool at his disposal. Like he drove the ancient
Chevy because he wanted to. Like he wasn't interested in
the new Fords. I could see that kind of stubborn old-timer
personality in the way he held himself. He was wide and
bulky in a plain dark suit made from some kind of heavy

wool. He was tall but stooped. An old man. He turned his head and looked north and south along the road and then craned his thick neck to glance back over his shoulder at the college gate. He was thirty yards away from me.

The college gate itself was purely a ceremonial thing. Two tall brick pillars just rose up from a long expanse of tended lawn behind the sidewalk. Connecting the pillars was a high double gate made from iron bars bent and folded and twisted into fancy shapes. It was shiny black. It looked like it had just been repainted. It was probably repainted after every winter. It had no security function. Anybody who wanted to avoid it could drive straight across the lawn. It was wide open, anyway. There was a driveway behind it with little knee-high iron posts set eight feet back on either side. They had latches. Each half of the gate was latched into one of them. Wide open. The driveway led on down to a huddle of mellow brick buildings about a hundred yards away. The buildings had steep mossy roofs and were overhung by trees. The driveway was lined with trees. The sidewalk was lined with trees. There were trees everywhere. Their leaves were just about coming in. They were tiny and curled and bright green. Six months from now they would be big and red and golden and photographers would be swarming all over the place taking pictures of them for the college brochure.

Twenty yards beyond the cop and his car and the gate was a pickup truck parked on the other side of the road. It was tight against the curb. It was facing toward me, fifty yards away. It looked a little out of place. It was faded red and had a big bull bar on the front. The bar was dull black and looked like it had been bent and straightened a couple of times. There were two men in the cab. They were young, tall, clean-cut, fair-haired. They were just sitting there, completely still, gazing forward, looking at nothing in particular. They weren't looking at the cop. They weren't looking at me.

I was set up to the south. I had an anonymous brown panel van parked outside a music store. The store was the kind of place you find near a college gate. It had used CDs in racks out on the sidewalk and posters in the windows behind them advertising bands people have never heard of. I had the van's rear doors open. There were boxes stacked inside. I had a sheaf of paperwork in my hands. I was wearing a coat, because it was a cold April morning. I was wearing gloves, because the boxes in the van had loose staples where they had been torn open. I was wearing a gun, because I often do. It was wedged in my pants, at the back, under the coat. It was a Colt Anaconda, which is a huge stainless steel revolver chambered for the .44 Magnum cartridge. It was thirteen and a half inches long and weighed almost four pounds. Not my first choice of weapon. It was hard and heavy and cold and I was aware of it all the time.

I paused in the middle of the sidewalk and looked up from my papers and heard the distant pickup's engine start. It stayed where it was, just idling. White exhaust pooled around its rear wheels. The air was cold. It was early and the street was deserted. I stepped behind my van and glanced down the side of the music store toward the college buildings. Saw a black Lincoln Town Car waiting outside one of them. There were two guys standing next to it. I was a hundred yards away but neither one of them looked like a limo driver. Limo drivers don't come in pairs and they don't look young and heavy and they don't act tense and wary. These guys looked exactly like bodyguards.

The building the Lincoln was waiting outside of looked like some kind of a small dormitory. It had Greek letters over a big wooden door. I watched and the big

wooden door opened up and a young thin guy stepped out.
He looked like a student. He had long messy hair and was
dressed like a homeless person but carried a bag that
looked like shiny expensive leather. One of the bodyguards stood point while the other held the car door and
the young thin guy tossed his bag onto the back seat and
slid right in after it. He pulled the door shut behind himself. I heard it slam, faint and muffled from a hundred
yards away. The bodyguards glanced around for a second
and then got in the front together and a short moment later
the car moved away. Thirty yards behind it a college security vehicle snuffled slowly in the same direction, not like
it was intending to make up a convoy but like it just happened to be there anyway. There were two rent-a-cops in
it. They were slumped down low in their seats and they
looked aimless and bored.

I took my gloves off and tossed them into the back of
my van. Stepped out into the road where my view was better. I saw the Lincoln come up the driveway at a moderate
speed. It was black and shiny and immaculate. It had
plenty of chrome on it. Plenty of wax. The college cops
were way behind it. It paused at the ceremonial gate and
turned left and came south toward the black police
Caprice. Toward me.

What happened next occupied eight seconds, but it
felt like the blink of an eye.

The faded red pickup moved off the curb twenty
yards back. It accelerated hard. It caught up with the Lincoln and pulled out and passed it exactly level with the
cop's Caprice. It came within a foot of the cop's knees.
Then it accelerated again and pulled a little ways ahead
and its driver swung the wheel hard and the corner of the
bull bar smashed square into the Lincoln's front fender.
The pickup driver kept the wheel turned and his foot hard

down and forced the Lincoln off the road onto the shoulder. The grass tore up and the Lincoln slowed radically and then hit a tree head-on. There was the *boom* of metal caving and tearing and headlight glass shattering and there was a big cloud of steam and the tree's tiny green leaves shook and quivered noisily in the still morning air.

Then the two guys in the pickup came out shooting. They had black machine pistols and were firing them at the Lincoln. The sound was deafening and I could see arcs of spent brass raining down on the blacktop. Then the guys were pulling at the Lincoln's doors. Hauling them open. One of them leaned into the back and started dragging the thin kid out. The other was still firing his gun into the front. Then he reached into his pocket left-handed and came out with some kind of a grenade. Tossed it inside the Lincoln and slammed the doors and grabbed his buddy and the kid by the shoulders and turned them away and hauled them down into a crouch. There was a loud bright explosion inside the Lincoln. All six windows shattered. I was more than twenty yards away and felt every bit of the concussion. Pebbles of glass blew everywhere. They made rainbows in the sun. Then the guy who had tossed the grenade scrambled up and sprinted for the passenger side of the pickup and the other straight-armed the kid inside the cab and crowded right in after him. The doors slammed shut and I saw the kid trapped in there on the center seat. I saw terror in his face. It was white with shock and right through the dirty windshield I saw his mouth opening in a silent scream. I saw the driver working the gears and heard the engine roaring and the tires squealing and then the truck was coming directly at me.

It was a Toyota. I could see TOYOTA on the grille behind the bull bar. It rode high on its suspension and I could see a big black differential at the front. It was the size of a soccer ball. Four-wheel drive. Big fat tires. Dents and faded paint that hadn't been washed since it left the factory. It was coming straight at me.

I had less than a second to decide.

I flipped the tail of my coat and pulled out the Colt. Aimed very carefully and fired once at the Toyota's grille. The big gun flashed and roared and kicked in my hand. The huge .44 slug shattered the radiator. I fired again at the left front tire. Blew it out in a spectacular explosion of black rubber debris. Yards of blown tread whipped through the air. The truck slewed and stopped with the driver's side facing me. Ten yards away. I ducked behind the back of my van and slammed the rear doors and came out on the sidewalk and fired again at the left rear tire. Same result. Rubber everywhere. The truck crashed down on its left-side rims at a steep angle. The driver opened his door and spilled out on the blacktop and scrambled up on one knee. He had his gun in the wrong hand. He juggled it across and I waited until I was fairly sure he was going to point it at me. Then I used my left hand to cradle my right forearm against the Colt's four-pound weight and aimed carefully at center mass like I had been taught a long time ago and pulled the trigger. The guy's chest seemed to explode in a huge cloud of blood. The skinny kid was rigid inside the cab. Just staring in shock and horror. But the second guy was out of the cab and scrambling around the front of the hood toward me. His gun was coming around at me. I swiveled left and paused a beat and cradled my forearm. Aimed at his chest. Fired. Same result. He went down on his back behind the fender in a cloud of red vapor.

Now the skinny kid was moving in the cab. I ran for him and pulled him out right over the first guy's body. Ran him back to my van. He was limp with shock and confusion. I shoved him into the passenger seat and slammed the door on him and spun around and headed for the driver's side. In the corner of my eye I saw a third guy coming right at me. Reaching into his jacket. Some tall heavy guy. Dark clothes. I braced my arm and fired and saw the big red explosion in his chest at exactly the same split second I realized it was the old cop from the Caprice and he had been reaching into his pocket for his badge. The badge was a gold shield in a worn leather holder and it flew up out of his hand and tumbled end over end and landed hard against the curb right in front of my van.

Time stood still.

I stared at the cop. He was on his back in the gutter. His whole chest was a mess of red. It was all over him. There was no welling or pumping. No sign of a heartbeat. There was a big ragged hole in his shirt. He was completely still. His head was turned and his cheek was hard against the blacktop. His arms were flung out and I could see pale veins in his hands. I was aware of the blackness of the road and the vivid green of the grass and the bright blue of the sky. I could hear the thrill of the breeze in the new leaves over the gunshots still roaring in my ears. I saw the skinny kid staring out through my van's windshield at the downed cop and then staring at me. I saw the college security cruiser coming left out of the gate. It was moving slower than it should have been. Dozens of shots had been fired. Maybe they were worried about where their jurisdiction began and where it ended. Maybe they were just scared. I saw their pale pink faces behind their windshield. They were turned in my direction. Their car was doing maybe fifteen miles an hour. It was crawling straight at me. I glanced at the gold shield in the gutter. The metal was worn smooth by a lifetime of use. I glanced at my van. Stood completely still. One thing I learned a long time ago is that it's easy enough to shoot a man. But there's absolutely no way to unshoot one.

I heard the college car rolling slowly toward me.

Heard its tires crushing grit on the blacktop. Everything else was silence. Then time restarted and a voice in my head screamed *go go go* and I ran for it. I scrambled into the van and threw the gun down on the middle seat and fired up the engine and pulled a U-turn so hard we came up on two wheels. The skinny kid was thrown all over the place. I got the wheel straight and stamped on the gas and took off south. I had a limited view in the mirror but I saw the college cops light up their roof bar and come right after me. The kid next to me was totally silent. His mouth was hanging open. He was concentrating on staying in his seat. I was concentrating on accelerating as hard as I could. Traffic was mercifully light. It was a sleepy New England town, early in the morning. I got the van wound up to about seventy miles an hour and tightened my hands on the wheel until my knuckles showed white and just stared at the road ahead, like I didn't want to see what was behind me.

"How far back are they?" I asked the kid.

He didn't respond. He was slack with shock and crunched up in the corner of his seat, as far away from me as he could get. He was staring at the roof. He had his right hand braced against the door. Pale skin, long fingers.

"How far back?" I asked again. The engine was roaring loud.

"You killed a cop," he said. "That old guy was a cop, you know."

"I know."

"You shot him."

"Accident," I said. "How far back are the others?"

"He was showing you his badge."

"How far back are the others?"

He stirred himself and turned around and ducked his head so he could line up the view out of the small rear windows.

"Hundred feet," he said. He sounded vague and scared. "Real close. One of them is hanging out the window with a gun."

Right on cue I heard the distant pop of a handgun over the roar of the engine and the whine of the tires. I picked up the Colt from the seat beside me. Dropped it again. It was empty. I had fired six times already. A radiator, two tires, two guys. And one cop.

"Glove compartment," I said.

"You should stop," the kid said. "Explain to them. You were helping me. It was a mistake." He wasn't looking at me. He was staring out of the back windows.

"I shot a cop," I said. I kept my voice completely neutral. "That's all they know. That's all they want to know. They aren't going to care about how or why."

The kid said nothing.

"Glove compartment," I said again.

He turned again and fumbled the lid open. There was another Anaconda in there. Identical. Shiny stainless steel, fully loaded. I took it from the kid. Wound my window all the way down. Cold air rushed in like a gale. It carried the sound of a handgun firing right behind us, fast and steady.

"Shit," I said.

The kid said nothing. The shots kept coming, loud and dull and percussive. *How were they missing?*

"Get down on the floor," I said.

I slid sideways until my left shoulder was jammed hard against the door frame and craned my right arm all the way around until the new gun was out of the window and pointing backward. I fired once and the kid stared at me in horror and then slid forward and crouched down in the space between the front edge of his seat and the dash with his arms wrapped around his head. A second later the rear window ten feet behind where his head had been exploded.

"Shit," I said again. Steered for the side of the road to improve my angle. Fired behind us again.

"I need you to watch," I said. "Stay down as far as you can."

The kid didn't move.

"Get up," I said. "*Now.* I need you to watch."

He raised himself and twisted around until his head was just high enough to see out the back. I saw him register the shattered rear window. Saw him realize that his head had been right in line with it.

"I'm going to slow down a little," I said. "Going to pull in so they'll pull out to pass me."

"Don't do it," the kid said. "You can still put this right."

I ignored him. Dropped the speed to maybe fifty and pulled right and the college car instinctively drifted left to come up on my flank. I fired my last three chambers at it and its windshield shattered and it slewed all the way across the road like maybe the driver was hit or a tire had gone. It plowed nose-first into the opposite shoulder and smashed through a line of planted shrubs and then it was lost to sight. I dropped the empty gun on the seat beside me and wound the window up and accelerated hard. The kid said nothing. Just stared into the rear of the van. The broken window back there was making a weird moaning sound as the air sucked out through it.

"OK," I said. I was out of breath. "Now we're good to go."

The kid turned to face me.

"Are you crazy?" he said.

"You know what happens to people who shoot cops?" I said back.

He had no reply to that. We drove on in silence for

maybe thirty whole seconds, more than half a mile, blinking and panting and staring straight ahead through the windshield like we were mesmerized. The inside of the van stank of gunpowder.

"It was an accident," I said. "I can't bring him back. So get over it."

"Who *are* you?" he asked.

"No, who are *you*?" I asked back.

He went quiet. He was breathing hard. I checked the mirror. The road was completely empty behind us. Completely empty ahead of us. We were way out in open country. Maybe ten minutes from a highway cloverleaf.

"I'm a target," he said. "For abduction."

It was an odd word to use.

"They were trying to kidnap me," he said.

"You think?"

He nodded. "It's happened before."

"Why?"

"Money," the kid said. "Why else?"

"You rich?"

"My father is."

"Who is he?"

"Just a guy."

"But a rich guy," I said.

"He's a rug importer."

"Rugs?" I said. "What, like carpets?"

"Oriental rugs."

"You can get rich importing Oriental rugs?"

"Very," the kid said.

"You got a name?"

"Richard," he said. "Richard Beck."

I checked the mirror again. The road was still empty behind. Still empty ahead. I slowed a little and steadied the van in the center of my lane and tried to drive on like a normal person.

"So who were those guys?" I asked.

Richard Beck shook his head. "I have no idea."

"They knew where you were going to be. And when."

"I was going home for my mother's birthday. It's tomorrow."

"Who would know that?"

"I'm not sure. Anybody who knows my family. Anybody in the rug community, I guess. We're well known."

"There's a community?" I said. "Rugs?"

"We all compete," he said. "Same sources, same market. We all know each other."

I said nothing. Just drove on, sixty miles an hour.

"*You* got a name?" he asked me.

"No," I said.

He nodded, like he understood. *Smart boy*.

"What are you going to do?" he asked.

"I'm going to let you out near the highway," I said. "You can hitch a ride or call a cab and then you can forget all about me."

He went very quiet.

"I can't take you to the cops," I said. "That's just not possible. You understand that, right? I killed one. Maybe three. You saw me do it."

He stayed quiet. *Decision time*. The highway was six minutes ahead.

"They'll throw away the key," I said. "I screwed up, it was an accident, but they aren't going to listen. They never do. So don't ask me to go anywhere near *anybody*. Not as a witness, not as nothing. I'm out of here like I don't exist. We absolutely clear on that?"

He didn't speak.

"And don't give them a description," I said. "Tell them you don't remember me. Tell them you were in shock. Or I'll find you and I'll kill you."

He didn't answer.

"I'll let you out somewhere," I said. "Like you never saw me."

He moved. Turned sideways on his seat and looked straight at me.

"Take me home," he said. "All the way. We'll give you money. Help you out. We'll hide you, if you want. My folks will be grateful. I mean, *I'm* grateful. Believe me. You saved my ass. The cop thing, it was an accident, right? Just an accident. You got unlucky. It was a pressure situation. I can understand that. We'll keep it quiet."

"I don't need your help," I said. "I just need to get rid of you."

"But I need to get home," he said. "We'd be helping each other."

The highway was four minutes ahead.

"Where's home?" I asked.

"Abbot," he said.

"Abbot what?"

"Abbot, Maine. On the coast. Between Kennebunkport and Portland."

"We're heading in the wrong direction."

"You can turn north on the highway."

"It's got to be two hundred miles, minimum."

"We'll give you money. We'll make it worth your while."

"I could let you out near Boston," I said. "Got to be a bus to Portland."

He shook his head, violently, like a seizure.

"No way," he said. "I can't take the bus. I can't be alone. Not now. I need protection. Those guys might still be out there."

"Those guys are dead," I said. "Like the damn cop."

"They might have associates."

It was another odd word to use. He looked small and thin and scared. There was a pulse jumping in his neck.

He used both hands to pull his hair away from his head and turned toward the windshield to let me see his left ear. It wasn't there. There was just a hard knob of scar tissue. It looked like a small piece of uncooked pasta. Like a raw tortellini floret.

"They cut it off and mailed it," he said. "The first time."

"When?"

"I was fifteen."

"Your dad didn't pay up?"

"Not quickly enough."

I said nothing. Richard Beck just sat there, showing me his scar, shocked and scared and breathing like a machine.

"You OK?" I asked.

"Take me home," he said. Like he was pleading. "I can't be alone now."

The highway was two minutes ahead.

"Please," he said. "Help me."

"Shit," I said, for the third time.

"Please. We can help each other. You need to hide out."

"We can't keep this van," I said. "We have to assume the description is on the air all over the state."

He stared at me, full of hope. The highway was one minute ahead.

"We'll have to find a car," I said.

"Where?"

"Anywhere. There are cars all over the place."

There was a big sprawling out-of-town shopping mall nestled south and west of the highway interchange. I could already see it in the distance. There were giant tan buildings with no windows and bright neon signs. There were giant parking lots about half-filled with cars. I pulled in and drove once around the whole place. It was as big as a town. There were people everywhere. They made me nervous. I came around again and headed in past a line of trash containers to the rear of a big department store.

"Where are we going?" Richard asked.

"Staff parking," I said. "Customers are in and out all day long. Unpredictable. But store people are in there for the duration. Safer."

He looked at me like he didn't understand. I headed for a line of eight cars parked head-on against a blank wall. There was an empty slot next to a dull-colored Nissan Maxima about three years old. It would do. It was a pretty anonymous vehicle. The lot was a backwater, quiet and private. I pulled beyond the empty slot and backed up into it. Put the van's rear doors tight against the wall.

"Got to hide the busted window," I said.

The kid said nothing. I put both empty Colts into my coat pockets and slid out. Tried the Maxima's doors.

"Find me some wire," I said. "Like heavy electrical cable or a coat hanger."

"You're going to steal this car?"

I nodded. Said nothing.

"Is that smart?"

"You'd think so if it was you who'd accidentally shot a cop."

The kid looked blank for a second and then came to and scouted around. I emptied the Anacondas and tossed the twelve spent shell cases into a garbage container. The kid came back with a three-foot length of electrical wire from a trash pile. I stripped the insulation with my teeth and made a little hook in the end and shoved it past the rubber sealing strip around the Maxima's window.

"You're the lookout," I said.

He stepped away and scanned the lot and I fed the wire down inside the car and jiggled it around and jiggled the door handle until it popped open. I tossed the wire back in the trash and bent down under the steering column and pulled off the plastic shroud. Sorted through the wires in there until I found the two I needed and touched them together. The starter motor whined and the engine turned over and caught and ran steadily. The kid looked suitably impressed.

"Misspent youth," I said.

"Is this smart?" he asked again.

I nodded. "Smart as we can get. It won't be missed until six tonight, maybe eight. Whenever the store closes. You'll be home long before then."

He paused with his hand on the passenger door and then kind of shook himself and ducked inside. I racked the driver's seat back and adjusted the mirror and backed out of the slot. Took it easy through the mall lot. There was a cop car crawling around about a hundred yards away. I parked again in the first place I saw and sat there with the engine running until the cop moved away. Then I hustled for the exit and around the cloverleaf and two minutes later we were heading north on a wide smooth highway at a respectable sixty miles an hour. The car smelled strongly of perfume and there were two boxes of tissues in it. There was some kind of furry bear stuck on the rear window with clear plastic suckers where its paws should have been. There was a Little League glove on the back seat and I could hear an aluminum bat rattling around in the trunk.

"Mom's taxi," I said.

The kid didn't answer.

"Don't worry," I said. "She's probably insured. Probably a solid citizen."

"Don't you feel bad?" he said. "About the cop?"

I glanced at him. He was thin and pale and crunched up again as far from me as he could get. His hand was resting against the door. His long fingers made him look a little like a musician. I think he wanted to like me, but I didn't need him to.

"Shit happens," I said. "No need to get all worked up about it."

"What the hell kind of answer is that?"

"The only kind. It was minor collateral damage. Means nothing unless it comes back to bite us. Bottom line, we can't change it, so we move on."

He said nothing.

"Anyway, it was your dad's fault," I said.

"For being rich and having a son?"

"For hiring lousy bodyguards."

He looked away. Said nothing.

"They *were* bodyguards, right?"

He nodded. Said nothing.

"So don't *you* feel bad?" I asked. "About them?"

"A little," he said. "I guess. I didn't know them well."

"They were useless," I said.

"It happened so fast."

"The bad guys were waiting right there," I said. "A ratty old pickup like that just hanging around in a prissy little college town? What kind of bodyguards don't notice a thing like that? They never heard of threat assessment?"

"You saying you noticed?"

"I noticed."

"Not bad for a van driver."

"I was in the army. I was a military cop. I understand bodyguarding. And I understand collateral damage."

The kid nodded, uncertainly.

"You got a name yet?" he asked.

"Depends," I said. "I need to understand your point of view. I could be in all kinds of trouble. At least one cop is dead and now I just stole a car."

He went quiet again. I matched him, mile for mile.

Gave him time to think. We were almost out of Massachusetts.

"My family appreciates loyalty," he said. "You did their son a service. And you did *them* a service. Saved them some money, at least. They'll show their gratitude. I'm sure the last thing they'll do is rat you out."

"You need to call them?"

He shook his head. "They're expecting me. As long as I show up there's no need to call them."

"The cops will call them. They think you're in big trouble."

"They don't have the number. Nobody does."

"The college must have your address. They can find your number."

He shook his head again. "The college doesn't have the address. Nobody does. We're very careful about stuff like that."

I shrugged and kept quiet and drove another mile.

"So what about you?" I said. "You going to rat me out?"

I saw him touch his right ear. The one that was still there. It was clearly a completely subconscious gesture.

"You saved my ass," he said. "I'm not going to rat you out."

"OK," I said. "My name is Reacher."

WE SPENT A FEW MINUTES CUTTING ACROSS A tiny corner of Vermont and then struck out north and east across New Hampshire. Settled in for the long, long drive. The adrenaline drained away and the kid got over his state of shock and we both ended up a little down and sleepy. I cracked the window to get some air in and some perfume out. It made the car noisy but it kept me awake. We talked a little. Richard Beck told me he was twenty years old. He was in his junior year. He was majoring in some kind of contemporary art expression thing that sounded a lot like finger painting to me. He wasn't good at relationships. He was an only child. There was a lot of ambivalence about his family. They were clearly some kind of tight close-knit clan and half of him wanted out and the other half needed to be in. He was clearly very traumatized by the previous kidnap. It made me wonder whether something had been done to him, apart from the ear thing. Maybe something much worse.

I told him about the army. I laid it on pretty thick about my bodyguarding qualifications. I wanted him to feel he was in good hands, at least temporarily. I drove fast and steady. The Maxima had just been filled. We didn't need to stop for gas. He didn't want lunch. I stopped once to use a men's room. Left the engine running so I wouldn't have to fiddle with the ignition wires again. Came back to the car and found him inert inside it. We got back on the road and passed by Concord in New Hampshire and headed toward Portland in Maine. Time passed. He got more relaxed, the closer we got to home. But he got quieter, too. Ambivalence.

We crossed the state line and then about twenty miles short of Portland he squirmed around and checked the view out of the back very carefully and told me to take the next exit. We turned onto a narrow road heading due east toward the Atlantic. It passed under I-95 and then ran more than fifteen miles across granite headlands to the sea. It was the kind of landscape that would have looked great in summer. But it was still cold and raw. There were trees stunted by salt winds and exposed rock outcrops where gales and storm tides had scoured the dirt away. The road twisted and turned like it was trying to fight its way as far east as it could get. I glimpsed the ocean ahead. It was as gray as iron. The road pushed on past inlets to the left and right. I saw small beaches made of gritty sand. Then the road curved left and immediately right and rose up onto a headland shaped like the palm of a hand. The palm narrowed abruptly into a single finger jutting directly out to sea. It was a rock peninsula maybe a hundred yards wide and half a mile long. I could feel the wind buffeting the car. I drove out onto the peninsula and saw a line of bent and stunted evergreen trees that were trying to hide a high granite wall but weren't quite tall enough or thick enough to succeed. The wall was maybe eight feet tall. It was topped with big coils of razor wire. It had security lights mounted at intervals. It ran laterally all the way across the hundred-yard width of the finger. It canted down suddenly at the ends and ran all the way into the sea, where its massive foundations were built on huge stone blocks. The blocks were mossy with seaweed. There was an iron gate set in the wall, dead-center. It was closed.

"This is it," Richard Beck said. "This is where I live."

The road led straight to the gate. Behind the gate it changed to a long straight driveway. At the end of the driveway was a gray stone house. I could see it there at the end of the finger, right out in the ocean. Right beside the gate was a one-story lodge. Same design and same stone as the house, but much smaller and lower. It shared its foundations with the wall. I slowed and stopped the car in front of the gate.

"Honk the horn," Richard Beck said.

The Maxima had a little bugle shape on the airbag lid. I pressed on it with one finger and the horn beeped politely. I saw a surveillance camera on the gatepost tilt and pan. It was like a little glass eye looking at me. There was a long pause and the lodge door opened. A guy in a dark suit stepped out. Clearly the suit came from a big-and-tall store and was probably the largest size it had ever offered but even so it was very tight in the shoulders and short in the arms for its owner. He was way bigger than me, which put him firmly in the freak category. He was a giant. He walked up close to his side of the gate and stared out. He spent a long time looking at me and a short time looking at the kid. Then he unlocked the gate and pulled it open.

"Drive straight up to the house," Richard told me. "Don't stop here. I don't like that guy very much."

I drove through the gate. Didn't stop. But I drove slow and looked around. The first thing you do going into a place is to look for your way out. The wall ran all the way into rough water on both sides. It was too high to jump and the razor wire along the top made it impossible to climb. There was a cleared area maybe thirty yards deep behind it. Like no-man's-land. Or a minefield. The security lights were set to cover all of it. There was no way out except through the gate. The giant was closing it behind us. I could see him in the mirror.

It was a long drive up to the house. Gray ocean on three sides. The house was a big old pile. Maybe some sea captain's place from way back when killing whales made people respectable fortunes. It was all stone, with intricate beadings and cornices and folds. All the north-facing surfaces were covered in gray lichen. The rest was spotted with green. It was three stories high. It had a dozen chimneys. The roofline was complex. There were gables all over the place with short gutters and dozens of fat iron pipes to drain the rainwater away. The front door was oak and was banded and studded with iron. The driveway widened into a carriage circle. I followed it around counterclockwise and stopped right in front of the door. The door opened and another guy in a dark suit stepped out. He was about my size, which made him a lot smaller than the guy in the lodge. But I didn't like him any better. He had a stone face and blank eyes. He opened the Maxima's passenger door like he had been expecting to see it, which

I guessed he was, because the big guy in the lodge would have called ahead.

"Will you wait here?" Richard asked me.

He slipped out of the car and walked away into the gloom inside the house and the guy in the suit closed the oak door from the outside and took up station right in front of it. He wasn't looking at me but I knew I was somewhere in his peripheral vision. I broke the wire connection under the steering column and turned the motor off and waited.

It was a reasonably long wait, probably close to forty minutes. Without the engine running the car grew cold. It rocked gently in the sea breeze eddying around the house. I stared straight ahead through the windshield. I was facing northeast and the air was whipped and clear. I could see the coastline curving in from the left. I could see a faint brown smudge in the air about twenty miles away. Probably pollution coming up out of Portland. The city itself was hidden behind a headland.

Then the oak door opened again and the guard stepped smartly aside and a woman came out. She was Richard Beck's mother. No doubt about that. No doubt at all. She had the same slight build and the same pale face. The same long fingers. She was wearing jeans and a heavy fisherman's sweater. She had windblown hair and was maybe fifty years old. She looked tired and strained. She stopped about six feet from the car, like she was giving me the opportunity to realize it would be more polite if I got out and met her halfway. So I opened the door and slid out. I was stiff and cramped. I stepped forward and she put out her hand. I took it. It was ice cold and full of bones and tendons.

"My son told me what happened," she said. Her voice was low and sounded a little husky, like maybe she smoked a lot or had been crying hard. "I can't begin to express how grateful I am that you helped him."

"Is he OK?" I asked.

She made a face, like she wasn't sure. "He's lying down now."

I nodded. Let go of her hand. It fell back to her side. There was a short awkward silence.

"I'm Elizabeth Beck," she said.

"Jack Reacher," I said.

"My son explained your predicament," she said.

It was a nice neutral word. I said nothing in reply.

"My husband will be home tonight," she said. "He'll know what to do."

I nodded. There was another awkward pause. I waited.

"Would you like to come in?" she asked.

She turned and walked back into the hallway. I followed her. I passed through the door and it beeped. I looked again and saw that a metal detector had been installed tight against the inside jamb.

"Would you mind?" Elizabeth Beck asked. She made a sort of sheepish apologetic gesture toward me and then toward the big ugly guy in the suit. He stepped up and made ready to pat me down.

"Two guns," I said. "Empty. In my coat pockets."

He pulled them out with the kind of easy practiced moves that suggested he had patted plenty of people down before. He laid them on a side table and squatted and ran his hands up my legs, and then stood and went over my arms, my waist, my chest, my back. He was very thorough, and not very gentle.

"I'm sorry," Elizabeth Beck said.

The guy in the suit stood back and there was another awkward silence.

"Do you need anything?" Elizabeth Beck asked.

I could think of a lot of things I needed. But I just shook my head.

"I'm kind of tired," I said. "Long day. I really need a nap."

She smiled briefly, like she was pleased, like having her own personal cop-killer asleep somewhere would relieve her of a social pressure.

"Of course," she said. "Duke will show you to a room."

She looked at me for a second longer. Underneath the strain and the pallor she was a handsome woman. She had fine bones and good skin. Thirty years ago she must have been fighting them off with a stick. She turned away and disappeared into the depths of the house. I turned to the guy in the suit. I assumed he was Duke.

"When do I get the guns back?" I asked.

He didn't answer. Just pointed me to the staircase and followed me up. Pointed to the next staircase and we came out on the third floor. He led me to a door and pushed it open. I went in and found a plain square room paneled with oak. There was heavy old furniture in it. A bed, an armoire, a table, a chair. There was an Oriental carpet on the floor. It looked thin and threadbare. Maybe it was a priceless old item. Duke pushed past me and walked across it and showed me where the bathroom was. He was acting like a bellboy in a hotel. He pushed past me again and headed back to the door.

"Dinner's at eight," he said. Nothing more.

He stepped out and closed the door. I didn't hear a sound but when I checked I found it was locked from the outside. There was no keyhole on the inside. I stepped to the window and looked out at the view. I was at the back of the house and all I could see was ocean. I was facing due east and there was nothing between me and Europe. I looked down. Fifty feet below were rocks with waves foaming all around them. The tide looked like it was coming in.

I stepped back to the door and put my ear against it and listened hard. Heard nothing. I scanned the ceiling and the cornices and the furniture, very carefully, inch by inch. Nothing there. No cameras. I didn't care about microphones. I wasn't going to make any noise. I sat on the bed and took my right shoe off. Flipped it over and used my fingernails to pull a pin out of the heel. Swiveled the heel rubber like a little door and turned the shoe the right way up and shook it. A small black plastic rectangle fell out on the bed and bounced once. It was a wireless e-mail device. Nothing fancy. It was just a commercial product, but it had been reprogrammed to send only to one address. It was about the size of a large pager. It had a small cramped keyboard with tiny keys. I switched the power on and typed a short message. Then I pressed *send now*.

The message said: *I'm in.*

CHAPTER **2**

TRUTH IS BY THAT POINT I HAD BEEN *IN* FOR
eleven whole days, since a damp shiny Saturday night in
the city of Boston when I saw a dead man walk across a
sidewalk and get into a car. It wasn't a delusion. It wasn't
an uncanny resemblance. It wasn't a double or a twin or a
brother or a cousin. It was a man who had died a decade
ago. There was no doubt about it. No trick of the light. He
looked older by the appropriate number of years and was
carrying the scars of the wounds that had killed him.

I was walking on Huntington Avenue with a mile to
go to a bar I had heard about. It was late. Symphony Hall
was just letting out. I was too stubborn to cross the street
and avoid the crowd. I just threaded my way through it.
There was a mass of well-dressed fragrant people, most of
them old. There were double-parked cars and taxis at the
curb. Their engines were running and their windshield
wipers were thumping back and forth at irregular intervals. I saw the guy step out of the foyer doors on my left.
He was wearing a heavy cashmere overcoat and carrying
gloves and a scarf. He was bareheaded. He was about
fifty. We almost collided. I stopped. He stopped. He
looked right at me. We got into one of those crowded-

sidewalk things where we both hesitated and then both started moving and then both stopped again. At first I thought he didn't recognize me. Then there was a shadow in his face. Nothing definitive. I held back and he walked across in front of me and climbed into the rear seat of a black Cadillac DeVille waiting at the curb. I stood there and watched as the driver eased out into the traffic and pulled away. I heard the hiss of the tires on the wet pavement.

I got the plate number. I wasn't panicking. I wasn't questioning anything. I was ready to believe the evidence of my own eyes. Ten years of history was overturned in a second. *The guy was alive.* Which gave me a huge problem.

That was day one. I forgot all about the bar. I went straight back to my hotel and started calling half-forgotten numbers from my Military Police days. I needed somebody I knew and trusted, but I had been out for six years by then and it was late on a Saturday night so the odds were against me. In the end I settled for somebody who claimed he had heard of me, which might or might not have made a difference to the eventual outcome. He was a warrant officer named Powell.

"I need you to trace a civilian plate," I told him. "Purely as a favor."

He knew who I was, so he didn't give me any grief about not being able to do it for me. I gave him the details. Told him I was pretty sure it was a private registration, not a livery car. He took my number and promised to call me back in the morning, which would be day two.

HE DIDN'T CALL ME BACK. HE SOLD ME OUT INstead. I think in the circumstances anybody would have. Day two was a Sunday and I was up early. I had room service for breakfast and sat waiting for the call. I got a knock on the door instead. Just after ten o'clock. I put my eye to the peephole and saw two people standing close together so they would show up well in the lens. One man, one woman. Dark jackets. No overcoats. The man was carrying a briefcase. They both had some kind of official IDs held up high and tilted so they would catch the hallway light.

"Federal agents," the man called, just loud enough for me to hear him through the door.

In a situation like that it doesn't work to pretend you're not in. I'd been the guys in the hallway often enough. One of them stays right there and the other goes down to get a manager with a passkey. So I just opened up and stood back to let them in.

They were wary for a moment. They relaxed as soon as they saw I wasn't armed and didn't look like a maniac. They handed over their IDs and shuffled around politely while I deciphered them. At the top they said: *United States Department of Justice.* At the bottom they said: *Drug Enforcement Administration.* In the middle were all kinds of seals and signatures and watermarks. There were photographs and typed names. The man was listed as Steven Eliot, one *l* like the old poet. *April is the cruelest month.* That was for damn sure. The photograph was a pretty good likeness. Steven Eliot looked somewhere between thirty and forty and was thickset and dark and a little bald and had a smile that looked friendly in the picture and even better in person. The woman was listed as Susan Duffy. Susan Duffy was a little younger than Steven Eliot. She was a little taller than him, too. She was pale and slender and attractive and had changed her hair since her photograph was taken.

"Go ahead," I said. "Search the room. It's a long time since I had anything worth hiding from you guys."

I handed back their IDs and they put them away in

their inside pockets and made sure they moved their jackets enough to let me see their weapons. They had them in neat shoulder rigs. I recognized the ribbed grip of a Glock 17 under Eliot's armpit. Duffy had a 19, which is the same thing only a little smaller. It was snug against her right breast. She must have been left-handed.

"We don't want to search the room," she said.

"We want to talk about a license plate," Eliot said.

"I don't own a car," I said.

We were all still standing in a neat little triangle just inside the door. Eliot still had the briefcase in his hand. I was trying to figure out who was the boss. Maybe neither one of them. Maybe they were equals. And fairly senior. They were well dressed but looked tired. Maybe they had worked most of the night and flown in from somewhere. From Washington D.C., maybe.

"Can we sit down?" Duffy asked.

"Sure," I said. But a cheap hotel room made that awkward. There was only one chair. It was shoved under a small desk crammed between a wall and the cabinet that held the television set. Duffy pulled it out and turned it around so it faced the bed. I sat on the bed, up near the pillows. Eliot perched on the foot of the bed and laid his briefcase down on it. He was still giving me the friendly smile and I couldn't find anything phony about it. Duffy looked great on the chair. The seat height was exactly right for her. Her skirt was short and she was wearing dark nylons that went light where her knees bent.

"You're Reacher, right?" Eliot asked.

I took my eyes off Duffy's legs and nodded. I felt I could count on them to know that much.

"This room is registered to somebody called Calhoun," Eliot said. "Paid for with cash, one night only."

"Habit," I said.

"You leaving today?"

"I take it one day at a time."

"Who's Calhoun?"

"John Quincy Adams's vice president," I said. "It seemed appropriate for this location. I used up the presidents long ago. Now I'm doing vice presidents. Calhoun was unusual. He resigned to run for the Senate."

"Did he get in?"

"I don't know."

"Why the phony name?"

"Habit," I said again.

Susan Duffy was looking straight at me. Not like I was nuts. Like she was interested in me. She probably found it to be a valuable interrogation technique. Back when I interrogated people I did the same thing. Ninety percent of asking questions is about listening to answers.

"We spoke to a military cop called Powell," she said. "You asked him to trace a plate."

Her voice was low and warm and a little husky. I said nothing.

"We have traps and flags in the computers against that plate," she said. "Soon as Powell's inquiry hit the wires we knew all about it. We called him and asked him what his interest was. He told us the interest came from you."

"Reluctantly, I hope," I said.

She smiled. "He recovered fast enough to give us a phony phone number for you. So you needn't worry about old unit loyalties."

"But in the end he gave you the right number."

"We threatened him," she said.

"Then MPs have changed since my day," I said.

"It's important to us," Eliot said. "He saw that."

"So now you're important to us," Duffy said.

I looked away. I've been around the block more times than I care to count but the sound of her voice saying that still gave me a little thrill. I began to think maybe she was the boss. And a hell of an interrogator.

"A member of the public calls in a plate," Eliot said. "Why would he do that? Maybe he got in a fender bender with the car the plate was on. Maybe it was a hit-and-run. But wouldn't he go to the cops for that? And you just told us you don't have a car anyway."

"So maybe you saw somebody *in* the car," Duffy said.

She let the rest of it hang. It was a neat Catch-22. If the person in the car was my friend, then I was probably her enemy. If the person in the car was my enemy, then she was ready to be my friend.

"You guys had breakfast?" I asked.

"Yes," she said.

"So have I," I said.

"We know," she said. "Room service, a short stack of pancakes with an egg on top, over easy. Plus a large pot of coffee, black. It was ordered for seven forty-five and delivered at seven forty-four and you paid cash and tipped the waiter three bucks."

"Did I enjoy it?"

"You ate it."

Eliot snapped the locks on his briefcase and lifted the lid. Pulled out a stack of paper secured with a rubber band. The paper looked new but the writing on it was blurred. Photocopies of faxes, probably made during the night.

"Your service record," he said.

I could see photographs in his briefcase. Glossy black-and-white eight-by-tens. Some kind of a surveillance situation.

"You were a military cop for thirteen years," Eliot said. "Fast-track promotion all the way from second lieutenant to major. Citations and medals. They liked you. You were good. Very good."

"Thank you."

"More than very good, actually. You were their special go-to guy on numerous occasions."

"I guess I was."

"But they let you go."

"I was riffed," I said.

"Riffed?" Duffy repeated.

"RIF, reduction in force. They love to make acronyms out of things. The Cold War ended, military spending got cut, the army got smaller. So they didn't need so many special go-to guys."

"The army still exists," Eliot said. "They didn't chop everybody."

"No."

"So why you in particular?"

"You wouldn't understand."

He didn't challenge me.

"You can help us," Duffy said. "Who did you see in the car?"

I didn't answer.

"Were there drugs in the army?" Eliot asked.

I smiled.

"Armies love drugs," I said. "They always have. Morphine, Benzedrine. The German Army invented Ecstasy. It was an appetite suppressant. CIA invented LSD, tested it on the U.S. Army. Armies march on their veins."

"Recreational?"

"Average age of a recruit is eighteen. What do you think?"

"Was it a problem?"

"We didn't make it much of a problem. Some grunt goes on furlough, smokes a couple of joints in his girlfriend's bedroom, we didn't care. We figured we'd rather see them with a couple of blunts than a couple of six-packs.

Outside of our care we liked them docile rather than aggressive."

Duffy glanced at Eliot and Eliot used his fingernails to scrape the photographs up out of his case. He handed them to me. There were four of them. All four were grainy and a little blurred. All four showed the same Cadillac DeVille I had seen the night before. I recognized it by the plate number. It was in some kind of a parking garage. There were two guys standing next to the trunk. In two of the pictures the trunk lid was down. In two of them it was up. The two guys were looking down at something inside the trunk. No way of telling what it was. One of the guys was a Hispanic gangbanger. The other was an older man in a suit. I didn't know him.

Duffy must have been watching my face.

"Not the man you saw?" she said.

"I didn't say I saw anybody."

"The Hispanic guy is a major dealer," Eliot said. "Actually he's *the* major dealer for most of Los Angeles County. Not provable, of course, but we know all about him. His profits must run to millions of dollars a week. He lives like an emperor. But he came all the way to Portland, Maine, to meet with this other guy."

I touched one of the photographs. "This is Portland, Maine?"

Duffy nodded. "A parking garage, downtown. About nine weeks ago. I took the pictures myself."

"So who's this other guy?"

"We're not exactly sure. We traced the Cadillac's plate, obviously. It's registered to a corporation called Bizarre Bazaar. Main office is in Portland, Maine. Far as we can tell it started out way back as some kind of hippy-dippy import-export trader with the Middle East. Now it specializes in importing Oriental rugs. Far as we can tell the owner is a guy called Zachary Beck. We're assuming that's him in the photographs."

"Which makes him huge," Eliot said. "If this guy from LA is prepared to fly all the way back east to meet with him, he's got to be a couple of rungs up the ladder. And anybody a couple of rungs above this LA guy is in the stratosphere, believe me. So Zachary Beck's a top boy, and he's fooling with us. Rug importer, drug importer. He's making jokes."

"I'm sorry," I said. "I never saw him before."

"Don't be sorry," Duffy said. She hitched forward on the chair. "It's better for us if he isn't the guy you saw. We already know about him. It's better for us if you saw one of his associates. We can try to get to him that way."

"You can't get to him head-on?"

There was a short silence. Seemed to me there was some embarrassment in it.

"We've got problems," Eliot said.

"Sounds like you've got probable cause against the LA player. And you've got photographs that put him side by side with this Beck guy."

"The photographs are tainted," Duffy said. "I made a mistake."

More silence.

"The garage was private property," she said. "It's under an office building. I didn't have a warrant. Fourth Amendment makes the pictures inadmissible."

"Can't you lie? Say you were outside the garage?"

"Physical layout makes that impossible. Defense counsel would figure it in a minute and the case would collapse."

"We need to know who you saw," Eliot said.

I didn't answer.

"We really need to know," Duffy said. She said it in the kind of soft voice that makes men want to jump tall buildings. But there was no artifice there. No pretense. She wasn't aware of how good she was sounding. *She really needed to know.*

"Why?" I asked.

"Because I need to put this right."

"Everybody makes mistakes."

"We sent an agent after Beck," she said. "Undercover. A woman. She disappeared."

Silence.

"When?" I asked.

"Seven weeks ago."

"You looked for her?"

"We don't know where to look. We don't know where Beck goes. We don't even know where he lives. He has no registered property. His house must be owned by some phantom corporation. It's a needle in a haystack."

"Haven't you tailed him?"

"We've tried. He has bodyguards and drivers. They're too good."

"For the DEA?"

"For us. We're on our own. The Justice Department disowned the operation when I screwed up."

"Even though there's an agent missing?"

"They don't know there's an agent missing. We put her in after they closed us down. She's off the books."

I stared at her.

"This whole thing is off the books," she said.

"So how are you working it?"

"I'm a team leader. Nobody's looking over my shoulder day to day. I'm pretending I'm working on something else. But I'm not. I'm working on this."

"So nobody knows this woman is missing?"

"Just my team," she said. "Seven of us. And now you."

I said nothing.

"We came straight here," she said. "We need a break. Why else would we fly up here on a Sunday?"

The room went quiet. I looked from her to Eliot and back to her. They needed me. I needed them. And I liked them. I liked them a lot. They were honest, likable people. They were like the best of the people I used to work with.

"I'll trade," I said. "Information for information. We'll see how we get along. And then we'll take it from there."

"What do you need?"

I TOLD HER I NEEDED TEN-YEAR-OLD HOSPITAL records from a place called Eureka in California. I told her what kind of a thing to look for. I told her I would stay in Boston until she got back to me. I told her not to put anything on paper. Then they left and that was it for day two. Nothing happened on day three. Or day four. I hung around. I find Boston acceptable for a couple of days. It's what I call a forty-eight town. Anything more than forty-eight hours, and it starts to get tiresome. Of course, most places are like that for me. I'm a restless person. So by the start of day five I was going crazy. I was ready to assume they had forgotten all about me. I was ready to call it quits and get back on the road. I was thinking about Miami. It would be a lot warmer down there. But late in the morning the phone rang. It was her voice. It was nice to hear.

"We're on our way up," she said. "Meet you by that big statue of whoever it is on a horse, halfway around the Freedom Trail, three o'clock."

It wasn't a very precise rendezvous, but I knew what she meant. It was a place in the North End, near a church. It was springtime and too cold to want to go there without a purpose but I got there early anyway. I sat on a bench next to an old woman feeding house sparrows and rock doves with torn-up crusts of bread. She looked at me and moved to another bench. The birds swarmed around her feet, pecking at the grit. A watery sun was fighting rainclouds in the sky. It was Paul Revere on the horse.

Duffy and Eliot showed up right on time. They were wearing black raincoats all covered in little loops and buckles and belts. They might as well have worn signs around their necks saying *Federal Agents from Washington D.C.* They sat down, Duffy on my left and Eliot on my right. I leaned back and they leaned forward with their elbows on their knees.

"Paramedics fished a guy out of the Pacific surf," Duffy said. "Ten years ago, just south of Eureka, California. White male, about forty. He had been shot twice in the head and once in the chest. Small-caliber, probably .22s. Then they figure he was thrown off a cliff into the ocean."

"He was alive when they fished him out?" I asked, although I already knew the answer.

"Barely," she said. "He had a bullet lodged near his heart and his skull was broken. Plus one arm and both legs and his pelvis, from the fall. And he was half-drowned. They operated on him for fifteen straight hours. He was in intensive care for a month and in the hospital recuperating for another six."

"ID?"

"Nothing on him. He's in the records as a John Doe."

"Did they try to ID him?"

"No fingerprint match," she said. "Nothing on any missing-persons lists. Nobody came to claim him."

I nodded. *Fingerprint computers tell you what they're told to tell you.*

"What then?" I asked.

"He recovered," she said. "Six months had passed.

They were trying to work out what to do with him when he suddenly discharged himself. They never saw him again."

"Did he tell them anything about who he was?"

"They diagnosed amnesia, certainly about the trauma, because that's almost inevitable. They figured he might be genuinely blank about the incident and the previous day or two. But they figured he must be able to remember things from before that, and they got the strong impression he was pretending not to. There's a fairly extensive case file. Psychiatrists, everything. They interviewed him regularly. He was extremely resolute. Never said a word about himself."

"What was his physical condition when he left?"

"Pretty fair. He had visible scars from the GSWs, that's about all."

"OK," I said. I leaned my head back and looked up at the sky.

"Who was he?"

"Your guess?" I said.

"Twenty-twos to the head and chest?" Eliot said. "Dumped in the ocean? It was organized crime. An assassination. Some kind of hit man got to him."

I said nothing. Looked up at the sky.

"Who was he?" Duffy said again.

I kept on looking up at the sky and dragged myself ten years backward through time, to a whole different world.

"You know anything about tanks?" I asked.

"Military tanks? Tracks and guns? Not really."

"There's nothing to them," I said. "I mean, you like them to be able to move fast, you want some reliability, you don't object to some fuel economy. But if I've got a tank and you've got a tank, what's the only thing I really want to know?"

"What?"

"Can I shoot you before you can shoot me? That's what I want to know. If we're a mile apart, can my gun reach you? Or can your gun reach me?"

"So?"

"Of course, physics being physics, the likely answer is if I can hit you at a mile, then you can hit me at a mile. So it comes down to ammunition. If I stand off another two hundred yards so your shell bounces off me without hurting me, can I develop a shell that doesn't bounce off you? That's what tanks are all about. The guy in the ocean was an army intelligence officer who had been blackmailing an army weapons specialist."

"Why was he in the ocean?"

"Did you watch the Gulf War on TV?" I asked.

"I did," Eliot said.

"Forget about the smart bombs," I said. "The real star of the show was the M1A1 Abrams main battle tank. It scored about four hundred to zip against the Iraqis, who were using the best anybody ever had to give them. But having the war on TV meant that we'd shown our hand to the whole world, so we better get on with dreaming up some new stuff for the next time around. So we got on with it."

"And?" Duffy asked.

"If you want a shell to fly farther and hit harder, you can stuff more propellant into it. Or make it lighter. Or both. Of course, if you're stuffing more propellant into it, you've got to do something pretty radical elsewhere to make it lighter. Which is what they did. They took the explosive charge out of it. Which sounds weird, right? Like, what's it going to do? Go *clang* and bounce off? But they changed the shape. They dreamed up this thing that looks like a giant lawn dart. Built-in fins and all. It's cast from tungsten and depleted uranium. The densest metals you can find. It goes real fast and real far. They called it the long-rod penetrator."

Duffy glanced at me with her eyelids low and smiled and blushed all at the same time. I smiled back.

"They changed the name," I said. "Now it's called the *APFSDS*. I told you they like initials. Armor Piercing Fin Stabilized Discarding Sabot. It's powered by its own little rocket motor, basically. It hits the enemy tank with tremendous kinetic energy. The kinetic energy changes to heat energy, just like they teach you in high school physics. It melts its way through in a split second and sprays the inside of the enemy tank with a jet of molten metal, which kills the tankers and blows up anything explosive or flammable. It's a very neat trick. And either way, you shoot, you score, because if the enemy armor is too thick or you've fired from too far away, the thing just sticks partway in like a dart and spalls, which means it fragments the inner layer of the armor and throws scabs of scalding metal around inside like a hand grenade. The enemy crew come apart like frogs in a blender. It was a brilliant new weapon."

"What about the guy in the ocean?"

"He got the blueprints from the guy he was blackmailing," I said. "Piece by piece, over a long period of time. We were watching him. We knew exactly what he was doing. He was aiming to sell them to Iraqi Intelligence. The Iraqis wanted to level the playing field for the next time around. The U.S. Army didn't want that to happen."

Eliot stared at me. "So they had the guy killed?"

I shook my head. "We sent a couple of MPs down to arrest him. Standard operating procedure, all legal and aboveboard, believe me. But it went wrong. He got away. He was going to disappear. The U.S. Army *really* didn't want that to happen."

"So *then* they had him killed?"

I looked up at the sky again. Didn't answer.

"That wasn't standard procedure," Eliot said. "Was it?"

I said nothing.

"It was off the books," he said. "Wasn't it?"

I didn't answer.

"But he didn't die," Duffy said. "What was his name?"

"Quinn," I said. "Turned out to be the single worst guy I ever met."

"And you saw him in Beck's car on Saturday?"

I nodded. "He was being chauffeured away from Symphony Hall."

I GAVE THEM ALL THE DETAILS I HAD. BUT AS I talked we all knew the information was useless. It was inconceivable that Quinn would be using his previous identity. So all I had to offer was a physical description of a plain-looking white man about fifty years old with two .22 GSW scars on his forehead. Better than nothing, but it didn't really get them anywhere.

"Why didn't his prints match?" Eliot asked.

"He was erased," I said. "Like he never existed."

"Why didn't he die?"

"Silenced .22," I said. "Our standard issue weapon for covert close work. But not a very powerful weapon."

"Is he still dangerous?"

"Not to the army," I said. "He's ancient history. This all was ten years ago. The APFSDS will be in the museum soon. So will the Abrams tank."

"So why try to trace him?"

"Because depending on exactly what he remembers he could be dangerous to the guy who went to take him out."

Eliot nodded. Said nothing.

"Did he look important?" Duffy asked. "On Saturday? In Beck's car?"

"He looked wealthy," I said. "Expensive cashmere overcoat, leather gloves, silk scarf. He looked like a guy who was accustomed to being chauffeured around. He just jumped right in, like he did it all the time."

"Did he greet the driver?"

"I don't know."

"We need to place him," she said. "We need context. How did he act? He was using Beck's car, but did he look entitled? Or like somebody was doing him a favor?"

"He looked entitled," I said. "Like he uses it every day of the week."

"So is he Beck's equal?"

I shrugged. "He could be Beck's boss."

"Partner at best," Eliot said. "Our LA guy wouldn't travel to meet with an underling."

"I don't see Quinn as somebody's partner," I said.

"What was he like?"

"Normal," I said. "For an intelligence officer. In most ways."

"Except for the espionage," Eliot said.

"Yes," I said. "Except for that."

"And whatever got him killed off the books."

"That, too."

Duffy had gone quiet. She was thinking hard. I was pretty sure she was thinking of ways she could use me. And I didn't mind at all.

"Will you stay in Boston?" she asked. "Where we can find you?"

I said I would, and they left, and that was the end of day five.

————

I FOUND A SCALPER IN A SPORTS BAR AND SPENT most of days six and seven at Fenway Park watching the Red Sox struggling through an early-season homestand. The Friday game went seventeen innings and ended very late. So I slept most of day eight and then went back to Symphony Hall at night to watch the crowd. Maybe Quinn had season tickets to a concert series. But he didn't show. I replayed in my mind the way he had glanced at me. It might have been just that rueful crowded-sidewalk thing. But it might have been more.

Susan Duffy called me again on the morning of day nine, Sunday. She sounded different. She sounded like a person who had done a lot more thinking. She sounded like a person with a plan.

"Hotel lobby at noon," she said.

She showed up in a car. Alone. The car was a Taurus built down to a very plain specification. It was grimy inside. A government vehicle. She was wearing faded denim jeans with good shoes and a battered leather jacket. Her hair was newly washed and combed back from her forehead. I got in on the passenger side and she crossed six lanes of traffic and drove straight into the mouth of a tunnel that led to the Mass Pike.

"Zachary Beck has a son," she said.

She took an underground curve fast and the tunnel ended and we came out into the weak midday April light, right behind Fenway.

"He's a college junior," she said. "Some small no-account liberal-arts place, not too far from here, as it happens. We talked to a classmate in exchange for burying a cannabis problem. The son is called Richard Beck. Not a popular person, a little strange. Seems very traumatized by something that happened about five years ago."

"What kind of something?"

"He was kidnapped."

I said nothing.

"You see?" Duffy said. "You know how often regular people get kidnapped these days?"

"No," I said.

"Doesn't happen," she said. "It's an extinct crime. So it must have been a turf war thing. It's practically proof his dad's a racketeer."

"That's a stretch."

"OK, but it's very persuasive. And it was never reported. FBI has no record of it. Whatever happened was handled privately. And not very well. The classmate says Richard Beck is missing an ear."

"So?"

She didn't answer. She just drove west. I stretched out on the passenger seat and watched her out of the corner of my eye. She looked good. She was long and lean and pretty, and she had life in her eyes. She was wearing no makeup. She was one of those women who absolutely didn't need to. I was very happy to let her drive me around. But she wasn't just driving me around. She was taking me somewhere. That was clear. She had come with a plan.

"I studied your whole service record," she said. "In great detail. You're an impressive guy."

"Not really," I said.

"And you've got big feet," she said. "That's good, too."

"Why?"

"You'll see," she said.

"Tell me," I said.

"We're very alike," she said. "You and me. We have something in common. I want to get close to Zachary Beck to get my agent back. You want to get close to him to find Quinn."

"Your agent is dead. Eight weeks now, it would be a miracle. You should face it."

She said nothing.

"And I don't care about Quinn."

She glanced right and shook her head.

"You do," she said. "You really do. I can see that from here. It's eating you up. He's unfinished business. And my guess is you're the sort of guy who hates unfinished business." Then she paused for a second. "And I'm proceeding on the assumption that my agent is still alive, unless and until you supply definitive proof to the contrary."

"Me?" I said.

"I can't use one of my people," she said. "You understand that, right? This whole thing is illegal as far as the Justice Department is concerned. So whatever I do next has to stay off the books. And my guess is you're the sort of guy who understands off-the-books operations. And is comfortable with them. Even prefers them, maybe."

"So?"

"I need to get somebody inside Beck's place. And I've decided it's going to be you. You're going to be my very own long-rod penetrator."

"How?"

"Richard Beck is going to take you there."

SHE CAME OFF THE PIKE ABOUT FORTY MILES west of Boston and turned north into the Massachusetts countryside. We passed through picture-perfect New England villages. Fire departments were out on the curbs polishing their trucks. Birds were singing. People were putting stuff on their lawns and pruning their bushes. There was the smell of woodsmoke in the air.

We stopped at a motel in the middle of nowhere. It was an immaculate place with quiet brick facings and blinding white trim. There were five cars in the lot. They were blocking access to the five end rooms. They were all government vehicles. Steven Eliot was waiting in the middle room with five men. They had hauled their desk chairs in from their own rooms. They were sitting in a neat semicircle. Duffy led me inside and nodded to Eliot. I figured it was a nod that meant: *I told him, and he hasn't said no. Yet.* She moved to the window and turned so that she faced the room. The daylight was bright behind her. It made her hard to see. She cleared her throat. The room went quiet.

"OK, listen up, people," she said. "One more time, this is off the books, this is not officially sanctioned, and this will be done on our own time and at our own risk. Anybody wants out, just leave now."

Nobody moved. Nobody left. It was a smart tactic. It showed me she and Eliot had at least five guys who would follow them to hell and back.

"We have less than forty-eight hours," she said. "Day after tomorrow Richard Beck heads home for his mother's birthday. Our source says he does it every year. Cuts classes and all. His father sends a car with two pro bodyguards because the kid is terrified of a repeat abduction. We're going to exploit that fear. We're going to take down the bodyguards and kidnap him."

She paused. Nobody spoke.

"Our aim is to get into Zachary Beck's house," she said. "We can assume the supposed kidnappers themselves wouldn't exactly be welcome there. So what will happen is that Reacher will immediately rescue the kid *from* the supposed kidnappers. It will be a tight sequence, kidnap, rescue, like that. The kid comes over all grateful and Reacher is greeted like a hero around the family hearth."

People sat quiet at first. Then they stirred. The plan

was so full of holes it made a Swiss cheese look solid. I stared straight at Duffy. Then I found myself staring out the window. *There were ways of plugging the holes.* I felt my brain start to move. I wondered how many of the holes Duffy had already spotted. I wondered how many of the answers she had already gotten. I wondered how she knew I loved stuff like this.

"We have an audience of one," she said. "All that matters is what Richard Beck thinks. The whole thing will be phony from beginning to end, but he's got to be absolutely convinced it's real."

Eliot looked at me. "Weaknesses?"

"Two," I said. "First, how do you take the bodyguards down without really hurting them? I assume you're not *that* far off the books."

"Speed, shock, surprise," he said. "The kidnap team will have machine pistols with plenty of blank ammunition. Plus a stun grenade. Soon as the kid is out of the car, we toss a flashbang in. Lots of sound and fury. They'll be dazed, nothing more. But the kid will assume they're hamburger meat."

"OK," I said. "But second, this whole thing is like method acting, right? I'm some kind of a passerby, and coincidentally I'm the type of guy who can rescue him. Which makes me smart and capable. So why wouldn't I just haul his ass around to the nearest cops? Or wait for the cops to come to us? Why wouldn't I stick around and give evidence and make all kinds of witness statements? Why would I want to immediately drive him all the way home?"

Eliot turned to Duffy.

"He'll be terrified," she said. "He'll want you to."

"But why would I agree? It doesn't matter what he wants. What matters is what is logical for me to do. Because we don't have an audience of one. We have an audience of *two.* Richard Beck and Zachary Beck. Richard Beck there and then, and Zachary Beck later. He'll be looking at it in retrospect. We've got to convince him just as much."

"The kid might ask you not to go to the cops. Like last time."

"But why would I listen to him? If I was Mr. Normal the cops would be the first thing on my mind. I'd want to do everything strictly by the book."

"He would argue with you."

"And I would ignore him. Why would a smart and capable adult listen to a crazy kid? It's a hole. It's too cooperative, too purposeful, too phony. Too *direct.* Zachary Beck would rumble it in a minute."

"Maybe you get him in a car and you're being chased."

"I'd drive straight to a police station."

"Shit," Duffy said.

"It's a plan," I said. "But we need to get real."

I looked out of the window again. It was bright out there. I saw a lot of green stuff. Trees, bushes, distant wooded hillsides dusted with new leaves. In the corner of my eye I saw Eliot and Duffy looking down at the floor of the room. Saw the five guys sitting still. They looked like a capable bunch. Two of them were a little younger than me, tall and fair. Two were about my age, plain and ordinary. One was a lot older, stooped and gray. I thought long and hard. Kidnap, rescue, Beck's house. *I need to be in Beck's house. I really do. Because I need to find Quinn. Think about the long game.* I looked at the whole thing from the kid's point of view. Then I looked at it again, from his father's point of view.

"It's a plan," I said again. "But it needs perfecting. So I need to be the sort of person who wouldn't go to the cops." Then I paused. "No, better still, right in front of

Richard Beck's eyes, I need to *become* the sort of person who *can't* go to the cops."

"How?" Duffy said.

I looked straight at her. "I'll have to hurt somebody. By accident, in the confusion. Another passerby. Some innocent party. Some kind of ambiguous circumstance. Maybe I run somebody over. Some old lady walking her dog. Maybe I even kill her. I panic and I run."

"Too difficult to stage," she said. "And not really enough to make you run, anyway. I mean, accidents happen, in circumstances like these."

I nodded. The room stayed quiet. I closed my eyes and thought some more and saw the beginnings of a sketchy scene take shape right there in my mind.

"OK," I said. "How about this? I'll kill a cop. By accident."

Nobody spoke. I opened my eyes.

"It's a grand slam," I said. "You see that? It's totally perfect. It puts Zachary Beck's mind at rest about why I didn't act normally and *go* to the cops. You don't go to the cops if you've just killed one of their own, even if it's an accident. He'll understand that. And it'll give me a reason to stay on at his house afterward. Which I'll need to do. He'll think I'm in hiding. He'll be grateful about the rescue and he's a criminal anyway so his conscience won't get in his way."

There were no objections. Just silence, and then a slow indefinable murmur of assessment, agreement, consent. I scoped it out, beginning to end. *Think about the long game.* I smiled.

"And it gets better," I said. "He might even hire me. In fact I think he'll be very *tempted* to hire me. Because we're creating the illusion that his family's suddenly under attack and he'll be down by two bodyguards and he'll know I'm better than they were anyway because they lost and I didn't. And he'll be happy to hire me because as long as he thinks I'm a cop-killer and he's sheltering me he'll think he *owns* me."

Duffy smiled, too.

"So let's go to work," she said. "We've got less than forty-eight hours."

THE TWO YOUNGER GUYS WERE TAGGED AS THE kidnap team. We decided they would be driving a Toyota pickup from the DEA's stock of impounded vehicles. They would be using confiscated Uzis filled with nine-millimeter blanks. They would have a stun grenade filched from the DEA SWAT stores. Then we started to rehearse my role as the rescuer. Like all good scam artists we decided I should stick as close to the truth as possible, so I would be an ex-military drifter, in the right place at the right time. I would be armed, which in the circumstances would be technically illegal in Massachusetts, but which would be in character and plausible.

"I need a big old-fashioned revolver," I said. "I have to be carrying something appropriate for a citizen. And the whole thing has to be a big drama, beginning to end. The Toyota comes at me, I need to disable it. I need to shoot it up. So I need three real bullets and three blanks, in strict sequence. The three real bullets for the truck, the three blanks for the people."

"We could load any gun like that," Eliot said.

"But I'll need to see the chambers," I said. "Right before I fire. I won't fire a mixed load without a visual check. I need to know I'm starting in the right place. So I need a revolver. A big one, not some small thing, so I can see clearly."

He saw my point. Made a note. Then we nominated

the old guy as the local cop. Duffy proposed he should just blunder into my field of fire.

"No," I said. "It has to be the right kind of mistake. Not just a careless shot. Beck senior needs to be impressed with me in the right kind of way. I need to do it deliberately, but recklessly. Like I'm a madman, but a madman who can shoot."

Duffy agreed and Eliot thought through a mental list of available vehicles and offered me an old panel van. Said I could be a delivery guy. Said it would give me a legitimate reason to be hanging out on the street. We made lists, on paper and in our heads. The two guys my age were sitting there without an assigned task, and they were unhappy about it.

"You're backup cops," I said. "Suppose the kid doesn't even see me shoot the first one? He might have fainted or something. You need to chase us in a car, and I'll take you out when I'm certain he's watching."

"Can't have backup cops," the old guy said. "I mean, what's going on here? Suddenly the whole place is swarming with cops for no good reason?"

"College cops," Duffy said. "You know, those rent-a-cop guys colleges have? They just happen to be there. I mean, where else would you find them?"

"Excellent," I said. "They can start from right inside the campus. They can control the whole thing by radio from the rear."

"How will you take them out?" Eliot asked me, like it was an issue.

I nodded. I saw the problem. I would have fired six shots by then.

"I can't reload," I said. "Not while I'm driving. Not with blanks. The kid might notice."

"Can you ram them? Force them off the road?"

"Not in a crummy old van. I'll have to have a second

revolver. Preloaded, waiting inside the van. In the glove compartment, maybe."

"You're running around with two six-shooters?" the old guy said. "That's a little odd, in Massachusetts."

I nodded. "It's a weak point. We're going to have to risk a few."

"So I should be in plain clothes," the old guy said. "Like a detective. Shooting at a uniformed cop is beyond reckless. That would be a weak point, too."

"OK," I said. "Agreed. Excellent. You're a detective, and you pull out your badge, and I think it's a gun. That happens."

"But how do we die?" the old guy asked. "We just clutch our stomachs and fall over, like an old Wild West show?"

"That's not convincing," Eliot said. "This whole thing has got to look exactly right. For Richard Beck's sake."

"We need Hollywood stuff," Duffy said. "Kevlar vests and condoms filled with fake blood that explode off of a radio signal."

"Can we get it?"

"From New York or Boston, maybe."

"We're tight for time."

"Tell me about it," Duffy said.

THAT WAS THE END OF DAY NINE. DUFFY WANTED me to move into the motel and offered to have somebody drive me back to my Boston hotel for my luggage. I told her I didn't have any luggage and she looked at me sideways but didn't say anything. I took a room next to the old guy. Somebody drove out and got pizza. Everybody was running around and making phone calls. They left me alone. I lay on my bed and thought the whole thing through again, beginning to end, from my point of view. I made a list in my head of all the things we hadn't considered. It was a long list. But there was one item bothering me above all. Not exactly *on* the list. Kind of parallel to it. I got off my bed and went to find Duffy. She was out in the lot, hurrying back to her room from her car.

"Zachary Beck isn't the story here," I told her. "He can't be. If Quinn's involved, then Quinn's the boss. He wouldn't play second fiddle. Unless Beck is a worse guy than Quinn, and I don't even want to think about that."

"Maybe Quinn changed," she said. "He was shot twice in the head. Maybe that kind of rewired his brains. Diminished him, somehow."

I said nothing. She hurried away. I went back to my room.

DAY TEN STARTED WITH THE ARRIVAL OF THE VE-hicles. The old guy got a seven-year-old Chevy Caprice to act as his police unmarked. It was the one with the Corvette motor in it, from the final model year before General Motors stopped making them. It looked just right. The pickup was a big thing painted faded red. It had a bull bar on the front. I saw the younger guys talking about how they would use it. My ride was a plain brown panel van. It was the most anonymous truck I had ever seen. It had no side windows and two small rear windows. I checked inside for a glove compartment. It had one.

"OK?" Eliot asked me.

I slapped its side like van people do and it boomed faintly in response.

"Perfect," I said. "I want the revolvers to be big .44 Magnums. I want three heavy soft-nosed bullets and nine blanks. Make the blanks as loud as you can get."

"OK," he said. "Why soft-nose?"

"I'm worried about ricochets," I said. "I don't want to

hurt anybody by accident. Soft-nose slugs will deform and stick to what they hit. I'm going to fire one into the radiator and two at the tires. I want you to pump the tires way high so they'll explode when I hit them. We've got to make it spectacular."

Eliot hurried away and Duffy came up to me.

"You'll need these," she said. She had a coat and a pair of gloves for me. "You'll look more realistic if you're wearing them. It'll be cold. And the coat will hide the gun."

I took them from her and tried on the coat. It fit pretty well. She was clearly a good judge of sizes.

"The psychology will be tricky," she said. "You're going to have to be flexible. The kid might be catatonic. You might need to coax some reaction out of him. But ideally he'll be awake and talking. In which case I think you need to show a little reluctance about getting yourself more and more involved. Ideally you need to let *him* talk *you* into driving him all the way home. But at the same time you need to be dominant. You need to keep events moving along so he doesn't have time to dwell on exactly what he's seeing."

"OK," I said. "In which case I'm going to change my ammunition requisition. I'm going to make the second bullet in the second gun a real one. I'll tell him to get down on the floor and then I'll blow out the window behind him. He'll think it was the college cops shooting at us. Then I'll tell him to get up again. It'll increase his sense of danger and it'll get him used to doing what I tell him and it'll make him a little happier to watch the college cops get it in the neck. Because I don't want him fighting me, trying to stop me. I might wreck the van and kill both of us."

"In fact you need to bond with him," she said. "He needs to speak well of you, later. Because I agree, getting hired on up there would hit the jackpot. It would give you access. So try to impress the kid. But keep it very subtle. You don't need him to like you. You just need to make him think you're a tough guy who knows what he's doing."

I went to find Eliot and then the two guys playing the college cops came to find me. We arranged that they would fire blanks at me first, then I would fire one blank at them, then I would shoot out the van's rear window, and then I would fire another blank, and finally I would fire my last three blanks in a spaced group. On the final shot they would blow out their own windshield with a real bullet from one of their own guns and then they would go sliding off the road like they had lost a tire or been hit.

"Don't get confused which load is which," one of them said.

"You either," I said back.

WE HAD MORE PIZZA FOR LUNCH AND THEN WENT out to cruise the target area. We parked a mile short and went over a couple of maps. Then we risked three separate passes in two cars right past the college gate. I would have preferred more time to study but we were worried about being conspicuous. We drove back to the motel in silence and regrouped in Eliot's room.

"Looks OK," I said. "Which way will they turn?"

"Maine is north of here," Duffy said. "We can assume he lives somewhere near Portland."

I nodded. "But I think they'll go south. Look at the maps. You get to the highway faster that way. And standard security doctrine is to get on wide busy roads as soon as possible."

"It's a gamble."

"They'll go south," I said.

"Anything else?" Eliot asked.

"I'd be nuts to stick with the van," I said. "Old man Beck will figure if I was doing this for real I'd ditch it and steal a car."

"Where?" Duffy asked.

"The map shows a mall next to the highway."

"OK, we'll stash one there."

"Spare keys under the bumper?" Eliot asked.

Duffy shook her head. "Too phony. We need this whole thing to be absolutely convincing. He'll have to steal it for real."

"I don't know how," I said. "I've never stolen a car."

The room went quiet.

"All I know is what I learned in the army," I said. "Military vehicles are never locked. And they don't have ignition keys. They start off a button."

"OK," Eliot said. "No problem is insuperable. We'll leave it unlocked. But you'll act like it *is* locked. You'll pretend to jimmy the door. We'll leave a load of wire and a bunch of coat hangers nearby. Maybe you could ask the kid to find something for you. Make him feel involved. It'll help the illusion. Then you screw around with it and, hey, the door pops open. We'll loosen the shroud on the steering column. We'll strip the right wires and *only* the right wires. You find them and touch them together and you're an instant bad guy."

"Brilliant," Duffy said.

Eliot smiled. "I do my best."

"Let's take a break," Duffy said. "Start again after dinner."

THE FINAL PIECES FELL INTO PLACE AFTER DIN-ner. Two of the guys got back with the last of the equipment. They had a matched pair of Colt Anacondas for me. They were big brutal weapons. They looked expensive. I didn't ask where they got them from. They came with a box of real .44 Magnums and a box of .44 blanks. The blanks came from a hardware store. They were designed for a heavy-duty nail gun. The sort of thing that punches nails straight into concrete. I opened each Anaconda cylinder and scratched an X against one of the chambers with the tip of a nail scissor. A Colt revolver's cylinder steps around clockwise, which is different from a Smith & Wesson, which rotates counterclockwise. The X would represent the first chamber to be fired. I would line it up at the ten o'clock position where I could see it and it would step around and fall under the hammer with the first pull of the trigger.

Duffy brought me a pair of shoes. They were my size. The right one had a cavity carved into the heel. She gave me a wireless e-mail device that fit snugly into the space.

"That's why I'm glad you've got big feet," she said. "Made it easier to fit."

"Is it reliable?"

"It better be. It's new government issue. All departments are doing their concealed communications with it now."

"Great," I said. In my career more foul-ups had been caused by faulty technology than any other single cause.

"It's the best we can do," she said. "They'd find anything else. They're bound to search you. And the theory is if they're scanning for radio transmissions all they'll hear is a brief burst of modem screech. They'll probably think it's static."

They had three blood effects from a New York theatrical costumier. They were big and bulky. Each was a foot-wide square of Kevlar that was to be taped to the victim's chest. They had rubber gore reservoirs and radio receivers and firing charges and batteries.

"Wear loose shirts, guys," Eliot said.

The radio triggers were separate buttons I would have to tape to my right forearm. They were wired to batteries I would have to carry in my inside pocket. The buttons were big enough to feel through my coat and my jacket and my shirt, and I figured I would look OK supporting the Colt's weight with my left hand. We rehearsed the sequence. First, the pickup driver. That button would be nearest my wrist. I would trigger it with my index finger. Second, the pickup passenger. That button would be in the middle. Middle finger. Third, the old guy playing the cop. That button would be nearest my elbow, ring finger.

"You'll have to lose them afterward," Eliot said. "They'll search you for sure at Beck's house. You'll have to stop at a men's room or something and get rid of them."

We rehearsed endlessly in the motel lot. We laid out the road in miniature. By midnight we were as solid as we were ever going to get. We figured we would need all of eight seconds, beginning to end.

"You have the critical decision," Duffy said to me. "It's your call. If there's anything wrong when the Toyota is coming at you, anything at all, then you abort and you watch it go on by. We'll clean it up somehow. But you'll be firing three live rounds in a public place and I don't want any stray pedestrians getting hit, or cyclists, or joggers. You'll have less than a second to decide."

"Understood," I said, although I really didn't see any easy way of cleaning it up if it had already gotten that far. Then Eliot took a last couple of phone calls and confirmed they had a college security cruiser on loan and were putting a plausible old Nissan Maxima behind the mall's flagship department store. The Maxima had been impounded from a small-time marijuana grower in New York State. They still had tough drug laws down there. They were putting phony Massachusetts plates on it and filling it with the kind of junk a department store sales lady might be expected to haul around with her.

"Bed now," Duffy called. "Big day tomorrow."

That was the end of day ten.

DUFFY BROUGHT DOUGHNUTS AND COFFEE TO my room for breakfast on day eleven, early. Her and me, alone. We went through the whole thing, one last time. She showed me photographs of the agent she had inserted fifty-nine days ago. She was a blond thirty-year-old who had gotten a clerk's job with Bizarre Bazaar using the name Teresa Daniel. Teresa Daniel was petite and looked resourceful. I looked hard at the pictures and memorized her features, but it was another woman's face I was seeing in my mind.

"I'm assuming she's still alive," Duffy said. "I have to."

I said nothing.

"Try hard to get hired," she said. "We checked your recent history, the same way Beck might. You come out pretty vague. Plenty missing that would worry me, but I don't think it would worry him."

I gave the photographs back to her.

"I'm a shoo-in," I said. "The illusion reinforces itself. He's left shorthanded and he's under attack, all at the same time. But I'm not going to try too hard. In fact I'm going to come across a little reluctant. I think anything else would seem phony."

"OK," she said. "You've got seven objectives, of which numbers one, two, and three are, take a lot of care. We can assume these are extremely dangerous people."

I nodded. "We can do more than assume it. If Quinn's involved, we can absolutely guarantee it."

"So act accordingly," she said. "Gloves off, from the start."

"Yes," I said. I put my arm across my chest and started massaging my left shoulder with my right hand. Then I stopped myself, surprised. An army psychiatrist once told me that type of unconscious gesture represents feelings of vulnerability. It's defensive. It's about covering up and hiding. It's the first step toward curling yourself into a ball on the floor. Duffy must have read the same books, because she picked up on it and looked straight at me.

"You're scared of Quinn, aren't you?" she said.

"I'm not scared of anybody," I said. "But certainly I preferred it when he was dead."

"We can cancel," she said.

I shook my head. "I'd like the chance to find him, believe me."

"What went wrong with the arrest?"

I shook my head again.

"I won't talk about that," I said.

She was quiet for a beat. But she didn't push it. Just looked away and paused and looked back and started up with the briefing again. Quiet voice, efficient diction.

"Objective number four is find my agent," she said. "And bring her back to me."

I nodded.

"Five, bring me solid evidence I can use to nail Beck."

"OK," I said.

She paused again. Just a beat. "Six, find Quinn and do whatever you need to do with him. And then seven, get the hell out of there."

I nodded. Said nothing.

"We won't tail you," she said. "The kid might spot us. He'll be pretty paranoid by then. And we won't put a homing device on the Nissan, because they'd probably find it later. You'll have to e-mail us your location, soon as you know it."

"OK," I said.

"Weaknesses?" she asked.

I forced my mind away from Quinn.

"Three weaknesses that I can see," I said. "Two minor and one major. First minor one is that I'm going to blow the back window out of the van but the kid will have about ten minutes to realize the broken glass is in the wrong place and there isn't a corresponding hole in the windshield."

"So don't do it."

"I think I really need to. I think we need to keep the panic level high."

"OK, we'll put a bunch of boxes back there. You should have boxes anyway if you're a delivery man. They might obscure his view. If they don't, just hope he doesn't put two and two together inside ten minutes."

I nodded. "And second, old man Beck is going to call the cops down here, sometime, somehow. Maybe the newspapers, too. He's going to be looking for corroborating information."

"We'll give the cops a script to follow. And they'll give the press something. They'll play ball for as long as they need to. What's the major weakness?"

"The bodyguards," I said. "How long can you hold them? You can't let them get near a phone, or they'll call Beck. So you can't formally arrest them. You can't put them in the system. You'll have to hold them incommunicado, completely illegally. How long can you keep that going?"

She shrugged. "Four or five days, tops. We can't protect you any longer than that. So be real fast."

"I plan to be," I said. "How long will the battery last on my e-mail thing?"

"About five days," she said. "You'll be out by then. We can't give you a charger. It would be too suspicious. But you can use a cell phone charger, if you can find one."

"OK," I said.

She just looked at me. There was nothing more to say. Then she moved close and kissed me on the cheek. It was sudden. Her lips were soft. They left a dusting of doughnut sugar on my skin.

"Good luck," she said. "I don't think we've missed anything."

But we had missed a lot of things. They were glaring errors in our thinking and they all came back to haunt me.

CHAPTER 3

DUKE THE BODYGUARD CAME BACK TO MY ROOM five minutes before seven in the evening, which was way too early for dinner. I heard his footsteps outside and a quiet click as the lock turned. I was sitting on the bed. The e-mail device was back in my shoe and my shoe was back on my foot.

"Get a nap, asshole?" he asked.

"Why am I locked up?" I asked back.

"Because you're a cop-killer," he said.

I looked away. Maybe he had been a cop himself, before he went private. Lots of ex-cops wind up in the security business, as consultants or private eyes or bodyguards. Certainly he had some kind of an agenda, which could be a problem for me. But it meant he was buying Richard Beck's story without question, which was the upside. He looked at me for a second with nothing much in his face. Then he led me out of the room and down the two flights of stairs to the ground floor and through dark passageways toward the side of the house that faced north. I could smell salt air and damp carpet. There were rugs everywhere. Some places they were laid two-deep on the floor. They glowed with muted colors. He stopped in front of a door and pushed it open and stepped back so I was channeled into a room. It was large and square and paneled with dark oak. Rugs all over the floor. There were small windows in deep recesses. Darkness and rock and gray ocean outside. There was an oak table. My two Colt Anacondas were lying on it, unloaded. Their cylinders were open. There was a man at the head of the table. He was sitting in an oak chair with arms and a tall back. He was the guy from Susan Duffy's surveillance photographs.

In the flesh he was mostly unremarkable. Not big, not small. Maybe six feet, maybe two hundred pounds. Gray hair, not thin, not thick, not short, not long. He was about fifty. He was wearing a gray suit made out of expensive cloth cut without any attempt at style. His shirt was white and his tie was no color at all, like gasoline. His hands and face were pale, like his natural habitat was underground parking garages at night, hawking samples of something from his Cadillac's trunk.

"Sit down," he said. His voice was quiet and strained, like it was all high up in his throat. I sat opposite him at the far end of the table.

"I'm Zachary Beck," he said.

"Jack Reacher," I said.

Duke closed the door gently and leaned his bulk against it from the inside. The room went quiet. I could hear the ocean. It wasn't a rhythmic wave sound like you hear at the beach. It was a continuous random crashing and sucking of surf on the rocks. I could hear pools draining and gravel rattling and breakers coming in like explosions. I tried to count them. People say every seventh wave is a big one.

"So," Beck said. He had a drink on the table in front of him. Some kind of amber liquid in a short heavy glass. Oily, like scotch or bourbon. He nodded to Duke. Duke picked up a second glass. It had been waiting there for me on a side table. It had the same oily amber liquid in it. He carried it awkwardly with his finger and thumb right down at the base. He walked across the room and bent a little to place it carefully in front of me. I smiled. I knew what it was for.

"So," Beck said again.

I waited.

"My son explained your predicament," he said. It was the same phrase his wife had used.

"The law of unintended consequences," I said.

"It presents me with difficulties," he said. "I'm just an ordinary businessman, trying to work out where my responsibilities lie."

I waited.

"We're grateful, naturally," he said. "Please don't misunderstand that."

"But?"

"There are legal issues, aren't there?" He said it with a little annoyance in his voice, like he was being victimized by complexities beyond his control.

"It's not rocket science," I said. "I need you to turn a blind eye. At least temporarily. Like one good turn deserves another. If your conscience can accommodate that kind of a thing."

The room went quiet again. I listened to the ocean. I could hear a full spectrum of sounds out there. I could hear brittle seaweed dragging on granite and a drawn-out undertow sucking backward toward the east. Zachary Beck's gaze was moving all over the place. He was looking at the table, then at the floor, then into space. His face was narrow. Not much of a jaw. His eyes were set fairly close together. His brow was lined with concentration. His lips were thin and his mouth was pursed. His head was moving a little. The whole thing was a reasonable facsimile of an ordinary businessman struggling with weighty issues.

"Was it a mistake?" he asked.

"The cop?" I said. "In retrospect, obviously. At the time, I was just trying to get the job done."

He spent a little more time thinking, and then he nodded.

"OK," he said. "In the circumstances, we might be willing to help you out. If we can. You did a great service for the family."

"I need money," I said.

"Why?"

"I'm going to need to travel."

"When?"

"Right now."

"Is that wise?"

"Not really. I'd prefer to wait here a couple of days until the initial panic is over. But I don't want to push my luck with you."

"How much money?"

"Five thousand dollars might do it."

He said nothing to that. Just started up with the gazing thing again. This time, there was a little more focus in his eyes.

"I've got some questions for you," he said. "Before you leave us. *If* you leave us. Two issues are paramount. First, who were they?"

"Don't you know?"

"I have many rivals and enemies."

"That would go this far?"

"I'm a rug importer," he said. "I didn't intend to be, but that's the way things worked out. Possibly you think I just deal with department stores and interior decorators, but the reality is I deal with all kinds of unsavory characters in various foreign hellholes where enslaved children are forced to work eighteen-hour days until their fingers bleed. Their owners are all convinced I'm ripping them off and raping their cultures, and the truth is I probably am, although no more than they are. They aren't fun companions. I need a certain toughness to prosper. And the point is, so do my competitors. This is a tough business all around. So between my suppliers and my competitors I can think of half a dozen separate people who would kidnap my son to get at me. After all, one of them *did,* five years ago, as I'm sure my son told you."

I said nothing.

"I need to know who they were," he said, like he really meant it. So I paused a beat and recounted the whole event for him, second by second, yard by yard, mile by mile. I described the two tall fair-haired DEA guys in the Toyota accurately and in great detail.

"They mean nothing to me," he said.

I didn't answer.

"Did you get the Toyota's license plate?" he asked.

I thought back and told him the truth.

"I only saw the front," I said. "There was no plate."

"OK," he said. "So they were from a state that doesn't require a front license plate. That narrows it down a little, I guess."

I said nothing. A long moment later he shook his head.

"Information is in very short supply," he said. "An associate of mine contacted the police department down there, in a roundabout way. One town cop is dead, one college cop is dead, two unexplained strangers in a Lincoln Town Car are dead, and two unexplained strangers in a Toyota pickup truck are dead. The only surviving eyewitness is a second college cop, and he's still unconscious after a car wreck nearly five miles away. So right now nobody knows what happened. Nobody knows why it happened. Nobody has made a connection to an attempted kidnap. All anybody knows is there was a bloodbath down there for no apparent reason. They're speculating about gang warfare."

"What happens when they run the Lincoln's plate?" I asked.

He hesitated.

"It's a corporate registration," he said. "It doesn't lead directly here."

I nodded. "OK, but I want to be on the West Coast before that other college cop wakes up. He got a good look at me."

"And I want to know who stepped out of line here."

I glanced at the Anacondas on the table. They had been cleaned and lightly oiled. I was suddenly very glad I had ditched the spent shells. I picked up my glass. Wrapped my thumb and all four fingers around it and sniffed the contents. I had no idea what they were. I would have preferred a cup of coffee. I put the glass back on the table.

"Is Richard OK?" I asked.

"He'll live," Beck said. "I'd like to know who exactly is attacking me."

"I told you what I saw," I said. "They didn't show me ID. They weren't known to me personally. I just happened to be there. What's your second paramount issue?"

There was another pause. The surf crashed and boomed outside the windows.

"I'm a cautious man," Beck said. "And I don't want to offend you."

"But?"

"But I'm wondering who you are, exactly."

"I'm the guy who saved your boy's other ear," I said.

Beck glanced at Duke, who stepped forward smartly and took my glass away. He used the same awkward pincer movement with his thumb and his index finger, right down at the base.

"And now you've got my fingerprints," I said. "Nice and clear."

Beck nodded again, like a guy making a judicious decision. He pointed at the guns, where they lay on the table.

"Nice weapons," he said.

I said nothing back. He moved his hand and nudged one of them with his knuckles. Then he sent it sliding across the wood toward me. The heavy steel made a hollow reverberant sound on the oak.

"You want to tell me why there's a mark scratched against one of the chambers?"

I listened to the ocean.

"I don't know why," I said. "They came to me like that."

"You bought them used?"

"In Arizona," I said.

"From a gun store?"

"From a gun show," I said.

"Why?"

"I don't like background checks," I said.

"Didn't you ask about the scratches?"

"I assumed they were reference marks," I said. "I assumed some gun nut had tested them and marked the most accurate chamber. Or the least accurate."

"Chambers differ?"

"Everything differs," I said. "That's the nature of manufacturing."

"Even with eight-hundred-dollar revolvers?"

"Depends on how discriminating you want to be. You feel the need to measure down to the hundred-thousandths of an inch, then everything in the world is different."

"Does it matter?"

"Not to me," I said. "I point a gun at somebody, I don't care which individual blood cell I'm targeting."

He sat quiet for a moment. Then he went into his

pocket and came out with a bullet. Shiny brass case, dull lead point. He stood it upright in front of him like a miniature artillery shell. Then he knocked it over and rolled it under his fingers on the table. Then he placed it carefully and flicked it with his fingertip so that it rolled all the way along to me. It came in a wide graceful curve. It made a slow droning sound on the wood. I let it roll off the end of the table and caught it in my hand. It was an unjacketed Remington .44 Magnum. Heavy, probably more than three hundred grains. It was a brutal thing. Probably cost the best part of a dollar. It was warm from his pocket.

"You ever played Russian roulette?" he asked.

"I need to get rid of the car I stole," I said.

"We've already gotten rid of it," he said.

"Where?"

"Where it won't be found."

He went quiet. I said nothing. Just looked at him, like I was thinking *Is that the sort of thing an ordinary businessman does*? As well as registering his limousines through shell corporations? And instantly recalling the retail on a Colt Anaconda? And trapping a guest's prints on a whiskey tumbler?

"You ever played Russian roulette?" he asked again.

"No," I said. "I never did."

"I'm under attack," he said. "And I just lost two guys. Time like this I need to be adding guys, not losing them."

I waited, five seconds, ten. I made out like I was struggling with the concept.

"You asking to hire me?" I said. "I'm not sure I can stick around."

"I'm not asking anything," he said. "I'm deciding. You look like a useful guy. You could have that five thousand dollars to stay, not to go. Maybe."

I said nothing.

"Hey, if I want you, I've got you," he said. "There's a

dead cop down in Massachusetts and I've got your name and I've got your prints."

"But?"

"But I don't know who you are."

"Get used to it," I said. "How do you know who anybody is?"

"I find out. I test people. Suppose I asked you to kill another cop? As a gesture of good faith?"

"I'd say no. I'd repeat that the first one was an unfortunate accident I regret very much. And I'd start wondering about what kind of an ordinary businessman you really are."

"My business is my business. It needn't concern you."

I said nothing.

"Play Russian roulette with me," he said.

"What would that prove?"

"A federal agent wouldn't do it."

"Why are you worried about federal agents?"

"That needn't concern you, either."

"I'm not a federal agent," I said.

"So prove it. Play Russian roulette with me. I mean, I'm already playing Russian roulette with you, in a manner of speaking, just letting you into my house without knowing exactly who you are."

"I saved your son."

"And I'm very grateful for that. Grateful enough that I'm still talking to you in a civilized manner. Grateful enough that I might yet offer you sanctuary and employment. Because I like a man who gets the job done."

"I'm not looking for work," I said. "I'm looking to hide out for maybe forty-eight hours and then move on."

"We'd look after you. Nobody would ever find you. You'd be completely safe here. If you pass the test."

"Russian roulette is the test?"

"The infallible test," he said. "In my experience."

I said nothing. The room was silent. He leaned forward in his chair.

"You're either with me or against me," he said. "Either way, you're about to prove it. I sincerely hope you choose wisely."

Duke moved against the door. The floor creaked under his feet. I listened to the ocean. Spray smashed upward and the wind whipped it and heavy foam drops arced lazily through the air and tapped against the window glass. The seventh wave came booming in, heavier than the others. I picked up the Anaconda in front of me. Duke pulled a gun out from under his jacket and pointed it at me in case I had something other than roulette on my mind. He had a Steyr SPP, which is most of a Steyr TMP submachine gun cut down into pistol form. It's a rare piece from Austria and it was big and ugly in his hand. I looked away from it and concentrated on the Colt. I thumbed the bullet into a random chamber and closed the cylinder and spun it free. The ratchet purred in the silence.

"Play," Beck said.

I spun the cylinder again and raised the revolver and touched the muzzle to my temple. The steel was cold. I looked Beck straight in the eye and held my breath and eased the trigger back. The cylinder turned and the hammer cocked. The action was smooth, like silk rubbing on silk. I pulled the trigger all the way. The hammer fell. There was a loud click. I felt the smack of the hammer pulse all the way through the steel to the side of my head. But I felt nothing else. I breathed out and lowered the gun and held it with the back of my hand resting on the table. Then I turned my hand over and pulled my finger out of the trigger guard.

"Your turn," I said.

"I just wanted to see you do it," he said.

I smiled.

"You want to see me do it again?" I said.

Beck said nothing. I picked up the gun again and spun the cylinder and let it slow and stop. Raised the muzzle to my head. The barrel was so long my elbow was forced up and out. I pulled the trigger, fast and decisive. There was a loud click in the silence. It was the sound of an eight-hundred-dollar piece of precision machinery working exactly the way it should. I lowered the gun and spun the cylinder a third time. Raised the gun. Pulled the trigger. Nothing. I did it a fourth time, fast. Nothing. I did it a fifth time, faster. Nothing.

"OK," Beck said.

"Tell me about Oriental rugs," I said.

"Nothing much to tell," he said. "They go on the floor. People buy them. Sometimes for a lot of money."

I smiled. Raised the gun again.

"Odds are six to one," I said. I spun the cylinder a sixth time. The room went completely silent. I put the gun to my head. Pulled the trigger. I felt the smack of the hammer falling on an empty chamber. Nothing else.

"Enough," Beck said.

I lowered the Colt and cracked the cylinder and dumped the bullet out on the table. Lined it up carefully and rolled it all the way back to him. It droned on the wood. He stopped it with the heel of his hand and sat there and said nothing for two or three minutes. He was looking at me like I was an animal in a zoo. Like maybe he wished there were some bars between him and me.

"Richard tells me you were a military cop," he said.

"Thirteen years," I said.

"Were you good?"

"Better than those bozos you sent to pick him up."

"He speaks well of you."

"So he should," I said. "I saved his ass. At considerable cost to myself."

"You going to be missed anywhere?"

"No."

"Family?"

"Haven't got any."

"Job?"

"I can't go back to it now," I said. "Can I?"

He played with the bullet for a moment, rolling it under the pad of his index finger. Then he scooped it up into his palm.

"Who can I call?" he said.

"For what?"

He jiggled the bullet in his palm, like shaking dice.

"An employment recommendation," he said. "You had a boss, right?"

Mistakes, coming back to haunt me.

"Self-employed," I said.

He put the bullet back on the table.

"Licensed and insured?" he said.

I paused a beat.

"Not exactly," I said.

"Why not?"

"Reasons," I said.

"Got a registration for your truck?"

"I might have mislaid it."

He rolled the bullet under his fingers. Gazed at me. I could see him thinking. He was running things through his head. Processing information. Trying to make it fit with his own preconceptions. I willed him onward. *An armed tough guy with an old panel van that doesn't belong to him. A car thief. A cop-killer.* He smiled.

"Used records," he said. "I've seen that store."

I said nothing. Just looked him in the eye.

"Let me take a guess," he said. "You were fencing stolen CDs."

His type of guy. I shook my head.

"Bootlegs," I said. "I'm not a thief. I'm ex-military, trying to scrape a living. And I believe in free expression."

"Like hell," he said. "You believe in making a buck."

His type of guy.

"That too," I said.

"Were you doing well?"

"Well enough."

He scooped the bullet into his palm again and tossed it to Duke. Duke caught it one-handed and dropped it into his jacket pocket.

"Duke is my head of security," Beck said. "You'll work for him, effective immediately."

I glanced at Duke, than back at Beck.

"Suppose I don't want to work for him?" I said.

"You have no choice. There's a dead cop down in Massachusetts, and we have your name and your prints. You'll be on probation, until we get a feel for exactly what kind of a person you are. But look on the bright side. Think about five thousand dollars. That's a lot of bootleg CDs."

THE DIFFERENCE BETWEEN BEING AN HONORED guest and a probationary employee was that I ate dinner in the kitchen with the other help. The giant from the gatehouse lodge didn't show, but there was Duke and one other guy I took to be some kind of an all-purpose mechanic or handyman. There was a maid and a cook. The five of us sat around a plain deal table and had a meal just as good as the family was getting in the dining room. Maybe better, because maybe the cook had spat in theirs, and I doubted if she would spit in ours. I had spent enough time around grunts and NCOs to know how they do things.

There wasn't much conversation. The cook was a sour woman of maybe sixty. The maid was timid. I got the impression she was fairly new. She was unsure about how to conduct herself. She was young and plain. She was wearing a cotton shift and a wool cardigan. She had clunky flat shoes on. The mechanic was a middle-aged guy, thin, gray, quiet. Duke was quiet too, because he was thinking. Beck had handed him a problem and he wasn't sure how he should deal with it. Could he use me? Could he trust me? He wasn't stupid. That was clear. He saw all the angles and he was prepared to spend a little time examining them. He was around my age. Maybe a little younger, maybe a little older. He had one of those hard ugly corn-fed faces that hides age well. He was about my size. I probably had heavier bones, he was probably a little bulkier. We probably weighed within a pound or two of each other. I sat next to him and ate my food and tried to time it right with the kind of questions a normal person would be expected to ask.

"So tell me about the rug business," I said, with enough tone in my voice that he knew I was saying I assumed Beck was into something else entirely.

"Not now," he said, like he meant *not in front of the help*. And then he looked at me in a way that had to mean *anyway I'm not sure I want to be talking to a guy crazy enough to chance shooting himself in the head six straight times*.

"The bullet was a fake, right?" I said.

"What?"

"No powder in it," I said. "Probably just cotton wadding."

"Why would it be a fake?"

"I could have shot him with it."

"Why would you want to do that?"

"I wouldn't, but he's a cautious guy. He wouldn't take the risk."

"I was covering you."

"I could have gotten you first. Used your gun on him."

He stiffened a little, but he didn't say anything. *Competitive.* I didn't like him very much. Which was OK with me, because I guessed he was going to wind up as a casualty before too long.

"Hold this," he said.

He took the bullet out of his pocket and handed it to me.

"Wait there," he said.

He got up off his chair and walked out of the kitchen. I stood the bullet upright in front of me, just like Beck had. I finished up my meal. There was no dessert. No coffee. Duke came back with one of my Anacondas swinging from his trigger finger. He walked past me to the back door and nodded me over to join him. I picked the bullet up and clamped it in my palm. Followed him. The back door beeped as we passed through it. Another metal detector. It was neatly integrated into the frame. But there was no burglar alarm. Their security depended on the sea and the wall and the razor wire.

Beyond the back door was a cold damp porch, and then a rickety storm door into the yard, which was nothing more than the tip of the rocky finger. It was a hundred yards wide and semicircular in front of us. It was dark and the lights from the house picked up the grayness of the granite. The wind was blowing and I could see luminescence from the whitecaps out in the ocean. The surf crashed and eddied. There was a moon and low torn clouds moving fast. The horizon was immense and black.

The air was cold. I twisted up and back and picked out my room's window way above me.

"Bullet," Duke said.

I turned back and passed it to him.

"Watch," he said.

He loaded it into the Colt. Jerked his hand to snap the cylinder shut. Squinted in the moonlit grayness and clicked the cylinder around until the loaded chamber was at the ten o'clock position.

"Watch," he said again.

He pointed the gun with his arm straight, aiming just below horizontal at the flat granite tables where they met the sea. He pulled the trigger. The cylinder turned and the hammer dropped and the gun kicked and flashed and roared. There was a simultaneous spark on the rocks and an unmistakable metallic *whang* of a ricochet. It feathered away to silence. The bullet probably skipped a hundred yards out into the Atlantic. Maybe it killed a fish.

"It wasn't a fake," he said. "I'm fast enough."

"OK," I said.

He opened the cylinder and shook the empty shell case out. It clinked on the rocks by his feet.

"You're an asshole," he said. "An asshole cop-killer."

"Were you a cop?"

He nodded. "Once upon a time."

"Is Duke your first name or your last?"

"Last."

"Why does a rug importer need armed security?"

"Like he told you, it's a rough business. There's a lot of money in it."

"You really want me here?"

He shrugged. "I might. If somebody's sniffing around, we might need some cannon fodder. Better you than me."

"I saved the kid."

"So what? Get in line. We've all saved the kid, one time or another. Or Mrs. Beck, or Mr. Beck himself."

"How many guys have you got?"

"Not enough," he said. "Not if we're under attack."

"What is this, a war?"

He didn't answer. Just walked past me toward the house. I turned my back on the restless ocean and followed him.

THERE WAS NOTHING DOING IN THE KITCHEN. The mechanic had disappeared and the cook and the maid were stacking dishes into a machine large enough to do duty in a restaurant. The maid was all fingers and thumbs. She didn't know what went where. I looked around for coffee. There still wasn't any. Duke sat down again at the empty deal table. There was no activity. No urgency. I was aware of time slipping away. I didn't trust Susan Duffy's estimate of five days' grace. Five days is a long time when you're guarding two healthy individuals off the books. I would have been happier if she had said three days. I would have been more impressed by her sense of realism.

"Go to bed," Duke said. "You'll be on duty as of six-thirty in the morning."

"Doing what?"

"Doing whatever I tell you."

"Is my door going to be locked?"

"Count on it," he said. "I'll unlock it at six-fifteen. Be down here by six-thirty."

I WAITED ON MY BED UNTIL I HEARD HIM COME up after me and lock the door. Then I waited some more until I was sure he wasn't coming back. Then I took my shoe off and checked for messages. The little device powered up and the tiny green screen was filled with a cheerful italic announcement: *You've Got Mail!* There was one item only. It was from Susan Duffy. It was a one-word question: *Location?* I hit *reply* and typed *Abbot, Maine, coast, 20m S of Portland, lone house on long rock finger.* That would have to do. I didn't have a mailing address or exact GPS coordinates. But she should be able to pin it down if she spent some time with a large-scale map of the area. I hit *send now.*

Then I stared at the screen. I wasn't entirely sure how e-mail worked. Was it instantaneous communication, like a phone call? Or would my reply wait somewhere in limbo before it got to her? I assumed she would be watching for it. I assumed she and Eliot would be spelling each other around the clock.

Ninety seconds later the screen announced *You've Got Mail!* again. I smiled. This might work. This time her message was longer. Only twenty-one words, but I had to scroll down the tiny screen to read it all. It said: *We'll work the maps, thanks. Prints show 2 bodyguards in our custody are ex-army. All under control here. You? Progress?*

I hit *reply* and typed *hired, probably.* Then I thought for a second and pictured Quinn and Teresa Daniel in my mind and added *otherwise no progress yet.* Then I thought some more and typed *re 2 bodyguards ask MP Powell quote 10-29, 10-30, 10-24, 10-36 unquote from me specifically.* Then I hit *send now.* I watched the machine announce *Your message has been sent* and looked away at the darkness outside the window and hoped Powell's generation still spoke the same language mine did. 10-29, 10-30, 10-24, and 10-36 were four standard Military Police radio codes that meant nothing much in themselves. 10-29 stood for *weak signal.* It was a procedural complaint about failing equipment. 10-30 meant *I am requesting nonemergency assistance.* 10-24 meant *suspicious person.* 10-36 meant *please forward my messages.* The 10-30 nonemergency call meant the whole string would attract no attention from anybody. It would be recorded and filed somewhere and ignored for the rest of history. But taken together the string was a kind of underground jargon. At least it used to be, way back when I was in uniform. The *weak signal* part meant *keep this quiet and under the radar.* The request for nonemergency assistance backed it up: *keep this away from the hot files.* *Suspicious person* was self-explanatory. *Please forward my messages* meant *put me in the loop.* So if Powell was on the ball he would understand the whole thing to mean *check these guys out on the quiet and give me the skinny.* And I hoped he was on the ball, because he owed me. He owed me big time. He had sold me out. My guess was he would be looking for ways to make it up to me.

I looked back at the tiny screen: *You've Got Mail!* It was Duffy, saying *OK, be fast.* I replied *trying* and switched off and nailed the device back into the heel of my shoe. Then I checked the window.

It was a standard two-part sliding thing. The bottom casement would slide upward in front of the top casement. There was no insect screen. The paint on the inside was thin and neat. The paint on the outside was thick and sloppy from where it had been continually redone to beat the climate. There was a brass catch. It was an ancient thing. There was no modern security. I slipped the catch and pushed the window up. It caught on the thick paint. But it moved. I got it open about five inches and cold sea air blew in on me. I bent down and looked for alarm pads. There weren't any. I heaved it all the way up and examined the whole of the frame. There was no sign of any security system at all. It was understandable. The window was fifty feet up above the rocks and the ocean. And the house itself was unreachable because of the high wall and the water.

I leaned out the window and looked down. I could see where I had been standing when Duke fired the bullet. I stayed half-in and half-out of the window for about five minutes, leaning on my elbows, staring at the black ocean, smelling the salt air, and thinking about the bullet. I had pulled the trigger six times. It would have made a hell of a mess. My head would have exploded. The rugs would have been ruined and the oak paneling would have splintered. I yawned. The thinking and the sea air were making me sleepy. I ducked back inside and slammed the casement down and went to bed.

I WAS ALREADY UP AND SHOWERED AND DRESSED when I heard Duke unlock the door at six-fifteen the next morning, day twelve, Wednesday, Elizabeth Beck's birthday. I had already checked my e-mail. There were no messages. None at all. I wasn't worried. I spent ten quiet minutes at the window. The dawn was right there in front of me and the sea was gray and oily and subdued. The tide was out. Rocks were exposed. Pools had formed here and there. I could see birds on the shore. They were black guillemots. Their spring feathers were coming in. Gray was changing to black. They had bright red feet. I could see cormorants and black-backed gulls wheeling in the distance. Herring gulls swooping low, searching for breakfast.

I waited until Duke's footsteps had receded and went downstairs and walked into the kitchen and met the giant from the gatehouse face-to-face. He was standing at the sink, drinking water from a glass. He had probably just swallowed his steroid pills. He was a very big guy. I stand six feet five inches tall and I have to center myself quite carefully to walk through a standard thirty-inch doorway. This guy was at least six inches taller than me and probably ten inches wider across the shoulders. He probably outweighed me by two hundred pounds. Maybe by more. I got that core shudder I get when I'm next to a guy big enough to make me feel small. The world seems to tilt a little.

"Duke is in the gym," the guy said.

"There's a gym?" I said.

"Downstairs," he said. His voice was light and high-pitched. He must have been gobbling steroids like candy for years. His eyes were dull and his skin was bad. He was somewhere in his middle thirties, greasy blond, dressed in a muscle shirt and sweatpants. His arms were bigger than my legs. He looked like a cartoon.

"We work out before breakfast," he said.

"Fine," I said. "Go right ahead."

"You too."

"I never work out," I said.

"Duke's expecting you. You work here, you work out."

I glanced at my watch. Six twenty-five in the morning. Time ticking away.

"What's your name?" I asked.

He didn't answer. Just looked at me like I was setting some kind of a trap for him. That's another problem with steroids. Too many of them can rewire your head. And this guy's head didn't look like it had started from a very positive place to begin with. He looked mean and stupid. No better way to put it. And not a good combination. There was something in his face. I didn't like him. I was oh-for-two, as far as liking my new colleagues went.

"It's not a difficult question," I said.

"Paulie," he said.

I nodded. "Pleased to meet you, Paulie. I'm Reacher."

"I know," he said. "You were in the army."

"You got a problem with that?"

"I don't like officers."

I nodded. *They had checked.* They knew what rank I had held. They had some kind of access.

"Why not?" I asked. "Did you fail the OCS exam?"

He didn't answer.

"Let's go find Duke," I said.

He put his glass of water down and led me out to a back hallway and through a door to a set of wooden cellar stairs. There was a whole basement under the house. It must have been blasted out of solid rock. The walls were raw stone patched and smoothed with concrete. The air was a little damp and musty. There were naked light-bulbs hanging in wire cages close to the ceiling. There were numerous rooms. One was a good-sized space with white paint all over it. The floor was covered with white linoleum. There was a smell of old sweat. There was an exercise bicycle and a treadmill and a weights machine. There was a heavy bag hanging from a ceiling joist. There was a speed bag near it. Boxing gloves on a shelf. There were dumbbells stored in wall racks. There were free weights stacked loose on the floor next to a bench. Duke was standing right next to it. He was wearing his dark suit. He looked tired, like he had been up all night. He hadn't showered. His hair was a mess and his suit was creased and wrinkled, especially low down on the back of the coat.

Paulie went straight into some kind of a complicated stretching routine. He was so muscle-bound that his legs and arms had limited articulation. He couldn't touch his shoulders with his fingers. His biceps were too big. I looked at the weights machine. It had all kinds of handles and bars and grips. It had strong black cables that led through pulleys to a tall stack of lead plates. You would have to be able to lift about five hundred pounds to move them all.

"You working out?" I said to Duke.

"None of your business," he replied.

"Me either," I said.

Paulie turned his giant neck and glanced at me. Then he lay down on his back on the bench and shuffled around until his shoulders were positioned underneath a bar resting on a stand. The bar had a bunch of weights on either end. He grunted a bit and wrapped his hands around the bar and flicked his tongue in and out like he was preparing for a major effort. Then he pressed upward and lifted the bar off the stand. The bar bent and wobbled. There was so much weight on it that it curved way down at the ends, like old film of Russian weight-lifters at the Olympics. He grunted again and heaved it up until his arms were locked straight. He held it like that for a second and then crashed it back into the stand. He turned his head and looked straight at me, like I was supposed to be impressed. I was, and I wasn't. It was a lot of weight, and he had a lot of muscle. But steroid muscle is dumb muscle. It looks real good, and if you want to pit it against dead weight it works just fine. But it's slow and heavy and tires you out just carrying it around.

"Can you bench-press four hundred pounds?" he called. He was a little out of breath.

"Never tried," I said.

"Want to try now?"

"No," I said.

"Wimpy little guy like you, it could build you up."

"I'm officer class," I said. "I don't need building up. I

want some four-hundred-pound weight bench-pressed, I just find some big stupid ape and tell him to do it for me."

He glowered at me. I ignored him and looked at the heavy bag. It was a standard piece of gym equipment. Not new. I pushed it with my palm and set it swinging gently on its chain. Duke was watching me. Then he was glancing at Paulie. He had picked up on some vibe I hadn't. I pushed the bag again. We had used heavy bags extensively in hand-to-hand combat training. We would be wearing dress uniforms to simulate street clothes and we used the bags to learn how to kick. I once split a heavy bag with the edge of my heel, years ago. The sand dumped right out on the floor. I figured that would impress Paulie. But I wasn't going to try it again. The e-mail thing was hidden in my heel and I didn't want to damage it. I made an absurd mental note to tell Duffy she should have put it in the left shoe instead. But then, she was left-handed. Maybe she had thought she was doing the right thing all along.

"I don't like you," Paulie called. He was looking straight at me, so I assumed he was talking to me. His eyes were small. His skin glittered. He was a walking chemical imbalance. Exotic compounds were leaking from his pores.

"We should arm wrestle," he said.

"What?"

"We should arm wrestle," he said again. He came up right next to me, light and quiet on his feet. He towered over me. He practically blotted out the light. He smelled of sharp acrid sweat.

"I don't want to arm wrestle," I said. I saw Duke watching me. Then I glanced at Paulie's hands. They were clenched into fists, but they weren't huge. And steroids don't do anything for a person's hands, unless they exercise them, and most people don't think to do that.

"Pussy," he said.

I said nothing.

"Pussy," he said again.

"What's in it for the winner?" I asked.

"Satisfaction," he said.

"OK."

"OK what?"

"OK, let's do it," I said.

He seemed surprised, but he moved back to the weights bench fast enough. I took my jacket off and folded it over the exercise bicycle. Unbuttoned my right cuff and rolled my sleeve up to my shoulder. My arm looked very thin next to his. But my hand was a shade bigger. My fingers were longer. And what little muscle I had in comparison to him came from pure genetics, not out of some pharmacist's bottle.

We knelt down facing each other across the bench and planted our elbows. His forearm was a little longer than mine, which was going to put a kink in his wrist, which was going to help me. We slapped our palms together and gripped. His hand felt cold and damp to me. Duke took up station at the head of the bench, like a referee.

"Go," he said.

I cheated from the first moment. The aim of arm wrestling is to use the strength in your arm and shoulder to rotate your hand downward, taking your opponent's hand with it, to the mat. I had no chance of doing that. Not against this guy. No chance at all. It was going to be all I could do to keep my own hand in place. So I didn't even try to win. I just squeezed. A million years of evolution have given us an opposable thumb, which means it can work against the other four fingers like a pincer. I got his knuckles lined up and squeezed them mercilessly. And I have very strong hands. I concentrated on keeping my arm upright. Stared into his eyes and squeezed his hand until I felt his knuckles start to crush. Then I squeezed harder. And harder. He didn't give up. He was immensely strong. He kept the pressure on. I was sweating and breathing hard, just trying not to lose. We held it like that for a whole minute, straining and quivering in the silence. I squeezed harder. I let the pain build up in his hand. Watched it register in his face. Then I squeezed harder still. That's what gets them. They think it's already gotten as bad as it's going to get, and then it gets worse. And then worse still, like a ratchet. Worse and worse, like there's an infinite universe of agony ahead of them, stepping *up* and *up* and *up,* remorselessly, like a machine. They start concentrating on their own distress. And then the decision starts flickering in their eyes. They know I'm cheating, but they realize they can't do anything about it. They can't look up helplessly and say *he's hurting me*! *It's not fair!* That makes them the pussy, not me. And they can't face that. So they swallow it. They swallow it and they start worrying about whether it's going to get any worse. And it is. For sure. There's plenty more to come. There's always more to come. I stared into Paulie's eyes and squeezed harder. Sweat was making his skin slick, so my hand was moving easily over his, tighter and tighter. There were no friction burns to distract him. The pain was all right there in his knuckles.

"Enough," Duke called. "It's a tie."

I didn't loosen my grip. Paulie didn't back off with the pressure. His arm was as solid as a tree.

"I said enough," Duke called. "You assholes have got work to do."

I raised my elbow up high so he couldn't surprise me with a last-second effort. He looked away and dragged his arm off the bench. We let go of each other. His hand was marked vivid red and white. The ball of my thumb felt like it was on fire. He pushed himself off his knees and stood up and walked straight out of the room. I heard his heavy tread on the wooden staircase.

"That was real stupid," Duke said. "You just made another enemy."

I was out of breath. "What, I was supposed to lose?"

"It would have been better."

"Not my way."

"Then you're stupid," he said.

"You're head of security," I said. "You should tell him to act his age."

"Not that easy."

"So get rid of him."

"That's not easy either."

I stood up slowly. Rolled my sleeve down and buttoned my cuff. Glanced at my watch. Nearly seven in the morning. Time ticking away.

"What am I doing today?" I asked.

"Driving a truck," Duke said. "You can drive a truck, right?"

I nodded, because I couldn't say no. I had been driving a truck when I rescued Richard Beck.

"I need to shower again," I said. "And I need some clean clothes."

"Tell the maid," he said. He was tired. "What am I, your damn valet?"

He watched me for a second and headed for the stairs and left me all alone in the basement. I stood and stretched and panted and shook my hand loose from the wrist to ease the strain. Then I retrieved my jacket and went looking for Teresa Daniel. Theoretically she could be locked up somewhere down there. But I didn't find her. The basement was a warren of spaces carved and blasted out of the rock. Most of them were self-explanatory. There was a furnace room filled with a roaring boiler and a bunch of pipes. There was a laundry room, with a big washing machine sitting high on a wooden table, so it would drain by gravity into a pipe that ran out through the wall at knee height. There were storage areas. There were two locked rooms. Their doors were solid. I listened hard but heard nothing from inside them. I knocked gently and got no response.

I headed back upstairs and met Richard Beck and his mother in the ground-floor hallway. Richard had washed his hair and parted it low on the right and swept it sideways so it hung down thickly on the left, to hide his missing ear. It looked like the thing old guys do to hide the fact they're going bald on top. The ambivalence was still there in his face. He looked comfortable in the dark safety of his house, but I could see he also felt a little trapped. He looked pleased enough to see me. Not just because I had saved his ass, but maybe because I was a random representation of the outside world, too.

"Happy birthday, Mrs. Beck," I said.

She smiled at me, like she was flattered that I'd remembered. She looked better than she had the day before. She was easily ten years older than me, but I might have paid her some attention if we'd met somewhere by chance, like a bar or a club or on a long train ride.

"You'll be with us for a while," she said. Then it seemed to dawn on her why I would be with them for a while. I was hiding out there because I had killed a cop. She looked confused and glanced away and moved on through the hallway. Richard went with her and looked back at me, once, over his shoulder. I found the kitchen again. Paulie wasn't there. Zachary Beck was waiting for me instead.

"What weapons did they have?" he asked. "The guys in the Toyota?"

"They had Uzis," I said. *Stick to the truth, like all good scam artists.* "And a grenade."

"Which Uzis?"

"The Micros," I said. "The little ones."

"Magazines?"

"The short ones. Twenty rounds."

"Are you absolutely sure?"

I nodded.

"You an expert?"

"They were designed by an Israeli Army lieutenant," I said. "His name was Uziel Gal. He was a tinkerer. He made all kinds of improvements to the old Czech models 23 and 25 until he had a whole new thing going. This was back in 1949. The original Uzi went into production in 1953. It's franchised to Belgium and Germany. I've seen a few, here and there."

"And you're absolutely sure these were Micro versions with the short mags?"

"I'm sure."

"OK," he said, like it meant something to him. Then he walked out of the kitchen and disappeared. I stood there and thought about the urgency of his questions and the wrinkles in Duke's suit. The combination worried me.

I FOUND THE MAID AND TOLD HER I NEEDED clothes. She showed me a long shopping list and said she was on her way out to the grocery store. I told her I wasn't asking her to go buy me clothes. I told her just to borrow them from somebody. She went red and bobbed her head and said nothing. Then the cook came back from somewhere and took pity on me and fried me some eggs and bacon. And made me some coffee, which put the whole day in a better light. I ate and drank and then I went up the two flights of stairs to my room. The maid had left some clothes in the corridor, neatly folded on the floor. There was a pair of black denim jeans and a black denim shirt. Black socks and white underwear. Every item was laundered and neatly pressed. I guessed they were Duke's. Beck's or Richard's would have been too small and Paulie's would look like I was wearing a tent. I scooped them up and carried them inside. Locked myself in my bathroom and took my shoe off and checked for e-mail. There was one message. It was from Susan Duffy. It said: *Your location pinpointed by map. We will move up 25m S and W of you to motel near I-95. Response from Powell quote your eyes only, both DD after 5, 10-2, 10-28 unquote. Progress?*

I smiled. Powell still talked the language. *Both DD after 5* meant both guys had served five years and then been dishonorably discharged. Five years is way too long for the discharges to have been related to inherent ineptitude or training screw-ups. Those things would have been evident very early. The only way to get fired after five years is to be a bad person. And *10-2, 10-28* left no doubt about it. 10-28 was a standard radio-check response meaning *loud and clear.* 10-2 was a standard radio call for *ambulance urgently needed.* But read together as MPs' covert slang *ambulance urgently needed, loud and clear* meant *these guys need to be dead, make no mistake about it.* Powell had been in the files, and he hadn't liked what he had seen.

I found the icon for *reply* and typed *no progress yet, stay tuned.* Then I hit *send now* and put the unit back in my shoe. I didn't spend long in the shower. Just rinsed the gymnasium sweat off and dressed in the borrowed clothes. I used my own shoes and jacket and the overcoat Susan Duffy had given me. I walked downstairs and found Zachary Beck and Duke standing together in the hallway. They both had coats on. Duke had car keys in his hand. He still hadn't showered. He still looked tired, and he was scowling. Maybe he didn't like me wearing his clothes. The front door was standing open and I saw the maid driving past in a dusty old Saab, off to do the household's marketing. Maybe she was going to buy a birthday cake.

"Let's go," Beck said, like there was work to be done and not much time to do it in. They led me out through the front door. The metal detector beeped twice, once for each of them but not for me. Outside the air was cold and fresh. The sky was bright. Beck's black Cadillac was waiting on the carriage circle. Duke held the rear door and Beck settled himself in the back. Duke got into the driver's seat. I took the front passenger seat. It seemed appropriate. There was no conversation.

Duke started the engine and put the car in gear and accelerated down the driveway. I could see Paulie far ahead in the distance, opening the gate for the maid in the Saab. He was back in his suit. He stood and waited for us and we swept past him and headed west, away from the sea. I turned around and saw him closing the gate again.

We drove the fifteen miles inland and turned north on the highway toward Portland. I stared ahead through the windshield and wondered exactly where they were taking me. And what they were going to do with me when they got me there.

THEY TOOK ME RIGHT TO THE EDGE OF THE PORT facilities outside the city itself. I could see the tops of ships' superstructures out on the water, and cranes all over the place. There were abandoned containers stacked in weedy lots. There were long low office buildings. There were trucks moving in and moving out. There were sea-gulls in the air everywhere. Duke drove through a gate into a small lot made of cracked concrete and patched black-top. There was nothing in it except for a panel van stand-ing all alone in the center. It was a medium-sized thing, made from a pickup frame with a big boxy body built onto it. The body was wider than the cab and wrapped up over it. It was the kind of thing you find in a rental line. Not the smallest they have to offer, not the largest. There was no writing on it. It was entirely plain, painted blue, with rust streaks here and there. It was old, and it had lived its life in the salt air.

"Keys are in the door pocket," Duke said.

Beck leaned forward from the back seat and handed me a slip of paper. It had directions on it, to some place in New London, Connecticut.

"Drive the truck to this exact address," he said. "It's a parking lot pretty much the same as this one. There'll be an identical truck already there. Keys in the door pocket. You leave this one, you bring the other one back here."

"And don't look inside either one," Duke said.

"And drive slow," Beck said. "Stay legal. Don't attract attention."

"Why?" I said. "What's in them?"

"Rugs," Beck said, from behind me. "I'm thinking of you, is all. You're a wanted man. Better to keep a low pro-file. So take your time. Stop for coffee. Act normally."

They said nothing more. I got out of the Cadillac. The air smelled of sea and oil and diesel exhaust and fish. The wind was blowing. There was indistinct industrial noise all around, and the shriek and caw of gulls. I walked over to the blue truck. Passed directly behind it and saw the roller door handle was secured by a little lead seal. I walked on and opened the driver's door. Found the keys in the pocket. Climbed inside and started the engine. Belted myself in and got comfortable and put the thing in gear and drove out of the lot. I saw Beck and Duke in the Cadillac, watching me go, nothing in their faces. I paused at the first turn and made the left and struck out south.

CHAPTER 4

TIME TICKING AWAY. THAT'S WHAT I WAS CON-
scious of. This was some kind of a trial or a test, and it
was going to take me at least ten precious hours to complete it. Ten hours that I didn't have to spare. And the
truck was a pig to drive. It was old and balky and there
was a constant roaring from the engine and a screaming
whine from the transmission. The suspension was soft
and worn out and the whole vehicle floated and wallowed.
But the rearview mirrors were big solid rectangular things
bolted to the doors and they gave me a pretty good view of
anything more than ten yards behind me. I was on I-95,
heading south, and it was quiet. I was pretty sure nobody
was tailing me. Pretty sure, but not completely certain.

I slowed as much as I dared and squirmed around and
put my left foot on the gas pedal and ducked down and
pulled off my right shoe. Juggled it up into my lap and ex-
tracted the e-mail device one-handed. I held it tight
against the rim of the steering wheel and drove and typed
all at the same time: *urgent meet me 1st I-95 rest area
southbound S of Kennebunk exit now immediately bring
soldering iron and lead solder Radio Shack or hardware
store.* Then I hit *send now* and dropped the thing on the

seat beside me. Kicked my foot back into the shoe and got it back on the pedal and straightened up in the seat. Checked the mirrors again. Nothing there. So I did some math. Kennebunk to New London was a distance of maybe two hundred miles, maybe a little more. Four hours at fifty miles an hour. Two hours fifty minutes at seventy, and seventy was probably the best I was going to get out of that particular truck. So I would have a maximum margin of an hour and ten minutes to do whatever I decided I needed to.

I drove on. I kept it at a steady fifty in the right lane. Everybody passed me. Nobody stayed behind me. I had no tail. I wasn't sure if that was good or bad. The alternative might be worse. I passed the Kennebunk exit after twenty-nine minutes. Saw a rest area sign a mile later. It promised food and gas and restrooms seven miles ahead. The seven miles took me eight and a half minutes. Then there was a shallow ramp that swooped right and rose up a slope through a thicket of trees. The view wasn't good. The leaves were small and new but there were so many of them that I couldn't see much. The rest area itself was invisible to me. I let the truck coast and crested the rise and drove down into a perfectly standard interstate facility. It was just a wide road with diagonal parking slots on both sides and a small huddle of low brick buildings on the right. Beyond the buildings was a gas station. There were maybe a dozen cars parked close to the bathrooms. One of them was Susan Duffy's Taurus. It was last in line on the left. She was standing next to it with Eliot at her side.

I drove slowly past her and made a *wait* gesture with my hand and parked four slots beyond her. I switched off the engine and sat gratefully in the sudden silence for a moment. I put the e-mail device back in my heel and laced my shoe. Then I tried to look like a normal person. I stretched my arms and opened the door and slid out and stumped around for a moment like a guy easing his cramped legs and relishing the fresh forest air. I turned a couple of complete circles and scanned the whole area and then stood still and kept my eyes on the ramp. Nobody came up it. I could hear light traffic out on the highway. It was close by and fairly loud, but the way it was all behind the trees made me feel private and isolated. I counted off seventy-two seconds, which represents a mile at fifty miles an hour. Nobody came up the ramp. And nobody follows at a distance of more than a mile. So I ran straight over to where Duffy and Eliot were waiting for me. He was in casual clothes and looked a little uneasy in them. She was in worn jeans and the same battered leather jacket I had seen before. She looked spectacular in them. Neither of them wasted any time on greetings, which I guess I was happy about.

"Where are you headed?" Eliot asked.

"New London, Connecticut," I said.

"What's in the truck?"

"I don't know."

"No tail," Duffy said, like a statement, not a question.

"Might be electronic," I said.

"Where would it be?"

"In the back, if they've got any sense. Did you get the soldering iron?"

"Not yet," she said. "It's on its way. Why do we need it?"

"There's a lead seal," I said. "We need to be able to remake it."

She glanced at the ramp, anxious. "Hard thing to get ahold of at short notice."

"Let's check the parts we can get to," Eliot said. "While we're waiting."

We jogged back to the blue truck. I got down on the ground and took a look at the underside. It was all caked in ancient gray mud and streaked with leaking oil and fluid.

"It won't be here," I said. "They'd need a chisel to get close to the metal."

Eliot found it inside the cab about fifteen seconds after he started looking. It was stuck to the foam on the bottom of the passenger's seat with a little dot of hook-and-loop fastener. It was a tiny bare metal can a little bigger than a quarter and about half an inch thick. It trailed a thin eight-inch wire that was presumably the transmitting antenna. Eliot closed the whole thing into his fist and backed out of the cab fast and stared at the mouth of the ramp.

"What?" Duffy asked.

"This is weird," he said. "Thing like this has a hearing-aid battery, nothing more. Low power, short range. Can't be picked up beyond about two miles. So where's the guy tracking it?"

The mouth of the ramp was empty. I had been the last guy up it. We stood there with our eyes watering in the cold wind, staring at nothing. Traffic hissed by behind the trees, but nothing came up the ramp.

"How long have you been here now?" Eliot asked.

"About four minutes," I said. "Maybe five."

"Makes no sense," he said. "That puts the guy maybe four or five miles behind you. And he can't hear this thing from four or five miles."

"Maybe there's no guy," I said. "Maybe they trust me."

"So why put this thing in there?"

"Maybe they didn't. Maybe it's been in there for years. Maybe they forgot all about it."

"Too many maybes," he said.

Duffy spun right and stared at the trees.

"They could have stopped on the highway shoulder,"

she said. "You know, exactly level with where we are now."

Eliot and I spun to our right and stared, too. It made good sense. It was no kind of clever surveillance technique to pull into a rest stop and park right next to your target.

"Let's take a look," I said.

There was a narrow strip of neat grass and then an equally narrow area where the highway people had tamed the edge of the woods with planted shrubs and bark chips. Then there were just trees. The highway had mown them down to the east and the rest area had leveled them to the west but in between was a forty-foot thicket that could have been growing there since the dawn of time. It was hard work getting through it. There were vines and scratchy brambles and low branches. But it was April. Getting through in July or August might have been impossible.

We stopped just before the trees petered out into lower growth. Beyond that was the flat grassy highway shoulder. We eased forward as far as we dared and craned left and right. There was nobody parked there. The shoulder was clear as far as we could see in both directions. Traffic was very light. Whole five-second intervals went by with no vehicles in view at all. Eliot shrugged like he didn't understand it and we turned around and forced our way back.

"Makes no sense," he said again.

"They're short of manpower," I said.

"No, they're on Route One," Duffy said. "They must be. It runs parallel with I-95 the whole way down the coast. From Portland, way down south. It's probably less than two miles away most of the time."

We turned east again, like we could see through the

trees and spot a car idling on the shoulder of a distant parallel road.

"It's how I'd do it," Duffy said.

I nodded. It was a very plausible scenario. There would be technical disadvantages. With up to two miles of lateral displacement any slight fore-aft discrepancy due to traffic would make the signal drift in and out of range. But then, all they wanted to know was my general direction.

"It's possible," I said.

"No, it's likely," Eliot said. "Duffy's right. It's pure common sense. They want to stay out of your mirrors as long as they can."

"Either way, we have to assume they're there. How far does Route One stay close to I-95?"

"Forever," Duffy said. "Way farther than New London, Connecticut. They split around Boston, but they come back together."

"OK," I said. Checked my watch. "I've been here about nine minutes now. Long enough for the bathroom and a cup of coffee. Time to put the electronics back on the road."

I told Eliot to put the transmitter in his pocket and drive Duffy's Taurus south at a steady fifty miles an hour. I told him I would catch him in the truck somewhere before New London. I figured I would worry about how to get the transmitter back in the right place later. Eliot took off and I was left alone with Duffy. We watched her car disappear south and then swiveled around north and watched the incoming ramp. I had an hour and one minute and I needed the soldering iron. *Time ticking away.*

"How is it up there?" Duffy asked.

"A nightmare," I said. I told her about the eight-foot granite wall and the razor wire and the gate and the metal detectors on the doors and the room with no inside keyhole. I told her about Paulie.

"Any sign of my agent?" she asked.

"I only just got there," I said.

"She's in that house," she said. "I have to believe that."

I said nothing.

"You need to make some progress," she said. "Every hour you spend there puts you deeper in trouble. And her."

"I know that," I said.

"What's Beck like?" she asked.

"Bent," I said. I told her about the fingerprints on the glass and the way the Maxima had disappeared. Then I told her about the Russian roulette.

"You played?"

"Six times," I said, and stared at the ramp.

She stared at me. "You're crazy. Six to one, you should be dead."

I smiled. "You ever played?"

"I wouldn't. I don't like those odds."

"You're like most people. Beck was the same. He thought the odds were six to one. But they're nearer six hundred to one. Or six thousand. You put a single heavy bullet in a well-made well-maintained gun like that Anaconda and it would be a miracle if the cylinder came to rest with the bullet near the top. The momentum of the spin always carries it to the bottom. Precision mechanism, a little oil, gravity helps you out. I'm not an idiot. Russian roulette is a lot safer than people think. And it was worth the risk to get hired."

She was quiet for a spell.

"You got a feeling?" she asked.

"He looks like a rug importer," I said. "There are rugs all over the damn place."

"But?"

"But he isn't," I said. "I'd bet my pension on it. I asked him about the rugs and he didn't say much. Like he wasn't very interested in them. Most people like to talk about their businesses. Most people, you can't shut them up."

"You get a pension?"

"No," I said.

Right then a gray Taurus identical to Duffy's except for the color burst up over the rise of the ramp. It slowed momentarily while the driver scanned around and then accelerated hard straight toward us. It was the old guy at the wheel, the one I had left in the gutter near the college gate. He slammed to a stop next to my blue truck and opened his door and heaved himself up and out in exactly the same way he had gotten out of the borrowed police Caprice. He had a big black-and-red Radio Shack bag in his hand. It was bulky with boxes. He held it up and smiled and stepped forward to shake my hand. He had a fresh shirt on, but his suit was the same. I could see blotches where he had tried to sponge the fake blood out. I could picture him, standing at his motel room sink, getting busy with the hand towel. He hadn't been very successful. It looked like he had been careless with the ketchup at dinner.

"They got you running errands already?" he asked.

"I don't know what they got me doing," I said. "We got a lead seal problem."

He nodded. "I figured. Shopping list like that, what else could it be?"

"You done one before?"

"I'm old-school," he said. "We did ten a day, once upon a time, way back. Truck stops all over the place, we'd be in and out before the guy had even ordered his soup."

He squatted down and emptied the Radio Shack bag on the blacktop. He had a soldering iron and a spool of dull solder. And an inverter that would power the iron from his car's cigar lighter. That meant he had to keep his engine running, so he started it up and reversed a little way so that the cord would reach.

The seal was basically a drawn lead wire with large tags molded on each end. The tags had been crushed together with some kind of a heated device so they had fused together in a large embossed blob. The old guy left the fused ends strictly alone. It was clear he had done this before. He plugged the iron in and let it heat. He tested it by spitting on the end. When he was satisfied he dabbed the tip on the sleeve of his suit coat and then touched it to the wire where it was thin. The wire melted and parted. He eased the gap wider like opening a tiny handcuff and slipped the seal out of its channel. He ducked into his car and laid it on the dash. I grabbed the door lever and turned it.

"OK," Duffy said. "So what have we got?"

We had rugs. The door rattled upward and daylight flooded the load area and we saw maybe two hundred rugs, all neatly rolled and tied with string and standing upright on their ends. They were all different sizes, with the taller rolls at the cab end and the shorter ones at the door end. They stepped down toward us like some kind of ancient basalt rock formation. They were rolled face-in, so all we saw were the back surfaces, coarse and dull. The string around them was rough sisal, old and yellowed. There was a strong smell of raw wool and a fainter smell of vegetable dye.

"We should check them," Duffy said. There was disappointment in her voice.

"How long have we got?" the old guy asked.

I checked my watch.

"Forty minutes," I said.

"Better just sample them," he said.

We hauled a couple out from the front rank. They were rolled tight. No cardboard tubes. They were just rolled in on themselves and tied tight with the string. One of them had a fringe. It smelled old and musty. The knots in the string were old and flattened. We picked at them with our nails but we couldn't get them undone.

"They must cut the string," Duffy said. "We can't do that."

"No," the old guy said. "We can't."

The string was coarse and looked foreign. I hadn't seen string like that for a long time. It was made from some kind of a natural fiber. Jute, maybe, or hemp.

"So what do we do?" the old guy asked.

I pulled another rug out. Hefted it in my hands. It weighed about what a rug should weigh. I squeezed it. It gave slightly. I rested it end-down on the road and punched it in the middle. It yielded a little, exactly how a tightly-rolled rug would feel.

"They're just rugs," I said.

"Anything under them?" Duffy asked. "Maybe those tall ones in back aren't tall at all. Maybe they're resting on something else."

We pulled rugs out one by one and laid them on the road in the order we would have to put them back in. We built ourselves a random zigzag channel through the load space. The tall ones were exactly what they appeared to be, tall rugs, rolled tight, tied with string, standing upright on their ends. There was nothing hidden. We climbed out of the truck and stood there in the cold surrounded by a crazy mess of rugs and looked at each other.

"It's a dummy load," Duffy said. "Beck figured you would find a way in."

"Maybe," I said.

"Or else he just wanted you out of the way."

"While he's doing what?"

"Checking you out," she said. "Making sure."

I looked at my watch. "Time to reload. I'm already going to have to drive like a madman."

"I'll come with you," she said. "Until we catch up with Eliot, I mean."

I nodded. "I want you to. We need to talk."

We put the rugs back inside, kicking and shoving them until they were neatly arranged in their original positions. Then I pulled the roller door down and the old guy got to work with the solder. He slipped the broken seal back through its channel and eased the parted ends close together. He heated the iron and bridged the gap with its tip and touched the free end of the solder roll to it. The gap filled with a large silvery blob. It was the wrong color and it was way too big. It made the wire look like a cartoon drawing of a snake that has just swallowed a rabbit.

"Don't worry," he said.

He used the tip of the iron like a tiny paintbrush and smoothed the blob thinner and thinner. He flicked the tip occasionally to get rid of the excess. He was very delicate. It took him three long minutes but at the end of them he had the whole thing looking pretty much like it had before he arrived. He let it cool a little and then blew hard on it. The new silvery color instantly turned to gray. It was as close to an invisible repair as I had ever seen. Certainly it was better than I could have done myself.

"OK," I said. "Very good. But you're going to have to do another one. I'm supposed to bring another truck back. We better take a look at that one, too. We'll meet up in the first northbound rest area after Portsmouth, New Hampshire."

"When?"

"Be there five hours from now."

DUFFY AND I LEFT HIM STANDING THERE AND headed south as fast as I could get the old truck to move. It wouldn't do much better than seventy. It was shaped like a brick and the wind resistance defeated any attempt to go faster. But seventy was OK. I had a few minutes in hand.

"Did you see his office?" she asked.

"Not yet," I said. "We need to check it out. In fact we need to check out his whole harbor operation."

"We're working on it," she said. She had to talk loud. The engine noise and gearbox whine were twice as bad at seventy as they had been at fifty. "Fortunately Portland is not too much of a madhouse. It's only the forty-fourth busiest port in the U.S. About fourteen million tons of imports a year. That's about a quarter-million tons a week. Beck seems to get about ten of them, two or three containers."

"Does Customs search his stuff?"

"As much as they search anybody's. Their current hit rate is about two percent. If he gets a hundred and fifty containers a year maybe three of them will be looked at."

"So how is he doing it?"

"He could be playing the odds by limiting the bad stuff to, say, one container in ten. That would bring the effective search rate down to zero-point-two percent. He could last years like that."

"He's already lasted years. He must be paying somebody off."

She nodded beside me. Said nothing.

"Can you arrange extra scrutiny?" I asked.

"Not without probable cause," she said. "Don't forget, we're way off the books here. We need some hard evidence. And the possibility of a payoff makes the whole thing a minefield, anyway. We might approach the wrong official."

We drove on. The engine roared and the suspension swayed. We were passing everything we saw. Now I was watching the mirrors for cops, not tails. I was guessing that Duffy's DEA papers would take care of any specific legal problems, but I didn't want to lose the time it would take for her to have the conversation.

"How did Beck react?" she asked. "First impression?"

"He was puzzled," I said. "And a little resentful. That was my first impression. You notice that Richard Beck wasn't guarded at school?"

"Safe environment."

"Not really. You could take a kid out of a college, easy as anything. No guards means no danger. I think the bodyguard thing for the trip home was just some kind of a sop to the fact that the kid is paranoid. I think it was purely an indulgence. I don't think old man Beck can have thought it was really necessary, or he would have provided security at school as well. Or kept him out of school altogether."

"So?"

"So I think there was some kind of a done deal somewhere in the past. As a result of the original kidnap, maybe. Something that guaranteed some kind of stability. Hence no bodyguards in the dorm. Hence Beck's resentment, like somebody had suddenly broken an agreement."

"You think?"

I nodded at the wheel. "He was surprised, and puzzled, and annoyed. His big question was who?"

"Obvious question."

"But this was a how-dare-they kind of a question. There was attitude in it. Like somebody was out of line. It wasn't just an inquiry. It was an expression of annoyance at somebody."

"What did you tell him?"

"I described the truck. I described your guys."

She smiled. "Safe enough."

I shook my head. "He's got a guy called Duke. First

name unknown. Ex-cop. His head of security. I saw him
this morning. He'd been up all night. He looked tired and
he hadn't showered. His suit coat was all creased, low
down at the back."

"So?"

"Means he was driving all night. I think he went
down there to get a look at the Toyota. To check the rear license plate. Where did you stash it?"

"We let the state cops take it. To keep the plausibility
going. We couldn't take it back to the DEA garage. It'll be
in a compound somewhere."

"Where will the plate lead?"

"Hartford, Connecticut," she said. "We busted a
small-time Ecstasy ring."

"When?"

"Last week."

I drove on. The highway was getting busier.

"Our first mistake," I said. "Beck's going to check it
out. And then he's going to be wondering why some
small-time Ecstasy dealers from Connecticut are trying to
snatch his son. And then he's going to be wondering *how*
some small-time Ecstasy dealers from Connecticut *can* be
trying to snatch his son a week after they all got hauled off
to jail."

"Shit," Duffy said.

"It gets worse," I said. "I think Duke got a look at the
Lincoln, too. It's got a caved-in front and no window glass
left, but it hasn't got any bullet holes in it. And it doesn't
look like a real grenade went off inside. That Lincoln is
living proof this whole thing was phony baloney."

"No," she said. "The Lincoln is hidden. It didn't go
with the Toyota."

"Are you sure? Because the first thing Beck asked me
this morning was chapter and verse about the Uzis. It was

like he was asking me to damn myself right out of my own mouth. Two Uzi Micros, twenty-round mags, forty shots fired, and not a single mark on the car?"

"No," she said again. "No way. The Lincoln is hidden."

"Where?"

"It's in Boston. It's in our garage, but as far as any paperwork goes it's in the county morgue building. It's supposed to be a crime scene. The bodyguards are supposed to be plastered all over the inside. We aimed for plausibility. We thought this thing through."

"Except for the Toyota's plate."

She looked deflated. "But the Lincoln is OK. It's a hundred miles away from the Toyota. This guy Duke would have to drive all night."

"I think he did drive all night. And why was Beck so uptight about the Uzis?"

She went still.

"We have to abort," she said. "Because of the Toyota. Not because of the Lincoln. The Lincoln's OK."

I checked my watch. Checked the road ahead. The van roared on. We would be coming up on Eliot sometime soon. I calculated time and distance.

"We have to abort," she said again.

"What about your agent?"

"Getting you killed won't help her."

I thought about Quinn.

"We'll discuss it later," I said. "Right now we stay in business."

WE PASSED ELIOT AFTER EIGHT MORE MINUTES. His Taurus was sitting rock-steady in the inside lane, holding a modest fifty. I pulled ahead of him and matched his speed and he fell in behind. We skirted all the way around Boston and pulled into the first rest area we saw south of the city. The world was a lot busier down there. I sat still with Duffy at my side and watched the ramp for seventy-two seconds and saw four cars follow me in. None of their drivers paid me any attention. A couple of them had passengers. They all did normal rest-stop things like standing and yawning by their open doors and looking around and then heading over to the bathrooms and the fast food.

"Where's the next truck?" Duffy asked.

"In a lot in New London," I said.

"Keys?"

"In it."

"So there will be people there, too. Nobody leaves a truck alone with the keys in it. They'll be waiting for you. We don't know what they've been told to do. We should consider termination."

"I won't walk into a trap," I said. "Not my style. And the next truck might have something better in it."

"OK," she said. "We'll check it in New Hampshire. If you get that far."

"You could lend me your Glock."

I saw her reach up and touch it under her arm. "How long for?"

"As long as I need it."

"What happened to the Colts?"

"They took them."

"I can't," she said. "I can't give up my service weapon."

"You're already way off the books."

She paused.

"Shit," she said. She took the Glock out of her holster and passed it to me. It was warm from the heat of her body. I held it in my palm and savored the feeling. She dug in her purse and came out with two spare magazines. I put them in one pocket and the gun in the other.

"Thanks," I said.

"See you in New Hampshire," she said. "We'll check the truck. And then we'll decide."

"OK," I said, although I had already decided. Eliot walked over and took the transmitter out of his pocket. Duffy got out of his way and he stuck it back under her seat. Then they went off together, back to the government Taurus. I waited a plausible amount of time and got back on the road.

I FOUND NEW LONDON WITHOUT ANY PROBLEM. It was a messy old place. I had never been there before. Never had a reason to go. It's a Navy town. I think they build submarines there. Or somewhere nearby. Groton, maybe. The directions Beck had given me brought me off the highway early and threaded me through failing industrial areas. There was plenty of old brick, damp and smoke-stained and rotten. I pulled into the side of the road about a mile short of where I guessed the lot would be. Then I made a right and a left and tried to circle around it. I parked at a busted meter and checked Duffy's gun. It was a Glock 19. It was maybe a year old. It was fully loaded. The spare magazines were full, too. I got out of the truck. I heard booming foghorns way out in the Sound. A ferry was heading in. The wind was scraping trash along the street. A hooker stepped out of a doorway and smiled at me. It's a Navy town. She couldn't smell an army MP the way her sisters could elsewhere.

I turned a corner and got a pretty good partial view of the lot I was headed for. The land sloped down toward the sea and I had some elevation. I could see the truck waiting for me. It was the twin of the one I was in. Same age, same type. Same color. It was sitting there all alone. It was in the exact center of the lot, which was just an empty square made of crushed brick and weeds. Some old building had been bulldozed two decades ago and nothing had been built to replace it.

I couldn't see anybody waiting for me, although there were a thousand dirty windows within range and theoretically all of them could have been full of watchers. But I didn't feel anything. Feeling is a lot worse than knowing, but sometimes it's all you've got. I stood still until I got cold and then I walked back to the truck. Drove it around the block and into the lot. Parked it nose to nose with its twin. Pulled the key and dropped it in the door pocket. Glanced around one last time and got out. I put my hand in my pocket and closed it around Duffy's gun. Listened hard. Nothing but grit blowing and the far-off sounds of a run-down city struggling through the day. I was OK, unless somebody was planning to drop me with a long-range rifle shot. And clutching a Glock 19 in my pocket wasn't going to defend against that.

The new truck was cold and still. The door was unlocked and the key was right there in the pocket. I racked the seat and fixed the mirrors. Dropped the key on the floor like I was clumsy and checked under the seats. No transmitter. Just a few gum wrappers and dust bunnies. I started the engine. Backed away from the truck I had just gotten out of and swooped the new one around the lot and aimed it back toward the highway. I didn't see anybody. Nobody came after me.

THE NEW TRUCK DROVE A LITTLE BETTER THAN the old one had. It was a little quieter and a little faster. Maybe it had been around the clock only twice. It reeled in the miles, taking me back north. I stared ahead through the windshield and felt like I could see the lonely house on the rock finger getting bigger and bigger with every minute. It was drawing me in and repelling me simultaneously with equal force. So I just sat there immobile with one hand on the wheel and my eyelids locked open. Rhode Island was quiet. Nobody followed me through it. Massachusetts was mostly a long loop around Boston and then a sprint through the northeastern bump with the dumps like Lowell on my left and the cute places like Newburyport and Cape Ann and Gloucester far away on my right. No tail. Then came New Hampshire. I-95 sees about twenty miles of it with Portsmouth as the last stop. I passed it by and watched for rest area signs. I found one just inside the Maine state line. It told me that Duffy and Eliot and the old guy with the stained suit would be waiting for me eight miles ahead.

IT WASN'T JUST DUFFY AND ELIOT AND THE OLD guy. They had a DEA canine unit with them. I guess if you give government types enough time to think they'll come up with something you don't expect. I pulled into an area pretty much identical to the Kennebunk one and saw their two Tauruses parked on the end of the row next to a plain van with a spinning ventilator on the roof. I parked four slots away from them and went through the cautious routine of waiting and watching, but nobody pulled in after me. I didn't worry about the highway shoulder. The trees made me invisible from the highway. There were trees everywhere. Maine has got a whole lot of trees, that was for damn sure.

I got out of the truck and the old guy pulled his car close and went straight into his thing with the soldering iron. Duffy pulled me out of his way by the elbow.

"I made some calls," she said. She held up her Nokia like she was proving it to me. "Good news and bad news."

"Good news first," I said. "Cheer me up."

"I think the Toyota thing might be OK."

"Might be?"

"It's complicated. We got Beck's shipping schedule from U.S. Customs. All his stuff comes out of Odessa. It's in the Ukraine, on the Black Sea."

"I know where it is."

"Plausible point of origin for rugs. They come north through Turkey from all over. But Odessa is a heroin port, from our point of view. Everything that doesn't come here direct from Colombia feeds through Afghanistan and Turkmenistan and across the Caspian and the Caucasus. So if Beck's using Odessa it means he's a heroin guy, and if he's a heroin guy it means he doesn't know any Ecstasy dealers from Adam. Not in Connecticut, not anywhere. There can't be a relationship. No way. How could there be? It's a completely different part of the business. So he's starting from scratch as far as finding anything out goes. I mean, the Toyota plate will give him a name and an address, sure, but that information won't mean anything to him. It's going to be a few days before he can find out who they are and pick up their trail."

"That's the good news?"

"It's good enough. Trust me, they're in separate worlds. And a few days is all you've got anyway. We can't hold those bodyguards forever."

"What's the bad news?"

She paused a beat. "It's actually not impossible that someone could have gotten a peek at the Lincoln."

"What happened?"

"Nothing specific. Just that security at the garage maybe wasn't as good as it might have been."

"What does that mean?"

"It means we can't say for sure that something bad didn't happen."

We heard the truck's roller door rattle upward. It banged against its stop and a second later we heard Eliot calling us urgently. We stepped over there expecting to find something good. We found another transmitter instead. It was the same tiny metal can with the same eight-inch filament antenna. It was glued to the inside of the sheetmetal, near the loading door, about head height.

"Great," Duffy said.

The load space was packed with rugs, exactly the same as we had seen before. It could have been the same van. They were rolled tight and tied with rough string and stacked on their ends in descending order of height.

"Do we check them?" the old guy asked.

"No time," I said. "If somebody's on the other end of that transmitter they'll figure I'm entitled to maybe ten minutes here, nothing more."

"Put the dog in," Duffy said.

A guy I hadn't met opened up the rear of the DEA van and came out with a beagle on a leash. It was a little fat low-slung thing wearing a working-dog harness. It had long ears and an eager expression. I like dogs. Sometimes I think about getting one. It could keep me company. This one ignored me completely. It just let its handler lead it over to the blue truck and then it waited to be told what to do. The guy lifted it up into the load space and put it down on the staircase of rugs. He clicked his fingers and spoke some kind of a command and took the leash off. The dog scampered up and down and side to side. Its legs were short and it had a problem making it up and down between the different levels. But it covered every inch and then came back to where it had started and stood there with its eyes bright and its tail wagging and its mouth open in an absurd wet smile like it was saying *so where's the action*?

"Nothing," its handler said.

"Legit load," Eliot said.

Duffy nodded. "But why is it coming back north? Nobody exports rugs back to Odessa. Why would they?"

"It was a test," I said. "For me. They figured maybe I'd look, maybe I wouldn't."

"Fix the seal," Duffy said.

The new guy hauled his beagle out and Eliot stretched up tall and pulled the door down. The old guy picked up his soldering iron and Duffy pulled me away again.

"Decision?" she said.

"What would you do?"

"Abort," she said. "The Lincoln is the wild card. It could kill you."

I looked over her shoulder and watched the old guy at work. He was already thinning the solder join.

"They bought the story," I said. "Impossible not to. It was a great story."

"They might have looked at the Lincoln."

"I can't see why they would have wanted to."

The old guy was finishing up. He was bending down, ready to blow on the join, ready to turn the wire dull gray. Duffy put her hand on my arm.

"Why was Beck talking about the Uzis?" she asked.

"I don't know."

"All done," the old guy called.

"Decision?" Duffy said.

I thought about Quinn. Thought about the way his gaze had traveled across my face, not fast, not slow. Thought about the .22 scars, like two extra eyes up there on the left of his forehead.

"I'm going back," I said. "I think it's safe enough. They'd have gone for me this morning if they had any doubts."

Duffy said nothing. She didn't argue. She just took her hand off my arm and let me go.

CHAPTER 5

SHE LET ME GO, BUT SHE DIDN'T ASK FOR HER gun back. Maybe it was subconscious. Maybe she wanted me to have it. I put it in the back of my waistband. It felt better there than the big Colt had. I hid the spare magazines in my socks. Then I hit the road and was back in the lot near the Portland docks exactly ten hours after I left it. There was nobody waiting there to meet me. No black Cadillac. I drove right in and parked. Dropped the key in the door pocket and slid out. I was tired and slightly deaf after five hundred highway miles.

It was six o'clock in the evening and the sun was way down behind the city on my left. The air was cold and dampness was blowing in from the sea. I buttoned my coat and stood still for a minute in case I was being watched. Then I wandered off. I tried to look aimless. But I headed generally north and took a good look at the buildings ahead of me. The lot was bordered by low offices. They looked like trailers without the wheels. They had been cheaply built and badly maintained. They had small untidy parking lots. The lots were full of mid-range cars. The whole place looked busy and down-to-earth. Real-world commerce happened there. That was clear. No fancy headquarters, no marble, no sculpture, just a bunch of ordinary people working hard for their money behind unwashed windows lined with broken venetian blinds.

Some of the offices were bumped-out additions built onto the sides of small warehouses. The warehouses were modern prefabricated metal structures. They had concrete loading platforms built up to waist height. They had narrow lots defined by thick concrete posts. The posts had every shade of automotive paint known to man scraped on them.

I found Beck's black Cadillac after about five minutes. It was parked on a rectangle of cracked blacktop at an angle against the side of a warehouse, near an office door. The door looked like it belonged on a house in the suburbs. It was a colonial design made from hardwood. It had never been painted and it was gray and grainy from the salt air. It had a faded sign screwed to it: *Bizarre Bazaar*. The script was handpainted and looked like something from Haight-Ashbury in the sixties. Like it should have been promoting a concert at the Fillmore West, like Bizarre Bazaar was a one-hit wonder opening for Jefferson Airplane or the Grateful Dead.

I heard a car approaching and backed off behind the adjacent building and waited. It was a big car, coming slowly. I could hear fat soft tires dropping into wet potholes. It was a Lincoln Town Car, shiny black, identical to the one we had trashed outside the college gate. The two of them had probably come off the line together, nose to tail. It drove slowly past Beck's Cadillac and rounded the corner and parked in back of the warehouse. A guy I hadn't seen before got out of the driver's seat. He stretched and yawned like maybe he had just driven five hundred highway miles, too. He was medium height and heavy with close-cropped black hair. Lean face, bad skin. He was scowling, like he was frustrated. He looked dangerous. But junior, somehow. Like he was low down on the totem pole. And like he might be all the more dangerous because of it. He leaned back into the car and came out again carrying a portable radio scanner. It had a long chrome antenna and a mesh-covered speaker that would whine and squawk whenever an appropriate transmitter was within a mile or two of it.

He walked around the corner and pushed in through the unpainted door. I stayed where I was. Reviewed the whole of the last ten hours in my head. As far as radio surveillance went I had stopped three times. Each stop had been short enough to be plausible. Visual surveillance would be a different matter entirely. But I was pretty sure there had been no black Lincoln in my line of sight at any point. I tended to agree with Duffy. The guy and his scanner had been on Route One.

I stood still for a minute. Then I came out into plain sight and walked to the door. Pushed it open. There was an immediate right-angle turn to the left. It led to a small open area filled with desks and file cabinets. There were no people in it. None of the desks was occupied. But they had been until very recently. That was clear. They were part of a working office. There were three of them and they were covered with the kind of stuff people leave behind at the end of the day. Half-finished paperwork, rinsed coffee cups, notes to themselves, souvenir mugs filled with pencils, packs of tissues. There were electric heaters on the walls and the air was very warm and it smelled faintly of perfume.

At the back of the open area was a closed door with low voices behind it. I recognized Beck's, and Duke's. They were talking with a third man, who I guessed was the guy with the tracking equipment. I couldn't make out what they were saying. Couldn't make out the tone. There was some urgency there. Some debate. No raised voices, but they weren't discussing the company picnic.

I looked at the stuff on the desks and the walls. There were two maps pinned up on boards. One showed the whole world. The Black Sea was more or less in the exact center. Odessa was nestling there to the left of the Crimean Peninsula. There was nothing marked on the paper but I could trace the route a little tramp steamer would take, through the Bosphorus, through the Aegean Sea, through the Mediterranean, out past Gibraltar, and then full steam across the Atlantic to Portland, Maine. A two-week voyage, probably. Maybe three. Most ships are pretty slow.

The other map showed the United States. Portland itself was obliterated by a worn and greasy stain. I guessed people had put their fingertips on it to span their hands and calculate time and distance. A small person's hand fully extended might represent a day's driving. In which case Portland wasn't the best location for a distribution center. It was a long way from everywhere else.

The papers on the desks were incomprehensible to me. At best I could just about interpret details about dates and loads. I saw some prices listed. Some were high, some were low. Opposite the prices were codes for something. They could have been for rugs. They could have been for something else. But on the surface the whole place looked exactly like an innocent shipping office. I wondered if Teresa Daniel had worked in it.

I listened to the voices some more. Now I was hearing anger and worry. I backed out to the corridor. Took the Glock out of my waistband and put it in my pocket with my finger inside the trigger guard. A Glock doesn't have a safety catch. It has a sort of trigger on the trigger. It's a tiny bar that latches back as you squeeze. I put a little pressure on it. Felt it give. I wanted to be ready. I figured I would shoot Duke first. Then the guy with the radio. Then Beck. Beck was probably the slowest and you always leave the slowest for last.

I put my other hand in my pocket, too. A guy with one hand in his pocket looks armed and dangerous. A guy with both hands in his pockets looks relaxed and lazy. No threat. I took a breath and walked back into the room, noisily.

"Hello?" I called.

The back office door opened up fast. The three of them crowded together to look out. Beck, Duke, the new guy. No guns.

"How did you get in here?" Duke asked. He looked tired.

"Door was open," I said.

"How did you know which door?" Beck asked.

I kept my hands in my pockets. I couldn't say I had seen the painted sign, because it was Duffy who had told me the name of his operation, not him.

"Your car's parked outside," I said.

He nodded.

"OK," he said.

He didn't ask about my day. The new guy with the scanner must have described it already. Now he was just standing there, looking straight at me. He was younger than Beck. Younger than Duke. Younger than me. He was maybe thirty-five. He still looked dangerous. He had flat cheekbones and dull eyes. He was like a hundred bad guys I had busted in the army.

"Enjoy the drive?" I asked him.

He didn't answer.

"I saw you bring the scanner in," I said. "I found the first bug. Under the seat."

"Why did you look?" he asked.

"Habit," I said. "Where was the second?"

"In the back," he said. "You didn't stop for lunch."

"No money," I said. "Nobody gave me any yet."

The guy didn't smile.

"Welcome to Maine," he said. "Nobody gives you money here. You earn it."

"OK," I said.

"I'm Angel Doll," he said, like he was expecting his name to impress me. But it didn't.

"I'm Jack Reacher," I said.

"The cop-killer," he said, with something in his voice.

He looked at me for a long moment and then looked away. I couldn't figure out where he fit in. Beck was the boss and Duke was his head of security but this junior guy seemed very relaxed about talking right over their heads.

"We're in a meeting," Beck said. "You can wait out by the car."

He ushered the other two back inside the room and shut the door on me. That in itself told me there was nothing worth hunting for in the secretarial area. So I wandered outside and took a good look at the security system on my way. It was fairly rudimentary, but effective. There were contact pads on the door and all the windows. They were small rectangular things. They had wires the size and color of spaghetti tacked all along the baseboards. The wires came together in a metal box mounted on the wall next to a crowded notice board. The notice board was full of yellowed paper. There was all kinds of stuff about employee insurance and fire extinguishers and evacuation points. The alarm box had a keypad and two small lights. There was a red one labeled *armed* and a green one labeled *unarmed*. There were no separate zones. No motion sensors. It was crude perimeter defense only.

I didn't wait by the car. I walked around a little, until I had gotten a feel for the place. The whole area was a warren of similar operations. There was a convoluted access road for trucks. I guessed it would operate as a one-way system. Containers would be hauled down from the piers to the north and unloaded into the warehouses. Then delivery trucks would be loaded in turn and take off south. Beck's warehouse itself wasn't very private. It was right in the middle of a row of five. But it didn't have an outside loading dock. No waist-high platform. It had a roller door instead. It was temporarily blocked by Angel Doll's Lincoln, but it was big enough to drive a truck through. Secrecy could be achieved.

There was no overall external security. It wasn't like a naval dockyard. There was no wire fencing. No gate, no barriers, no guards in booths. It was just a big messy hundred-acre area full of random buildings and puddles and dark corners. I guessed there would be some kind of activity all around the clock. How much, I didn't know. But probably enough to mask some clandestine comings and goings.

I WAS BACK AT THE CADILLAC AND LEANING on the fender when the three of them came out. Beck and Duke came first and Doll hung back in the doorway. I still had my hands in my pockets. I was still ready to go for Duke first. But there was no overt aggression in the way anybody was moving. No wariness. Beck and Duke just walked over toward the car. They looked tired and preoccupied. Doll stayed where he was in the doorway, like he owned the place.

"Let's go," Beck said.

"No, wait," Doll called. "I need to talk to Reacher first."

Beck stopped walking. Didn't turn around.

"Five minutes," Doll said. "That's all. Then I'll lock up for you."

Beck didn't say anything. Neither did Duke. They looked irritated, but they weren't going to object. I kept my hands in my pockets and walked back. Doll turned and led me through the secretarial pen and into the back office. Through another door and into a glass-walled cubicle inside the warehouse itself. I could see a forklift on the warehouse floor and steel racks loaded with rugs. The racks were easily twenty feet high and the rugs were all tightly rolled and tied with string. The cubicle had a personnel door to the outside and a metal desk with a computer on it. The desk chair was worn out. Dirty yellow foam showed through at every seam. Doll sat down on it and looked up at me and moved his mouth into the approximate shape of a smile. I stood sideways at the end of the desk and looked down on him.

"What?" I said.

"See this computer?" he said. "It's got taps into every Department of Motor Vehicles in the country."

"So?"

"So I can check license plates."

I said nothing. He took a handgun out of his pocket. A neat move, fast and fluid. But then, it was a good pocket gun. It was a Soviet-era PSM, which is a small automatic pistol built as smooth and slim as possible, so it won't snag on clothing. It uses weird Russian ammunition, which is hard to get. It has a safety catch at the rear of the slide. Doll's was in the forward position. I couldn't remember whether that represented *safe* or *fire*.

"What do you want?" I asked him.

"I want to confirm something with you," he said. "Before I go public with it and move myself up a rung or two."

There was silence.

"How would you do that?" I asked.

"By telling them an extra little thing they don't know

about yet," he said. "Maybe I'll even earn myself a nice big bonus. Like, maybe I'll get the five grand they ear-marked for you."

I pressed the Glock's trigger lock in my pocket. Glanced to my left. I could see all the way through to the back office window. Beck and Duke were standing by the Cadillac. They had their backs to me. They were forty feet away. *Too close.*

"I dumped the Maxima for you," Doll said.

"Where?"

"Doesn't matter," he said. Then he smiled again.

"What?" I said again.

"You stole it, right? At random, from a shopping mall."

"So?"

"It had Massachusetts plates," he said. "They were phony. No such number has ever been issued."

Mistakes, coming back to haunt me. I said nothing.

"So I checked the VIN," he said. "The vehicle identi-fication number. All cars have them. On a little metal plate, top of the dash."

"I know," I said.

"It came back as a Maxima," he said. "So far, so good. But it was registered in New York. To a bad boy who was arrested five weeks ago. By the government."

I said nothing.

"You want to explain all that?" he said.

I didn't answer.

"Maybe they'll let me waste you myself," he said. "I might enjoy that."

"You think?"

"I've wasted people before," he said, like he had something to prove.

"How many?" I said.

"Enough."

I glanced through the back office window. Let go of the Glock and took my hands out of my pockets, empty.

· "The New York DMV list must be out-of-date," I said. "It was an old car. Could have been sold out of state a year ago. You check the authentication code?"

"Where?"

"Top of the screen, on the right. It needs to have the right numbers in it to be up-to-date. I was a military cop. I've been in the New York DMV system more times than you have."

"I hate MPs," he said.

I watched his gun.

"I don't care who you hate," I said. "I'm just telling you I know how those systems work. And that I've made the same mistake. More than once."

He was quiet for a beat.

"That's bullshit," he said.

Now I smiled.

"So go ahead," I said. "Embarrass yourself. No skin off my nose."

He sat still for a long moment. Then he swapped the gun from his right hand to his left and got busy with the mouse. He tried to keep one eye on me while he clicked and scrolled. I moved a little, like I was interested in the screen. The New York DMV search page came up. I moved a little more, around behind his shoulder. He entered what must have been the Maxima's original plate number, apparently from memory. He hit *search now*. The screen redrew. I moved again, like I was all set to prove him wrong.

"Where?" he asked.

"Right there," I said, and started to point at the monitor. But I was pointing with both hands and all ten fingers and they didn't make it to the screen. My right hand stopped at his neck. My left took the gun out of his left. It dropped on the floor and sounded exactly like a pound of steel hitting a plywood board covered with linoleum. I kept my eyes on the office window. Beck and Duke still had their backs to me. I got both hands around Doll's neck and squeezed. He thrashed around wildly. Fought back. I shifted my grip. The chair fell over under him. I squeezed harder. Watched the window. Beck and Duke were just standing there. Their backs to me. Their breath was misting in front of them. Doll started clawing at my wrists. I squeezed harder still. His tongue came out of his mouth. Then he did the smart thing and gave up on my wrists and reached up behind him and went for my eyes. I pulled my head back and hooked one hand under his jaw and put the other flat against the side of his head. Wrenched his jaw hard to the right and smashed his head downward to the left and broke his neck.

I STOOD THE CHAIR UPRIGHT AGAIN AND PUSHED it in neatly behind the desk. Picked up his gun and ejected the magazine. It was full. Eight bottle-necked 5.45 millimeter Soviet Pistol shells. They're roughly the same size as a .22, and they're slow, but they're supposed to hit pretty hard. Soviet security forces were supposed to be happy enough with them. I checked the chamber. There was a round in it. I checked the action. It had been set to *fire*. I reassembled the whole thing and left it cocked and locked. Put it in my left-hand pocket.

Then I went through his clothes. He had all the usual stuff. A wallet, a cell phone, a money clip without much money in it, a big bunch of keys. I left it all there. Opened the rear personnel door to the outside and checked the view. Beck and Duke were now hidden from me by the corner of the building. I couldn't see them, they couldn't see me. There was nobody else around. I walked over to

Doll's Lincoln and opened the driver's door. Found the trunk release. The latch popped quietly and the lid rose an inch. I went back inside and dragged the body out by the collar. Opened the trunk all the way and heaved it inside. Latched the lid down gently and closed the driver's door. Glanced at my watch. The five minutes were up. I would have to finish the garbage disposal later. I walked back through the glass cubicle, through the back office, through the secretarial pen, through the front door, and outside. Beck and Duke heard me and turned around. Beck looked cold and annoyed by the delay. I thought: *so why stand still for it?* Duke was shivering a little and his eyes were watering and he was yawning. He looked exactly like a guy who hadn't slept for thirty-six hours. I thought: *I see a triple benefit in that.*

"I'll drive," I said. "If you want."

He hesitated. Said nothing.

"You know I can drive," I said. "You just had me driving all day. I did what you wanted. Doll told you all about it."

He said nothing.

"Was it another test?" I asked.

"You found the bug," he said.

"Did you think I wouldn't?"

"You might have acted different if you hadn't found the bug."

"Why would I? I just wanted to get back here, fast and safe. I was exposed, ten straight hours. It was no fun for me. I've got more to lose than you, whatever you're into."

He said nothing to that.

"Your call," I said, like I didn't care.

He hesitated a fraction more and then exhaled and handed me the keys. That was the first benefit. There's something symbolic about handing over a set of keys. It's about trust and inclusion. It moved me closer to the center of their circle. Made me less of an outsider. And it was a big bunch of keys. There were house keys and office keys as well as the car keys. Maybe a dozen keys in total. A lot of metal. A big symbol. Beck watched the whole transaction and made no comment about it. Just turned away and settled himself in the back of the car. Duke dumped himself in the passenger seat. I got in the driver's seat and started the engine. Arranged my coat around me so that both of the guns in my pockets were resting in my lap. I was ready to pull them out and use them if a cell phone rang. It was a fifty-fifty chance that the next call these guys got would be because someone had found Doll's body. Therefore the next call these guys got would also be their last. I was happy with odds of six hundred or six thousand to one, but fifty-fifty was a little too rich for me.

But no phones rang the whole way home. I drove smoothly and gently and found all the right roads. I turned east toward the Atlantic. It was already full dark out there. I came up on the palm-shaped promontory and drove out onto the rock finger and aimed straight for the house. The lights were blazing all along the top of the wall. The razor wire glittered. Paulie was waiting to open the gate. He glared at me as I drove past. I ignored him and hustled up the driveway and stopped on the carriage circle right next to the door. Beck got straight out. Duke shook himself awake and followed him.

"Where do I put the car?" I asked.

"In the garage, asshole," he said. "Around the side."

That was the second benefit. I was going to get five minutes alone.

I looped all the way around the carriage circle again and headed down the south side of the house. The garage block stood on its own inside a small walled courtyard. It had probably been a stable back when the house was built.

It had granite cobblestones in front of it and a vented cupola on the roof to let the smell out. The horse stalls had been knocked together to make four garages. The hayloft had been converted into an apartment. I guessed the quiet mechanic lived up there.

The garage on the left-hand end had its door open and was standing empty. I drove the Cadillac inside and killed the motor. It was gloomy in there. There were shelves filled with the kind of junk that piles up in a garage. There were oil cans and buckets and old bottles of wax polish. There was an electric tire compressor and a pile of used rags. I put the keys in my pocket and slid out of the seat. Listened for the sound of a phone in the house. Nothing. I strolled over and checked the rags. Picked up a thing the size of a hand towel. It was dark with grime and dirt and oil. I used it to wipe an imaginary spot off the Cadillac's front fender. Glanced around. Nobody there. I wrapped Doll's PSM and Duffy's Glock and her two spare magazines in the rag. Put the whole bundle under my coat. It might have been possible to get the guns into the house. Maybe. I could have gone in the back door and let the metal detector beep and looked puzzled for a second and then pulled out the big bunch of keys. I could have held them up like they explained everything. A classic piece of misdirection. It might have worked. Maybe. It would depend on their level of suspicion. But whatever, getting the guns out of the house again would have been very difficult. Assuming there were no panic phone calls anytime soon the chances were I would be leaving with Beck or Duke or both in the normal way and there was no guarantee I would have the keys again. So I had a choice. Take a chance, or play it safe? My decision was to play it safe and keep the firepower outside.

I walked out of the garage courtyard and wandered

around toward the back of the house. Stopped at the corner of the courtyard wall. Stood still for a second and then turned ninety degrees and followed the wall out toward the rocks like I wanted to take a look at the ocean. It was still calm. There was a long oily swell coming in from the southeast. The water looked black and infinitely deep. I gazed at it for a moment and then ducked down and put the wrapped guns in a little dip tight against the wall. There were scrawny weeds growing there. Somebody would have to trip over them to find them.

I strolled back, hunched into my coat, trying to look like a reflective guy getting a couple of minutes' peace. It was quiet. The shore birds were gone. It was too dark for them. They would be safe in their roosts. I turned around and headed for the back door. Went in through the porch and into the kitchen. The metal detector beeped. Duke and the mechanic guy and the cook all turned to look at me. I paused a beat and pulled out the keys. Held them up. They looked away. I walked in and dropped the keys on the table in front of Duke. He left them there.

THE THIRD BENEFIT OF DUKE'S EXHAUSTION UNfolded steadily all the way through dinner. He could barely stay awake. He didn't say a word. The kitchen was warm and steamy and we ate the kind of food that would put anybody to sleep. We had thick soup and steak and potatoes. There was a lot of it. The plates were piled high. The cook was working like a production line. There was a spare plate with a whole portion of everything just sitting untouched on a counter. Maybe somebody was in the habit of eating twice.

I ate fast and kept my ears open for the phone. I figured I could grab the car keys and be outside before the first ring finished. Inside the Cadillac before the second.

Halfway down the drive before the third. I could smash through the gate. I could run Paulie over. But the phone didn't ring. There was no sound in the house at all, except people chewing. There was no coffee. I was on the point of taking that personally. I like coffee. I drank water instead. It came from the faucet over the sink and tasted like chlorine. The maid came in from the family dining room before I finished my second glass. She walked over to where I was sitting, awkward in her unfashionable shoes. She was shy. She looked Irish, like she had just come all the way from Connemara to Boston and couldn't find a job down there.

"Mr. Beck wants to see you," she said.

It was only the second time I had heard her speak. She sounded a little Irish, too. Her cardigan was wrapped tight around her.

"Now?" I asked.

"I think so," she said.

He was waiting for me in the square room with the oak dining table where I had played Russian roulette for him.

"The Toyota was from Hartford, Connecticut," he said. "Angel Doll traced the plate this morning."

"No front plates in Connecticut," I said, because I had to say something.

"We know the owners," he said.

There was silence. I stared straight at him. It took me a fraction of a second just to understand him.

"How do you know them?" I asked.

"We have a business relationship."

"In the rug trade?"

"The nature of the relationship needn't concern you."

"Who are they?"

"That needn't concern you either," he said.

I said nothing.

"But there's a problem," he said. "The people you described aren't the people who own the truck."

"Are you sure?"

He nodded. "You described them as tall and fair. The guys who own the truck are Spanish. Small and dark."

"So who were the guys I saw?" I asked, because I had to ask something.

"Two possibilities," he said. "One, maybe somebody stole their truck."

"Or?"

"Two, maybe they expanded their personnel."

"Either one is possible," I said.

He shook his head. "Not the first. I called them. There was no answer. So I asked around. They've disappeared. No reason why they should disappear just because someone stole their truck."

"So they expanded their roster."

He nodded. "And decided to bite the hand that feeds them."

I said nothing.

"Are you certain they used Uzis?" he asked.

"That's what I saw," I said.

"Not MP5Ks?"

"No," I said. I looked away. No comparison. Not even close. The MP5K is a short Heckler & Koch submachine gun designed early in the 1970s. It has two big fat handles molded from expensive plastic. It looks very futuristic. Like a movie prop. Next to it an Uzi looks like something hammered together by a blind man in his basement.

"No question," I said.

"No possibility the kidnap was random?" he asked.

"No," I said. "Million to one."

He nodded again.

"So they've declared war," he said. "And they've gone to ground. They're hiding out somewhere."

"Why would they do that?"

"I have no idea."

There was silence. No sound from the sea. The swells came and went inaudibly.

"Are you going to try to find them?" I asked.

"You bet your ass," Beck said.

DUKE WAS WAITING FOR ME IN THE KITCHEN. He was angry and impatient. He wanted to take me upstairs and get me locked down for the night. I didn't protest. A locked door with no inside keyhole is a very good alibi.

"Tomorrow, six-thirty," he said. "Back on duty."

I listened hard and heard the lock click and waited for his footsteps to recede. Then I got busy with my shoe. There was a message waiting. It was from Duffy: *back OK?* I hit *reply* and typed: *Bring a car one mile short of the house. Leave it there with key on seat. Quiet approach, no lights.*

I hit *send*. There was a short delay. I guessed she was using a laptop. She would be waiting in her motel room with it plugged in and switched on. It would go: *Bing! You've Got Mail!*

She came back with: *Why? When?*

I sent: *Don't ask. Midnight.*

There was a long delay. Then she sent: *OK.*

I sent: *Retrieve it six am, stealthy.*

She replied: *OK.*

I sent: *Beck knows the Toyota owners.*

Ninety painful seconds later she came back with: *How?*

I sent: *quote business relationship unquote.*

She asked: *Specifics?*

I sent: *Not given.*

She replied with one simple word: *Shit.*

I waited. She sent nothing more. She was probably conferring with Eliot. I could picture them, talking fast, not looking at each other, trying to decide. I sent a question: *How many did you arrest in Hartford?* She came back with: *All of them, i.e. three.* I asked: *Are they talking?* She replied: *Not talking at all.* I asked: *Lawyers?* She came back with: *No lawyers.*

It was a very ponderous way to have a conversation. But it gave me plenty of time to think. Lawyers would have been fatal. Beck could have gotten to their lawyers, easily. Sooner or later it would have occurred to him to check if his buddies had been arrested.

I sent: *Can you keep them incommunicado?*

She sent: *Yes, two or three days.*

I sent: *Do it.*

There was a long pause. Then she came back with: *What is Beck thinking?*

I sent: *That they've declared war and gone to ground.*

She asked: *What are you going to do?*

I sent: *Not sure.*

She sent: *Will leave car, advise use it to pull out.*

I replied: *Maybe.*

There was another long pause. Then she sent: *Turn unit off, save battery.* I smiled to myself. Duffy was a very practical woman.

I LAY FULLY DRESSED ON THE BED FOR THREE hours, listening for a phone. I didn't hear one. I got up just before midnight and rolled the Oriental rug back and lay down on the floor with my head against the oak boards and listened. It's the best way to pick up the small sounds inside a building. I could hear the heating system running. I could hear the wind around the house. It was moaning softly. The ocean itself was quiet. The house was still. It was a solid stone structure. No creaking, no cracking. No human activity. No talking, no movement. I guessed Duke was sleeping the sleep of the dead. That was the third benefit of his exhaustion. He was the only one I was worried about. He was the only professional.

I laced my shoes tight and took off my jacket. I was still dressed in the black denim the maid had supplied. I slid the window all the way up and sat on the sill, facing the room. I stared at the door. Twisted around and looked outside. There was a slim sliver of moon. Some starlight. A little wind. Ragged silver clouds. The air was cold and salty. The ocean was moving slow and steady.

I swung my legs out into the night and shuffled sideways. Then I rolled over onto my stomach and scrabbled with my toes until I found a fold in the stone carving where an accent line had been set into the facade. I got my feet set and held the sill with both hands and craned my body outward. Used one hand to pull the window down to within two inches of closed. Eased sideways and felt for a drainpipe running down from the roof gutter. I found one about a yard away. It was a fat cast-iron pipe maybe six inches in diameter. I got my right palm flat on it. It felt solid. But it felt distant. I'm not an agile person. Put me in the Olympics and I'd be a wrestler or a boxer or a weightlifter. Not a gymnast.

I brought my right hand back and shuffled sideways with my toes until I was as far to the right as I could get. I jumped my left hand along the sill until it was tight in the corner of the window frame. Stretched out with my right. Got it hooked around the far side of the pipe. The iron was painted and it felt cold and a little slick with night dew. I put my thumb in front and my fingers behind. Tested my grip. Craned out a little more. I was spread-eagled on the wall. I equalized the pressure between my hands and pulled inward. Kicked my feet off the ledge and jumped them sideways, one each side of the pipe. Pulled inward again and let go of the sill and brought my left hand over to join my right. Now I had the pipe in both hands. My grip held. My feet were flat on the wall. My ass was sticking right out, fifty feet above the rocks. The wind caught my hair. It was cold.

A boxer, not a gymnast. I could hold on there all night. No problem with that. But I wasn't certain how to move myself down. I tensed my arms and pulled myself in toward the wall. Slid my hands downward as I did so, six inches. Slid my feet down a matching distance. Let my weight fall backward. That seemed to work. I did it again. I bounced down, six inches at a time. Wiped each palm in turn to fight the dew. I was sweating, even though it was cold. My right hand hurt from my bout with Paulie. I was still forty-five feet above the ground. I inched downward. Got myself level with the second floor. It was slow progress, but it was safe. Except that I was putting two hundred and fifty pounds of shock into an old iron pipe every few seconds. The pipe was probably a hundred years old. And iron rusts and rots.

It moved a little. I felt it shudder and shake and shiver. And it was slippery. I had to lock my fingers behind it to make sure my grip would hold. My knuckles were scraping on the stone. I bounced down, six inches at a time. I developed a rhythm. I would pull close, then fall back and slide my hands down and try to cushion the shock by easing my arms out straight. I let my shoulders take the impact. Then I would be bent at the waist at a tighter angle than before so I would move my feet down six inches and start again. I made it down to the first-floor windows. The pipe felt stronger there. Maybe it was anchored in a concrete base. I bounced down, faster. Made it all the way to the ground. Felt the solid rock under my feet and breathed out in relief and stepped away from the wall. Wiped my hands on my pants and stood still and listened. It felt good to be out of the house. The air was like velvet. I heard nothing. There were no lights in the windows. I felt the sting of cold on my teeth and realized I was smiling. I glanced up at the hunter's moon. Shook myself and walked quietly away to reclaim the guns.

They were still there in the rag in the dip behind the weed stalks. I left Doll's PSM where it was. I preferred the Glock. I unwrapped it and checked it carefully, out of habit. Seventeen bullets in the gun, seventeen in each of the spare magazines. Fifty-one nine-millimeter Parabellums. If I fired one, I'd probably have to fire them all. By which time somebody would have won and somebody would have lost. I put the magazines in my pockets and the gun itself in my waistband and tracked all the way around the far side of the garage block for a preliminary distant look at the wall. It was still all lit up. The lights blazed harsh and blue and angry, like a stadium. The lodge was bathed in the glow. The razor wire glittered. The light was a solid bar, thirty yards deep, bright as day, with absolute darkness beyond. The gate stood closed and chained. The whole thing looked like the outer perimeter of a nineteenth-century prison. Or an asylum.

I gazed at it until I had figured out how to get past it and then I headed around inside the cobbled courtyard. The apartment above the garages was dark and quiet. The garage doors were all closed, but none of them had locks. They were big old-fashioned timber things. They had been installed way back before anybody had thought of stealing cars. Four sets of doors, four garages. The left-hand one held the Cadillac. I had already been in there. So I checked the others, slow and quiet. The second had yet another Lincoln Town Car in it, black, the same as Angel

Doll's, the same as the one the bodyguards had used. It was waxed and shiny and its doors were locked.

The third garage was completely empty. Nothing in it at all. It was clean and swept. I could see broom tracks in the dusty oil patches on the floor. There were a few carpet fibers here and there. Whoever had swept up had missed them. They were short and stiff. I couldn't make out the color in the darkness. They looked gray. They looked like they had been pulled out of a rug's burlap backing. They meant nothing to me. So I moved on.

I found what I wanted in the fourth garage. I opened the doors wide and let in just about enough moonlight to see by. The dusty old Saab the maid had used for her marketing was in there, parked head-in close to a workbench. There was a grimy window behind the bench. Gray moonlight on the ocean outside. The bench had a vise screwed to it and was covered in tools. The tools were old. Their handles were wood that had darkened with age and oil. I found a bradawl. It was just a blunt steel spike set into a handle. The handle was bulbous, turned from oak. The spike was maybe two inches long. I put it into the vise, maybe a quarter-inch deep. Tightened the vise hard. Pulled on the handle and bent the spike into a neat right angle. Loosened the vise and checked my work and put it away in my shirt pocket.

Then I found a chisel. It was a woodworking item. It had a half-inch blade and a nice ash handle. It was probably seventy years old. I hunted around and found a carborundum whetstone and a rusty can of sharpening fluid. Dabbed some fluid on the stone and spread it with the tip of the chisel. Worked the steel back and forth until it showed bright. One of the many high schools I went to was an old-fashioned place in Guam where shop was graded by how well you did with the scut work, like sharpening tools. We all scored high. It was the kind of accomplishment we were interested in. That class had the best knives I ever saw. I turned the chisel over and did the other face. I got the edge square and true. It looked like high-grade Pittsburgh steel. I wiped it on my pants. Didn't test the edge on my thumb. I didn't particularly want to bleed. I knew it was razor sharp just by looking at it.

I came out into the courtyard and squatted down in the angle of the walls and loaded my pockets. I had the chisel if things needed to stay quiet, and I had the Glock if it was OK to go noisy. Then I scoped out my priorities. *The house first,* I decided. There was a strong possibility that I would never get another look at it.

THE OUTER DOOR TO THE KITCHEN PORCH WAS locked, but the mechanism was crude. It was a token three-lever affair. I put the bent spike of the bradawl in like a key and felt for the tumblers. They were big and obvious. It took me less than a minute to get inside. I stopped again and listened carefully. I didn't want to walk in on the cook. Maybe she was up late, baking a special pie. Or maybe the Irish girl was in there doing something. But there was only silence. I crossed the porch and knelt down in front of the inner door. Same crude lock. Same short time. I backed off a foot and swung the door open. Smelled the kitchen smells. Listened again. The room was cold and deserted. I put the bradawl on the floor in front of me. Put the chisel next to it. Added the Glock and the spare magazines. I didn't want to set the metal detector off. In the still of the night it would have sounded like a siren. I slid the bradawl along the floor, tight against the boards. Pushed it right through the doorway and into the kitchen. Did the same with the chisel. Kept it tight against the floor and rolled it all the way inside. Almost all commercial metal detectors have a dead zone right at the bottom. That's because men's dress shoes are made with a steel shank in the sole. It gives the shoe flexibility and strength. Metal detectors are designed to ignore shoes. It makes sense, because otherwise they would beep every time a guy with decent footwear passed through.

I slid the Glock through the dead zone and followed it with one magazine at a time. Pushed everything as far inside as I could reach. Then I stood up and walked through the door. Closed it quietly behind me. Picked up all my gear and reloaded my pockets. Debated taking my shoes off. It's easier to creep around quietly in socks. But if it comes to it, shoes are great weapons. Kick somebody with your shoes on, and you disable them. With your shoes off, you break a toe. And they take time to put back on. If I had to get out fast, I didn't want to be running around on the rocks barefoot. Or climbing the wall. I decided to keep them on and walk carefully. It was a solidly-built house. Worth the risk. I went to work.

First I searched the kitchen for a flashlight. Didn't find one. Most houses on the end of a long power line spur have outages from time to time, so most people who live in them keep something handy. But the Becks didn't seem to. The best I could find was a box of kitchen matches. I put three in my pocket and struck one on the box. Used the flickering light to look for the big bunch of keys I had left on the table. Those keys would have helped me a lot, but they weren't there. Not on the table, not on some hook near the door, not anywhere. I wasn't very surprised. It would have been too good to be true to find them.

I blew out the match and found my way in the dark to the head of the basement stairs. Crept all the way down and struck another match with my thumbnail at the bottom. Followed the tangle of wires on the ceiling back to the breaker box. There was a flashlight on a shelf right next to it. Classic dumb place to keep a flashlight. If a breaker pops the box is your destination, not your starting point.

The flashlight was a big black Maglite the length of a nightstick. Six D cells inside. We used to use them in the army. They were guaranteed unbreakable, but we found that depended on what you hit with them, and how hard. I lit it up and blew out the match. Spat on the burned stub and put it in my pocket. Used the flashlight to check the breaker box. It had a gray metal door with twenty circuit breakers inside. None of them was labeled *gatehouse*. It must have been separately supplied, which made sense. No point in running power all the way to the main house and then running some of it all the way back to the lodge. Better to give the lodge its own tap on the incoming power line. I wasn't surprised, but I was vaguely disappointed. It would have been sweet to be able to turn the wall lights off. I shrugged and closed the box and turned around and went to look at the two locked doors I had found that morning.

They weren't locked anymore. First thing you always do before attacking a lock is to check it's not already open. Nothing makes you feel stupider than picking a lock that isn't locked. These weren't. Both doors opened easily with a turn of the handle.

The first room was completely empty. It was more or less a perfect cube, maybe eight feet on a side. I played the flashlight beam all over it. It had rock walls and a cement floor. No windows. It looked like a storeroom. It was immaculately clean and there was nothing in it. Nothing at all. No carpet fibers. Not even trash or dirt. It had been swept and vacuumed, probably earlier that day. It was a little dank and damp. Exactly how you would expect a stone cellar to feel. I could smell the distinctive dusty smell of a vacuum cleaner bag. And there was a trace of something else in the air. A faint, tantalizing odor right at the edge of imperceptibility. It was vaguely familiar. Rich, and papery. Something I should know. I stepped right inside the room and shut off the flashlight. Closed my eyes and stood in the absolute blackness and concentrated. The smell disappeared. It was like my movements had disturbed the air molecules and the one part in a billion I was interested in had diffused itself into the clammy background of underground granite. I tried hard, but I couldn't get it. So I gave it up. It was like memory. To chase it meant to lose it. And I didn't have time to waste.

I switched the flashlight back on and came out into the basement corridor and closed the door quietly behind me. Stood still and listened. I could hear the furnace. Nothing else. I tried the next room. It was empty, too. But only in the sense that it was currently unoccupied. It had stuff in it. It was a bedroom.

It was a little larger than the storeroom. It was maybe twelve-by-ten. The flashlight beam showed me rock walls, a cement floor, no windows. There was a thin mattress on the floor. It had wrinkled sheets and an old blanket strewn across it. No pillows. It was cold in the room. I could smell stale food, stale perfume, sleep, and sweat, and fear.

I searched the whole room carefully. It was dirty. But I found nothing of significance until I pulled the mattress aside. Under it, scratched into the cement of the floor, was a single word: *JUSTICE*. It was written all in spidery capital letters. They were uneven and chalky. But they were clear. And emphatic. And underneath the letters were numbers. Six of them, in three groups of two. Month, day, year. Yesterday's date. The letters and the numbers were scratched deeper and wider than marks made with a pin or a nail or the tip of a scissor. I guessed they had been made with the tine of a fork. I put the mattress back in position and took a look at the door. It was solid oak. It was thick and heavy. It had no inside keyhole. Not a bedroom. A prison cell.

I stepped outside and closed the door and stood still again and listened hard. Nothing. I spent fifteen minutes on the rest of the basement and found nothing at all, not that I expected to. I wouldn't have been left to run around there that morning if there was anything for a person to find. So I killed the flashlight and crept back up the stairs in the dark. Went back to the kitchen and searched it until I found a big black trash can liner. Then I wanted a towel. Best thing I could find was a worn linen square designed to dry dishes with. I folded both items neatly and jammed them in my pockets. Then I came back out into the hallway and went to look at the parts of the house I hadn't seen before.

There were a lot to choose from. The whole place was a warren. I started at the front, where I had first come in the day before. The big oak door was closed tight. I gave it a wide berth, because I didn't know how sensitive the metal detector was. Some of them beep when you're a foot away. The floors were solid oak planks, covered in rugs. I stepped carefully, but I wasn't too worried about noise. The rugs and the drapes and the paneling would soak up sound.

I scouted the whole of the ground floor. Only one place caught my attention. On the north side next to the room where I had spent the time with Beck was another locked door. It was opposite the family dining room, across a wide interior hallway. It was the only locked door on the ground floor. Therefore it was the only room that interested me. Its lock was a big brass item from back when things were manufactured with pride and aplomb. It had all kinds of fancy filigree edges where it was screwed into the wood. The screw heads themselves were rubbed smooth by a hundred and fifty years of polishing. It was probably original to the house. Some old artisan up in nineteenth-century Portland had probably fashioned it by hand, in between making boat chandlery. It took me about a second and a half to open.

The room was a den. Not an office, not a study, not a family room. I covered every inch with the flashlight beam. There was no television in there. No desk, no computer. It was just a room, simply furnished in an old-fashioned style. There were heavy velvet drapes pulled across the window. There was a big armchair padded with buttoned red leather. There was a glass-fronted collector's cabinet. And rugs. They were three-deep on the floor. I checked my watch. It was nearly one o'clock. I had been on the loose for nearly an hour. I stepped into the room and closed the door quietly.

The collector's cabinet was nearly six feet tall. It had two full-width drawers at the bottom and locked glass doors above them. Behind the glass were five Thompson submachine guns. They were the classic drum-magazine gangster weapons from the 1920s, the pieces you see in old grainy black-and-white photographs of Al Capone's soldiers. They were displayed alternately facing left and right, resting on custom hardwood pegs that held them exactly level. They were all identical. And they all looked brand new. They looked like they had never been fired. Like they had never even been touched. The armchair was set to face the cabinet. There was nothing else of significance in the room. I sat down in the chair and got to wondering why anybody would want to spend time gazing at five old grease guns.

Then I heard footsteps. A light tread, upstairs, directly over my head. Three paces, four, five. Fast quiet steps. Not just deference to the time of night. A real attempt at concealment. I got up out of the chair. Stood still. Turned the flashlight off and put it in my left hand. Put the chisel in my right. I heard a door close softly. Then there was silence. I listened hard. Focused on every tiny sound.

The background rush of the heating system built to a roar in my ears. My breathing was deafening. Nothing from above. Then the footsteps started again.

They were heading for the stairs. I locked myself inside the room. I knelt behind the door and tripped the tumblers, *one, two,* and listened to the creak of the staircase. It wasn't Richard coming down. It wasn't a twenty-year-old. There was a measured caution in the tread. Some kind of stiffness. Somebody getting slower and quieter as they approached the bottom. The sound disappeared altogether in the hallway. I pictured someone standing on the thick rugs, surrounded by the drapes and the paneling, looking around, listening hard. Maybe heading my way. I picked up the flashlight and the chisel again. The Glock was in my waistband. I had no doubt I could fight my way out of the house. No doubt at all. But approaching an alert Paulie over hundreds of yards of open ground and through the stadium lights would be difficult. And a firefight now would bury the mission forever. Quinn would disappear again.

There was no sound from the hallway. No sound at all. Just a crushing silence. Then I heard the front door open. I heard the rattle of a chain and a lock springing back and the click of a latch and the sucking sound of a copper insulating strip releasing its grip on the edge of the door. A second later the door closed again. I felt a tiny shudder in the structure of the house as the heavy oak hit the frame. *No beep from the metal detector.* Whoever had passed through it wasn't carrying a weapon. Or even a set of car keys.

I waited. Duke was surely fast asleep. And he wasn't the trusting type. I guessed he wouldn't walk around at night without a gun. Neither would Beck. But either one of them might be smart enough just to stand there in the hallway and open and close the door to make me think they had gone out through it. When in fact they hadn't. When in fact they were still standing right there, gun drawn, staring back into the gloom, waiting for me to show myself.

I sat down sideways in the red leather chair. Took the Glock out of my pants and aimed it left-handed at the door. Soon as they opened it wider than nine millimeters I would fire. Until then, I would wait. I was good at waiting. If they thought they were going to wait me out, they had picked the wrong guy.

BUT A WHOLE HOUR LATER THERE WAS STILL AB-solute silence out in the hallway. No sound of any kind. No vibrations. There was nobody there. Certainly not Duke. He would have fallen asleep by then and hit the deck. Not Beck, either. He was an amateur. It takes tremendous skill to keep absolutely still and silent for a whole hour. So the door thing hadn't been a trick. Somebody had gone out unarmed into the night.

I knelt down and used the bradawl on the tumblers again. Lay full-length on the floor and reached up and pulled the door open. A precaution. Anybody waiting for the door to open would have their eyes locked at head height. I would see them before they saw me. But there was nobody waiting. The hallway was empty. I stood up-right and locked the door behind me. Walked silently down the basement stairs and put the flashlight back in its place. Felt my way back upstairs. Crept to the kitchen and slid all my hardware along the floor and out the door into the porch. Locked it behind me and crouched down and picked up all my stuff and checked the view out back. Saw nothing except an empty gray world of moonlit rocks and ocean.

I locked the porch door behind me and kept very

close to the side of the house. Ducked through deep black shadows and made it back to the courtyard wall. Found the dip in the rock and wrapped the chisel and the bradawl in the rag and left them there. I couldn't take them with me. They would tear the trash bag. I followed the courtyard wall onward toward the ocean. I aimed to get down on the rocks right behind the garage block, to the south, completely out of sight of the house.

I made it halfway there. Then I froze.

Elizabeth Beck was sitting on the rocks. She was wearing a white bathrobe over a white nightgown. She looked like a ghost, or an angel. She had her elbows on her knees and she was staring into the darkness in the east like a statue.

I kept completely still. I was thirty feet away from her. I was dressed all in black but if she glanced to her left I would show up against the horizon. And sudden movement would give me away. So I just stood there. The ocean swell lapped in and out, quiet and lazy. It was a peaceful sound. Hypnotic motion. She was staring at the water. She must have been cold. There was a slight breeze and I could see it in her hair.

I inched downward like I was trying to melt into the rock. Bent my knees and spread my fingers and eased myself down into a crouch. She moved. Just a quizzical turn of her head, like something had suddenly occurred to her. She looked right at me. Gave no sign of surprise. She stared directly at me for minute after minute. Her long fingers were laced together. Her pale face was lit by moonlight reflected off the lapping water. Her eyes were open, but clearly she wasn't seeing anything. Or else I was low enough down against the sky that she thought I was a rock or a shadow.

She sat like that for maybe ten more minutes, staring in my direction. She started shivering in the cold. Then she moved her head again, decisively, and looked away from me at the sea to her right. She unlaced her fingers and moved her hands and smoothed her hair back. Turned her face up to the sky. She stood up slowly. She was barefoot. She shuddered, like she was cold, or sad. She held her arms out sideways like a tightrope walker and stepped toward me. The ground was hurting her feet. That was clear. She balanced herself with her arms and tested every step. She came within a yard of me. Went right on by and headed back to the house. I watched her go. The wind caught her robe. Her nightdress flattened against her body. She disappeared behind the courtyard wall. A long moment later I heard the front door open. There was a tiny pause and then a soft *clump* as it closed. I dropped flat to the ground and rolled onto my back. Stared up at the stars.

I LAY LIKE THAT AS LONG AS I DARED AND THEN got up and scrambled the final fifty feet to the edge of the sea. Shook out the trash bag and stripped off my clothes and packed them neatly into it. I wrapped the Glock inside my shirt with the spare magazines. Stuffed my socks into my shoes and packed them on top and followed them with the small linen towel. Then I tied the bag tight and held it by the neck. Slipped into the water, dragging it behind me.

The ocean was cold. I had figured it would be. I was on the coast of Maine in April. But this was *cold*. It was icy. It was jarring and numbing. It took my breath away. Inside a second I was chilled to the bone. Five yards offshore my teeth were chattering and I was going nowhere and the salt stung my eyes.

I kicked onward until I was ten yards out and I could see the wall. It glared with light. I couldn't get through it. Couldn't get over it. So I had to go around it. No choice. I reasoned with myself. I had to swim a quarter-mile. I was strong but not fast and I was towing a bag, so it would take me maybe ten minutes. Fifteen, at the absolute maximum. That was all. And nobody dies of exposure in fifteen minutes. Nobody. Not me, anyway. Not tonight.

I fought the cold and the swell and built a kind of sidestroke rhythm. I towed the bag with my left hand for ten leg-kicks. Then I changed to my right and kicked on. There was a slight current. The tide was coming in. It was helping me. But it was freezing me, too. It was coming in all the way from the Grand Banks. It was arctic. My skin was dead and slick. My breath was rasping. My heart was thumping. I started to worry about thermal shock. I thought back to books I had read about the *Titanic*. The people who didn't make it into the lifeboats all died within an hour.

But I wasn't going to be in the water for an hour. And there were no actual icebergs around. And my rhythm was working. I was about level with the wall. The light spill stopped well short of me. I was naked and pale from the winter but I felt invisible. I passed the wall. Halfway there. I kicked onward. Pounded away. Raised my wrist clear of the water and checked the time. I had been swimming for six minutes.

I swam for six more. Trod water and gasped for air and floated the bag ahead of me and looked back. I was well clear of the wall. I changed direction and headed for the shore. Came up through slick mossy rocks onto a gritty beach. Threw the bag up ahead of me and crawled out of the water on my knees. I stayed on all fours for a whole minute, panting and shivering. My teeth were chattering wildly. I untied the bag. Found the towel. Rubbed myself furiously. My arms were blue. My clothes snagged on my skin. I got my shoes on and stowed the Glock.

Folded the bag and the towel and put them wet in my pocket. Then I ran, because I needed to get warm.

I ran for nearly ten minutes before I found the car. It was the old guy's Taurus, gray in the moonlight. It was parked facing away from the house, all set to go, no delay. Duffy was a practical woman, that was for sure. I smiled again. The key was on the seat. I started the motor and eased away slowly. Kept the lights off and didn't touch the brake until I was off the palm-shaped promontory and around the first curve on the road inland. Then I lit up the headlights and turned up the heater and hit the gas hard.

I WAS OUTSIDE THE PORTLAND DOCKS FIFTEEN minutes later. I left the Taurus parked on a quiet street a mile short of Beck's warehouse. Walked the rest of the way. This was the moment of truth. If Doll's body had been found the place would be in an uproar and I would melt away and never be seen again. If it hadn't, I would live to fight another day.

The walk took the best part of twenty minutes. I saw nobody. No cops, no ambulances, no police tape, no medical examiners. No unexplained men in Lincoln Town Cars. I circled Beck's warehouse itself on a wide radius. I glimpsed it through gaps and alleys. The lights were all on in the office windows. But that was the way I had left it. Doll's car was still there by the roller door. Exactly where I had left it.

I walked away from the building and came back toward it from a new angle, from the blind side where there was no window. I took the Glock out. Held it hidden low down by my leg. Doll's car faced me. Beyond it on the left was the personnel door into the warehouse cubicle. Beyond that was the back office. I passed the car and the door and dropped to the floor and crawled under the window. Raised my head and looked inside. Nobody there. The secretarial area was empty, too. All quiet. I breathed out and put the gun away. Retraced my steps to Doll's car. Opened the driver's door and popped the trunk. He was still in there. He hadn't gone anywhere. I took his keys out of his pocket. Closed the lid on him again and carried the keys in through the personnel door. Found the right key and locked it behind me.

I was willing to risk fifteen minutes. I spent five in the warehouse cubicle, five in the back office, and five in the secretarial area. I wiped everything I touched with the linen towel, so I wouldn't leave any prints behind. I found no specific trace of Teresa Daniel. Or of Quinn. But then, there were no names named anywhere. Everything was coded, people and merchandise alike. I came away with only one solid fact. Bizarre Bazaar sold several tens of thousands of individual items every year, to several hundred individual customers, in transactions totaling several tens of millions of dollars. Nothing made clear what the items were or who the customers were. Prices were clustered around three levels: some around fifty bucks, some around a thousand bucks, and some much more than that. There were no shipping records at all. No FedEx, no UPS, no postal service. Clearly distribution was handled privately. But an insurance file I found told me that the corporation owned only two delivery trucks.

I walked back to the warehouse cubicle and shut the computer down. Retraced my steps to the entrance hallway and turned all the lights off as I went and left everything neat and tidy. I tested Doll's keys in the front door and found the one that fit and clamped it in my palm. Turned back to the alarm box.

Doll was clearly trusted to lock up, which meant he

knew how to set the alarm. I was sure Duke would do it himself, from time to time. And Beck, obviously. Probably one or two of the clerks as well. A whole bunch of people. One of them would have a lousy memory. I looked at the notice board next to the box. Flipped through the memos where they were pinned three-deep. Found a four-figure code written on the bottom of a two-year-old note from the city about new parking regulations. I entered it on the keypad. The red light started flashing and the box started beeping. I smiled. It never fails. Computer passwords, unlisted numbers, alarm codes, someone always writes them down.

I went out the front door and closed it behind me. The beeping stopped. I locked it and walked around the corner and slid into Doll's Lincoln. Started it up and drove it away. I left it in a downtown parking garage. It could have been the same one that Susan Duffy had photographed. I wiped everything I had touched and locked it up and put the keys in my pocket. I thought about setting it on fire. It had gas in the tank and I still had two dry kitchen matches. Burning cars is fun. And it would increase the pressure on Beck. But in the end I just walked away. It was probably the right decision. It would take most of a day for anybody to grow aware of it parked there. Most of another day for them to decide to do something about it. Then another day for the cops to respond. They would trace the plate and come up against one of Beck's shell corporations. So they would tow it away, pending further inquiry. They would bust open the trunk for sure, worried about terrorist bombs or because of the smell, but by then a whole bunch of other deadlines would have been reached and I would be long gone.

I WALKED BACK TO THE TAURUS AND DROVE IT
to within a mile of the house. Returned Duffy's compliment by U-turning and leaving it facing the right way for
her. Then I went through my previous routine in reverse. I
stripped on the gritty beach and packed the garbage bag.
Waded into the sea. I wasn't keen to do it. It was just as
cold. But the tide had turned. It was going my way. Even
the ocean was cooperating. I swam the same twelve minutes. Looped right around the end of the wall and came
ashore behind the garage block. I was shaking with cold
and my teeth were chattering again. But I felt good. I
dried myself as well as I could on the damp linen rag and
dressed fast before I froze. Left the Glock and the spare
magazines and Doll's set of keys hidden with the PSM
and the chisel and the bradawl. Folded the bag and the
towel and wedged them under a rock a yard away. Then I
headed for my drainpipe. I was still shivering.

The climb was easier going up than coming down. I
walked my hands up the pipe and my feet up the wall. Got
level with my window and grabbed the sill with my left
hand. Jumped my feet across to the stone ledge. Brought
my right hand over and pushed the window up. Hauled
myself inside as quietly as I could.

The room was icy. The window had been open for
hours. I closed it tight and stripped again. My clothes
were damp. I laid them out on the radiator and headed for
the bathroom. Took a long hot shower. Then I locked myself in there with my shoes. It was exactly six in the morning. They would be picking up the Taurus. Probably Eliot
and the old guy would be doing it. Probably Duffy would
have stayed back at base. I took the e-mail device out and
sent: *Duffy?* Ninety seconds later she came back with:
Here. You OK? I sent: *Fine. Check these names anywhere
you can, inc. with MP Powell—Angel Doll, poss. associate Paulie, both poss. ex-military.*

She sent: *Will do.*

Then I sent the question that had been on my mind for five and a half hours: *What is Teresa Daniel's real name?*

There was the usual ninety-second delay, and then she came back with: *Teresa Justice.*

CHAPTER 6

NO POINT IN GOING TO BED, SO I JUST STOOD at the window and watched the dawn. It was soon in full flow. The sun came up over the sea. The air was fresh and clear. I could see fifty miles. I watched an arctic tern coming in low from the north. It skimmed the rocks as it passed them. I guessed it was looking for a place to build a nest. The low sun behind it threw shadows as big as vultures. Then it gave up on the search for shelter and looped and wheeled and swooped away over the water and tumbled into the ocean. It came out a long moment later and silver droplets of freezing water trailed it back into the sky. It had nothing in its beak. But it flew on like it was happy enough. It was better adapted than me.

There wasn't much to see after that. There were a few herring gulls far in the distance. I squinted against the glare and looked for signs of whales or dolphins and saw nothing. I watched mats of seaweed drift around on circular currents. At six-fifteen I heard Duke's footsteps in the corridor and the click of my lock. He didn't come in. He just tramped away again. I turned and faced the door and took a deep breath. Day thirteen, Thursday. Maybe that was better than day thirteen falling on a Friday. I wasn't sure. *Whatever, bring it on.* I took another breath and walked out through the door and headed down the stairs.

Nothing was the same as the morning before. Duke was fresh and I was tired. Paulie wasn't around. I went down to the basement gym and found nobody there. Duke didn't stay for breakfast. He disappeared somewhere. Richard Beck came in to eat in the kitchen. There was just him and me at the table. The mechanic wasn't there. The cook stayed busy at the stove. The Irish girl came in and out from the dining room. She was moving fast. There was a buzz in the air. Something was happening.

"Big shipment coming in," Richard Beck said. "It's always like this. Everybody gets excited about the money they're going to make."

"You heading back to school?" I asked him.

"Sunday," he said. He didn't seem worried about it. But I was. Sunday was three days away. My fifth full day there. The final deadline. Whatever was going to happen would have happened by then. The kid was going to be in the crossfire throughout.

"You OK with that?" I asked.

"With going back?"

I nodded. "After what happened."

"We know who did it now," he said. "Some assholes from Connecticut. It won't happen again."

"You can be that sure?"

He looked at me like I was nuts. "My dad handles stuff like this all the time. And if it's not done by Sunday, then I'll just stay here until it is."

"Does your dad run this whole thing by himself? Or does he have a partner?"

"He runs it all by himself," he said. His ambivalence was gone. He looked happy to be home, secure and comfortable, proud of his dad. His world had contracted to a barren half-acre of lonely granite, hemmed in by the restless sea and a high stone wall topped by razor wire.

"I don't think you really killed that cop," he said.

The kitchen went quiet. I stared at him.

"I think you just wounded him," he said. "I'm hoping so, anyway. You know, maybe he's recovering right now. In a hospital somewhere. That's what I'm thinking. You should try to do the same. Think positive. It's better that way. Then you can have the silver lining without the cloud."

"I don't know," I said.

"So just pretend," he said. "Use the power of positive thinking. Say to yourself, I did a good thing and there was no downside."

"Your dad called the local police," I said. "I don't think there was any room for doubt."

"So just pretend," he said again. "That's what I do. Bad things didn't happen unless you choose to recall them."

He had stopped eating and his left hand was up at the left side of his head. He was smiling brightly, but his subconscious was recalling some bad things, right there and then. That was clear. It was recalling them big time.

"OK," I said. "It was just a flesh wound."

"In and out," he said. "Clean as a whistle."

I said nothing.

"Missed everything by a fraction," he said. "It was a miracle."

I nodded. It would have been some kind of a miracle. That was for damn sure. Shoot somebody in the chest with a soft-nose .44 Magnum and you blow a hole in them the size of Rhode Island. Death is generally instantaneous. The heart stops immediately, mostly because it isn't there anymore. I figured the kid hadn't seen anybody shot before. Then I thought, but maybe he has. And maybe he didn't like it very much.

"Positive thinking," he said. "That's the key. Just assume he's warm and comfortable somewhere, making a full recovery."

"What's in the shipment?" I asked.

"Fakes, probably," he said. "From Pakistan. We get two-hundred-year-old Persians made there. People are such suckers."

"Are they?"

He looked at me and nodded. "They see what they want to see."

"Do they?"

"All the time."

I looked away. There was no coffee. After a while you realize that caffeine is addictive. I was irritated. And tired.

"What are you doing today?" he asked me.

"I don't know," I said.

"I'm just going to read," he said. "Maybe stroll a little. Walk the shoreline, see what washed up in the night."

"Things wash up?"

"Sometimes. You know, things fall off boats."

I looked at him. *Was he telling me something?* I had heard of smugglers floating bales of marijuana ashore in isolated places. I guessed the same system would work for heroin. *Was he telling me something?* Or was he warning me? Did he know about my hidden bundle of hardware? And what was all that stuff about the shot cop? Psychobabble? Or was he playing games with me?

"But that's mostly in the summer," he said. "It's too cold for boats right now. So I guess I'll stay inside. Maybe I'll paint."

"You paint?"

"I'm an art student," he said. "I told you that."

I nodded. Stared at the back of the cook's head, like I

could induce her to make coffee by telepathy. Then Duke came in. He walked over to where I was sitting. Placed one hand on the back of my chair and the other flat on the table. Bent low, like he needed to have a confidential conversation.

"Your lucky day, asshole," he said.

I said nothing.

"You're driving Mrs. Beck," he said. "She wants to go shopping."

"Where?"

"Wherever," he said.

"All day?"

"It better be."

I nodded. *Don't trust the stranger on shipment day.*

"Take the Cadillac," he said. He dropped the keys on the table. "Make sure she doesn't rush back."

Or, don't trust Mrs. Beck on shipment day.

"OK," I said.

"You'll find it very interesting," he said. "Especially the first part. Gives me a hell of a kick, anyway, every single time."

I had no idea what he meant, and I didn't waste time speculating about it. I just stared at the empty coffee pot and Duke left and a moment later I heard the front door open and close. The metal detector beeped twice. Duke and Beck, guns and keys. Richard got up from the table and wandered out and I was left alone with the cook.

"Got any coffee?" I asked her.

"No," she said.

I sat there until I finally figured that a dutiful chauffeur should be ready and waiting, so I headed out through the back door. The metal detector beeped politely at the keys. The tide was all the way in and the air was cold and fresh. I could smell salt and seaweed. The swell was gone and I could hear waves breaking. I walked around to the garage block and started the Cadillac and backed it out. Drove it around to the carriage circle and waited there with the motor running to get the heater going. I could see tiny ships on the horizon heading in and out of Portland. They crawled along just beyond the line where the sky met the water, half-hidden, infinitely slow. I wondered if one of them was Beck's, or whether it was in already, all tied up and set for unloading. I wondered whether a Customs officer was already walking right past it, eyes front, heading for the next ship in line, a wad of crisp new bills in his pocket.

Elizabeth Beck came out of the house ten minutes later. She was wearing a knee-length plaid skirt and a thin white sweater with a wool coat over it. Her legs were bare. No panty hose. Her hair was pulled back with a rubber band. She looked cold. And defiant, and resigned, and apprehensive. Like a noblewoman walking to the guillotine. I guessed she was used to having Duke drive her. I guessed she was a little conflicted about riding with the cop-killer. I got out and made ready to open the rear door. She walked right past it.

"I'll sit in front," she said.

She settled herself in the passenger seat and I slid back in next to her.

"Where to?" I asked politely.

She stared out her window.

"We'll talk about that when we're through the gate," she said.

The gate was closed and Paulie was standing dead-center in front of it. His shoulders and arms looked like he had basketballs stuffed inside his suit. The skin on his face was red with cold. He had been waiting there for us. I stopped the car six feet in front of him. He made no move toward the gate. I looked straight at him. He ignored me and tracked around to Elizabeth Beck's window. Smiled at her and tapped on the glass with his knuckles and made a winding motion with his hand. She stared straight ahead through the windshield. Tried to ignore him. He tapped again. She turned to look at him. He raised his eyebrows. Made the winding motion again. She shuddered. It was enough of a definite physical spasm to rock the car on its springs. She stared hard at one of her fingernails and then placed it on the window button and pressed. The glass buzzed down. Paulie squatted with his right forearm on the door frame.

"Good morning," he said.

He leaned in and touched her cheek with the back of his forefinger. Elizabeth Beck didn't move. Just stared straight ahead. He tucked a stray wisp of hair behind her ear.

"I enjoyed our visit last night," he said.

She shuddered again. Like she was deathly cold. He moved his hand. Dropped it to her breast. Cupped it. Squeezed it. She sat still for it. I used the button on my side. Her glass buzzed up. Then it stalled against Paulie's giant arm and the safety feature kicked in and it came back down again. I opened my door and slid out. Rounded the hood. Paulie was still squatting down. He still had his hand inside the car. It had moved a little lower.

"Back off," he said, looking at her, talking to me.

I felt like a lumberjack confronting a redwood tree without an ax or a chainsaw. *Where do I start?* I kicked him in the kidney. It was the kind of kick that would have sent a football out of the stadium and into the parking lot. It would have cracked a utility pole. It would have put most guys in the hospital all by itself. It would have killed some of them. It had about as much effect on Paulie as a polite tap on the shoulder. He didn't even make a noise. He just put both hands on the door frame and slowly pushed himself upright. Turned around to face me.

"Relax, Major," he said. "Just my way of saying good morning to the lady."

Then he moved away from the car and looped right around me and unlocked the gate. I watched him. He was very calm. No sign of a reaction. It was like I hadn't touched him at all. I stood still and let the adrenaline drain away. Then I looked at the car. At the trunk, and at the hood. To walk around the trunk would say *I'm scared of you.* So I walked around the hood instead. But I made sure to stay well out of his reach. I had no desire to give some surgeon six months' work rebuilding the bones in my face. The closest I got to him was about five feet. He made no move on me. Just cranked the gate all the way open and stood there patiently waiting to close it again.

"We'll talk about that kick later, OK?" he called.

I didn't reply.

"And don't get the wrong impression, Major," he said. "She likes it."

I got back in the car. Elizabeth Beck had closed her window. She was staring straight ahead, pale and silent and humiliated. I drove through the gate. Headed west. Watched Paulie in the mirror. He closed the gate and headed back inside the lodge. Disappeared from sight.

"I'm sorry you had to see that," Elizabeth said quietly.

I said nothing.

"And thank you for your intervention," she said. "But it will prove futile. And I'm afraid it will bring you a lot of trouble. He already hates you, you know. And he's not very rational."

I said nothing.

"It's a control thing, of course," she said. It was like she was explaining it to herself. It wasn't like she was talking to me. "It's a demonstration of power. That's all it is. There's no actual sex. He can't do it. Too many steroids, I suppose. He just paws me."

I said nothing.

"He makes me undress," she said. "Makes me parade around for him. Paws me. There's no sex. He's impotent."

I said nothing. Just drove slow, keeping the car steady and level through the coastal curves.

"It usually lasts about an hour," she said.

"Have you told your husband?" I asked.

"What could *he* do?"

"Fire the guy."

"Not possible," she said.

"Why not?"

"Because Paulie doesn't work for my husband."

I glanced at her. Recalled telling Duke: *You should get rid of him.* Duke had answered: *That's not easy.*

"So who does he work for?" I said.

"Somebody else."

"Who?"

She shook her head. It was like she couldn't speak the name.

"It's a control thing," she said again. "I can't object to what they do to me, just like my husband can't object to what they do to him. Nobody can object. To *anything,* you see. That's the point. You won't be allowed to object to anything, either. Duke wouldn't think to object, of course. He's an animal."

I said nothing.

"I just thank God I have a son," she said. "Not a daughter."

I said nothing.

"Last night was very bad," she said. "I was hoping he would start leaving me alone. Now that I'm getting old."

I glanced at her again. Couldn't think of anything to say.

"It was my birthday yesterday," she said. "That was Paulie's present to me."

I said nothing.

"I turned fifty," she said. "I suppose you don't want to think about a naked fifty-year-old, parading around."

I didn't know what to say.

"But I keep in shape," she said. "I use the gym when the others aren't around."

I said nothing.

"He pages me," she said. "I have to carry a pager at all times. It buzzed in the middle of the night. Last night. I had to go, right away. It's much worse if I keep him waiting."

I said nothing.

"I was on my way back when you saw me," she said. "Out there on the rocks."

I PULLED ONTO THE SIDE OF THE ROAD, BRAKED gently and stopped the car. Eased the gearshift into Park.

"I think you work for the government," she said.

I shook my head.

"You're wrong," I said. "I'm just a guy."

"Then I'm disappointed."

"I'm just a guy," I said again.

She said nothing.

"You shouldn't say stuff like that," I said. "I'm in enough trouble already."

"Yes," she said. "They'd kill you."

"Well, they'd try," I said. Then I paused. "Have you told them what you think?"

"No," she said.

"Well don't. And you're wrong anyway."

She said nothing.

"There'd be a battle," I said. "They'd come for me and

I wouldn't go quietly. People would get hurt. Richard, maybe."

She stared at me. "Are you *bargaining* with me?"

I shook my head again.

"I'm warning you," I said. "I'm a survivor."

She smiled a bitter smile.

"You have absolutely no idea," she said. "Whoever you are, you're in way over your head. You should leave now."

"I'm just a guy," I said. "I've got nothing to hide from them."

The wind rocked the car. I could see nothing but granite and trees. We were miles from the nearest human being.

"My husband is a criminal," she said.

"I figured that," I said.

"He's a hard man," she said. "He can be violent, and he's always ruthless."

"But he's not his own boss," I said.

"No," she said. "He isn't. He's a hard man who literally quakes in front of the person who *is* his boss."

I said nothing.

"There's an expression," she said. "People ask, why do bad things happen to good people? But in my husband's case, bad things are happening to a bad person. Ironic, isn't it? But they *are* bad things."

"Who does Duke belong to?"

"My husband. But Duke's as bad as Paulie, in his way. I wouldn't care to choose between them. He was a corrupt cop, and a corrupt federal agent, and a killer. He's been in prison."

"Is he the only one?"

"On my husband's payroll? Well, he had the two bodyguards. They were his. Or they were provided for him, anyway. But they were killed, of course. Outside

Richard's college. By the men from Connecticut. So yes, Duke's the only one now. Apart from the mechanic, of course. But he's just a technician."

"How many has the other guy got?"

"I'm not sure. They seem to come and go."

"What exactly are they importing?"

She looked away. "If you're not a government man, then I guess you wouldn't be interested."

I followed her gaze toward the distant trees. *Think, Reacher.* This could be an elaborate con game designed to flush me out. They could all be in it together. His gate man's hand on his wife's breast would be a small price for Beck to pay for some crucial information. And I believed in elaborate con games. I had to. I was riding one myself.

"I'm not a government man," I said.

"Then I'm disappointed," she said again.

I put the car in Drive. Held my foot on the brake.

"Where to?" I asked.

"Do you think I care where the hell we go?"

"You want to get some coffee?"

"Coffee?" she said. "Sure. Go south. Let's stay well away from Portland today."

I MADE THE TURN SOUTH ONTO ROUTE ONE, about a mile short of I-95. It was a pleasant old road, like roads used to be. We passed through a place called Old Orchard Beach. It had neat brick sidewalks and Victorian streetlights. There were signs pointing left to a beach. There were faded French flags. I guessed Quebec Canadians had vacationed there before cheap airfares to Florida and the Caribbean had changed their preferences.

"Why were you out last night?" Elizabeth Beck asked me.

I said nothing.

"You can't deny it," she said. "Did you think I hadn't seen you?"

"You didn't react," I said.

"I was in Paulie mode," she said. "I've trained myself not to react."

I said nothing.

"Your room was locked," she said.

"I climbed out the window," I said. "I don't like to be locked in."

"What did you do then?"

"I took a stroll. Like I thought you were doing."

"Then you climbed back in?"

I nodded. Said nothing.

"The wall is your big problem," she said. "There are the lights and the razor wire, obviously, but there are sensors too, in the ground. Paulie would hear you from thirty yards away."

"I was just getting some air," I said.

"No sensors under the driveway," she said. "They couldn't make them work under the blacktop. But there's a camera on the lodge. And there's a motion alarm on the gate itself. Do you know what an NSV is?"

"Soviet tank-turret machine gun," I said.

"Paulie's got one," she said. "He keeps it by the side door. He's been told to use it if he hears the motion alarm."

I breathed in, and then I breathed out. An NSV is more than five feet long and weighs more than fifty-five pounds. It uses cartridges four and a half inches long and a half-inch wide. It can fire twelve of them in a second. It has no safety mechanism. The combination of Paulie and an NSV would be nobody's idea of fun.

"But I think you swam," she said. "I can smell the sea on your shirt. Very faintly. You didn't dry yourself properly when you got back."

We passed a sign for a town called Saco. I coasted to the shoulder and stopped again. Cars and trucks whined past us.

"You were incredibly lucky," she said. "There are some bad riptides off the point. Strong undertow. But I expect you went in behind the garages. In which case you missed them by about ten feet."

"I don't work for the government," I said.

"Don't you?"

"Don't you think you're taking a hell of a chance?" I said. "Let's say I wasn't exactly what I appeared to be. Just for the sake of argument. Let's say I was from a rival organization, for instance. Don't you see the risk? You think you would make it back to the house alive? Saying what you're saying?"

She looked away.

"Then I guess that will be the test," she said. "If you're a government man, you won't kill me. If you're not, you will."

"I'm just a guy," I said. "You could get me in trouble."

"Let's find coffee," she said. "Saco is a nice town. All the big mill owners lived there, way back."

WE ENDED UP ON AN ISLAND IN THE MIDDLE OF the Saco River. There was an enormous brick building on it that had been a gigantic mill, way back in history. Now it was being gentrified into hundreds of offices and stores. We found a glass-and-chrome coffee shop called *Café Café*. A pun in French, I guessed. But the smell alone was worth the trip. I ignored the lattes and the flavored foamy stuff and ordered regular coffee, hot, black, large. Then I turned to Elizabeth Beck. She shook her head.

"You stay," she said. "I've decided to go shopping. Alone. I'll meet you back here in four hours."

I said nothing.

"I don't need your permission," she said. "You're just my driver."

"I don't have any money," I said.

She gave me twenty bucks from her purse. I paid for the coffee and carried it to a table. She came with me and watched me sit down.

"Four hours," she said. "Maybe a little more, but no less. In case there's something you need to do."

"I've got nothing to do," I said. "I'm just your driver."

She looked at me. Zipped her purse. The space around my table was tight. She twisted a little to get the strap of her purse square on her shoulder. Jackknifed slightly to avoid touching the table and spilling my coffee. There was a *clunk,* like plastic hitting the floor. I looked down. Something had fallen out from under her skirt. She stared at it and her face slowly turned a deep shade of red. She bent and picked the thing up and clutched it in her hand. Fumbled her way onto the chair opposite me like all the strength had gone out of her. Like she was utterly humiliated. She was holding a pager. It was a black plastic rectangle a little smaller than my own e-mail device. She stared at it. Her neck was bright red all the way down under her sweater. She spoke in a low rueful whisper.

"He makes me carry it there," she said. "Inside my underpants. He likes it to have what he calls the appropriate effect when it buzzes. He checks that it's there every time I go through the gate. Normally I take it out and put it in my bag afterward. But I didn't want to do that, you know, this time, with you watching."

I said nothing. She stood up. Blinked twice and took a breath and swallowed.

"Four hours," she said. "In case there's something you need to do."

Then she walked away. I watched her go. She turned left outside the door and disappeared. *An elaborate con game?* It was possible that they could try to set me up with her story. Possible that she could carry a pager in her pants to back it up. Possible that she could contrive to shake it loose at exactly the right moment. All possible. But what wasn't even remotely possible was that she could manufacture a deep red blush, right on cue. Nobody can do that. Not even the world's finest actress at the peak of her powers could do that. So Elizabeth Beck was for real.

I DIDN'T ABANDON SENSIBLE PRECAUTIONS ENtirely. They were too deeply ingrained for that. I finished my coffee like an innocent person with all the time in the world. Then I strolled out to the mall's internal sidewalks and turned random lefts and rights until I was sure I was alone. Then I went back to the coffee shop and bought another cup. Borrowed their restroom key and locked myself in. Sat on the lid of the john and took off my shoe. There was a message waiting from Duffy: *Why interest in Teresa Daniel's real name?* I ignored it and sent: *Where is your motel?* Ninety seconds later she answered: *What did you have for breakfast first day in Boston?* I smiled. Duffy was a practical woman. She was worried my e-mail device had been compromised. She was asking a security question. I sent: *Short stack with egg, coffee, three-dollar tip, I ate it.* Any other answer than that and she would be running for her car. Ninety seconds later she came back with: *West side of Route One 100 yards south of Kennebunk River.* I figured that was about ten miles away. I sent: *See you in 10 minutes.*

IT TOOK ME MORE LIKE FIFTEEN MINUTES BY THE
time I had gotten back to the car and fought the traffic
where Route One bottlenecked through Saco. I kept one
eye on the mirror the whole way and saw nothing to worry
about. I crossed the river and found a motel on my right. It
was a cheerful bright gray place pretending to be a string
of classic New England saltboxes. It was April and not
very busy. I saw the Taurus I had been a passenger in out
of Boston parked next to the end room. It was the only
plain sedan I could see. I put the Cadillac thirty yards
away behind a wooden shed hiding a big propane tank. No
sense in leaving it visible to everybody passing by on
Route One.

I walked back and knocked once and Susan Duffy
opened the door fast and we hugged. We just went straight
into it. It took me completely by surprise. I think it took
her by surprise, too. We probably wouldn't have done it if
we had thought about it first. But I guess she was anxious
and I was stressed and it just happened. And it felt real
good. She was tall, but she was slight. My hand spanned
almost the whole width of her back and I felt her ribs give
a little. She smelled fresh and clean. No perfume. Just
skin, not long out of the shower.

"What do you know about Teresa?" she asked.

"You alone?" I asked.

She nodded. "The others are in Portland. Customs
says Beck's got a boat coming in today."

We let go of each other. Moved on into the room.

"What are they going to do?" I asked.

"Observation only," she said. "Don't worry. They're
good at it. Nobody will see them."

It was a very generic motel room. One queen bed, a
chair, a desk, a TV, a window, a through-the-wall air con-
ditioner. The only things that distinguished it from a hundred thousand other motel rooms were a blue-and-gray

color scheme and nautical prints on the wall. They gave it a definite New England coastal flavor.

"What do you know about Teresa?" she asked again.

I told her about the name carved into the basement room floor. And the date. Duffy stared at me. Then she closed her eyes.

"She's alive," she said. "Thank you."

"Well, she was alive yesterday," I said.

She opened her eyes. "You think she's alive today?"

I nodded. "I think the odds are pretty good. They want her for something. Why keep her alive nine weeks and kill her now?"

Duffy said nothing.

"I think they just moved her," I said. "That's all. That's my best guess. The door was locked in the morning, she was gone by the evening."

"You think she's been treated OK?"

I didn't tell her what Paulie liked to do with Elizabeth Beck. She already had enough to worry about.

"I think she scratched her name with a fork," I said. "And there was a spare plate of steak and potatoes lying around last night, like they took her out in such a hurry they forgot to tell the cook. So I think they were probably feeding her. I think she's a prisoner, plain and simple."

"Where would they have taken her?"

"I think Quinn's got her," I said.

"Why?"

"Because it seems to me what we're looking at here is one organization superimposed over another. Beck's a bad guy for sure, but he's been taken over by a worse guy."

"Like a corporate thing?"

"Exactly," I said. "Like a hostile takeover. Quinn's put his staff into Beck's operation. He's riding it like a parasite."

"But why would they move Teresa?"

"A precaution," I said.

"Because of you? How worried are they?"

"A little," I said. "I think they're moving things and hiding things."

"But they haven't confronted you yet."

I nodded. "They're not really sure about me."

"So why are they taking a risk with you?"

"Because I saved the boy."

She nodded. Went quiet. She looked a little tired. I guessed maybe she hadn't slept at all since I asked her for the car at midnight. She was wearing jeans and a man's Oxford shirt. The shirt was pure white and neatly tucked in. The top two buttons were undone. She was wearing boat shoes over bare feet. The room heat was set on high. There was a laptop computer on the desk, next to the room phone. The phone was a console thing all covered in fast-dial buttons. I checked the number and memorized it. The laptop was plugged through a complex adapter into a data port built into the base of the phone. There was a screensaver playing on it. It showed the Justice Department shield drifting around. Every time it reached the edge of the screen it would bounce off in a new random direction like that ancient video tennis game. There was no sound with it.

"Have you seen Quinn yet?" she asked.

I shook my head.

"Know where he operates out of?"

I shook my head again. "I haven't really seen anything. Except their books are coded and they don't have enough of a distribution fleet to be moving what they seem to move. Maybe their customers collect."

"That would be insane," she said. "They wouldn't show their customers their base of operations. In fact we already know they don't. Beck met with the LA dealer in a parking garage, remember."

"So maybe they rendezvous somewhere neutral. For the actual sales. Somewhere close by, in the northeast."

She nodded. "How did you see their books?"

"I was in their office last night. That's why I wanted the car."

She moved to the desk and sat down and tapped the laptop's touch pad. The screensaver disappeared. My last e-mail was displayed under it: *See you in 10 minutes.* She went into the deleted items directory and clicked on a message from Powell, the MP who had sold me out.

"We traced those names for you," she said. "Angel Doll did eight years in Leavenworth for sexual assault. Should have been life for rape and murder, but the prosecution screwed up. He was a communications technician. Raped a female lieutenant colonel, left her to bleed to death from the inside. He's not a very nice guy."

"He's a very dead guy," I said.

She just looked at me.

"He checked the Maxima's plates," I said. "Confronted me. Big error. He was the first casualty."

"You killed him?"

I nodded. "Broke his neck."

She said nothing.

"His choice," I said. "He was about to compromise the mission."

She was pale.

"You OK?" I said.

She looked away. "I wasn't really expecting casualties."

"There might be more. Get used to it."

She looked back at me. Took a breath. Nodded.

"OK," she said. Then she paused. "Sorry about the plates. That was a mistake."

"Anything about Paulie?"

She scrolled down the screen. "Doll had a buddy in

Leavenworth called Paul Masserella, a bodybuilder, serving eight for assault on an officer. His defense counsel pleaded it down on account of steroid rage. Tried to blame the army for not monitoring Masserella's intake."

"His intake is all over the place now."

"You think he's the same Paulie?"

"Must be. He told me he doesn't like officers. I kicked him in the kidney. It would have killed you or Eliot. He didn't even notice."

"What's he going to do about it?"

"I hate to think."

"You OK with going back?"

"Beck's wife knows I'm phony."

She stared at me. "How?"

I shrugged. "Maybe she doesn't *know*. Maybe she just wants me to be. Maybe she's trying to convince herself."

"Is she broadcasting it?"

"Not yet. She saw me out of the house last night."

"You can't go back."

"I'm not a quitter."

"You're not an idiot, either. It's out of control now."

I nodded. "But it's my decision."

She shook her head. "It's our decision, jointly. You're depending on our backup."

"We need to get Teresa out of there. We really do, Duffy. It's a hell of a situation for her to be in."

"I could send SWAT teams for her. Now you've confirmed she's alive."

"We don't know where she is right now."

"She's my responsibility."

"And Quinn is mine."

She said nothing.

"You can't send SWAT teams," I said. "You're off the books. Asking for SWAT teams is the same thing as asking to be fired."

"I'm prepared to get fired, if it comes to it."

"It's not just you," I said. "Six other guys would get fired with you."

She said nothing.

"And I'm going back anyway," I said. "Because I want Quinn. With you or without you. So you might as well use me."

"What did Quinn *do* to you?"

I said nothing. She was quiet for a long moment.

"Would Mrs. Beck talk to us?" she said.

"I don't want to ask her," I said. "Asking her is the same thing as confirming her suspicions. I can't be sure exactly where that would lead."

"What would you do if you went back?"

"Get promoted," I said. "That's the key. I need to move up into Duke's job. Then I'll be top boy on Beck's side. Then I'll get some kind of official liaison with Quinn's side. That's what I need. I'm working in the dark without it."

"We need progress," she said. "We need evidence."

"I know," I said.

"How will you get promoted?"

"Same way anybody gets promoted," I said.

She didn't reply to that. Just switched her e-mail program back to *inbox* and stood up and stepped away to the window to look at the view. I looked at her. The light behind her was coming right through her shirt. Her hair was swept back and a couple of inches of it was on her collar. It looked like a five-hundred-dollar style to me, but I guessed on a DEA salary she probably did it herself. Or got a girlfriend to do it for her. I could picture her in someone's kitchen, on a chair set out in the middle of the floor, an old towel around her neck, interested in how she looked but not interested enough to spend big bucks in a city salon.

Her butt looked spectacular in the jeans. I could see the label on the back: *Waist 24. Leg 32*. That made her inseam five inches short of mine, which I was prepared to accept. But a waist a whole foot smaller than mine was ridiculous. I carry almost no body fat. All I've got in there are the necessary organs, tight and dense. She must have had miniature versions. I see a waist like that and all I want to do is span it with my hands and marvel at it. Maybe bury my head somewhere a little higher up. I couldn't tell what that might feel like with her unless she turned around. But I suspected it might feel very nice indeed.

"How dangerous is it now?" she asked. "Realistic assessment?"

"Can't tell," I said. "Too many variables. Mrs. Beck is running on intuition, that's all. Maybe a little wish-fulfillment with it. She's got no hard evidence. In terms of hard evidence I think I'm holding up OK. So even if Mrs. Beck talks to somebody it all depends on whether they choose to take a woman's intuition seriously or not."

"She saw you out of the house. That's hard evidence."

"But of what? That I'm restless?"

"This guy Doll was killed while you weren't locked up."

"They'll assume I didn't get past the wall. And they won't find Doll. No way. Not in time."

"Why did they move Teresa?"

"Precaution."

"It's out of control now," she said again.

I shrugged, even though she couldn't see the gesture. "This kind of thing is always out of control. It's to be expected. Nothing ever works like you predict it. All plans fall apart as soon as the first shot is fired."

She went quiet. Turned around.

"What are you going to do now?" she asked.

I paused a beat. The light was still behind her. *Very nice indeed.*

"I'm going to take a nap," I said.

"How long have you got?"

I checked my watch. "About three hours."

"You tired?"

I nodded. "I was up all night, swimming, mostly."

"You swam past the wall?" she said. "Maybe you *are* an idiot."

"Are you tired too?" I asked.

"Very. I've been working hard for weeks."

"So take a nap with me," I said.

"Doesn't feel right. Teresa's in danger somewhere."

"I can't go yet anyway," I said. "Not until Mrs. Beck is ready."

She paused a beat. "There's only one bed."

"Not a huge problem. You're thin. You won't take up much room."

"Wouldn't be right," she said.

"We don't have to get *in*," I said. "We could just lie on top."

"Right next to each other?"

"Fully dressed," I said. "I'll even keep my shoes on."

She said nothing.

"It's not against the law," I said.

"Maybe it is," she said. "Some states have weird old statutes. Maine might be one of them."

"I've got other Maine statutes to worry about."

"Not right this minute."

I smiled. Then I yawned. I sat on the bed and lay down on my back. Rolled over on my side and turned away from the middle and jammed my arms up under my head. Closed my eyes. I sensed her standing there, minute after minute. Then I felt her lie down next to me. She shuffled around a little. Then she went still. But she was tense. I could feel it. It was coming through the mattress springs, tiny high-frequency thrills of concern.

"Don't panic," I said. "I'm way too tired."

BUT I WASN'T, REALLY. THE PROBLEM STARTED when she moved slightly and touched my butt with hers. It was a very faint contact, but she might as well have plugged me into a power outlet. I opened my eyes and stared at the wall and tried to figure out whether she was asleep and had moved involuntarily or whether she had done it on purpose. I spent a couple of minutes thinking it through. But I guess mortal danger is an aphrodisiac because I found myself erring on the side of optimism. Then I wasn't certain about the required response. What was the correct etiquette? I settled for moving an inch myself and firming up the connection. I figured that would put the ball back in her court. Now she could struggle with the interpretation.

Nothing happened for a whole minute. I was on the point of getting disappointed when she moved again. Now the connection was pretty damn solid. If I didn't weigh two hundred and fifty pounds she might have slid me right across the shiny bedcover. I was fairly certain I could feel the rivets on her back pockets. *My turn.* I disguised it with a sort of sleepy sound and rolled over so we were stacked like spoons and my arm was accidentally touching her shoulder. Her hair was in my face. It was soft and smelled like summer. The cotton of her shirt was crisp. It plunged down to her waist and then the denim of her jeans swooped back up over her hips. I squinted down. She had taken her shoes off. I could see the soles of her feet. Ten little toes, all in a line.

She made a sleepy sound of her own. I was pretty sure it was fake. She nestled backward until she was jammed tight against me from top to bottom. I put my hand on her upper arm. Then I moved it down until it fell off her elbow and came to rest on her waist. The tip of my little finger was under the waistband of her jeans. She made another sound. Almost certainly a fake. I held my breath. Her butt was tight against my groin. My heart was thumping. My head was spinning. No way could I resist. No way at all. It was one of those insane hormone-driven moments when I would have risked eight years in Leavenworth for it. I slid my hand up and forward and cupped her breast. After that, things got completely out of control.

SHE WAS ONE OF THOSE WOMEN WHO IS FAR more attractive naked than clothed. Not all women are, but she was. She had a body to die for. She had no tan, but her skin was not pale. It was as soft as silk, but it was not translucent. She was very slim, but I couldn't see her bones. She was long, and she was lean. She was made for one of those bathing suits that swoop way up at the sides. She had small firm breasts, perfectly shaped. Her neck was long and slender. She had great ears and ankles and knees and shoulders. She had a little hollow at the base of her throat. It was very slightly damp.

She was strong, too. I must have outweighed her by a hundred and thirty pounds, but she had worn me out. She was young, I guess. She had maybe ten years on me. She had left me exhausted, which made her smile. She had a great smile.

"Remember my hotel room in Boston?" I said. "The way you sat on the chair? I wanted you right then."

"I was just sitting on a chair. There wasn't a *way* to it."

"Don't kid yourself."

"Remember the Freedom Trail?" she said. "You told

me about the long-rod penetrator? I wanted *you* right then."

I smiled.

"It was part of a billion-dollar defense contract," I said. "So I'm glad this particular citizen got something out of it."

"If Eliot hadn't been with me I'd have done it right there in the park."

"There was a woman feeding the birds."

"We could have gone behind a bush."

"Paul Revere would have seen us," I said.

"He rode all night," she said.

"I'm not Paul Revere," I said.

She smiled again. I felt it against my shoulder.

"All done, old guy?" she asked.

"I didn't say that, exactly."

"Danger is an aphrodisiac, isn't it?" she said.

"I guess it is."

"So you admit you're in danger?"

"I'm in danger of having a heart attack."

"You really shouldn't go back," she said.

"I'm in danger of not being able to."

She sat up on the bed. Gravity had no effect on her perfection.

"I'm serious, Reacher," she said.

I smiled up at her. "I'll be OK. Two or three more days. I'll find Teresa and I'll find Quinn and then I'll get out."

"Only if I let you."

I nodded.

"The two bodyguards," I said.

She nodded in turn. "That's why you need my end of the operation. You can forget all about the heroic stuff. With you or without you, my ass. We turn those guys loose and you're a dead man, one phone call later."

"Where are they now?"

"In the first motel, back in Massachusetts. Where we made the plans. The guys from the Toyota and the college car are sitting on them."

"Hard, I hope."

"Very."

"That's hours away," I said.

"By road," she said. "Not by telephone."

"You want Teresa back."

"Yes," she said. "But I'm in charge."

"You're a control freak," I said.

"I don't want anything bad to happen to you, is all."

"Nothing bad ever happens to me."

She leaned down and traced her fingertips over the scars on my body. Chest, stomach, arms, shoulders, forehead. "You've taken a lot of damage for a guy nothing bad ever happens to."

"I'm clumsy," I said. "I fall over a lot."

She stood up and walked to the bathroom, naked, graceful, completely unself-conscious.

"Hurry back," I called.

BUT SHE DIDN'T HURRY BACK. SHE WAS IN THE bathroom a long time and when she came out again she was wearing a robe. Her face had changed. She looked a little awkward. A little rueful.

"We shouldn't have done that," she said.

"Why not?"

"It was unprofessional."

She looked straight at me. I nodded. I guessed it was a little unprofessional.

"But it was fun," I said.

"We shouldn't have."

"We're grown-ups. We live in a free country."

"It was just taking comfort. Because we're both stressed and uptight."

"Nothing really wrong with that."

"It's going to complicate things," she said.

I shook my head.

"Not if we don't let it," I said. "Doesn't mean we have to get married or anything. We don't owe each other anything because of it."

"I wish we hadn't."

"I'm glad we did. I think if a thing feels right, you should do it."

"That's your philosophy?"

I looked away.

"It's the voice of experience," I said. "I once said no when I wanted to say yes and I lived to regret it."

She hugged the robe tight around her.

"It did feel good," she said.

"For me too," I said.

"But we should forget it now. It meant what it meant, nothing more, OK?"

"OK," I said.

"And you should think hard about going back."

"OK," I said again.

I lay on the bed and thought about how it felt to say no when you really wanted to say yes. On balance saying yes had been better, and I had no regrets. Duffy was quiet. It was like we were just waiting for something to happen. I took a long hot shower and dressed in the bathroom. We were done talking by then. There was nothing left to say. We both knew I was going back. I liked the fact that she didn't really try to stop me. I liked the fact that we were both focused, practical people. I was lacing my shoes when her laptop went *ping,* like a muffled high-pitched bell. Like a microwave when your food is ready. No artificial voice saying *You've got mail.* I came out of the bathroom and she sat down in front of the computer and clicked a button.

"Message from my office," she said. "Records show eleven dubious ex-cops called Duke. I put the request in yesterday. How old is he?"

"Forty, maybe," I said.

She scrolled through her list.

"Southern guy?" she asked. "Northern?"

"Not Southern," I said.

"Choice of three," she said.

"Mrs. Beck said he'd been a federal agent, too."

She scrolled some more.

"John Chapman Duke," she said. "He's the only one who went federal afterward. Started in Minneapolis as a patrolman and then a detective. Subject of three investigations by Internal Affairs. Inconclusive. Then he joined us."

"DEA?" I said. "Really?"

"No, I meant the federal government," she said. "He went to the Treasury Department."

"To do what?"

"Doesn't say. But he was indicted within three years. Some kind of corruption. Plus suspicion of multiple homicides, no real hard evidence. But he went to prison for four years anyway."

"Description?"

"White, about your size. The photo makes him look uglier, though."

"That's him," I said.

She scrolled some more. Read the rest of the report.

"Take care," she said. "He sounds like a piece of work."

"Don't worry," I said. I thought about kissing her good-bye at the door. But I didn't. I figured she wouldn't want me to. I just ran over to the Cadillac.

I WAS BACK IN THE COFFEE SHOP AND ALMOST
at the end of my second cup when Elizabeth Beck appeared. She had nothing to show for her shopping. No
purchases, no gaudy bags. I guessed she hadn't actually
been inside any stores. She had hung around for four long
hours to let the government guy do whatever he needed
to. I raised my hand. She ignored me and headed straight
for the counter. Bought herself a tall white coffee and carried it over to my table. I had decided what I was going to
tell her.

"I don't work for the government," I said.

"Then I'm disappointed," she said, for the third time.

"How could I?" I said. "I killed a cop, remember."

"Yes," she said.

"Government people don't do stuff like that."

"They might," she said. "By accident."

"But they wouldn't run away afterward," I said. "They
would stick around and face the music."

She went quiet and stayed quiet for a long time.
Sipped her coffee slowly.

"I've been there maybe eight or ten times," she said.
"Where the college is, I mean. They run events for the students' families, now and then. And I try to be there at the
start and finish of every semester. One summer I even
rented a little U-Haul and helped him move his stuff
home."

"So?"

"It's a small school," she said. "But even so, on the
first day of the semester it gets very busy. Lots of parents,
lots of students, SUVs, cars, vans, traffic everywhere. The
family days are even worse. And you know what?"

"What?"

"I've never seen a town policeman there. Not once. Certainly not a detective in plain clothes."

I looked out the window to the internal mall sidewalk.

"Just a coincidence, I suppose," she said. "A random Tuesday morning in April, early in the day, nothing much going on, and there's a detective waiting right by the gate, for no very obvious reason."

"What's your point?" I asked.

"That you were terribly unlucky," she said. "I mean, what were the odds?"

"I don't work for the government," I said.

"You took a shower," she said. "Washed your hair."

"Did I?"

"I can see it and smell it. Cheap soap, cheap shampoo."

"I went to a sauna."

"You didn't have any money. I gave you twenty dollars. You bought at least two cups of coffee. That would leave maybe fourteen dollars."

"It was a cheap sauna."

"It must have been," she said.

"I'm just a guy," I said.

"And I'm disappointed about it."

"You sound like you want your husband to get busted."

"I do."

"He'd go to prison."

"He already lives in a prison. And he deserves to. But he'd be freer in a real prison than where he is now. And he wouldn't be there forever."

"You could call somebody," I said. "You don't need to wait for them to come to you."

She shook her head. "That would be suicide. For me and Richard."

"Just like it would be if you talked about me like this

in front of anybody else. Remember, I wouldn't go quietly. People would get hurt. You and Richard, maybe."

She smiled. "Bargaining with me again?"

"Warning you again," I said. "Full disclosure."

She nodded.

"I know how to keep my mouth shut," she said, and then she proved it by not saying another word. We finished our coffee in silence and walked back to the car. We didn't talk. I drove her home, north and east, completely unsure whether I was carrying a ticking time bomb with me or turning my back on the only inside help I would ever get.

PAULIE WAS WAITING BEHIND THE GATE. HE MUST have been watching from his window and then taken up position as soon as he saw the car in the distance. I slowed and stopped and he stared out at me. Then he stared at Elizabeth Beck.

"Give me the pager," I said.

"I can't," she said.

"Just do it," I said.

Paulie unlatched the chain and pushed the gate. Elizabeth unzipped her bag and handed me the pager. I let the car roll forward and buzzed my window down. Stopped level with where Paulie was waiting to shut the gate again.

"Check this out," I called.

I tossed the pager overarm out in front of the car. It was a left-handed throw. It was weak and lacked finesse. But it got the job done. The little black plastic rectangle looped up in the air and landed dead-center on the driveway maybe twenty feet in front of the car. Paulie watched its trajectory and then froze when he realized what it was.

"Hey," he said.

He went after it. I went after him. I stamped on the

gas and the tires howled and the car jumped forward. I aimed the right-hand corner of the front bumper at the side of his left knee. I got very close. But he was incredibly quick. He scooped the pager off the blacktop and skipped back and I missed him by a foot. The car shot straight past him. I didn't slow down. Just accelerated away and watched him in the mirror, standing in my wake, staring after me, blue tire smoke drifting all around him. I was severely disappointed. If I had to fight a guy who outweighed me by two hundred pounds I'd have been much happier if he was crippled first. Or at least if he wasn't so damn *fast*.

I STOPPED ON THE CARRIAGE CIRCLE AND LET Elizabeth Beck out at the front door. Then I put the car away and was heading for the kitchen when Zachary Beck and John Chapman Duke came out looking for me. They were agitated and walking quickly. They were tense and upset. I thought they were going to give me a hard time about Paulie. But they weren't.

"Angel Doll is missing," Beck said.

I stood still. The wind was blowing in off the ocean. The lazy swell was gone and the waves were as big and noisy as they had been on the first evening. There was spray in the air.

"He spoke with you last thing," Beck said. "Then he locked up and left and he hasn't been seen since."

"What did he want with you?" Duke asked.

"I don't know," I said.

"You don't know? You were in there five minutes."

I nodded. "He took me back to the warehouse office."

"And?"

"And nothing. He was all set to say something but his cell phone rang."

"Who was it?"

I shrugged. "How would I know? Some kind of an urgent thing. He talked on the phone the whole five minutes. He was wasting my time and yours so I just gave it up and walked back out."

"What was he saying on the phone?"

"I didn't listen," I said. "Didn't seem polite."

"Hear any names?" Beck asked.

I turned to him. Shook my head.

"No names," I said. "But they knew each other. That was clear. Doll did a lot of listening, I guess. I think he was taking instructions about something."

"About what?"

"No idea," I said.

"Something urgent?"

"I guess so. He seemed to forget all about me. Certainly he didn't try to stop me when I walked away."

"That's all you know?"

"I assumed it was some kind of a plan," I said. "Instructions for the following day, maybe."

"Today?"

I shrugged again. "I'm just guessing. It was a very one-sided conversation."

"Terrific," Duke said. "You're a real big help, you know that?"

Beck looked out at the ocean. "So he took an urgent call on his cell and then he locked up and left. That's all you can tell us?"

"I didn't see him lock up," I said. "And I didn't see him leave. He was still on the phone when I came out."

"Obviously he locked up," Beck said. "And obviously he left. Everything was perfectly normal this morning."

I said nothing. Beck turned through ninety degrees and faced east. The wind came off the sea and flattened his clothes against him. His trouser legs flapped like flags.

He moved his feet, scuffing the soles of his shoes against the grit, like he was trying to get warm.

"We don't need this now," he said. "We really don't *need* this. We've got a big weekend coming up."

I said nothing. They turned around together and headed back to the house and left me there, alone.

I WAS TIRED, BUT I WASN'T GOING TO GET ANY rest. That was clear. There was bustle in the air and the routine I had seen on the previous two nights was all shot to hell. There was no food in the kitchen. No dinner. The cook wasn't there. I heard people moving in the hallway. Duke came into the kitchen and walked straight past me and went out the back door. He was carrying a blue Nike sports bag. I followed him out and stood and watched from the corner of the house and saw him go into the second garage. Five minutes later he backed the black Lincoln out and drove off in it. He had changed the plates. When I had seen it in the middle of the night it had six-digit Maine plates on it. Now it was showing a seven-digit New York number. I went back inside and looked for coffee. I found the machine, but I couldn't find any filter papers. I settled for a glass of water instead. I was halfway through drinking it when Beck came in. He was carrying a sports bag, too. The way it hung from its handles and the noise it made when it bumped against his leg told me it was full of heavy metal. Guns, probably, maybe two of them.

"Get the Cadillac," he said. "Right now. Pick me up at the front."

He took the keys out of his pocket and dropped them on the table in front of me. Then he crouched down and unzipped his bag and came out with two New York license plates and a screwdriver. Handed them to me.

"Put these on it first," he said.

I saw guns in the bag. Two Heckler & Koch MP5Ks, short and fat and black with big bulbous molded handles. Futuristic, like movie props.

"Where are we going?" I said.

"We're following Duke down to Hartford, Connecticut," he said. "We've got some business there, remember?"

He zipped the bag and stood up and carried it back out into the hallway. I sat still for a second. Then I raised my glass of water and toasted the blank wall in front of me.

"Here's to bloody wars and dread diseases," I said to myself.

CHAPTER 7

I LEFT THE REST OF THE WATER IN THE KITCHEN and headed out toward the garage block. Dusk was gathering on the ocean horizon, a hundred miles away in the east. The wind was blowing hard and the waves were pounding. I stopped walking and turned a casual circle. Saw nobody else out and about. So I ducked out of sight down the side of the courtyard wall. Found my hidden bundle and laid the phony plates and the screwdriver on the rocks and unwrapped both guns. Duffy's Glock went into my right-hand coat pocket. Doll's PSM went into my left. I put the spare Glock mags in my socks. Stowed the rag and picked up the plates and the screwdriver and backtracked to the courtyard entrance.

The mechanic was busy in the third garage. The empty one. He had the doors wide open and was oiling the hinges. The space behind him was even cleaner than when I had seen it in the night. It was immaculate. The floor had been hosed. I could see it drying in patches. I nodded to the guy and he nodded back. I opened up the left-hand garage. Squatted down and unscrewed the Maine plate off the Cadillac's trunk lid and replaced it with the New York number. Did the same at the front. Left the old plates and the screwdriver on the floor and got in and fired it up. Backed it out and headed around to the carriage circle. The mechanic watched me go.

Beck was waiting there for me. He opened the rear door himself and dropped his sports bag on the back seat. I heard the guns shifting inside. Then he closed the rear door again and slid in the front beside me.

"Go," he said. "Use I-95 south as far as Boston."

"We need gas," I said.

"OK, first place you see," he said.

Paulie was waiting at the gate. His face was all twisted up with anger. He was a problem that wouldn't keep much longer. He glared in at me. Turned his head left and right and kept his eyes on me the whole time he was opening the gate. I ignored him and drove on through. I didn't look back at him. *Out of sight, out of mind* was the way I wanted to play it, as far as he was concerned.

The coast road west was empty. We were on the highway twelve minutes after we left the house. I was getting used to the way the Cadillac drove. It was a nice car. Smooth, and quiet. But it was heavy on gas. That was for sure. The needle was getting seriously low. I could almost see it moving. The way I recalled it the first gas stop was the one south of Kennebunk. The place where I had met with Duffy and Eliot on the way down to New London. We reached it within fifteen minutes. It felt very familiar to me. I drove past the parking lot where we had broken into the van and headed down to the pumps. Beck said nothing. I got out and filled the tank. It took a long time. Eighteen gallons. I screwed the cap back on and Beck buzzed his window down and gave me a wad of cash.

"Always buy gas with cash," he said. "Safer that way."

I kept the change, which was a little over fifteen bucks. I figured I was entitled. I hadn't been paid yet. I got back on the road and settled in for the trip. I was tired.

Nothing worse than mile after mile of lonely highway when you're tired. Beck was quiet beside me. At first I thought he was just morose. Or shy, or inhibited. Then I realized he was nervous. I guessed he wasn't entirely comfortable heading into battle. I was. Especially because I knew for sure we weren't going to find anybody to fight.

"How's Richard?" I asked him.

"He's fine," he said. "He's got inner strength. He's a good son."

"Is he?" I said, because I needed to say something. I needed him to talk to keep me awake.

"He's very loyal. A father can't ask for more."

Then he went quiet again, and I fought to stay awake. Five miles, ten.

"Have you ever dealt with small-time dope dealers?" he asked me.

"No," I said.

"There's something unique about them," he said.

He didn't say anything more for twenty miles. Then he picked it up again like he had spent the entire time chasing an elusive thought.

"They're completely dominated by fashion," he said.

"Are they?" I said, like I was interested. I wasn't, but I still needed him to talk.

"Of course lab drugs are fashion items anyway," he said. "Really their customers are just as bad as they are. I can't even keep track of the stuff they sell. Some different weird name every week."

"What's a lab drug?" I asked.

"A drug made in a lab," he said. "You know, something manufactured, something chemical. Not the same as something that grows naturally in the ground."

"Like marijuana."

"Or heroin. Or cocaine. Those are natural products.

Organic. They're refined, obviously, but they aren't created in a beaker."

I said nothing. Just fought to keep my eyes open. The car was way too warm. You need cold air when you're tired. I bit my bottom lip to stay awake.

"The fashion thing infects everything they do," he said. "Every single thing. Shoes, for instance. These guys we're looking for tonight, every time I've seen them they've had different shoes."

"What, like sneakers?"

"Sure, like they play basketball for a living. One time they've got two-hundred-dollar Reeboks, brand new out of the box. Next time I see them, Reeboks are completely unacceptable and it's got to be Nikes or something. Air-this, air-that. Or it's suddenly Caterpillar boots, or Timberlands. Leather, then Gore-Tex, then leather again. Black, then that yellow color like a work boot. Always with the laces undone. Then it's back to the running shoes again, only this time it's Adidas, with the little stripes. Two, three hundred dollars a pop. For no reason. It's insane."

I said nothing. Just drove, with my eyelids locked open and my eyeballs stinging.

"You know why it is?" he said. "Because of the money. They've got so much money they don't know what to do with it. Like jackets. Have you seen the jackets they wear? One week it's got to be North Face, all shiny and puffy, full of goose feathers, doesn't matter whether it's winter or summer because these guys are only out at night. The next week, shiny is yesterday's news. Maybe North Face is still OK, but now it's got to be microfiber. Then it's letter jackets, wool with leather sleeves. Two, three hundred dollars a pop. Each style lasts about a week."

"Crazy," I said, because I had to say something.

"It's the money," he said again. "They don't know

what to do with it, so they get into change for change's sake. It infects everything. Guns, too, of course. Like these particular guys, they liked Heckler and Koch MP5Ks. Now they have Uzis, according to you. You see what I mean? With these guys, even their weapons are fashion items, the same as their sneakers, or their jackets. Or their actual product, which brings everything full circle. Their demands change all the time, in every arena. Cars, even. They like Japanese mostly, which is about fashions coming in from the West Coast, I guess. But one week it's Toyotas, next week it's Hondas. Then it's Nissans. The Nissan Maxima was a big favorite, two, three years ago. Like the one you stole. Then it's Lexuses. It's a mania. Watches, too. They're wearing Swatches, then they're wearing Rolexes. They don't see a difference. Complete madness. Of course, being in the market, speaking as a supplier, I'm not complaining. Market obsolescence is what we aim for, but it gets a little rapid at times. Gets hard to keep up."

"So you're in the market?"

"What's your guess?" he said. "You thought I was an accountant?"

"I thought you were a rug importer."

"I am," he said. "I import a lot of rugs."

"OK."

"But that's fundamentally a cover," he said. Then he laughed. "You think you don't have to take precautions these days, selling athletic shoes to people like that?"

He kept on laughing. There was a lot of nervous tension in there. I drove on. He calmed down. Looked through the side window, looked through the windshield. Started talking again, like it served his own purpose as much as it served mine.

"Do you ever wear sneakers?" he asked.

"No," I said.

"Because I'm looking for somebody to explain it to me. There's no rational difference between a Reebok and a Nike, is there?"

"I wouldn't know."

"I mean, they're probably made in the same factory. Out in Vietnam somewhere. They're probably the same shoe until they put the logo on."

"Maybe," I said. "I really wouldn't know. I was never an athlete. Never wore that type of footwear."

"Is there a difference between a Toyota and a Honda?"

"I wouldn't know."

"Why not?"

"Because I never had a POV."

"What's a POV?"

"A privately owned vehicle," I said. "What the army would call a Toyota or a Honda. Or a Nissan or a Lexus."

"So what *do* you know?"

"I know the difference between a Swatch and a Rolex."

"OK, what's the difference?"

"There isn't one," I said. "They both tell the time."

"That's no answer."

"I know the difference between an Uzi and a Heckler and Koch."

He turned on his seat. "Good. Great. Explain it to me. Why would these guys junk their Heckler and Kochs in favor of Uzis?"

The Cadillac hummed onward. I shrugged at the wheel. Fought a yawn. It was a nonsense question, of course. The Hartford guys hadn't junked their MP5Ks in favor of Uzis. Not in reality. Eliot and Duffy hadn't been aware of Hartford's weapon *du jour* and they hadn't been aware that Beck knew anything about Hartford, that's all, so they had given their guys Uzis, probably because they were lying around closest to hand.

But theoretically it was a very good question. An Uzi is a fine, fine weapon. A little heavy, maybe. Not the world's fastest cyclic rate, which might matter to some people. Not much rifling inside the barrel, which compromises accuracy a little bit. On the other hand, it's very reliable, very simple, totally proven, and you can get a forty-round magazine for it. A fine weapon. But any Heckler & Koch MP5 derivative is a better weapon. They fire the same ammunition faster and harder. They're very, very accurate. As accurate as a good rifle, in some hands. Very reliable. Flat-out better. A great 1970s design up against a great 1950s design. Doesn't hold true in all fields, but with military ordnance, modern is better, every time.

"There's no reason," I said. "Makes no sense to me."

"Exactly," Beck said. "It's about fashion. It's an arbitrary whim. It's a compulsion. Keeps everybody in business, but drives everybody nuts, too."

His cell phone rang. He juggled it up out of his pocket and answered it by saying his name, short and sharp. And a little nervously. *Beck.* It sounded like a cough. He listened for a long time. Made his caller repeat an address and directions and then clicked off and put the phone back in his pocket.

"That was Duke," he said. "He made some calls. Our boys aren't anywhere in Hartford. But they're supposed to have some country place a little ways south and east. Duke figures that's where they're holed up. So that's where we're going."

"What are we going to do when we get there?"

"Nothing spectacular," Beck said. "We don't need to make a big deal out of it. Nothing neat, nothing fancy. Situation like this, I favor just mowing them down. An impression of inevitability, you know? But casual. Like you mess with me, then punishment is definitely swift and certain, but not like I'm in a sweat about it."

"You lose customers that way."

"I can replace them. I've got people lining up around the block. That's the truly great thing about this business. Supply and demand is tilted way in favor of demand."

"You going to do this yourself?"

He shook his head. "That's what you and Duke are for."

"Me? I thought I was just driving."

"You already wasted two of them. Couple more shouldn't bother you."

I turned the heater down a click and worked on keeping my eyes open. *Bloody wars,* I said to myself.

WE LOOPED HALFWAY AROUND BOSTON AND then he told me to strike out south and west on the Mass Pike and then I-84. We did sixty more miles, which took about an hour. He didn't want me to drive too fast. He didn't want to be conspicuous. Phony plates, a bag full of automatic weapons on the back seat, he didn't want the Highway Patrol to get involved. I could see the sense in that. I drove like an automaton. I hadn't slept in forty hours. But I wasn't regretting passing up the chance of a nap in Duffy's motel. I was very happy with the way I had spent my time there, even if she wasn't.

"Next exit," he said.

Right then I-84 was spearing straight through the city of Hartford. There was low cloud and the city lights made it orange. The exit led to a wide road that narrowed after a mile and headed south and east into open country. There was blackness ahead. There were a few closed country stores, bait and tackle, beer on ice, motorcycle parts, and then nothing at all except the dark shape of trees.

"Make the next right," he said, eight minutes later.

I turned onto a smaller road. The surface was bad and there were random curves. Darkness everywhere. I had to concentrate. I wasn't looking forward to driving back.

"Keep going," he said.

We did eight or nine more miles. I had no idea where we were.

"OK," he said. "Pretty soon we should see Duke waiting up ahead."

A mile and a half later my headlight beams picked out Duke's rear plate. He was parked on the shoulder. His car was canted over where the grade fell away into a ditch.

"Stop behind him."

I pulled up nose-to-tail with the Lincoln and jammed the selector into Park. I wanted to go to sleep. Five minutes would have made a lot of difference to me. But Duke swung out of his seat as soon as he identified us and hurried around to Beck's window. Beck buzzed the glass down and Duke squatted and leaned his face inside.

"Their place is about two miles ahead," he said. "Long curved driveway on the left. Not much more than a dirt path. We can make it about halfway up in the cars, if we do it quiet and slow, no lights. We'll have to walk the rest of the way."

Beck said nothing. Just buzzed his window up again. Duke went back to his car. It bounced off the shoulder and straightened up. I followed him through the two miles. We killed our lights a hundred yards short of the driveway and made the turn. Took it slow. There was some moonlight. The Lincoln ahead of me lurched and rolled as it crawled over ruts. The Cadillac did the same thing, out of phase, up where the Lincoln was down, corkscrewing right where the Lincoln was twisting left. We slowed to a crawl. Used idle speed to inch us closer. Then Duke's brake lights flared bright and he stopped dead. I stopped behind him. Beck twisted around in his seat and hauled the sports bag through the gap between us and unzipped it on his knee. Handed me one of the MP5Ks from it, with two spare thirty-round magazines.

"Get the job done," he said.

"You waiting here?"

He nodded. I broke the gun down and checked it. Put it back together and jacked a round into the chamber and clicked the safety on. Then I put the spare mags in my pockets very carefully so they wouldn't rattle against the Glock and the PSM. Eased myself out of the car. Stood and breathed the cold night air. It was a relief. It woke me up. I could smell a lake nearby, and trees, and leaf mold on the ground. I could hear a small waterfall in the distance, and the mufflers on the cars ticking gently as they cooled. There was a gentle breeze in the trees. Other than that there was nothing to hear. Just absolute silence.

Duke was waiting for me. I could see tension and impatience in the way he was holding himself. He had done this stuff before. That was clear. He looked exactly like a veteran cop before a major bust. Some degree of routine familiarity, mixed in with an acute awareness that no two situations are ever quite alike. He had his Steyr in his hand, with the long thirty-round magazine in it. It protruded way down out of the grip. Made the gun look bigger and uglier than ever.

"Let's go, asshole," he whispered.

I stayed five feet behind him and walked on the opposite side of the driveway, like an infantryman would. I had to be convincing, like I was worried about presenting a grouped target. I knew the place was going to be empty, but he didn't.

We walked on around a bend and saw the house in front of us. There was a light burning in a window. On a security timer, probably. Duke slowed and stopped.

"See a door?" he whispered.

I peered into the gloom. Saw a small porch. Pointed at it.

"You wait at the entrance," I whispered back. "I'll check the lighted window."

He was happy enough to agree to that. We made it to the porch. He stopped there and waited and I peeled off and looped around toward the window. Dropped to the ground and crawled the last ten feet in the dirt. Raised my head at the sill and peered inside. There was a low-wattage bulb burning in a table lamp with a yellow plastic shade. There were battered sofas and armchairs. Cold ash from an old fire in the hearth. Pine paneling on the walls. No people.

I crawled backward until the light spill let Duke see me and held two forked fingers below my eyes. Standard sniper-spotter visual code for *I see.* Then I held my hand palm out, all my fingers extended. *I see five people.* Then I went into a complicated series of gestures that might have indicated their disposition and their weaponry. I knew Duke wouldn't understand them. I didn't understand them either. As far as I knew they were entirely meaningless. I had never been a sniper-spotter. But the whole thing looked real good. It looked professional and clandestine and urgent.

I crawled back ten more feet and then stood up and walked quietly back to join him at the door.

"They're out of it," I whispered. "Drunk or stoned. We get a good jump, we'll be home and dry."

"Weapons?"

"Plenty, but nothing within reach." I pointed at the porch. "Looks like there's going to be a short hallway on the other side. Outer door, inner door, then the hallway. You take left, I'll take right. We'll wait there in the hallway. Take them down when they come out of the room to see what the noise is all about."

"You giving the orders now?"

"I did the recon."

"Just don't screw up, asshole."

"You either."

"I never do," he said.

"OK," I said.

"I mean it," he said. "You get in my way, I'll be more than happy to put you down with the rest of them, no hesitation."

"We're on the same side here."

"Are we?" he said. "I think we're about to find out."

"Relax," I said.

He paused. Tensed. Nodded in the dark. "I'll hit the outer door, you hit the inner. Like leapfrog."

"OK," I said again. I turned away and smiled. Just like a veteran cop. If I hit the inner door, he would leapfrog through it first and I would go second, and the second guy is the guy who usually gets shot, given normal reaction times from the enemy.

"Safeties off," I whispered.

I clicked the H&K to single-round fire and he clicked the catch on his Steyr to the right. I nodded and he nodded and kicked in the outer door. I was right there on his shoulder and slid past him and kicked in the inner door without breaking stride. He slid past me and jumped left and I followed him and went right. He was good enough. We made a pretty good team. We were crouched in perfect position even before the shattered doors had stopped swinging on their hinges. He was staring ahead at the entry to the room in front of us. He had the Steyr in a fixed two-handed grip, arms straight out, eyes wide open. He was breathing hard. Almost panting. Getting himself through a long moment of danger, the best way he could. I pulled Angel Doll's PSM out of my pocket. Held it left-handed and snicked the safety off and scrambled across the floor and jammed it in his ear.

"Keep very quiet," I said to him. "And make a choice. I'm going to ask you one question. Just one. If you lie, or if you refuse to answer, I'm going to shoot you in the head. You understand?"

He held perfectly still, five seconds, six, eight, ten. Stared desperately at the door in front of him.

"Don't worry, *asshole*," I said. "There's nobody here. They were all arrested last week. By the government."

He was motionless.

"You understand what I said before? About the question?"

He nodded, hesitantly, awkwardly, with the gun still jammed hard in his ear.

"You answer it, or I shoot you in the head. Got it?"

He nodded again.

"OK, here it comes," I said. "You ready?"

He nodded, just once.

"Where is Teresa Daniel?" I asked.

There was a long pause. He turned half toward me. I tracked my hand around to keep the PSM's muzzle in place. Realization dawned slowly in his eyes.

"In your dreams," he said.

I shot him in the head. Just jerked the muzzle out of his ear and fired once left-handed into his right temple. The sound was shattering in the dark. Blood and brain and bone chips hit the far wall. The muzzle flash burned his hair. Then I fired a double-tap from the H&K right-handed into the ceiling and fired another from the PSM left-handed into the floor. Switched the H&K to automatic fire and stood up and emptied it point-blank into his body. Picked up his Steyr from where it had fallen and blasted the ceiling with it, again and again, fifteen fast shots, *bam bam bam bam,* half the magazine. The hallway was instantly full of bitter smoke and chips of wood and plaster were flying everywhere. I switched magazines on the H&K and sprayed the walls, all around. The noise was deafening. Spent shell cases were spitting out and bouncing around and raining down everywhere. The H&K clicked empty and I fired the rest of the PSM's ammo into the hallway wall and kicked open the door to the lighted room and blew up the table lamp with the Steyr. I found a side table and tossed it through the window and used up the second spare magazine for the H&K by spraying the trees in the distance while I fired the Steyr left-handed into the floor until it clicked empty. Then I piled the Steyr and the H&K and the PSM together in my arms and ran for it with my head ringing like a bell. I had fired a hundred and twenty-eight rounds in about fifteen seconds. They had deafened me. They must have sounded like World War Three to Beck.

I ran straight down the driveway. I was coughing and trailing gunsmoke like a cloud. I headed for the cars. Beck had already scrambled across into the Cadillac's driver's seat. He saw me coming and opened his door an inch. Faster than using the window.

"Ambush," I said. I was out of breath and I could hear my own voice loud inside my head. "There were at least eight of them."

"Where's Duke?"

"Dead. We got to go. *Right now,* Beck."

He froze for a second. Then he moved.

"Take his car," he said.

He already had the Cadillac rolling. He jammed his foot down and slammed his door and reversed down the driveway and out of sight. I jumped into the Lincoln. Fired it up. Stuck the selector in Reverse and got one elbow up on the back of the seat and stared through the rear window and hit the gas. We shot out backward onto the road one after the other and slewed around and took off again north, side by side like a stoplight drag race. We howled around the curves and fought the camber and stayed up around seventy miles an hour. Didn't slow until we reached the turn that would take us back toward Hartford. Beck edged ahead of me and I fell in behind him and followed. He drove five fast miles and turned in at a closed package store and parked at the back of the lot. I parked ten feet from him and just lay back in the seat and let him come to me. I was too tired to get out. He ran around the Cadillac's hood and pulled my door open.

"It was an ambush?" he said.

I nodded. "They were waiting for us. Eight of them. Maybe more. It was a massacre."

He said nothing. There was nothing for him to say. I picked up Duke's Steyr from the seat beside me and handed it over.

"I recovered it," I said.

"Why?"

"I thought you might want me to. I thought it might be traceable."

He nodded. "It isn't. But that was good thinking."

I gave him the H&K, too. He stepped back to the Cadillac and I watched him zip both pieces into his bag. Then he turned around. Clenched both hands and looked up at the black sky. Then at me.

"See any faces?" he asked.

I shook my head. "Too dark. But we hit one of them. He dropped this."

I handed him the PSM. It was like punching him in the gut. He turned pale and put out a hand and steadied himself against the Lincoln's roof.

"What?" I said.

He looked away. "I don't believe it."

"What?"

"You hit somebody and he dropped this?"

"I think Duke hit him."

"You saw it happen?"

"Just shapes," I said. "It was dark. Lots of muzzle flashes. Duke was firing and he hit a shape and this was on the floor when I came out."

"This is Angel Doll's gun."

"Are you sure?"

"Million to one it isn't. You know what it is?"

"Never saw one like it."

"It's a special KGB pistol," he said. "From the old Soviet Union. Very rare in this country."

Then he stepped away into the darkness of the lot. I closed my eyes. I wanted to sleep. Even five seconds would have made a difference.

"Reacher," he called. "What evidence did you leave?"

I opened my eyes.

"Duke's body," I said.

"That won't lead anybody anywhere. Ballistics?"

I smiled in the dark. Imagined Hartford PD forensic scientists trying to make sense of the trajectories. Walls, floors, ceilings. They would conclude the hallway had been full of heavily-armed disco dancers.

"A lot of bullets and shell cases," I said.

"Untraceable," he said.

He moved deeper into the dark. I closed my eyes again. I had left no fingerprints. No part of me had touched any part of the house except for the soles of my shoes. And I hadn't fired Duffy's Glock. I had heard something about a central registry somewhere that stored data on rifling marks. Maybe her Glock was a part of it. But I hadn't used it.

"Reacher," Beck called. "Drive me home."

I opened my eyes.

"What about this car?" I called back.

"Abandon it here."

I yawned and forced myself to move and used the tail of my coat to wipe the wheel and all the controls I had touched. The unused Glock nearly fell out of my pocket. Beck didn't notice. He was so preoccupied I could have taken it out and twirled it around my finger like the Sundance Kid and he wouldn't have noticed. I wiped the door handle and then leaned in and pulled the keys and wiped them and tossed them into the scrub at the edge of the lot.

"Let's go," Beck said.

HE WAS SILENT UNTIL WE WERE THIRTY MILES NORTH and east of Hartford. Then he started talking. He had spent the time getting it all worked out in his mind.

"The phone call yesterday," he said. "They were laying their plans. Doll was working with them all along."

"From when?"

"From the start."

"Doesn't make sense," I said. "Duke went south and got the Toyota's plate number for you. Then you gave it to Doll and told him to trace it. But why would Doll tell you the truth about the trace? If they were his buddies, he'd have dead-ended it, surely. Led you away from them. Left you in the dark."

Beck smiled a superior smile.

"No," he said. "They were setting up the ambush. That was the point of the phone call. It was good improvisation on their part. The kidnap gambit failed, so they switched tactics. They let Doll point us in the right direction. So that what happened tonight could happen."

I nodded slowly, like I was deferring to his point of view. The best way to clinch a pending promotion is to let them think you're just a little dumber than they are. It had worked for me before, three straight times, in the military.

"Did Doll actually know what you were planning for tonight?" I asked.

"Yes," he said. "We were all discussing it, yesterday. In detail. When you saw us talking, in the office."

"So he set you up."

"Yes," he said again. "He locked up last night and then left Portland and drove all the way down to wait with them. Told them all who was coming, and when, and why."

I said nothing. Just thought about Doll's car. It was about a mile away from Beck's office. I began to wish I had hidden it better.

"But there's one big question," Beck said. "Was it *just* Doll?"

"Or?"

He went quiet. Then he shrugged.

"Or any of the others that work with him," he said.

The ones you don't control, I thought. *Quinn's people.*

"Or all of them together," he said.

He started thinking again, another thirty, forty miles. He didn't speak another word until we were back on I-95, heading north around Boston.

"Duke is dead," he said.

"I'm sorry," I said.

Here it comes, I thought.

"I knew him a long time," he said.

I said nothing.

"You're going to have to take over," he said. "I need somebody right now. Somebody I can trust. And you've done well for me so far."

"Promotion?" I said.

"You're qualified."

"Head of security?"

"At least temporarily," he said. "Permanently, if you'd like."

"I don't know," I said.

"Just remember what *I* know," he said. "I own you."

I was quiet for a mile. "You going to pay me anytime soon?"

"You'll get your five grand plus what Duke got on top."

"I'll need some background," I said. "I can't help you without it."

He nodded.

"Tomorrow," he said. "We'll talk tomorrow."

Then he went quiet again. Next time I looked, he was fast asleep beside me. Some kind of a shock reaction. He thought his world was falling apart. I fought to stay awake and keep the car on the road. And I thought back to texts I had read from the British Army in India, during the Raj, at the height of their empire. Young subalterns trapped in junior ranks had their own mess. They would dine together in splendid dress uniforms and talk about their chances of promotion. But they had none, unless a superior officer died. Dead men's shoes was the rule. So they would raise their crystal glasses of fine French wine and toast *bloody wars and dread diseases,* because a casualty further up the chain of command was their only way to get ahead. Brutal, but that's how it's always been, in the military.

I MADE IT BACK TO THE MAINE COAST PURELY on autopilot. I couldn't recall a single mile of the drive. I was numb with exhaustion. Every part of me ached. Paulie was slow about opening the gate. I guess we got him out of bed. He made a big point about staring in at me. I dropped Beck at the front door and put the car in the garage. Stashed the Glock and the spare magazines just for safety's sake and went in through the back door. The metal detector beeped at the car keys. I dropped them on the kitchen table. I was hungry, but I was too tired to eat. I climbed all the stairs and fell down on my bed and went to sleep, fully dressed, overcoat and shoes and all.

THE WEATHER WOKE ME SIX HOURS LATER. HORI-zontal rain was battering my window. It sounded like gravel on the glass. I rolled off the bed and checked the view. The sky was iron gray and thick with cloud and the sea was raging. It was laced with angry foam a half-mile out. The waves were swamping the rocks. No birds. It was nine in the morning. Day fourteen, a Friday. I lay down on the bed again and stared at the ceiling and tracked back seventy-two hours to the morning of day eleven, when Duffy gave me her seven-point plan. One, two, and three, take a lot of care. I was doing OK under that heading. I was still alive, anyway. Four, find Teresa Daniel. No real progress there. Five, nail down some evidence against Beck. I didn't have any. Not a thing. I hadn't even seen him do anything wrong, except maybe operate a vehicle with phony license plates and carry a bag full of subma-chine guns that were probably illegal in all four states he'd been in. Six, find Quinn. No progress there, either. Seven, get the hell out. That item was going to have to wait. Then Duffy had kissed me on the cheek. Left doughnut sugar on my face.

I got up again and locked myself in my bathroom to check for e-mail. My bedroom door wasn't locked any-more. I guessed Richard Beck wouldn't presume to walk in on me. Or his mother. But his father might. He owned me. I was promoted, but I was still walking a tightrope. I sat on the floor and took my shoe off. Opened the heel and switched the machine on. *You've Got Mail!* It was a message from Duffy: *Beck's containers unloaded and trucked to warehouse. Not inspected by Customs. Total of five. Largest shipment for some time.*

I hit *reply* and typed: *Are you maintaining surveillance?*

Ninety seconds later she answered: *Yes.*

I sent: *I got promoted.*

She sent: *Exploit it.*

I sent: *I enjoyed yesterday.*

She sent: *Save your battery.*

I smiled and switched the unit off and put it back in my heel. I needed a shower, but first I needed breakfast, and then I needed to find clean clothes. I unlocked the bathroom and walked through my room and downstairs to the kitchen. The cook was back in business. She was serving toast and tea to the Irish girl and dictating a long shopping list. The Saab keys were on the table. The Cadillac keys weren't. I scratched around and ate everything I could find and then went looking for Beck. He wasn't around. Neither was Elizabeth or Richard. I went back to the kitchen.

"Where's the family?" I asked.

The maid looked up and said nothing. She had put a raincoat on, ready to go out shopping.

"Where's Mr. Duke?" the cook asked.

"Indisposed," I said. "I'm replacing him. Where are the Becks?"

"They went out."

"Where to?"

"I don't know."

I looked out at the weather. "Who drove?"

The cook looked down at the floor.

"Paulie," she said.

"When?"

"An hour ago."

"OK," I said. I was still wearing my coat. I had put it on when I left Duffy's motel and I hadn't taken it off since. I went straight out the back door and into the gale. The rain was lashing and it tasted of salt. It was mixed with sea spray. The waves were hitting the rocks like bombs. White foam was bursting thirty feet in the air. I ducked my face into my collar and ran around to the garage block. Into the walled courtyard. It was sheltered in there. The first garage was empty. The doors were standing open. The Cadillac was gone. The mechanic was inside the third garage, doing something by himself. The maid ran into the courtyard. I watched her haul open the fourth garage's doors. She was getting soaked. She went in and a moment later backed the old Saab out. It rocked in the wind. The rain turned the dust on it to a thin film of gray mud that ran down the sides like rivers. She drove away, off to market. I listened to the waves. Started worrying about how high they might be getting. So I hugged the courtyard wall and looped all the way around it to the seaward side. Found my little dip in the rocks. The weed stalks around it were wet and bedraggled. The dip was full of water. It was rainwater. Not seawater. It was safely above the tide. The waves hadn't reached it. But rainwater was all it was full of. Apart from the water, it was completely empty. No bundle. No rag, no Glock. The spare magazines were gone, Doll's keys were gone, the bradawl was gone, and the chisel was gone.

CHAPTER 8

I CAME AROUND TO THE FRONT OF THE HOUSE and faced west and stood in the lashing rain and stared at the high stone wall. Right at that moment I came as close as I ever got to bailing out. It would have been easy. The gate was wide open. I guessed the maid had left it that way. She had gotten out in the rain to open it and she hadn't wanted to get out again to close it. Paulie wasn't there to do it for her. He was out, driving the Cadillac. So the gate was open. And unguarded. The first time I had ever seen it that way. I could have slipped straight through it. But I didn't. I stayed.

Time was part of the reason. Beyond the gate was at least twelve miles of empty road before the first significant turning. Twelve miles. And there were no cars to use. The Becks were out in the Cadillac and the maid was out in the Saab. We had abandoned the Lincoln in Connecticut. So I would be on foot. Three hours' fast walk. I didn't have three hours. Almost certainly the Cadillac would return within three hours. And there was nowhere to hide on the road. The shoulders were bare and rocky. It was an exposed situation. Beck would pass me head-on. I would be walking. He would be in a car. And he had a gun. And Paulie. I had nothing.

Therefore strategy was part of the reason, too. To be caught in the act of walking away would confirm whatever Beck might think he knew, assuming it was Beck who had discovered the stash. But if I stayed I had some kind of a chance. Staying would imply innocence. I could deflect suspicion onto Duke. I could say it must have been Duke's stash. Beck might find that plausible. Maybe. Duke had enjoyed the freedom to go wherever he wanted, any time of night or day. I had been locked up and supervised the whole time. And Duke wasn't around anymore to deny anything. But I would be right there in Beck's face, talking loud and fast and persuasive. He might buy it.

Hope was part of the reason, too. Maybe it wasn't Beck who had found the stash. Maybe it was Richard, walking the shoreline. His reaction would be unpredictable. I figured it at fifty-fifty whether he would approach me or his father first. Or maybe it was Elizabeth who had found it. She was familiar with the rocks out there. She knew them well. Knew their secrets. I guessed she had spent plenty of time on them, for one reason or another. And her reaction would favor me. Probably.

The rain was part of the reason for staying, too. It was cold and hard and relentless. I was too tired to road march three hours in the rain. I knew it was just weakness. But I couldn't move my feet. I wanted to go back inside the house. I wanted to get warm and eat again and rest.

Fear of failure was part of the reason, too. If I walked away now I would never come back. I knew that. And I had invested two weeks. I had made good progress. People were depending on me. I had been beaten many times. But I had never just quit. Not once. Not ever. If I quit now, it would eat me up the rest of my days. *Jack Reacher, quitter. Walked away when the going got tough.*

I stood there with the rain driving against my back. Time, strategy, hope, the weather, fear of failure. All parts of the reason for staying. All right there on the list.

But top of the list was a woman.

Not Susan Duffy, not Teresa Daniel. A woman from long ago, from another life. She was called Dominique Kohl. I was a captain in the army when I met her. I was one year away from my final promotion to major. I got to my office early one morning and found the usual stack of paperwork on my desk. Most of it was junk. But among it was a copy of an order assigning an E-7 Sergeant First Class Kohl, D.E. to my unit. Back then we were in a phase where all written references to personnel had to be gender-neutral. The name *Kohl* sounded German to me and I pictured some big ugly guy from Texas or Minnesota. Big red hands, big red face, older than me, maybe thirty-five, with a whitewall haircut. Later in the morning the clerk buzzed through to say the guy was reporting for duty. I made him wait ten minutes just for the fun of it and then called him in. But the him was a her and she wasn't big and ugly. She was wearing a skirt. She was about twenty-nine years old. She wasn't tall, but she was too athletic to be called petite. And she was too pretty to be called athletic. It was like she had been exquisitely molded from the stuff they make the inside of tennis balls out of. There was an elasticity about her. A firmness and a softness, all at the same time. She looked sculpted, but she had no hard edges. She stood rigidly at attention in front of my desk and snapped a smart salute. I didn't return it, which was rude of me. I just stared at her for five whole seconds.

"At ease, Sergeant," I said.

She handed me her copy of her orders and her personnel file. We called them *service jackets*. They contained everything anybody needed to know. I left her standing easy in front of me while I read hers through, which was rude of me too, but there was no other option. I didn't have a visitor's chair. Back then the army didn't provide them below the rank of full colonel. She stood completely still, hands clasped behind her back, staring at a point in the air exactly a foot above my head.

Her jacket was impressive. She had done a little of everything and succeeded at it all in spectacular fashion. Expert marksman, specialist in a number of skills, tremendous arrest record, excellent clear-up percentage. She was a good leader and had been promoted fast. She had killed two people, one with a firearm, one unarmed, both incidents rated righteous by the subsequent investigating panels. She was a rising star. That was clear. I realized that her transfer represented a substantial compliment to me, in some superior's mind.

"Glad to have you aboard," I said.

"Sir, thank you, sir," she said, with her eyes fixed in space.

"I don't do all that shit," I said. "I'm not afraid I'm going to vaporize if you look at me and I don't really like one *sir* in a sentence, let alone two, OK?"

"OK," she said. She caught on fast. She never called me *sir* again, the whole rest of her life.

"Want to jump right in at the deep end?" I said.

She nodded. "Sure."

I rattled open a drawer and slid a slim file out and passed it across to her. She didn't look at it. Just held it one-handed down by her side and looked at me.

"Aberdeen, Maryland," I said. "At the proving grounds. There's a weapons designer acting weird. Confidential tip from a buddy who's worried about espionage. But I think it's more likely blackmail. Could be a long and sensitive investigation."

"No problem," she said.

She was the reason I didn't walk out through the open and unguarded gate.

I WENT INSIDE INSTEAD AND TOOK A LONG HOT shower. Nobody likes to risk confrontation when they're wet and naked, but I was way past caring. I guess I was feeling fatalistic. *Whatever, bring it on.* Then I wrapped up in a towel and went down a flight and found Duke's room. Stole another set of his clothes. I dressed in them and put my own shoes and jacket and coat on. Went back to the kitchen to wait. It was warm in there. The way the sea was pounding and the rain was beating on the windows made it feel warmer still. It was like a sanctuary. The cook was in there, doing something with a chicken.

"Got coffee?" I asked her.

She shook her head.

"Why not?"

"Caffeine," she said.

I looked at the back of her head.

"Caffeine is the whole point of coffee," I said. "Anyway, tea's got caffeine, and I've seen you make that."

"Tea has tannin," she said.

"And caffeine," I said.

"So drink tea instead," she said.

I looked around the room. There was a wooden block standing vertically on a counter with black knife handles protruding at angles. There were bottles and glasses. I guessed under the sink there might be ammonia sprays. Maybe some chlorine bleach. Enough improvised weapons for a close-quarters fight. If Beck was even a little inhibited about shooting in a crowded room, I might be OK. I might be able to take him before he took me. All I would need was half a second.

"You want coffee?" the cook asked. "Is that what you're saying?"

"Yes," I said. "It is."

"All you have to do is ask."

"I did ask."

"No, you asked if there was any," she said. "Not the same thing."

"So will you make me some? Please?"

"What happened to Mr. Duke?"

I paused. Maybe she was planning on marrying him, like in old movies where the cook marries the butler and they retire and live happily ever after.

"He was killed," I said.

"Last night?"

I nodded. "In an ambush."

"Where?"

"In Connecticut."

"OK," she said. "I'll make you some coffee."

She set the machine going. I watched where she got everything from. The filter papers were stored in a cupboard next to the paper napkins. The coffee itself was in the freezer. The machine was old and slow. It made a loud ponderous gulping sound. Combined with the rain lashing on the windows and the waves pounding on the rocks it meant I didn't hear the Cadillac come back. First I knew, the back door was thrown open and Elizabeth Beck burst in with Richard crowding after her and Beck himself bringing up the rear. They were moving with the kind of exhilarated breathless urgency people show after a short fast dash through heavy rain.

"Hello," Elizabeth said to me.

I nodded. Said nothing.

"Coffee," Richard said. "Great."

"We went out for breakfast," Elizabeth said. "Old Orchard Beach. There's a little diner there we like."

"Paulie figured we shouldn't wake you," Beck said. "He figured you looked pretty tired last night. So he offered to drive us instead."

"OK," I said. Thought: *Did* Paulie *find my stash? Did he tell them yet?*

"You want coffee?" Richard asked me. He was over by the machine, rattling cups in his hand.

"Black," I said. "Thanks."

He brought me a cup. Beck was peeling off his coat and shaking water off it onto the floor.

"Bring it through," he called. "We need to talk."

He headed out to the hallway and looked back like he expected me to follow him. I took my coffee with me. It was hot and steaming. I could toss it in his face if I had to. He led me toward the square paneled room we had used before. I was carrying my cup, which slowed me down a little. He got there well ahead of me. When I entered he was already all the way over by one of the windows with his back to me, looking out at the rain. When he turned around he had a gun in his hand. I just stood still. I was too far away to use the coffee. Maybe fourteen feet. It would have looped up and curled and dispersed in the air and probably missed him altogether.

The gun was a Beretta M9 Special Edition, which was a civilian Beretta 92FS all dressed up to look exactly like a standard military-issue M9. It used nine-millimeter Parabellum ammunition. It had a fifteen-round magazine and military dot-and-post sights. I remembered with bizarre clarity that the retail price had been $861. I had carried an M9 for thirteen years. I had fired many thousands of practice rounds with it and more than a few for real. Most of them had hit their targets, because it's an accurate weapon. Most of the targets had been destroyed, because it's a powerful weapon. It had served me well. I even remembered the original sales pitch from the ordnance people: *It's got manageable recoil and it's easy to strip in the field.* They had repeated it like a mantra. Over and over again. I guess there were contracts at stake. There was some controversy. Navy SEALs hated it. They claimed they'd had dozens blow up in their faces. They even made up a cadence song about it: *No way are you a Navy Seal, until you eat some Italian steel.* But the M9 always served me well. It was a fine weapon, in my opinion. Beck's example looked like a brand-new gun. The finish was immaculate. Dewy with oil. There was luminescent paint on the sights. It glowed softly in the gloom.

I waited.

Beck just stood there, holding the gun. Then he moved. He slapped the barrel into his left palm and took his right hand away. Leaned over the oak table and held the thing out to me, butt-first, left-handed, politely, like he was a clerk in a store.

"Hope you like it," he said. "I thought you might feel at home with it. Duke was into the exotics, like that Steyr he had. But I figured you'd be more comfortable with the Beretta, you know, given your background."

I stepped forward. Put my coffee on the table. Took the gun from him. Ejected the magazine, checked the chamber, worked the action, looked down the barrel. It wasn't spiked. It wasn't a trick. It was a working piece. The Parabellums were real. It was brand new. It had never been fired. I slapped it back together and just held it for a moment. It was like shaking hands with an old friend. Then I cocked it and locked it and put it in my pocket.

"Thanks," I said.

He put his hand in his own pocket and came out with two spare magazines.

"Take these," he said.

He passed them across. I took them.

"I'll get you more later," he said.

"OK," I said.

"You ever tried laser sights?"

I shook my head.

"There's a company called Laser Devices," he said. "They do a universal handgun sight that mounts under the barrel. Plus a little flashlight that clips under the sight. Very cool device."

"Gives a little red spot?"

He nodded. Smiled. "Nobody likes to get lit up with that little red spot, that's for sure."

"Expensive?"

"Not really," he said. "Couple hundred bucks."

"How much weight does it add?"

"Four and a half ounces," he said.

"All at the front?"

"It helps, actually," he said. "Stops the muzzle kicking upward when you fire. It adds about thirteen percent of the weight of the gun. More with the flashlight, of course. Maybe forty, forty-five ounces total. Still way less than those Anacondas you were using. What were they, fifty-nine ounces?"

"Unloaded," I said. "More with six shells in them. Am I ever going to get them back?"

"I put them away somewhere," he said. "I'll get them for you later."

"Thanks," I said again.

"You want to try the laser?"

"I'm happy without it," I said.

He nodded again. "Your choice. But I want the best protection I can get."

"Don't worry," I said.

"I've got to go out now," he said. "Alone. I've got an appointment."

"You don't want me to drive you?"

"This sort of appointment, I have to do them alone.

You stay here. We'll talk later. Move into Duke's room, OK? I like my security closer to where I sleep."

I put the spare magazines in my other pocket.

"OK," I said.

He walked past me into the hallway, back toward the kitchen.

IT WAS THE KIND OF MENTAL SOMERSAULT THAT can slow you down. Extreme tension, and then extreme puzzlement. I walked to the front of the house and watched from a hallway window. Saw the Cadillac sweep around the carriage circle in the rain and head for the gate. It paused in front of it and Paulie came out of the gatehouse. They must have dropped him there on their way back from breakfast. Beck must have driven the final length of the driveway himself. Or Richard, or Elizabeth. Paulie opened the gate. The Cadillac drove through it and away into the rain and the mist. Paulie closed the gate. He was wearing a slicker the size of a circus tent.

I shook myself and turned back and went to find Richard. He had the kind of guileless eyes that hide nothing. He was still in the kitchen, drinking his coffee.

"You walk the shoreline this morning?" I asked him.

I asked it innocently and amiably, like I was just making conversation. If he had anything to hide, I would know. He would go red, look away, stammer, shuffle his feet. But he did none of those things. He was completely relaxed. He looked straight at me.

"Are you kidding?" he said. "Seen the weather?"

I nodded.

"Pretty bad," I said.

"I'm quitting college," he said.

"Why?"

"Because of last night," he said. "The ambush. Those

Connecticut guys are still on the loose. Not safe to go back. I'm staying right here for a spell."

"You OK with that?"

He nodded. "It was mostly a waste of time."

I looked away. *The law of unintended consequences.* I had just short-circuited a kid's education. Maybe ruined his life. But then, I was about to send his father to jail. Or waste him altogether. So I guessed a BA didn't matter very much, compared to that.

I WENT TO FIND ELIZABETH BECK. SHE WOULD BE harder to read. I debated my approach and couldn't come up with anything guaranteed to work. I found her in a parlor tucked into the northwest corner of the house. She was in an armchair. She had a book open on her lap. It was *Doctor Zhivago,* by Boris Pasternak. Paperback. I had seen the movie. I remembered Julie Christie, and the music. "Lara's Theme." Train journeys. And a lot of snow. Some girl had made me go.

"It's not you," she said.

"What's not me?"

"You're not the government spy."

I breathed out. She wouldn't say that if she'd found my stash.

"Exactly," I said. "Your husband just gave me a gun."

"You're not smart enough to be a government spy."

"Aren't I?"

She shook her head. "Richard was desperate for a cup of coffee just now. When we came in."

"So?"

"Do you think he would have been if we'd really been out for breakfast? He could have had all the coffee he wanted."

"So where did you go?"

"We were called to a meeting."

"With who?"

She just shook her head, like she couldn't speak the name.

"Paulie didn't *offer* to drive us," she said. "He summoned us. Richard had to wait in the car."

"But you went in?"

She nodded. "They've got a guy called Troy."

"Silly name," I said.

"But a very smart guy," she said. "He's young, and he's very good with computers. I guess he's what they call a hacker."

"And?"

"He just got partial access to one of the government systems in Washington. He found out they put a federal agent in here. Undercover. At first they assumed it was you. Then they checked a little further and found out it was a woman and she's actually been here for weeks."

I stared at her, not understanding. *Teresa Daniel was off the books. The government computers knew nothing about her.* Then I remembered Duffy's laptop, with the Justice Department logo as the screensaver. I remembered the modem wire, trailing across the desk, going through the complex adapter, going into the wall, hooking up with all the other computers in the world. Had Duffy been compiling private reports? For her own use? For postaction justification?

"I hate to think what they're going to do," Elizabeth said. "To a woman."

She shuddered visibly and looked away. I made it as far as the hallway. Then I stopped dead. There were no cars. And twelve miles of road before I would even begin to get anywhere. Three hours' fast walk. Two hours, running.

"Forget it," Elizabeth called. "Nothing to do with you."

I turned around and stared in at her.

"Forget it," she said again. "They'll be doing it right now. It'll be all over soon."

THE SECOND TIME I EVER SAW SERGEANT FIRST Class Dominique Kohl was the third day she worked for me. She was wearing green battledress pants and a khaki T-shirt. It was very hot. I remember that. We were having some kind of a major heat wave. Her arms were tanned. She had the kind of skin that looks dusty in the heat. She wasn't sweating. The T-shirt was great. She had her tapes on it, *Kohl* on the right and *US Army* on the left, both of them kicked up just a little by the curve of her breasts. She was carrying the file I had given her. It had gotten a little thicker, padded out with her notes.

"I'm going to need a partner," she said to me. I felt a little guilty. Her third day, and I hadn't even partnered her up. I wondered whether I'd given her a desk. Or a locker, or a room to sleep in.

"You met a guy called Frasconi yet?" I said.

"Tony? I met him yesterday. But he's a lieutenant."

I shrugged. "I don't mind commissioned and non-commissioned working together. There's no regulation against it. If there was, I'd ignore it anyway. You got a problem with it?"

She shook her head. "But maybe he does."

"Frasconi? He won't have a problem."

"So will you tell him?"

"Sure," I said. I made a note for myself, on a slip of blank paper, *Frasconi, Kohl, partners.* I underlined it twice, so I would remember. Then I pointed at the file she was carrying. "What have you got?"

"Good news and bad news," she said. "Bad news is their system for signing out eyes-only paper is all shot to hell. Could be routine inefficiency, but more likely it's been deliberately compromised to conceal stuff that shouldn't be happening."

"Who's the guy in question?"

"A pointy-head called Gorowski. Uncle Sam recruited him right out of MIT. A nice guy, by all accounts. Supposed to be very smart."

"Is he Russian?"

She shook her head. "Polish, from a million years ago. No hint of any ideology."

"Was he a Red Sox fan up at MIT?"

"Why?"

"They're all weird," I said. "Check it."

"It's probably blackmail," she said.

"So what's the good news?"

She opened her file. "This thing they're working on is a kind of small missile, basically."

"Who are they working with?"

"Honeywell and the General Defense Corporation."

"And?"

"This missile needs to be slim. So it's going to be sub-caliber. The tanks use hundred and twenty millimeter cannons, but the thing is going to be smaller than that."

"By how much?"

"Nobody knows yet. But they're working on the sabot design right now. The sabot is a kind of sleeve that surrounds the thing to make it up to the right diameter."

"I know what a sabot is," I said.

She ignored me. "It's going to be a discarding sabot, which means it comes apart and falls away immediately after the thing leaves the gun muzzle. They're trying to figure whether it has to be a metal sabot, or whether it could be plastic. *Sabot* means boot. From the French. It's like the missile starts out wearing a little boot."

"I know that," I said. "I speak French. My mother was French."

"Like sabotage," she said. "From old French labor disputes. Originally it meant to smash new industrial equipment by kicking it."

"With your boots," I said.

She nodded. "Right."

"So what's the good news again?"

"The sabot design isn't going to tell anybody anything," she said. "Nothing important, anyway. It's just a sabot. So we've got plenty of time."

"OK," I said. "But make it a priority. With Frasconi. You'll like him."

"You want to get a beer later?"

"Me?"

She looked right at me. "If all ranks can work together, they should be able to have a beer together, right?"

"OK," I said.

DOMINIQUE KOHL LOOKED NOTHING AT ALL LIKE the photographs I had seen of Teresa Daniel, but it was a blend of both their faces I saw in my head. I left Elizabeth Beck with her book and headed up to my original room. I felt more isolated up there. Safer. I locked myself in the bathroom and took my shoe off. Opened the heel and fired up the e-mail device. There was a message from Duffy waiting: *No activity at warehouse. What are they doing?*

I ignored it and hit *new message* and typed: *We lost Teresa Daniel.*

Four words, eighteen letters, three spaces. I stared at them for a long time. Put my finger on the *send* button.

But I didn't press it. I went to *backspace* instead and erased the message. It disappeared from right to left. The little cursor ate it up. I figured I would send it only when I had to. When I knew for sure.

I sent: *Possibility your computer is penetrated.*

There was a long delay. Much longer than the usual ninety seconds. I thought she wasn't going to answer. I thought she must be ripping her wires out of the wall. But maybe she was just getting out of the shower or something because about four minutes later she came back with a simple: *Why?*

I sent: *Talk of a hacker with partial access to government systems.*

She sent: *Mainframes or LANs?*

I had no idea what she meant. I sent: *Don't know.*

She asked: *Details?*

I sent: *Just talk. Are you keeping a log on your laptop?*

She sent: *Hell no!*

I sent: *Anywhere?*

She sent: *Hell no!!*

I sent: *Eliot?*

There was another four-minute delay. Then she came back with: *Don't think so.*

I asked: *Think or know?*

She sent: *Think.*

I stared at the tiled wall in front of me. Breathed out. *Eliot had killed Teresa Daniel.* It was the only explanation. Then I breathed in. Maybe it wasn't. Maybe he hadn't. I sent: *Are these e-mails vulnerable?*

We had been e-mailing back and forth furiously for more than sixty hours. She had asked for news of her agent. I had asked for her agent's real name. And I had asked in a way that definitely wasn't gender-neutral. Maybe I had killed Teresa Daniel.

I held my breath until Duffy came back with: *Our*

e-mail is encrypted. Technically might be visible as code but no way is it readable.

I breathed out and sent: *Sure?*

She sent: *Totally.*

I sent: *Coded how?*

She sent: *NSA billion-dollar project.*

That cheered me up, but only a little. Some of NSA's billion-dollar projects are in the *Washington Post* before they're even finished. And communications snafus screw more things up than any other reason in the world.

I sent: *Check with Eliot immediately about computer logs.*

She sent: *Will do. Progress?*

I typed: *None.*

Then I deleted it and sent: *Soon.* I thought it might make her feel better.

I WENT ALL THE WAY DOWN TO THE GROUND-floor hallway. The door to Elizabeth's parlor was standing open. She was still in the armchair. *Doctor Zhivago* was facedown in her lap and she was staring out the window at the rain. I opened the front door and stepped outside. The metal detector squawked at the Beretta in my pocket. I closed the door behind me and headed straight across the carriage circle and down the driveway. The rain was hard on my back. It ran down my neck. But the wind helped me. It blew me west, straight toward the gatehouse. I felt light on my feet. Coming back again was going to be harder. I would be walking directly into the wind. Assuming I was still walking at all.

Paulie saw me coming. He must have spent his whole time crouched inside the tiny building, prowling from the front windows to the back windows, watching, like a restless animal in its lair. He came out, in his slicker. He had to duck his head and turn sideways to get through the door. He stood with his back against the wall of his house, where the eaves were low. But the eaves didn't help him. The rain drove horizontally under them. I could hear it lashing against the slicker, hard and loud and brittle. It drove against his face and ran down it like torrents of sweat. He had no hat. His hair was plastered against his forehead. It was dark with water.

I had both hands in my pockets with my shoulders hunched forward and my face ducked into my collar. My right hand was tight around the Beretta. The safety was off. But I didn't want to use it. Using it would require complicated explanations. And he would only be replaced. I didn't want to have him replaced until I was ready to have him replaced. So I didn't want to use the Beretta. But I was prepared to.

I stopped six feet from him. Out of his reach.

"We need to talk," I said.

"I don't want to talk," he said.

"You want to arm wrestle instead?"

His eyes were pale blue and his pupils were tiny. I guessed his breakfast had been taken entirely in the form of capsules and powder.

"Talk about what?" he said.

"New situation," I said.

He said nothing.

"What's your MOS?" I asked.

MOS is an army acronym. The army loves acronyms. It stands for *Military Occupational Specialty*. And I used the present tense. *What is,* not *what was.* I wanted to put him right back there. Being ex-military is like being a lapsed Catholic. Even though they're way in the back of your mind, the old rituals still exert a powerful pull. Old rituals like obeying an officer.

"Eleven bang bang," he said, and smiled.

Not a great answer. *Eleven bang bang* was grunt slang for *11B,* which meant *11-Bravo, Infantry,* which meant *Combat Arms.* Next time I face a four-hundred-pound giant with veins full of meth and steroids I would prefer it if his MOS had been mechanical maintenance, or typewriting. Not combat arms. Especially a four-hundred-pound giant who doesn't like officers and who had served eight years in Fort Leavenworth for beating up on one.

"Let's go inside," I said. "It's wet out here."

I said it with the kind of tone you develop when you get promoted past captain. It's a reasonable tone, almost conversational. It's not the sort of tone you use as a lieutenant. It's a suggestion, but it's an order, too. It's heavy with inclusion. It says: *Hey, we're just a couple of guys here. We don't need to let formalities like rank get in our way, do we?*

He looked at me for a long moment. Then he turned and slid sideways through his door. Ducked his chin to his chest so he could get through. Inside, the ceiling was about seven feet high. It felt low to me. His head was almost touching it. I kept my hands in my pockets. Water from his slicker was pooling on the floor.

The house stank with a sharp acrid animal smell. Like a mink. And it was filthy. There was a small living room that opened to a kitchen area. Beyond the kitchen was a short hallway with a bathroom off it and a bedroom at the end. That was all. It was smaller than a city apartment, but it was all dressed up to look like a miniature stand-alone house. There was mess everywhere. Unwashed dishes in the sink. Used plates and cups and articles of athletic clothing all over the living room. There was an old sofa opposite a new television set. The sofa had been crushed by his bulk. There were pill bottles on shelves, on tables, everywhere. Some of them were vitamins. But not many of them.

There was a machine gun in the room. The old Soviet NSV. It belonged on a tank turret. Paulie had it suspended from a chain in the middle of the room. It hung there like a macabre sculpture. Like the Alexander Calder thing they put in every new airport terminal. He could stand behind it and swing it through a complete circle. He could fire it through the front window or the back window, like they were gunports. Limited field of fire, but he could cover forty yards of the road to the west, and forty yards of the driveway to the east. It was fed by a belt that came up out of an open ammunition case placed on the floor. There were maybe twenty more cases stacked against the wall. The cases were dull olive, all covered with Cyrillic letters and red stars.

The gun was so big I had to back up against the wall to get around it. I saw two telephones. One was probably an outside line. The other was probably an internal phone that reached the house. There were alarm boxes on the wall. One would be for the sensors out in no-man's-land. The other would be for the motion detector on the gate itself. There was a video monitor, showing a milky monochrome picture from the gatepost camera.

"You kicked me," he said.

I said nothing.

"Then you tried to run me over," he said.

"Warning shots," I said.

"About what?"

"Duke's gone," I said.

He nodded. "I heard."

"So it's me now," I said. "You've got the gate, I've got the house."

He nodded again. Said nothing.

"I look after the Becks now," I said. "I'm responsible

for their security. Mr. Beck trusts me. He trusts me so much he gave me a weapon."

I was giving him a stare the whole time I was talking. The kind of stare that feels like pressure between the eyes. This would be the moment when the meth and the steroids should kick in and make him grin like an idiot and say, *Well he ain't going to trust you anymore when I tell him what I found out there on the rocks, is he? When I tell him you already had a weapon.* He would shuffle and grin and use a singsong voice. But he said nothing. Did nothing. Didn't react at all, beyond a slight defocus in his eyes, like he was having trouble computing the implications.

"Understand?" I said.

"It used to be Duke and now it's you," he said neutrally.

It wasn't him who had found my stash.

"I'm looking out for their welfare," I said. "Including Mrs. Beck's. That game is over now, OK?"

He said nothing. I was getting a sore neck from looking up into his eyes. My vertebrae are much more accustomed to looking downward at people.

"OK?" I said again.

"Or?"

"Or you and I will have to go around and around."

"I'd like that."

I shook my head.

"You wouldn't like it," I said. "Not one little bit. I'd take you apart, piece by piece."

"You think?"

"You ever hit an MP?" I asked. "Back in the service?"

He didn't answer. Just looked away and stayed quiet. He was probably remembering his arrest. He probably resisted a little, and needed to be subdued. So consequently he probably tripped down some stairs somewhere and suffered a fair amount of damage. Somewhere between the scene of the crime and the holding cell, probably. Purely by accident. That kind of thing happens, in certain circumstances. But then, the arresting officer probably sent six guys to pick him up. I would have sent eight.

"And then I'd fire you," I said.

His eyes came back, slow and lazy.

"You can't fire me," he said. "I don't work for you. Or Beck."

"So who do you work for?"

"Somebody."

"This somebody got a name?"

He shook his head.

"No dice," he said.

I kept my hands in my pockets and eased my way around the machine gun. Headed for the door.

"We straight now?" I said.

He looked at me. Said nothing. But he was calm. His morning dosages must have been well balanced.

"Mrs. Beck is off-limits, right?" I said.

"While you're here," he said. "You won't be here forever."

I hope not, I thought. His telephone rang. The outside line, I guessed. I doubted if Elizabeth or Richard would be calling him from the house. The ring was loud in the silence. He picked it up and said his name. Then he just listened. I heard a trace of a voice in the earpiece, distant and indistinct with plastic peaks and resonances that obscured what was being said. The voice spoke for less than a minute. Then the call was over. He put the phone down and moved his hand quite delicately and used the flat of his palm to set the machine gun swinging gently on its chain. I realized it was a conscious imitation of the thing I had done with the heavy bag down in the gym on our first morning together. He grinned at me.

"I'm watching you," he said. "I'll always be watching you."

I ignored him and opened the door and stepped outside. The rain hit me like a fire hose. I leaned forward and walked straight into it. Held my breath and had a very bad feeling in the small of my back until I was all the way through the forty-yard arc the back window could cover. Then I breathed out.

Not Beck, not Elizabeth, not Richard. Not Paulie.

No dice.

DOMINIQUE KOHL SAID *NO DICE* TO ME THE NIGHT we had our beer. Something unexpected had come up and I had to rain-check the first evening and then she rain-checked my makeup date, so it was about a week before we got together. Maybe eight days. Sergeants drinking with captains was difficult on-post back then because the clubs were rigorously separate, so we went out to a bar in town. It was the usual kind of place, long and low, eight pool tables, plenty of people, plenty of neon, plenty of jukebox noise, plenty of smoke. It was still very hot. The air conditioners were running flat out and getting nowhere. I was wearing fatigue pants and an old T-shirt, because I didn't own any personal clothes. Kohl arrived wearing a dress. It was a simple A-line, no sleeves, knee-length, black, with little white dots on it. Very small dots. Not like big polka dots or anything. A very subtle pattern.

"How's Frasconi working out?" I asked her.

"Tony?" she said. "He's a nice guy."

She didn't say anything more about him. We ordered Rolling Rocks, which suited me because it was my favorite drink that summer. She had to lean very close to talk, because of the noise. I enjoyed the proximity. But I wasn't fooling myself. It was the decibel level making her do it, nothing else. And I wasn't going to try anything with her. No formal reason not to. There were rules back then, I guess, but there were no regulations yet. The notion of sexual harassment was slow coming to the army. But I was already aware of the potential unfairness. Not that there was any way I could help or hurt her career. Her jacket made it plain she was going to make master sergeant and then first sergeant like night follows day. It was only a matter of time. Then came the leap up to E-9 status, sergeant major. That was hers for the taking, too. After that, she would have a problem. After sergeant major came command sergeant major, and there's only one of those in each regiment. After that came sergeant major of the army, and there's only one of those, period. So she would rise and then stop, whatever I said about it.

"We have a tactical problem," she said. "Or strategic, maybe."

"Why?"

"The pointy-head, Gorowski? We don't think it's blackmail in the sense that he's got some terrible secret or anything. Looks to us more like straightforward threats against his family. Coercion, rather than blackmail."

"How can you tell?"

"His file is clean as a whistle. He's been background-checked to hell and back. That's why they do it. They're trying to avoid the possibility of blackmail."

"Was he a Red Sox fan?"

She shook her head. "Yankees. He's from the Bronx. Went to the High School of Science there."

"OK," I said. "I like him already."

"But the book says we should bust him right now."

"What's he doing?"

"We've seen him taking papers out of the lab."

"Are they still doing the sabot?"

She nodded. "But they could publish the sabot design

in *Stars and Stripes* and it wouldn't tell anybody anything. So the situation isn't critical yet."

"What does he do with the papers?"

"He dead-drops them in Baltimore."

"Have you seen who picks them up?"

She shook her head.

"No dice," she said.

"What are you thinking about the pointy-head?"

"I don't want to bust him. I think we should get whoever it is off his back and leave him be. He's got two baby girls."

"What does Frasconi think?"

"He agrees."

"Does he?"

She smiled.

"Well, he will," she said. "But the book says different."

"Forget the book," I said.

"Really?"

"Direct order from me," I said. "I'll put it in writing, if you want. Go with your instinct. Trace the chain the whole way to the other end. If we can, we'll keep this Gorowski guy out of trouble. That's my usual approach, with Yankees fans. But don't let it get away from you."

"I won't," she said.

"Wrap it up before they get done with the sabot," I said. "Or we'll have to think of another approach."

"OK," she said.

Then we talked about other things, and drank a couple more beers. After an hour there was something good on the jukebox and I asked her to dance. For the second time that night she told me *No dice*. I thought about that phrase later. Clearly it came from crapshooters' jargon. It must have originally meant *foul,* like a call, like the dice hadn't been properly rolled. *No dice!* Like a baseball umpire calling a grounder over the bag. *Foul ball!* Then much later it became just another negative, like *no way, no how, no chance.* But how far back in its etymology was she mining? Had she meant a plain *no,* or was she calling a foul? I wasn't sure.

I WAS COMPLETELY SOAKED WHEN I GOT BACK to the house so I went upstairs and took possession of Duke's room and toweled off and dressed in a fresh set of his clothes. The room was at the front of the house, more or less central. The window gave me a view west all the way along the driveway. The elevation meant I could see over the wall. I saw a Lincoln Town Car in the far distance. It was heading straight for us. It was black. It had its headlights on, because of the weather. Paulie came out in his slicker and opened the gate well ahead of time so it didn't have to slow down. It came straight through, moving fast. The windshield was wet and smeared and the wipers were beating back and forth. Paulie had been expecting it. He had been alerted by the phone call. I watched it approach until it was lost to sight below me. Then I turned away.

Duke's room was square and plain, like most of the rooms in the house. It had dark paneling and a big Oriental carpet. There was a television set and two telephones. External and internal, I guessed. The sheets were clean and there were no personal items anywhere, except for clothes in the closet. I guessed maybe early in the morning Beck had told the maid about the personnel change. I guessed he had told her to leave the clothes for me.

I went back to the window and about five minutes later I saw Beck coming back in the Cadillac. Paulie was ready for him, too. The big car barely had to slow. Paulie swung the gate shut after it. Then he chained it and locked it. The gate was a hundred yards from me, but I could make out what he was doing. The Cadillac disappeared from view beneath me and headed around to the garage block. I headed downstairs. I figured since Beck was back it might be time for lunch. I figured maybe Paulie had chained the gate because he was heading on down to join us.

But I was wrong.

I made it to the hallway and met Beck coming out of the kitchen. His coat was spotted with rain. He was looking for me. He had a sports bag in his hand. It was the same bag he had carried the guns to Connecticut in.

"Job to do," he said. "Right now. You need to catch the tide."

"Where?"

He moved away. Turned his head and called over his shoulder.

"The guy in the Lincoln will tell you," he said.

I went through the kitchen and outside. The metal detector beeped at me. I walked back into the rain and headed for the garage block. But the Lincoln was parked right there at the corner of the house. It had been turned and backed up so its trunk faced the sea. There was a guy in the driver's seat. He was sheltering from the rain, and he was impatient. He was tapping on the wheel with his thumbs. He saw me in the mirror and the trunk popped and he opened his door and slid out fast.

He looked like somebody had dragged him out of a trailer park and shoved him in a suit. He had a long graying goatee hiding a weak chin. He had a greasy pony tail held together by a pink rubber band. The band was speckled with glitter. It was the kind of thing you see on drugstore carousels, placed low down so little girls will choose them. He had old acne scars. He had prison tattoos on his neck. He was tall and very thin, like a regular person split lengthwise into two.

"You the new Duke?" he said to me.

"Yes," I said. "I'm the new Duke."

"I'm Harley," he said.

I didn't tell him my name.

"So let's do it," he said.

"Do what?"

He came around and raised the trunk lid all the way.

"Garbage disposal," he said.

There was a military-issue body bag in the trunk. Heavy black rubber, zipped all along its length. I could see by the way it was folded into the space that it held a small person. A woman, probably.

"Who is it?" I asked, although I already knew the answer.

"The government bitch," he said. "Took us long enough, but we got her in the end."

He leaned in and grabbed his end of the bag. Clamped both corners in his hands. Waited for me. I just stood there, feeling the rain against my neck, listening to it snapping and popping against the rubber.

"Got to catch the tide," he said. "It's going to turn."

I leaned down and took hold of the corners at my end. We glanced at each other to coordinate our efforts and heaved the bag up and out. It wasn't heavy, but it was awkward, and Harley was not strong. We carried it a few steps toward the shore.

"Put it down," I said.

"Why?"

"I want to see," I said.

Harley just stood there.

"I don't think you do," he said.

"Put it down," I said again.

He hesitated a second longer and then we squatted together and laid the bag on the rocks. The body settled inside with its back arched upward. I stayed squatted down and duck-walked around to the head. Found the zipper tag and pulled.

"Just look at the face," Harley said. "That part's not too bad."

I looked. It was very bad. She had died in extreme agony. That was clear. Her face was blasted with pain. It was still twisted into the shape of her final ghastly scream.

But it wasn't Teresa Daniel.

It was Beck's maid.

CHAPTER 9

I INCHED THE ZIPPER DOWN A LITTLE MORE UN-
til I saw the same mutilation I had seen ten years previously. Then I stopped. Turned my head into the rain and
closed my eyes. The water on my face felt like tears.

"Let's get on with it," Harley said.

I opened my eyes. Stared at the waves. Pulled the zipper back up without looking anymore. Stood slowly and
stepped around to the foot of the bag. Harley waited. Then
we each grasped our corners and lifted. Carried the bur-
den over the rocks. He led me south and east, way out to a
place on the shore where two granite shelves met. There
was a steep V-shaped cleft between them. It was half-full
of moving water.

"Wait until after the next big wave," Harley said.

It came booming in and we both ducked our heads
away from the spray. The cleft filled to the top and the tide
ran up over the rocks and almost reached our shoes. Then
it pulled away again and the cleft emptied out. Gravel rattled and drained. The surface of the sea was laced with
dull gray foam and pitted by the rain.

"OK, put it down," Harley said. He was out of breath.
"Hold your end."

We laid the bag down so the head end was hanging out over the granite shelf and into the cleft. The zipper faced upward. The body was on its back. I held both corners at the foot. The rain plastered my hair to my head and ran into my eyes. It stung. Harley squatted and straddled the bag and humped the head end farther out into space. I went with him, inch by inch, small steps on the slippery rocks. The next wave came in and eddied under the bag. It floated it up a little. Harley used the temporary buoyancy to slide it a little farther into the sea. I moved with it. The wave receded. The cleft drained again. The bag drooped down. The rain thrashed against the stiff rubber. It battered our backs. It was deathly cold.

Harley used the next five waves to ease the bag out more and more until it was hanging right down into the cleft. I was left holding empty rubber. Gravity had jammed the body tight up against the top of the bag. Harley waited and looked out to sea and then ducked low and pulled the zipper all the way down. Scrambled back fast and took a corner from me. Held tight. The seventh wave came booming in. We were soaked with its spray. The cleft filled and the bag filled and then the big wave receded and sucked the body right out of the bag. It floated motionless for a split second and then the undertow caught it and took it away. It went straight down, into the depths. I saw long fair hair streaming in the water and pale skin flashing green and gray and then it was gone. The cleft foamed red as it drained.

"Hell of a riptide here," Harley said.

I said nothing.

"The undertow takes them right out," he said. "We never had one come back, anyways. It pulls them a mile or two, going down all the way. Then there's sharks out there, I guess. They cruise the coast here. Plus all kinds of other creatures. You know, crabs, suckerfish, things like that."

I said nothing.

"Never had one come back," he said again.

I glanced at him and he smiled at me. His mouth was like a caved-in hole above the goatee. He had rotten yellow stumps for teeth. I glanced away again. The next wave came in. It was only a small one, but when it receded the cleft was washed clean. It was like nothing had happened. Like nothing had ever been there. Harley stood up awkwardly and zipped the empty bag. Pink water sluiced out of it and ran over the rocks. He started rolling it up. I glanced back at the house. Beck was standing in the kitchen doorway, alone, watching us.

WE WENT BACK TOWARD THE HOUSE, SOAKED with rain and salt water. Beck ducked back into the kitchen. We followed him in. Harley hung around on the edge of the room, like he felt he shouldn't be there.

"She was a federal agent?" I said.

"No question," Beck said.

His sports bag was on the table, in the center, prominent, like a prosecution exhibit in a courtroom. He zipped it open and rummaged inside.

"Check this out," he said.

He lifted a bundle onto the table. Something wrapped in a damp dirty oil-stained rag the size of a hand towel. He unfolded it and took out Duffy's Glock 19.

"This all was hidden in the car we let her use," he said.

"The Saab?" I said, because I had to say something.

He nodded. "In the well where the spare tire is. Under the trunk floor." He laid the Glock on the table. Took the two spare magazines out of the rag and laid them next to the gun. Then he put the bent bradawl next to them, and the sharpened chisel. And Angel Doll's keyring.

I couldn't breathe.

"The bradawl is a lock pick, I guess," Beck said.

"How does this prove she was federal?" I asked.

He picked up the Glock again and turned it around and pointed to the right-hand side of the slide.

"Serial number," he said. "We checked with Glock in Austria. By computer. We have access to that kind of thing. This particular gun was sold to the United States government about a year ago. Part of a big order for the law enforcement agencies, 17s for the male agents and 19s for the women. So that's how we know she was federal."

I stared at the serial number. "Did she deny it?"

He nodded. "Of course she did. She said she just found it. Gave us a big song and dance. She blamed you, actually. Said it was your stuff. But then, they always deny it, don't they? They're trained to, I guess."

I looked away. Stared through the window at the sea. *Why had she picked it all up? Why hadn't she just left it there? Was it some kind of a housekeeping instinct? She didn't want it to get wet? Or what?*

"You look upset," Beck said.

And how did she even find it? Why would she even be looking?

"You look upset," he said again.

I was beyond upset. She had died in agony. And I had done it to her. She probably thought she was doing me a favor. By keeping my stuff dry. By keeping it from rusting. She was just a dumb naive kid from Ireland, trying to help me out. And I had killed her, as surely as if I had stood there and butchered her myself.

"I'm responsible for security," I said. "I should have suspected her."

"You're responsible only since last night," Beck said. "So don't beat yourself up over it. You haven't even got your feet under the table yet. It was Duke who should have made her."

"But I never would have suspected her," I said. "I thought she was just the maid."

"Hey, me too," he said. "Duke, also."

I looked away again. Stared at the sea. It was gray and heaving. I didn't really understand. *She found it. But why would she hide it so well?*

"This is the clincher," Beck said.

I looked back in time to see him lifting a pair of shoes out of the bag. They were big square clunky items, black, the shoes she had been wearing every single time I had seen her.

"Look at this," he said.

He turned the right shoe over and pulled a pin out of the heel with his fingernails. Then he swiveled the heel rubber like a little door and turned the shoe the right way up. He shook it. A small black plastic rectangle clattered out on the table. It landed facedown. He turned it over.

It was a wireless e-mail device, exactly identical to my own.

HE PASSED ME THE SHOE. I TOOK IT. STARED AT it, blankly. It was a woman's size six. Made for a small foot. But it had a wide bulbous toe, and therefore a wide thick heel to balance it visually. Some kind of a clumsy fashion statement. The heel had a rectangular cavity carved out of it. Identical to mine. It had been done neatly. It had been done with patience. But not by a machine. It showed the same faint tool marks that mine did. I pictured some guy in a lab somewhere, a line of shoes on a bench in front of him, the smell of new leather, a small arc of woodcarving tools laid out in front of him, curls and slivers of rubber accumulating on the floor around him as he labored. Most government work is surprisingly low-tech. It's not all exploding ballpoint pens and cameras built into watches. A trip to the mall to buy a commercial e-mail device and a pair of plain shoes is about as cutting-edge as most of it gets.

"What are you thinking?" Beck asked.

I was thinking about how I was feeling. I was on a roller-coaster. She was still dead, but I hadn't killed her anymore. The government computers had killed her again. So I was relieved, personally. But I was more than a little angry, too. *Like, what the hell was Duffy doing?* What the hell was she playing at? It was an absolute rule of procedure that you never put two or more people undercover in the same location unless they're aware of each other. That was absolutely *basic*. She had told me about Teresa Daniel. *So why the hell hadn't she told me about this other woman?*

"Unbelievable," I said.

"The battery is dead," he said. He was holding the device in both hands. Using both thumbs on it, like a video game. "It doesn't work, anyway."

He passed it to me. I put the shoe down and took it from him. Pressed the familiar *power* button. But the screen stayed dead.

"How long was she here?" I asked.

"Eight weeks," Beck said. "It's hard for us to keep domestic staff. It's lonely here. And there's Paulie, you know. And Duke wasn't a very hospitable guy, either."

"I guess eight weeks would be a long time for a battery to last."

"What would be their procedure now?" he asked.

"I don't know," I said. "I was never federal."

"In general," he said. "You must have seen stuff like this."

I shrugged.

"I guess they'd have expected it," I said. "Communications are always the first things to get screwed up. She drops off the radar, they wouldn't worry right away. They'd have no choice but to leave her in the field. I mean, they can't contact her to order her home, can they? So I guess they would trust her to get the battery charged up again, as soon as she could." I turned the unit on its edge and pointed to the little socket on the bottom. "Looks like it needs a cell phone charger, something like that."

"Would they send people after her?"

"Eventually," I said. "I guess."

"When?"

"I don't know. Not yet, anyway."

"We plan to deny she was ever here. Deny we ever saw her. There's no evidence she was ever here."

"You better clean her room real good," I said. "There'll be fingerprints and hair and DNA all over the place."

"She was recommended to us," he said. "We don't advertise in the paper or anything. Some guys we know in Boston put her in touch."

He glanced at me. I thought: *Some guys in Boston begging for a plea bargain, helping the government any which way they could.* I nodded.

"Tricky," I said. "Because what does that say about them?"

He nodded back sourly. He agreed with me. He knew what I was saying. He picked up the big bunch of keys from where they were lying next to the chisel.

"I think these are Angel Doll's," he said.

I said nothing.

"So it's a three-way nightmare," he said. "We can tie Doll to the Hartford crew, and we can tie our Boston friends to the feds. Now we can tie Doll to the feds, too. Because he gave his keys to the undercover bitch. Which means the Hartford crew must be in bed with the feds as well. Doll's dead, thanks to Duke, but I've still got Hartford, Boston, *and* the government on my back. I'm going to need you, Reacher."

I glanced at Harley. He was looking out the window at the rain.

"Was it just Doll?" I asked.

Beck nodded. "I've been through all of that. I'm satisfied. It was just Doll. The rest are solid. They're still with me. They were very apologetic about Doll."

"OK," I said.

There was silence for a long moment. Then Beck rewrapped my stash in its rag and dumped it back in his bag. He threw the dead e-mail device in after it and piled the maid's shoes on top. They looked sad and empty and forlorn.

"I've learned one thing," he said. "I'm going to start searching people's shoes, that's for damn sure. You can bet your life on that."

I BET MY LIFE ON IT RIGHT THERE AND THEN. I kept my own shoes on. I got back up to Duke's room and checked his closet. There were four pairs in there. Nothing I would have picked out for myself in a store, but they looked reasonable and they were close to the right size. But I left them there. To show up so soon in different shoes would raise a red flag. And if I was going to ditch mine, I was going to ditch them properly. No point leaving them in my room for casual inspection. I would have to get them out of the house. And there was no easy way of doing that right then. Not after the scene in the kitchen. I couldn't just walk downstairs with them in my hands. What was I supposed to say? *What, these? Oh, they're the shoes I was wearing when I arrived. I'm just going out to throw them in the ocean.* Like I was suddenly bored with them? So I kept them on.

And I still needed them, anyway. I was tempted, but I wasn't ready to cut Duffy out. Not just yet. I locked myself in Duke's bathroom and took the e-mail device out. It was an eerie feeling. I hit *power* and the screen came up with a message: *We need to meet.* I hit *reply* and sent: *You bet your ass we do.* Then I turned the unit off and nailed it back into my heel and went down to the kitchen again.

"Go with Harley," Beck told me. "You need to bring the Saab back."

The cook wasn't there. The counters were neat and clean. They had been scrubbed. The stove was cold. It felt like there should be a *Closed* sign hanging on the door.

"What about lunch?" I said.

"You hungry?"

I thought back to the way the sea had swelled the bag and claimed the body. Saw the hair under the water, fluid and infinitely fine. Saw the blood rinsing away, pink and diluted. I wasn't hungry.

"Starving," I said.

Beck smiled sheepishly. "You're one cold son of a bitch, Reacher."

"I've seen dead people before. I expect to see them again."

He nodded. "The cook is off duty. Eat out, OK?"

"I don't have any money."

He put his hand in his pants pocket and came out with a wad of bills. Started to count them out and then just shrugged and gave it up and handed the whole lot to me. It must have been close to a thousand dollars.

"Walking-around money," he said. "We'll do the salary thing later."

I put the cash in my pocket.

"Harley is waiting in the car," he said.

I went outside and pulled my coat collar up. The wind was easing. The rain was reverting to vertical. The Lincoln was still there at the corner of the house. The trunk lid was closed. Harley was drumming his thumbs on the wheel. I slid into the passenger seat and buzzed it backward to get some legroom. He fired up the engine and set the wipers going and took off. We had to wait while Paulie unchained the gate. Harley fiddled with the heater and set it on high. Our clothes were wet and the windows were steaming up. Paulie was slow. Harley started drumming again.

"You two work for the same guy?" I asked him.

"Me and Paulie?" he said. "Sure."

"Who is he?"

"Beck didn't tell you?"

"No," I said.

"Then I won't either, I guess."

"Hard for me to do my job without information," I said.

"That's your problem," he said. "Not mine."

He gave me his yellow gappy smile again. I figured if I hit him hard enough my fist would take out all the little stumps and end up somewhere in the back of his scrawny throat. But I didn't hit him. Paulie got the chain loose and swung the gate back. Harley took off immediately and squeezed through with about an inch of clearance on each side. I settled back in my seat. Harley clicked the headlights on and accelerated hard and rooster tails of spray kicked up behind us. We drove west, because there was no choice for the first twelve miles. Then we turned north on Route One, away from where Elizabeth Beck had taken me, away from Old Orchard Beach and Saco, toward Portland. I had no view of anything because the weather was so dismal. I could barely see the tail lights on the traffic ahead of us. Harley didn't speak. Just rocked back and forth in the driver's seat and drummed his thumbs on the wheel and drove. He wasn't a smooth driver. He was always either on the gas or the brake. We sped up, slowed down, sped up, slowed down. It was a long twenty miles.

Then the road swerved hard to the west and I saw I-295 close by on our left. There was a narrow tongue of gray seawater beyond it and beyond that was the Portland airport. There was a plane taking off in a huge cloud of spray. It roared low over our heads and swung south over the Atlantic. Then there was a strip mall on our left with a long narrow parking lot out front. The mall had the sort of stores you expect to find in a low-rent place trapped between two roads near an airport. The parking lot held maybe twenty cars in a line, all of them head-in and square-on to the curb. The old Saab was fifth from the left. Harley pulled the Lincoln in and stopped directly behind it. Drummed his thumbs on the wheel.

"All yours," he said. "Key is in the door pocket."

I got out in the rain and he drove off as soon as I shut my door. But he didn't get back on Route One. At the end of the lot he made a left. Then an immediate right. I saw him ease the big car through an improvised exit made of lumpy poured concrete that led into the adjoining lot. I pulled my collar up again and watched as he drove slowly through it and then disappeared behind a set of brand-new buildings. They were long low sheds made of bright corrugated metal. Some kind of a business park. There was a network of narrow blacktop roads. They were wet and shiny with rain. They had high concrete curbs, smooth and new. I saw the Lincoln again, through a gap between buildings. It was moving slow and lazy, like it was looking to park somewhere. Then it slid behind another building and I didn't see it again.

I turned around. The Saab was nose-in to a discount liquor store. Next to the liquor store on one side was a place that sold car stereos and on the other side was a place with a window full of fake crystal chandeliers. I doubted if the maid had been sent out to buy a new ceiling fixture. Or to get a CD player installed in the Saab. So she must have been sent to the liquor store. And then she must have found a whole bunch of people waiting there for her. Four of them, maybe five. At least. After the first moment of surprise she would have changed from a bewildered maid to a trained agent fighting for her life. They would have anticipated that. They would have come mob-handed. I looked up and down the sidewalk. Then I looked at the liquor store. It had a window full of boxes. There was no real view out. But I went in anyway.

The store was full of boxes but empty of people. It felt like it spent most of its time that way. It was cold and dusty. The clerk behind the counter was a gray guy of about fifty. Gray hair, gray shirt, gray skin. He looked like he hadn't been outside in a decade. He had nothing I wanted to buy as an ice-breaker. So I just went right ahead and asked him my question.

"See that Saab out there?" I said.

He made a big show of lining up his view out front.

"I see it," he said.

"You see what happened to the driver?"

"No," he said.

People who say *no* right away are usually lying. A truthful person is perfectly capable of saying *no,* but generally they stop and think about it first. And they add *sorry* or something like that. Maybe they come out with some questions of their own. It's human nature. They say *Sorry, no, why, what happened?* I put my hand in my pocket and peeled off a bill from Beck's wad purely by feel. Took it out. It was a hundred. I folded it in half and held it up between my finger and my thumb.

"Now did you see?" I said.

He glanced to his left. My right. Toward the business park beyond his walls. Just a fast glance, furtive, out and back.

"No," he said again.

"Black Town Car?" I said. "Drove off that way?"

"I didn't see," he said. "I was busy."

I nodded. "You're practically rushed off your feet in here. I can see that. It's a miracle one man can handle the pressure."

"I was in the back. On the phone, I guess."

I kept the hundred up there in my hand for another long moment. I guessed a hundred tax-free dollars would represent a healthy slice of his week's net take. But he looked away from it. That told me plenty, too.

"OK," I said. I put the money back in my pocket and walked out.

I DROVE THE SAAB TWO HUNDRED YARDS SOUTH on Route One and stopped at the first gas station I saw. Went in and bought a bottle of spring water and two candy bars. I paid four times more for the water than I would have for gasoline, if you calculated it by the gallon. Then I came out and sheltered near the door and peeled a candy bar and started eating it. Used the time to look around. No surveillance. So I stepped over to the pay phones and used my change to call Duffy. I had memorized her motel number. I crouched under the plastic bubble and tried to stay dry. She answered on the second ring.

"Drive north to Saco," I said. "Right now. Meet me in the big brick mall on the river island in a coffee shop called *Café Café*. Last one there buys."

I finished my candy bar as I drove south. The Saab rode hard and it was noisy compared to Beck's Cadillac or Harley's Lincoln. It was old and worn. The carpets were thin and loose. It had six figures on the clock. But it got the job done. It had decent tires and the wipers worked. It made it through the rain OK. And it had nice big mirrors. I watched them all the way. Nobody came after me. I got to the coffee shop first. Ordered a tall espresso to wash the taste of chocolate out of my mouth.

Duffy showed up six minutes later. She paused in the doorway and looked around and then headed over toward me and smiled. She was in fresh jeans and another cotton shirt, but it was blue, not white. Over that was her leather jacket and over that was a battered old raincoat that was way too big for her. Maybe it was the old guy's. Maybe she had borrowed it from him. It wasn't Eliot's. That was clear. He was smaller than she was. She must have come north not expecting bad weather.

"Is this place safe?" she said.

I didn't answer.

"What?" she said.

"You're buying," I said. "You got here second. I'll have another espresso. And you owe me for the first one."

She looked at me blankly and then went to the counter and came back with an espresso for me and a cappuccino for herself. Her hair was a little wet. She had combed it with her fingers. She must have parked her car on the street and walked in through the rain and checked her reflection in a store window. She counted her change in silence and dealt me bills and coins equal to the price of my first cup. Coffee was another thing way more expensive than gasoline, up here in Maine. But I guessed it was the same everywhere.

"What's up?" she said.

I didn't answer.

"Reacher, what's the matter?"

"You put another agent in eight weeks ago," I said. "Why didn't you tell me?"

"What?"

"What I said."

"What agent?"

"She died this morning. She underwent a radical double mastectomy without the benefit of anesthetic."

She stared at me. "Teresa?"

I shook my head.

"Not Teresa," I said. "The other one."

"What other one?"

"Don't bullshit me," I said.

"What other one?"

I stared at her. Hard. Then softer. There was something about the light in that coffee shop. Maybe it was the way it came off all the blond wood and the brushed metal and the glass and the chrome. It was like X-ray light. Like a truth serum. It had shown me Elizabeth Beck's genuine uncontrollable blush. Now I was expecting it to show me the exact same thing from Duffy. I was expecting it to show me a deep red blush of shame and embarrassment, because I had found her out. But it showed me total surprise instead. It was right there in her face. She had gone very pale. She had gone stark white with shock. It was like the blood had drained right out of her. And nobody can do that on command, any more than they can blush.

"What *other* one?" she said again. "There was only Teresa. What? Are you telling me she's dead?"

"Not Teresa," I said again. "There was another one. Another woman. She got hired on as a kitchen maid."

"No," she said. "There's only Teresa."

I shook my head again. "I saw the body. It wasn't Teresa."

"A kitchen maid?"

"She had an e-mail thing in her shoe," I said. "Exactly the same as mine. The heel was scooped out by the same guy. I recognized the handiwork."

"That's not possible," she said.

I looked straight at her.

"I would have told you," she said. "Of course I would have told you. And I wouldn't have *needed* you if I had another agent in there. Don't you see that?"

I looked away. Looked back. Now I was embarrassed.

"So who the hell was she?" I asked.

She didn't answer. Just started nudging her cup around and around on her saucer, prodding at the handle with her forefinger, turning it ten degrees at a time. The heavy foam and the chocolate dust stayed still while the cup rotated. She was thinking like crazy.

"Eight weeks ago?" she said.

I nodded.

"What alerted them?" she asked.

"They got into your computer," I said. "This morning, or maybe last night."

She looked up from her cup. "That's what you were asking me about?"

I nodded. Said nothing.

"Teresa isn't in the computer," she said. "She's off the books."

"Did you check with Eliot?"

"I did better than check," she said. "I searched the whole of his hard drive. And all of his files on the main server back in D.C. I've got total access everywhere. I looked for *Teresa, Daniel, Justice, Beck, Maine,* and *undercover.* And he didn't write any of those words anywhere."

I said nothing.

"How did it go down?" she asked.

"I'm not really sure," I said. "I guess at first the computer told them you had somebody in there, and then it told them it was a woman. No name, no details. So they looked for her. And I think it was partly my fault they found her."

"How?"

"I had a stash," I said. "Your Glock, and the ammo, and a few other things. She found them. She hid them in the car she was using."

Duffy was quiet for a second.

"OK," she said. "And you're thinking they searched the car and your stuff made her look bad, right?"

"I guess so."

"But maybe they searched *her* first and found the shoe."

I looked away. "I sincerely hope so."

"Don't beat up on yourself. It's not your fault. As soon as they got into the computer it was only a matter of time for the first one they looked at. They both fit the bill. I mean, how many women were there to choose from? Presumably just her and Teresa. They couldn't miss."

I nodded. There was Elizabeth, too. And there was the cook. But neither one of them would figure very high on a list of suspicious persons. Elizabeth was the guy's wife. And the cook had probably been there twenty years.

"But who was she?" I said.

She played with her cup until it was back in its starting position. The unglazed rim on the bottom made a tiny grinding sound.

"It's obvious, I'm afraid," she said. "Think of the time line here. Count backward from today. Eleven weeks ago I screwed up with the surveillance photographs. Ten weeks ago they pulled me off the case. But because Beck is a big fish I couldn't give it up and so nine weeks ago I put Teresa in without their knowledge. But also because Beck is a big fish, and without *my* knowledge, they must have reassigned the case to someone else and eight weeks ago that someone else put this maid person in, right on top of

Teresa. Teresa didn't know the maid was coming and the maid didn't know Teresa was already there."

"Why would she have nosed into my stuff?"

"I guess she wanted to control the situation. Standard procedure. As far as she was concerned, you weren't anybody kosher. You were just a loose cannon. Some kind of troublemaker. You were a cop-killer, and you were hiding weapons. Maybe she thought you were from a rival operation. She was probably thinking of selling you out to Beck. It would have enhanced her credibility with him. And she needed you out of the way, because she didn't need extra complications. If she didn't sell you out to Beck, she would have turned you in to us, as a cop-killer. I'm surprised she didn't already."

"Her battery was dead."

She nodded. "Eight weeks. I guess kitchen maids don't have good access to cell phone chargers."

"Beck said she was out of Boston."

"Makes sense," she said. "They probably farmed it out to the Boston field office. That would work, geographically. And it would explain why we didn't pick up any kind of water-cooler whispers in D.C."

"He said she was recommended by some friends of his."

"Plea-bargainers, for sure. We use them all the time. They set each other up quite happily. No code of silence with these people."

Then I remembered something else Beck had said.

"How was Teresa communicating?" I asked.

"She had an e-mail thing, like yours."

"In her shoe?"

Duffy nodded. Said nothing. I heard Beck's voice, loud in my head: *I'm going to start searching people's shoes, that's for damn sure. You can bet your life on that.*

"When did you last hear from her?"

"She fell off the air the second day."

She went quiet.

"Where was she living?" I asked.

"In Portland. We put her in an apartment. She was an office clerk, not a kitchen maid."

"You been to the apartment?"

She nodded. "Nobody's seen her there since the second day."

"You check her closet?"

"Why?"

"We need to know what shoes she was wearing when she was captured."

Duffy went pale again.

"Shit," she said.

"Right," I said. "What shoes were left in her closet?"

"The wrong ones."

"Would she think to ditch the e-mail thing?"

"Wouldn't help her. She'd have to ditch the shoes, too. The hole in the heel would tell the story, wouldn't it?"

"We need to find her," I said.

"We sure do," she said. Then she paused a beat. "She was very lucky today. They went looking for a woman, and they happened to look at the maid first. We can't count on her staying that lucky much longer."

I said nothing. *Very lucky for Teresa, very unlucky for the maid.* Every silver lining has a cloud. Duffy sipped her coffee. Grimaced slightly like the taste was off and put the cup back down again.

"But what gave her away?" she said. "In the first place? That's what I want to know. I mean, she only lasted two days. And that was nine whole weeks before they broke into the computer."

"What background story did you give her?"

"The usual, for this kind of work. Unmarried, unattached, no family, no roots. Like you, except you didn't have to fake it."

I nodded slowly. *A good-looking thirty-year-old woman who would never be missed.* A huge temptation for guys like Paulie or Angel Doll. Maybe irresistible. *A fun thing to have around.* And the rest of their crew might be even worse. Like Harley, for instance. He didn't strike me as much of an advertisement for the benefits of civilization.

"Maybe nothing gave her away," I said. "Maybe she just went missing, you know, like women do. Lots of women go missing. Young women especially. Single, unattached women. Happens all the time. Thousands a year."

"But you found the room they were keeping her in."

"All those missing women have to be somewhere. They're only missing as far as the rest of us are concerned. They know where they are, and the men who took them know where they are."

She looked at me. "You think it's like that?"

"Could be."

"Will she be OK?"

"I don't know," I said. "I hope so."

"Will they keep her alive?"

"I think they want to keep her alive. Because they don't know she's a federal agent. They think she's just a woman."

A fun thing to have around.

"Can you find her before they check her shoes?"

"They might never check them," I said. "You know, if they're seeing her in one particular light, as it were, it would be a leap to start seeing her as something else."

She looked away. Went quiet.

"One particular light," she repeated. "Why don't we just say what we mean?"

"Because we don't want to," I said.

She stayed quiet. One minute. Two. Then she looked straight back at me. A brand-new thought.

"What about your shoes?" she said.

I shook my head.

"Same thing," I said. "They're getting used to me. It would be a leap to start seeing me as something else."

"It's still a big risk."

I shrugged.

"Beck gave me a Beretta M9," I said. "So I'll wait and see. If he bends down to take a look I'll shoot him through the middle of the forehead."

"But he's just a businessman, right? Basically? Would he really do bad stuff to Teresa without knowing she was a threat to his business?"

"I don't know," I said.

"Did he kill the maid?"

I shook my head. "Quinn did."

"Were you a witness?"

"No."

"So how do you know?"

I looked away.

"I recognized the handiwork," I said.

THE FOURTH TIME I EVER SAW SERGEANT FIRST Class Dominique Kohl was a week after the night we spent in the bar. The weather was still hot. There was talk of a tropical storm blowing in from the direction of Bermuda. I had a million files on my desk. We had rapes, homicides, suicides, weapons thefts, assaults, and there had been a riot the night before because the refrigeration had broken down in the enlisted mess kitchens and the ice cream had turned to water. I had just gotten off the phone with a buddy at Fort Irwin in California who told me it was the same over there whenever the desert winds were blowing.

Kohl came in wearing shorts and a tank top shirt. She still wasn't sweating. Her skin was still dusty. She was carrying her file, which was then about eight times as thick as when I had first given it to her.

"The sabot has got to be metal," she said. "That's their final conclusion."

"Is it?" I said.

"They'd have preferred plastic, but I think that's just showboating."

"OK," I said.

"I'm trying to tell you they've finished with the sabot design. They're ready to move on with the important stuff now."

"You still feel all warm and fuzzy about this Gorowski guy?"

She nodded. "It would be a tragedy to bust him. He's a nice guy and an innocent victim. And the bottom line is he's good at his job and useful to the army."

"So what do you want to do?"

"It's tricky," she said. "I guess what I want to do is bring him on board and get him to feed phony stuff to whoever it is who's got the hook in. That way we keep the investigation going without risking putting anything real out there."

"But?"

"The real thing looks phony in itself. It's a very weird device. It's like a big lawn dart. It has no explosive in it."

"So how does it work?"

"Kinetic energy, dense metals, depleted uranium, heat, all that kind of stuff. Were you a physics postgrad?"

"No."

"Then you won't understand it. But my feeling is if we screw with the designs the bad guy is going to know. It'll put Gorowski at risk. Or his baby girls, or whatever."

"So you want to let the real blueprints out there?"

"I think we have to."

"Big risk," I said.

"Your call," she said. "That's why you get the big bucks."

"I'm a captain," I said. "I'd be on food stamps if I ever got time to eat."

"Decision?"

"Got a line on the bad guy yet?"

"No."

"Feel confident you won't let it get away?"

"Totally," she said.

I smiled. Right then she looked like the most self-possessed human being I had ever seen. Shining eyes, serious expression, hair hooked behind her ears, short khaki shorts, tiny khaki shirt, socks and parachute boots, dark dusty skin everywhere.

"So go for it," I said.

"I never dance," she said.

"What?"

"It wasn't just you," she said. "In fact, I'd have liked to. I appreciated the invitation. But I never dance with anybody."

"Why not?"

"Just a thing," she said. "I feel self-conscious. I'm not very coordinated."

"Neither am I."

"Maybe we should practice in private," she said.

"Separately?"

"One-on-one mentoring helps," she said. "Like with alcoholism."

Then she winked and walked out and left a very faint trace of her perfume behind her in the hot heavy air.

DUFFY AND I FINISHED OUR COFFEE IN SILENCE. Mine tasted thin and cold and bitter. I had no stomach for it. My right shoe pinched. It wasn't a perfect fit. And it was starting to feel like a ball and chain. It had felt ingenious at first. Smart, and cool, and clever. I remembered the first time I opened the heel, three days ago, soon after I first arrived at the house, soon after Duke locked the door to my room. *I'm in.* I had felt like a guy in a movie. Then I remembered the last time I opened it. Up in Duke's bathroom, an hour and a half ago. I had fired up the unit and Duffy's message had been waiting there for me: *We need to meet.*

"Why did you want to meet?" I asked her.

She shook her head. "Doesn't matter now. I'm revising the mission. I'm scrapping all our objectives except getting Teresa back. Just find her and get her out of there, OK?"

"What about Beck?"

"We're not going to get Beck. I screwed up again. This maid person was a legitimate agent and Teresa wasn't. Nor were you. And the maid died, so they're going to fire me for going off the books with Teresa and you, and they're going to abandon the case against Beck because I compromised procedure so badly they could never make it stand up in court anymore. So just get Teresa the hell out and we'll all go home."

"OK," I said.

"You'll have to forget about Quinn," she said. "Just let it go."

I said nothing.

"We failed anyway," she said. "You haven't found anything useful. Not a thing. No evidence at all. It's been a complete waste of time, beginning to end."

I said nothing.

"Like my career," she said.

"When are you going to tell the Justice Department?"

"About the maid?"

I nodded.

"Right away," she said. "Immediately. I'll have to. No choice. But I'll search the files first and find out who put her in there. Because I'd prefer to break the news face-to-face, I guess, at my own level. It'll give me a chance to apologize. Any other way all hell will break loose before I get the opportunity. All my access codes will be canceled and I'll be handed a cardboard box and told to clear my desk within thirty minutes."

"How long have you been there?"

"A long time. I thought I was going to be the first woman director."

I said nothing.

"I would have told you," she said. "I promise, if I'd had another agent in there I would have told you."

"I know," I said. "I'm sorry for jumping to conclusions."

"It's the stress," she said. "Undercover is tough."

I nodded. "It's like a hall of mirrors up there. One damn thing after another. Everything feels unreal."

We left our half-finished cups on the table and headed out, into the mall's interior sidewalks, and then outside into the rain. We had parked near each other. She kissed me on the cheek. Then she got into her Taurus and headed south and I got into the Saab and headed north.

PAULIE TOOK HIS OWN SWEET TIME ABOUT OPEN-ing the gate for me. He made me wait a couple of minutes before he even came lumbering out of his house. He still had his slicker on. Then he stood and stared for a minute before he went near the latch. But I didn't care. I was busy thinking. I was hearing Duffy's voice in my head: *I'm revising the mission.* Most of my military career a guy named Leon Garber was either directly or indirectly my boss. He explained everything to himself by making up little phrases or sayings. He had one for every occasion. He used to say: *Revising objectives is smart because it stops you throwing good money after bad.* He didn't mean money in any literal sense. He meant manpower, resources, time, will, effort, energy. He used to contradict himself, too. Just as often he would say: *Never ever get distracted from the exact job in hand.* Of course, proverbs are like that generally. *Too many cooks spoil the broth, many hands make light work, great minds think alike, fools never differ.* But overall, after you canceled out a few layers of contradiction, Leon approved of revision. He approved of it big time. Mainly because revision was about thinking, and he figured thinking never hurt anybody. So I was thinking, and thinking hard, because I was aware that something was slowly and imperceptibly creeping up on me, just outside of my conscious grasp. Something connected to something Duffy had said to me: *You haven't found anything useful. Not a thing. No evidence at all.*

I heard the gate swing back. Looked up to see Paulie waiting for me to drive through. The rain was beating on his slicker. He still had no hat. I exacted some petty revenge by waiting a minute myself. Duffy's revision suited me well enough. I didn't care much about Beck. I really didn't, either way. But I wanted Teresa. And I would get her. I wanted Quinn, too. And I would get him too, whatever Duffy said. The revision was only going to go so far.

I checked on Paulie again. He was still waiting. He was an idiot. He was out in the rain, I was in a car. I took my foot off the brake and rolled slowly through the gate. Then I accelerated hard and headed down to the house.

I put the Saab away in the slot I had once seen it in and walked out into the courtyard. The mechanic was still in the third garage. The empty one. I couldn't see what he was doing. Maybe he was just sheltering from the rain. I ran back to the house. Beck heard the metal detector announce my arrival and came into the kitchen to meet me. He pointed at his sports bag. It was still there on the table, right in the center.

"Get rid of this shit," he said. "Throw it in the ocean, OK?"

"OK," I said. He went back out to the hallway and I picked up the bag and turned around. Headed outside again and slipped down the ocean side of the garage block wall. I put my bundle right back in its hidden dip. *Waste not, want not.* And I wanted to be able to return Duffy's Glock to her. She was already in enough trouble without having to add the loss of her service piece to the list. Most agencies take that kind of a thing very seriously.

Then I walked on to the edge of the granite tables and swung the bag and hurled it far out to sea. It pinwheeled end over end in the air and the shoes and the e-mail unit were thrown clear. I saw the e-mail thing hit the water. It sank immediately. The left shoe hit toe-first and followed it. The bag parachuted a little and landed gently facedown and filled with water and turned over and slipped under. The right shoe floated for a moment, like a tiny black boat. It pitched and yawed and bobbed urgently like it was trying to escape to the east. It rode up over a peak and rode down on the far side of the crest. Then it started to list sideways. It floated maybe ten more seconds and then it filled with water and sank without a trace.

THERE WAS NO ACTIVITY IN THE HOUSE. THE cook wasn't around. Richard was in the family dining room eating a sandwich he must have made for himself and staring out at the rain. Elizabeth was still in her parlor, still working on *Doctor Zhivago*. By a process of elimination I figured Beck must be in his den, maybe sitting in his red leather chair and looking at his machine gun collection. There was quiet everywhere. I didn't understand it. Duffy had said they had five containers in and Beck had said he had a big weekend coming up, but nobody was doing anything.

I went up to Duke's room. I didn't think of it as my room. I hoped I never would. I lay down on the bed and started thinking again. Tried to chase whatever it was hovering way in the back of my mind. *It's easy,* Leon Garber would have said. *Work the clues. Go through everything you've seen, everything you've heard.* So I went through it. But I kept coming back to Dominique Kohl. The fifth time I ever saw her, she drove me to Aberdeen, Maryland, in an olive-green Chevrolet. I was having second thoughts about letting genuine blueprints out into the world. It was a big risk. Not usually something I would worry about, but I needed more progress than we were making. Kohl had identified the dead-drop site, and the drop technique, and where and when and how Gorowski was letting his contact know that the delivery had been made. But she still hadn't seen the contact make the pickup. Still didn't know who he was.

Aberdeen was a small place twenty-some miles north and east of Baltimore. Gorowski's method was to drive down to the big city on a Sunday and make the drop in the Inner Harbor area. Back then the renovations were in full swing and it was a nice bright place to be but the public hadn't caught on all the way yet and it stayed pretty empty most of the time. Gorowski had a POV. It was a two-year-old Mazda Miata, bright red. It was a plausible car, all things considered. Not new, but not cheap either, because it was a popular model back then and nobody could get a discount off sticker, so used values held up well. And it was a two-seater, which was no good for his baby girls. So he had to have another car, too. We knew his wife wasn't rich. It might have worried me in someone else, but the guy was an engineer. It was a characteristic choice. He didn't smoke, didn't drink. Entirely plausible that he would hoard his spare dollars and spring for something with a sweet manual change and rear-wheel drive.

The Sunday we followed him he parked in a lot near one of the Baltimore marinas and went to sit on a bench. He was a squat hairy guy. Wide, but not tall. He had the Sunday newspaper with him. He spent some time gazing out at the sailboats. Then he closed his eyes and turned his face up to the sky. The weather was still wonderful. He spent maybe five minutes just soaking up the sun like a lizard. Then he opened his eyes and opened his paper and started to read it.

"This is his fifth time," Kohl whispered to me. "Third trip since they finished with the sabot stuff."

"Standard procedure so far?" I asked.

"Identical," she said.

He kept busy with the paper for about twenty minutes. I could tell he was actually reading it. He paid attention to all the sections, except for sports, which I thought was a little odd for a Yankees fan. But then, I guessed a Yankees fan wouldn't like the Orioles stuffed down his throat all the time.

"Here we go," Kohl whispered.

He glanced up and slipped a buff army envelope out of the newspaper. Snapped his left hand up and out to take a kink out of the section he was reading. And to distract, because at the exact same time his right hand dropped the envelope into the garbage can beside him at the end of the bench.

"Neat," I said.

"You bet," she said. "This boy is no dummy."

I nodded. He was pretty good. He didn't get up right away. He sat there for maybe ten more minutes, reading. Then he folded the paper slowly and carefully and stood up and walked to the edge of the water and looked out at the boats some more. Then he turned around and walked back toward his car, with the newspaper tucked up under his left arm.

"Now watch," Kohl said.

I saw him take a nub of chalk out of his pants pocket with his right hand. He scuffed against an iron lamp post and left a tick of chalk on it. It was the fifth mark on the post. Five weeks, five marks. The first four were fading away with age, in sequence. I stared at them through my field glasses while he walked on into the parking lot and got into his roadster and drove slowly away. I turned back and focused on the garbage can.

"Now what happens?" I said.

"Absolutely nothing," Kohl said. "I've done this twice before. Two whole Sundays. Nobody's going to come. Not today, not tonight."

"When is the trash emptied?"

"Tomorrow morning, first thing."

"Maybe the garbage man is a go-between."

She shook her head. "I checked. The truck compacts everything into a solid mass as it's loaded and then it goes straight into the incinerator."

"So our secret blueprints are getting burned up in a municipal incinerator?"

"That's safe enough."

"Maybe one of these sailboat guys is sneaking out in the middle of the night."

"Not unless the Invisible Man bought a sailboat."

"So maybe there's no guy," I said. "Maybe the whole thing was set up way in advance and then the guy got arrested for something else. Or he got cold feet and left town. Or he got sick and died. Maybe it's a defunct scheme."

"You think?"

"Not really," I said.

"Are you going to pull the plug?" she said.

"I have to. I might be an idiot, but I'm not completely stupid. This is way out of hand now."

"Can I go to plan B?"

"Haul Gorowski in and threaten him with a firing squad. Then tell him if he plays ball and delivers phony plans we'll be nice to him."

"Tough to make them convincing."

"Tell him to draw them himself," I said. "It's his ass on the line."

"Or his children's."

"All part of being a parent," I said. "It'll concentrate his mind."

She was quiet for a moment. Then she said, "You want to go dancing?"

"Here?"

"We're a long way from home. Nobody knows us."

"OK," I said.

Then we figured it was too early for dancing, so we had a couple of beers and waited for evening. The bar we were in was small and dark. There was wood and brick. It was a nice place. It had a jukebox. We spent a long time leaning on it, side by side, trying to choose our debut number. We debated it with intensity. It began to assume enormous significance. I tried to interpret her suggestions by analyzing the tempos. Were we going to be holding on to each other? That sort of dancing? Or was it going to be the usual sort of separate-but-equal leaping about? In the end we would have needed a United Nations resolution, so we just put our quarter in the machine and closed our eyes and hit buttons at random. We got "Brown Sugar" by the Rolling Stones. It was a great number. It always has been. She was actually a pretty good dancer. But I was terrible.

Afterward we were out of breath, so we sat down and ordered more beers. And I suddenly figured out what Gorowski had been up to.

"It's not the envelope," I said. "The envelope is empty. It's the newspaper. The blueprints are in the newspaper. In the sports section. He should have checked the box scores. The envelope is a diversion, in case of surveillance. He's been well rehearsed. He dumps the newspaper in another garbage can, later. *After* making his chalk mark. Probably on his way out of the lot."

"Shit," Kohl said. "I wasted five weeks."

"And somebody got three real blueprints."

"One of us," she said. "Military, or CIA, or FBI. A professional, to be that cute."

THE NEWSPAPER, NOT THE ENVELOPE. TEN YEARS later I was lying on a bed in Maine thinking about Dominique Kohl dancing and a guy called Gorowski folding his newspaper, slowly and carefully, and staring out at a hundred sailboat masts on the water. *The newspaper, not the envelope.* It seemed to be still relevant, somehow. *This, not that.* Then I thought about the maid hiding my stash under the floor of the Saab's trunk. She couldn't have hidden anything else there, or Beck would have found it and added it to the prosecution exhibits on his kitchen table. But the Saab's carpets were old and loose. If I was the sort of person who hid a gun under a spare tire I might hide papers under a car's carpets. And I might be the sort of person who made notes and kept records.

I rolled off the bed and stepped to the window. The afternoon had already happened. Full dark was on its way.

Day fourteen, a Friday, nearly over. I went downstairs, thinking about the Saab. Beck was walking through the hallway. He was in a hurry. Preoccupied. He went into the kitchen and picked up the phone. Listened to it for a second and then held it out to me.

"The phones are all dead," he said.

I put the receiver to my ear and listened. There was nothing there. No dial tone, no scratchy hiss from open circuits. Just dull inert silence, and the sound of blood rushing in my head. Like a seashell.

"Go try yours," he said.

I went back upstairs to Duke's room. The internal phone worked OK. Paulie answered on the third ring. I hung up on him. But the outside line was stone dead. I held the receiver like it would make a difference and Beck appeared in the doorway.

"I can speak to the gate," I said.

He nodded.

"That's a completely separate circuit," he said. "We put it in ourselves. What about the outside line?"

"Dead," I said.

"Weird," he said.

I put the receiver down. Glanced at the window.

"Could be the weather," I said.

"No," he said. He held up his cell phone. It was a tiny silver Nokia. "This is out too."

He handed it to me. There was a tiny screen on the front. A bar chart on the right showed that the battery was fully charged. But the signal meter was all the way down. *No service* was displayed, big and black and obvious. I handed it back.

"I need to use the bathroom," I said. "I'll be right down."

I locked myself in. Pulled off my shoe. Opened the heel. Pressed *power*. The screen came up: *No service*. I turned it off and nailed it back in. Flushed the toilet for form's sake and sat there on the lid. I was no kind of a telecommunications expert. I knew phone lines came down, now and then. I knew cell phone technology was sometimes unreliable. But what were the chances that one location's land lines would fail at the exact same time its nearest cell tower went down? Pretty small, I guessed. Pretty damn small. So it had to be a deliberate outage. But who had requested it? Not the phone company. They wouldn't do disruptive maintenance at commuting time on a Friday. Early on a Sunday morning, maybe. And they wouldn't have the land lines down at the same time as the cell towers, anyway. They would stagger the two jobs, surely.

So who had organized it? A heavy-duty government agency, maybe. Like the DEA, perhaps. Maybe the DEA was coming for the maid. Maybe its SWAT team was rolling up the harbor operation first and it didn't want Beck to know before it was ready to come on out to the house.

But that was unlikely. The DEA would have more than one SWAT team available. It would go for simultaneous operations. And even if it didn't, it would be the easiest thing in the world to close the road between the house and the first turning. They could seal it forever. There was a twelve-mile stretch of unlimited opportunity. Beck was a sitting duck, phones or no phones.

So who?

Maybe Duffy, off the books. Duffy's status might just get her a major once-in-a-lifetime favor, one-on-one with a phone company manager. Especially a favor that was limited geographically. One minor land line spur. And one cell tower, probably somewhere out near I-95. It would give a thirty-mile dead spot for people to drive through, but she might have been able to swing it. Maybe. Especially if the favor was strictly limited in duration. Not open-ended. Four or five hours, say.

And why would Duffy suddenly be afraid of phones for four or five hours? Only one possible answer. She was afraid for me.

The bodyguards were loose.

CHAPTER 10

TIME. DISTANCE DIVIDED BY SPEED ADJUSTED for direction equals time. Either I had enough, or I had none at all. I didn't know which it would be. The bodyguards had been held in the Massachusetts motel where we planned the original eight-second sting. Which was less than two hundred miles south. That much, I knew for sure. Those were facts. The rest was pure speculation. But I could put together some kind of a likely scenario. They had broken out of the motel and stolen a government Taurus. Then they had driven like hell for maybe an hour, breathless with panic. They had wanted to get well clear before they did another thing. They might have even gotten a little lost, way out there in the wilds. Then they had gotten their bearings and hit the highway. Accelerated north. Then they had calmed down, checked the view behind, slowed up, stayed legal, and started looking for a phone. But by then Duffy had already killed the lines. She had acted fast. So their first stop represented a waste of time. Ten minutes, maybe, to allow for slowing down, parking, calling the house, calling the cell, starting up again, rejoining the highway traffic. Then they would have done it all again a second time at the next rest area. They would have blamed the first failure on a random technical hitch. Another ten minutes. After that, either they would have seen the pattern, or they would have figured they were getting close enough just to press on regardless. Or both.

Beginning to end, a total of four hours, maybe. But when did those four hours start? I had no idea. That was clear. Obviously somewhere between four hours ago and, say, thirty minutes ago. So either I had enough time or no time at all.

I came out of the bathroom fast and checked the window. The rain had stopped. It was night outside. The lights along the wall were on. They were haloed with mist. Beyond them was absolute darkness. No headlights in the distance. I headed downstairs. Found Beck in the hallway. He was still prodding at his Nokia, trying to get it to work.

"I'm going out," I said. "Up the road a little."

"Why?"

"I don't like this thing with the phones. Could be nothing, could be something."

"Something like what?"

"I don't know," I said. "Maybe somebody's coming. You just got through telling me how many people you got on your back."

"We've got a wall and a gate."

"You got a boat?"

"No," he said. "Why?"

"If they get as far as the gate, you're going to need a boat. They could sit there and starve you out."

He said nothing.

"I'll take the Saab," I said.

"Why?"

Because it's lighter than the Cadillac.

"Because I want to leave the Cadillac for you," I said. "It's bigger."

"What are you going to do?"

"Whatever I need to," I said. "I'm your head of security now. Maybe nothing's happening, but if it is, then I'm going to try to take care of it for you."

"What do I do?"

"You keep a window open and listen," I said. "At night with all this water around, you'll hear me from a couple miles away if I'm shooting. If you do, put everybody in the Cadillac and get the hell out. Drive fast. Don't stop. I'll hold them off long enough for you to get past. Have you got someplace else to go?"

He nodded. Didn't tell me where.

"So go there," I said. "If I make it, I'll get to the office. I'll wait there, in the car. You can check there later."

"OK," he said.

"Now call Paulie on the internal phone and tell him to stand by to let me through the gate."

"OK," he said again.

I left him there in the hallway. Walked out into the night. I detoured around the courtyard wall and retrieved my bundle from its hole. Carried it back to the Saab and put it on the rear seat. Then I slid into the front and fired up the engine and backed out. Drove slow around the carriage circle and accelerated down the drive. The lights on the wall were bright in the distance. I could see Paulie at the gate. I slowed a little and timed it so I didn't have to stop. I went straight through. Drove west, staring through the windshield, looking for headlight beams coming toward me.

I DROVE FOUR MILES, AND THEN I SAW A GOVernment Taurus. It was parked on the shoulder. Facing toward me. No lights. The old guy was sitting behind the wheel. I killed my lights and slowed and stopped window to window with him. Wound down my glass. He did the same. Aimed a flashlight and a gun at my face until he saw who I was. Then he put them both away.

"The bodyguards are out," he said.

I nodded. "I figured. When?"

"Close to four hours ago."

I glanced ahead, involuntarily. *No time.*

"We got two men down," he said.

"Killed?"

He nodded. Said nothing.

"Did Duffy report it?"

"She can't," he said. "Not yet. We're off the books. This whole situation isn't even happening."

"She'll have to report it," I said. "It's two guys."

"She will," he said. "Later. After you deliver. Because the objectives are right back in place again. She needs Beck for justification, now more than ever."

"How did it go down?"

He shrugged. "They bided their time. Two of them, four of us. Should have been easy. But our boys got sloppy, I guess. It's tough, locking people down in a motel."

"Which two got it?"

"The kids who were in the Toyota."

I said nothing. It had lasted roughly eighty-four hours. Three and a half days. Actually a little better than I had expected, at the start.

"Where is Duffy now?" I asked.

"We're all fanned out," he said. "She's up in Portland with Eliot."

"She did good with the phones."

He nodded. "Real good. She cares about you."

"How long are they off?"

"Four hours. That's all she could get. So they'll be back on soon."

"I think they'll come straight here."

"Me too," he said. "That's why I came straight here."

"Close to four hours, they'll be off the highway by now. So I guess the phones don't matter anymore."

"That's how I figure it."

"Got a plan?" I said.

"I was waiting for you. We figured you'd make the connection."

"Did they get guns?"

"Two Glocks," he said. "Full mags."

Then he paused a beat. Looked away.

"Less four shots fired at the scene," he said. "That's how it was described to us. Four shots, two guys. They were all head shots."

"Won't be easy."

"It never is," he said.

"We need to find a place."

I told him to leave his car where it was and get in with me. He came around and slid into the passenger seat. He was wearing the same raincoat Duffy had been wearing in the coffee shop. He had reclaimed it. We drove another mile, and then I started looking for a place. I found one where the road narrowed sharply and went into a long gentle curve. The blacktop was built up a little, like a shallow causeway. The shoulders were less than a foot wide and fell away fast into rocky ground. I stopped the car and then turned it sharply and backed it up and pulled forward again until it was square across the road. We got out and checked. It was a good roadblock. There was no room to get around it. But it was a very obvious roadblock, like I knew it would be. The two guys would come tearing around the curve and jam on the brakes and then start backing up and shooting.

"We need to roll it over," I said. "Like a bad accident."

I took my bundle out of the back seat. Put it down on

the shoulder, just in case. Then I made the old guy put his coat down on the road. I emptied my pockets and put mine beyond his. I wanted to roll the Saab onto the coats. I needed to bring it back relatively undamaged. Then we stood shoulder to shoulder with our backs to the car and started rocking it. It's easy enough to turn a car over. I've seen it done all over the world. You let the tires and the suspension help you. You rock it, and then you bounce it, and then you keep it going until it's coming right up in the air, and then you time it just right and flip it all the way over. The old guy was strong. He did his part. We got it bouncing through about forty-five degrees and then we spun around together and hooked our hands under the sill and heaved it all the way onto its side. Then we kept the momentum going and tipped it right onto its roof.

The coats meant it slid around easily enough without scratching, so we positioned it just right. Then I opened the upside-down driver's door and told the old guy to get in and play dead for the second time in three days. He threaded his way inside and lay down on his front, half-in and half-out, with his arms thrown up above his head. In the dark, he looked pretty convincing. In the harsh shadows of bright headlights he would look no worse. The coats weren't visible, unless you really looked for them. I moved away and retrieved my bundle and climbed down the rocks beyond the shoulder and crouched low.

Then we waited.

It seemed like a long wait. Five minutes, six, seven. I collected rocks, three of them, each a little larger than my palm. I watched the horizon to the west. The sky was still full of low clouds and I figured headlight beams would reflect off them as they bounced and dipped. But the horizon stayed black. And quiet. I could hear nothing at all except the distant surf and the old guy breathing.

"They got to be coming," he called.

"They'll come," I said.

We waited. The night stayed dark and quiet.

"What's your name?" I called.

"Why?" he called back.

"I just want to know," I said. "Doesn't seem right that I've killed you twice and I don't even know your name."

"Terry Villanueva," he called.

"Is that Spanish?"

"Sure is."

"You don't look Spanish."

"I know," he said. "My mom was Irish, my dad was Spanish. But my brother and I took after our mom. My brother changed his name to Newton. Like the old scientist, or the suburb. Because that's what *Villanueva* means, new town. But I stuck with the Spanish. Out of respect for the old guy."

"Where was this?"

"South Boston," he said. "Wasn't easy, years ago, a mixed marriage and all."

We went quiet again. I watched and listened. Nothing. Villanueva shifted his position. He didn't look comfortable.

"You're a trooper, Terry," I called.

"Old school," he called back.

Then I heard a car.

And Villanueva's cell phone rang.

The car was maybe a mile away. I could hear the faint feathery sound of a faraway V-6 motor revving fast. I could see the distant glow of headlights trapped between the road and the clouds. Villanueva's phone was set to ring with an insane speeded-up version of Bach's *Toccata and Fugue in D*. He stopped playing dead and scrambled halfway up to his knees and dragged it out of his pocket. Thumbed a button and killed the music and answered it. It was a tiny thing, lost in his hand. He held it to his ear. He listened for a second. I heard him say, "OK." Then, "We're doing it right now." Then, "OK." Then he said "OK" again and clicked the phone off and lay back down. His cheek was on the blacktop. The phone was half-in and half-out of his hand.

"Service was just restored," he called to me.

And a new clock started ticking. I glanced to my right into the east. Beck would keep trying the lines. I guessed as soon as he got a dial tone he would come out to find me and tell me the panic was over. I glanced to my left into the west. I could hear the car, loud and clear. The headlight beams bounced and swung, bright in the darkness.

"Thirty seconds," I called.

The sound got louder. I could hear the tires and the automatic gearbox and the engine all as separate noises. I ducked lower. Ten seconds, eight, five. The car raced around the corner and its lights whipped across my hunched back. Then I heard the thump of hydraulics and the squeal of brake rotors and the howl of locked rubber grinding on the blacktop and the car came to a complete stop, slightly off line, twenty feet from the Saab.

I looked up. It was a Taurus, plain blue paint, gray in the cloudy moonlight. A cone of white light ahead of it. Brake lights flaring red behind. Two guys in it. Their faces were lit by their lights bouncing back off the Saab. They held still for a second. Stared forward. They recognized the Saab. They must have seen it a hundred times. I saw the driver move. Heard him shove the gearshift forward into Park. The brake lights died. The engine idled. I could smell exhaust fumes and the heat from under the hood.

The two guys opened their doors in unison. Got out and stood up, behind the doors. They had the Glocks in their hands. They waited. They came out from behind the doors. Walked forward, slowly, with the guns held low. The headlight beams lit them brightly from the waist down. Their upper bodies were harder to see. But I could make out their features. Their shapes. They were the bodyguards. No doubt about it. They were young and heavy, tense and wary. They were dressed in dark suits, creased and crumpled and stained. They had no ties. Their shirts had turned from white to gray.

They squatted next to Villanueva. He was in their shadow. They moved a little and turned his face into the light. I knew they had seen him before. Just a brief glimpse as they passed him, outside the college gate, eighty-four hours ago. I didn't expect them to remember him. And I don't think they did. But they had been fooled once, and they didn't want to get fooled again. They were very cautious. They didn't start in with immediate first aid. They just squatted there and did nothing. Then the one nearest me stood up.

By then I was five feet from him. I had my right hand cupped around a rock. It was a little bigger than a softball. I swung my arm, wide and flat and fast, like I was going to slap him in the face. The momentum would have taken my arm off at the shoulder if I had missed. But I didn't miss. The rock hit him square on the temple and he went straight down like a weight had fallen on him from above. The other guy was faster. He scrambled away and twisted to his feet. Villanueva flailed at his legs and missed them. The guy danced away and whipped around. His Glock came up toward me. All I wanted to do was stop him firing it so I hurled the rock straight at his head. He spun away again and took it square in the back of his neck, right where his cranium curved in to meet his spine. It was like a ferocious punch. It pitched him straight forward. He dropped the Glock and went down on his face like a tree and lay still.

I stood there and watched the darkness in the east. Saw nothing. No lights. Heard nothing, except the distant sea. Villanueva crawled out of the upside-down car on his hands and knees and crouched over the first guy.

"This one's dead," he said.

I checked, and he was. Hard to survive a ten-pound rock sideways into the temple. His skull was neatly caved in and his eyes were wide open and there was nothing much happening behind them. I checked the pulses in his neck and his wrist and went to look at the second guy. Crouched down over him. He was dead, too. His neck was broken, but good. I wasn't very surprised. The rock weighed ten pounds and I had pitched it like Nolan Ryan.

"Two birds, one stone," Villanueva said.

I said nothing.

"What?" he said. "You wanted to take them back into custody? After what they did to us? This was suicide by cop, plain and simple."

I said nothing.

"You got a problem?" Villanueva said.

I wasn't *us*. I wasn't DEA, and I wasn't a cop. But I thought about Powell's private signal to me: *My eyes only, 10-2, 10-28. These guys need to be dead, make no mistake about it.* And I was prepared to take Powell's word for it. That's what unit loyalties are for. Villanueva had his, and I had mine.

"No problem," I said.

I found the rock where it had come to rest and rolled it back to the shoulder. Then I got to my feet and walked away and leaned in and killed the Taurus's lights. Waved Villanueva over toward me.

"We need to be real quick now," I said. "Use your phone and get Duffy to bring Eliot down here. We need him to take this car back."

Villanueva used a speed dial and started talking and I found the two Glocks on the road and stuffed them back into the dead guys' pockets, one each. Then I stepped over to the Saab. Getting it the right way up again was going to be a whole lot harder than turning it over. For a second I worried that it was going to be impossible. The coats killed any friction against the road. If we shoved it, it was just going to slide on its roof. I closed the upside-down driver's door and waited.

"They're coming," Villanueva called.

"Help me with this," I called back.

We manhandled the Saab on the coats back toward the house as far as we could get it. It slid off Villanueva's coat onto mine. Slid to the far edge of mine and then stopped dead when the metal caught against the road.

"It's going to get scratched," Villanueva said.

I nodded.

"It's a risk," I said. "Now get in their Taurus and bump it."

He drove their Taurus forward until its front bumper touched the Saab. It connected just above the waistline, against the B-pillar between the doors. I signaled him for more gas and the Saab jerked sideways and the roof ground against the blacktop. I climbed up on the Taurus's hood and pushed hard against the Saab's sill. Villanueva kept the Taurus coming, slow and steady. The Saab jacked up on its side, forty degrees, fifty, sixty. I braced my feet against the base of the Taurus's windshield and walked my hands down the Saab's flank and then put them flat on its roof. Villanueva hit the gas and my spine compressed about an inch and the Saab rolled all the way over and landed on its wheels with a thump. It bounced once and Villanueva braked hard and I fell forward off the hood and banged my head on the Saab's door. Ended up flat on the road under the Taurus's front fender. Villanueva backed it away and stopped and hauled himself out.

"You OK?" he said.

I just lay there. My head hurt. I had hit it hard.

"How's the car?" I said.

"Good news or bad news?"

"Good first," I said.

"The side mirrors are OK," he said. "They'll spring back."

"But?"

"Big gouges in the paint," he said. "Small dent in the door. I think you did it with your head. The roof is a little caved-in, too."

"I'll say I hit a deer."

"I'm not sure they have deer out here."

"A bear, then," I said. "Or whatever. A beached whale. A sea monster. A giant squid. A huge woolly mammoth recently released from a melting glacier."

"You OK?" he said again.

"I'll live," I said.

I rolled over and got up on all fours. Pushed myself upright, slow and easy.

"Can you take the bodies?" he said. "Because we can't."

"Then I guess I'll have to," I said.

We opened the Saab's rear hatch with difficulty. It was a little misaligned because the roof was a little distorted. We carried the dead guys one at a time and folded them into the load space. They almost filled it. I went back to the shoulder and retrieved my bundle and carried it over and put it in on top of them. There was a parcel shelf that would hide everything from view. It took both of us to close the hatch. We had to take a side each and lean down hard. Then we picked up our coats off the road and shook them out and put them on. They were damp and crushed and a little torn up in places.

"You OK?" he asked again.

"Get in the car," I said.

We sprung the door mirrors back into place and

climbed in together. I turned the key. It wouldn't start. I tried again. No luck. In between the two tries I heard the fuel pump whining.

"Leave the ignition on for a moment," Villanueva said. "The gasoline drained out of the engine. When it was upside down. Wait a moment, let it pump back in."

I waited and it started on the third attempt. So I put it in gear and got it straight on the road and drove the mile back to where we had left the other Taurus. The one that Villanueva had arrived in. It was waiting right there for us on the shoulder, gray and ghostly in the moonlight.

"Now go back and wait for Duffy and Eliot," I said. "Then I suggest you get the hell out of here. I'll see you all later."

He shook my hand.

"Old school," he said.

"Ten-eighteen," I said. 10-18 was MP radio code for *assignment completed*. But I guess he didn't know that, because he just looked at me.

"Stay safe," I said.

He shook his head.

"Voice mail," he said.

"What about it?"

"When a cell phone is out of service you usually get routed to voice mail."

"The whole tower was down."

"But the cell network didn't know that. Far as the machinery knew, Beck just had his individual phone switched off. So they'll have gotten his voice mail. In a central server somewhere. They might have left him a message."

"What would have been the point?"

Villanueva shrugged. "They might have told him they were on their way back. You know, maybe they expected him to check his messages right away. They might have left him the whole story. Or maybe they weren't really thinking straight, and they figured it was like a regular answering machine, and they were saying, *Hey, Mr. Beck, pick up, will you?*"

I said nothing.

"They might have left their voices on there," he said. "Today. That's the bottom line."

"OK," I said.

"What are you going to do?"

"Start shooting," I said. "Shoes, voice mail, he's one step away now."

Villanueva shook his head.

"You can't," he said. "Duffy needs to bring him in. It's the only way she can save her own ass now."

I looked away. "Tell her I'll do my best. But if it's him or me, he goes down."

Villanueva said nothing.

"What?" I said. "Now I'm a human sacrifice?"

"Just do your best," he said. "Duffy's a good kid."

"I know she is," I said.

He hauled himself out of the Saab, one hand on the door frame, the other on the seat back. He stepped across and got into his own car and drove away, slow and quiet, no lights. I saw him wave. I watched until he was lost to sight and then I backed up and turned and got the Saab straddling the middle of the road, facing west. I figured when Beck came out to find me he would think I was doing a good defensive job.

BUT EITHER BECK WASN'T TRYING THE PHONES very often or he wasn't thinking very much about me because I sat there for ten minutes with no sign of him. I spent part of the time testing my earlier hypothesis that a person who hides a gun under the spare wheel might also hide notes under the carpets. The carpets were already loose and they hadn't been helped by being turned upside down. But there was nothing at all under them, except for rust stains and a damp layer of acoustical padding that looked like it had been made out of old red and gray sweaters. No notes. Bad hypothesis. I put the carpets back in place as well as I could and kicked them around until they were reasonably flat.

Then I got out and checked the exterior damage. Nothing I could do about the scratches in the paint. They were bad, but not disastrous. Nothing I could do about the dent in the door either, unless I wanted to take it apart and press the panel out. The roof was a little caved in. I remembered it as having a definite dome shape. Now it was fairly flat. But I figured I could maybe do something about that from the inside. I climbed into the back seat and put both palms up flat on the headliner and pushed hard. I was rewarded by two sounds. One of them was the pop of sheet metal springing back into shape. The other was the crackle of paper.

It wasn't a new car, so the headliner wasn't the one-piece molded mouse-fur thing that everybody uses now. It was the old-fashioned cream vinyl thing with the side-to-side wire ribs that pleated it into three accordion sections. The edges were trapped under a black rubber gasket that ran all around the roof. The vinyl was a little puckered in the front corner, over the driver's seat. The gasket looked a little loose there. I guessed a person could stress the vinyl by pushing up on it and then peel it out from under the gasket. Then tug on it until it pulled away all along its length. That would give sideways access into any one of the three pleated sections the person chose to use. Then it would take time and fingernails to get the vinyl back under the gasket. A little care would make the intrusion hard to see, in a car as worn as that one.

I leaned forward and checked the section that ran above the front seats. I stabbed the vinyl upward until I felt the underside of the roof, all the way across the width of the car. Nothing there. Nothing in the next section, either. But the section above the rear seats had paper hidden in it. I could even judge the size and weight. Legal-size paper, maybe eight or ten stacked sheets.

I got out of the back and slid into the driver's seat and looked at the gasket. Put some tension into the vinyl and picked at the edge. I got a fingernail under the rubber and eased it down into a little mouth a half-inch long. Scraped my other hand sideways across the roof and the vinyl obediently pulled out from under the gasket and gave me enough of a hole to get my thumb into.

I worked my thumb backward and I had gotten about nine inches unzipped when I was suddenly lit up from behind. Bright light, harsh shadows. The road came in over my right shoulder so I glanced across at the passenger-door mirror. The glass was cracked. It was filled with multiple sets of bright headlights. I saw the etched warning: *OBJECTS IN MIRROR ARE CLOSER THAN THEY APPEAR*. I twisted around in the seat and saw a single set of high beams sweeping urgently left and right through the curves. A quarter-mile back. Coming on fast. I dropped my window an inch and heard the distant hiss of fat tires and the growl of a quiet V-8 kicked down into second gear. The Cadillac, in a hurry. I stabbed the vinyl back into place. No time to secure it under the gasket. I just shoved it upward and hoped it would stay there.

The Cadillac came right up behind me and stopped hard. The headlights stayed on. I watched in the mirror and saw the door open and Beck step out. I put my hand in my pocket and clicked the Beretta to *fire*. Duffy or no Duffy, I wasn't interested in a long discussion about voice mail. But Beck had nothing in his hands. No gun, no

Nokia. He stepped forward and I slid out and met him level with the Saab's rear bumper. I wanted to keep him away from the dents and the scratches. It put him about eighteen inches from the guys he had sent down to pick up his son.

"Phones are back on," he said.

"The cell too?" I said.

He nodded.

"But look at this," he said.

He took the little silver phone out of his pocket. I kept my hand around the Beretta, out of sight. It would blow a hole in my coat, but it would blow a bigger hole in his coat. He passed me the phone. I took it, left-handed. Held it low, in the spread of the Cadillac's headlights. Looked at the screen. I didn't know what I was looking for. Some cell phones I had seen signaled a voice mail message with a little pictogram of an envelope. Some used a little symbol made up of two small circles joined together by a bar at the bottom, like a reel-to-reel tape, which I thought was weird, because I guessed most cell phone users had never seen a reel-to-reel tape in their lives. And I was pretty sure that the cell phone companies didn't record the messages themselves on reel-to-reel tape. I guessed they did it digitally, inert inside some kind of a solid-state circuit. But then, the signs at railroad crossings still show the sort of locomotive that Casey Jones would have been proud of.

"See that?" Beck said.

I saw nothing. No envelopes, no reel-to-reel tapes. Just the signal strength bar, and the battery bar, and the *menu* thing, and the *names* thing.

"What?" I said.

"The signal strength," he said. "It's only showing three out of five. Normally I get four."

"Maybe the tower was down," I said. "Maybe it powers up again slowly. Some kind of electrical reason."

"You think?"

"There are microwaves involved," I said. "It's probably complicated. You should look again later. Maybe it'll come back up."

I handed the phone back to him, left-handed. He took it and put it away in his pocket, still fretting about it.

"All quiet here?" he said.

"As the grave," I said.

"So it was nothing," he said. "Not something."

"I guess," I said. "I'm sorry."

"No, I appreciate your caution. Really."

"Just doing my job," I said.

"Let's go get dinner," he said.

He went back to the Cadillac and got in. I clicked the Beretta back to *safe* and slid into the Saab. He backed up and turned in the road and waited for me. I guessed he wanted to go in through the gate together, so Paulie would only have to open and close it once. We drove back in convoy, four short miles. The Saab rode badly and the headlights pointed way up at an angle and the steering felt light. There were four hundred pounds of weight in the trunk. And the corner of the headliner fell down when I hit the first bump in the road and flapped in my face the whole way back.

WE PUT THE CARS IN THE GARAGES AND BECK waited for me in the courtyard. The tide was coming in. I could hear the waves behind the walls. They were dumping huge volumes of water on the rocks. I could feel its impact through the ground. It was a definite physical sensation. Not just sound. I joined Beck and we walked back together and used the front door. The metal detector beeped twice, once for him, once for me. He handed me a set of house keys. I accepted them, like a badge of office.

Then he told me dinner would be served in thirty minutes and he invited me to eat it with the family.

I went up to Duke's room and stood at the high window. Five miles to the west, I thought I saw red taillights moving away into the distance. Three pairs of lights. Villanueva and Eliot and Duffy, I hoped, in the government Tauruses. *10-18, assignment completed.* But it was hard to be sure if they were real because of the glare from the lights on the wall. They might have been spots in my vision, from fatigue, or from the bang on the head.

I took a fast shower and stole another set of Duke's clothes. Kept my own shoes and jacket on, left my ruined coat in the closet. I didn't check for e-mail. Duffy had been too busy for messages. And at that point we were on the same page, anyway. There was nothing more she could tell me. Pretty soon I would be telling her something, just as soon as I got a chance to rip the headliner out of the Saab.

I wasted the balance of the thirty-minute lull and then walked downstairs. Found the family dining room. It was huge. There was a long rectangular table in it. It was oak, heavy, solid, not stylish. It would have seated twenty people. Beck was at the head. Elizabeth was all the way at the other end. Richard was alone on the far side. The place set for me put me directly opposite him, with my back to the door. I thought about asking him to swap with me. I don't like sitting with my back to a door. But I decided against it and just sat down.

Paulie wasn't there. Clearly he hadn't been invited. The maid wasn't there either, of course. The cook was having to do all the scut work, and she didn't look very pleased about it. But she had done a good job with the food. We started with French onion soup. It was pretty authentic. My mother wouldn't have approved, but there are always twenty million individual Frenchwomen who think they alone possess the perfect recipe.

"Tell us about your service career," Beck said to me, like he wanted to make conversation. He wasn't going to talk about business. That was clear. Not in front of the family. I guessed maybe Elizabeth knew more than was good for her, but Richard seemed fairly oblivious. Or maybe he was just blocking it out. What had he said? Bad things don't happen unless you choose to recall them?

"Nothing much to tell," I said. I didn't want to talk about it. Bad things had happened, and I didn't choose to recall them.

"There must be something," Elizabeth said.

They were all three looking at me, so I shrugged and gave them a story about checking a Pentagon budget and seeing eight-thousand-dollar charges for maintenance tools called RTAFAs. I told them I was bored enough to be curious and had made a couple of calls and been told the acronym stood for *rotational torque-adjustable fastener applicators.* I told them I had tracked one down and found a three-dollar screwdriver. That had led to three-thousand-dollar hammers, thousand-dollar toilet seats, the whole nine yards. It's a good story. It's the sort of thing that suits any audience. Most people respond to the audacity and anti-government types get to seethe. But it isn't true. It happened, I guess, but not to me. It was a different department entirely.

"Have you killed people?" Richard asked.

Four in the last three days, I thought.

"Don't ask questions like that," Elizabeth said.

"The soup is good," Beck said. "Maybe not enough cheese."

"Dad," Richard said.

"What?"

"You need to think about your arteries. They're going to get all clogged up."

"They're my arteries."

"And you're my dad."

They glanced at each other. They both smiled shy smiles. Father and son, best buddies. *Ambivalence.* It was all set to be a long meal. Elizabeth changed the subject away from cholesterol. She started talking about the Portland Museum of Art instead. She said it had an I. M. Pei building and a collection of American and Impressionist masters. I couldn't tell if she was trying to educate me or to tempt Richard to get out of the house and do something. I tuned her out. I wanted to get to the Saab. But I couldn't, right then. So I tried to predict exactly what I would find there. Like a game. I heard Leon Garber in my head: *Think about everything you've seen and everything you've heard. Work the clues.* I hadn't heard much. But I had seen a lot of things. I guessed they were all clues, of a sort. The dining table, for instance. The whole house, and everything in it. The cars. The Saab was a piece of junk. The Cadillac and the Lincolns were nice automobiles, but they weren't Rolls-Royces and Bentleys. The furniture was all old and dull and solid. Not cheap, but then, it didn't represent current expenditure anyway. It was all paid for long ago. What had Eliot said in Boston? About the LA gangbanger? *His profits must run to millions of dollars a week. He lives like an emperor.* Beck was supposed to be a couple of rungs up the ladder. But Beck didn't live like an emperor. Why not? Because he was a cautious Yankee, unimpressed by consumer baubles?

"Look," he said.

I surfaced and saw him holding his cell phone out to me. I took it from him and looked at the screen. The signal strength was back up to four bars.

"Microwaves," I said. "Maybe they ramp up slowly."

Then I looked again. No envelopes, no reel-to-reel tapes. No voice-mail messages. But it was a tiny phone and I have big thumbs and I accidentally touched the up-down arrow key underneath the screen. The display instantly changed to a list of names. His virtual phone book, I guessed. The screen was so small it could show only three contacts at a time. At the top was *house*. Then came *gate*. Third on the list was *Xavier.* I stared at it so hard the room went silent around me and blood roared in my ears.

"The soup was very good," Richard said.

I handed the phone back to Beck. The cook reached across in front of me and took my bowl away.

THE FIRST TIME I EVER HEARD THE NAME *XAVIER* was the sixth time I ever saw Dominique Kohl. It was seventeen days after we danced in the Baltimore bar. The weather had broken. The temperature had plummeted and the skies were gray and miserable. She was in full dress uniform. For a moment I thought I must have scheduled a performance review and forgotten all about it. But then, I had a company clerk to remind me about stuff like that, and he hadn't mentioned anything.

"You're going to hate this," Kohl said.

"Why? You got promoted and you're shipping out?"

She smiled at that. I realized it had come out as more of a personal compliment than I should have risked.

"I found the bad guy," she said.

"How?"

"Exemplary application of relevant skills," she said.

I looked at her. "Did we schedule a performance review?"

"No, but I think we should."

"Why?"

"Because I found the bad guy. And I think performance reviews always go better just after a big break in a case."

"You're still working with Frasconi, right?"

"We're partners," she said, which wasn't strictly an answer to the question.

"Is he helping?"

She made a face. "Permission to speak freely?"

I nodded.

"He's a waste of good food," she said.

I nodded again. That was my impression, too. Lieutenant Anthony Frasconi was solid, but he wasn't the crispest shirt in the closet.

"He's a nice man," she said. "I mean, don't get me wrong."

"But you're doing all the work," I said.

She nodded. She was holding the original file, the one that I had given her just after I found out she wasn't a big ugly guy from Texas or Minnesota. It was bulging with her notes.

"*You* helped, though," she said. "You were right. The document in question is in the newspaper. Gorowski dumps the whole newspaper in a trash can at the parking lot exit. Same can, two Sundays in a row."

"And?"

"And two Sundays in a row the same guy fishes it out again."

I paused. It was a smart plan, except that the idea of fishing around in a garbage can gave it a certain vulnerability. A certain lack of plausibility. The garbage can thing is hard to do, unless you're willing to go the whole way and dress up like a homeless person. And that's hard to do in itself, if you want to be really convincing. Homeless people walk miles, spend all day, check every can along their route. To imitate their behavior plausibly takes infinite time and care.

"What kind of a guy?" I said.

"I know what you're thinking," she said. "Who roots around in trash cans except street people, right?"

"So who does?"

"Imagine a typical Sunday," she said. "A lazy day, you're strolling, maybe the person you're meeting is a little late, maybe the impulse to go out for a walk has turned out to be a little boring. But the sun is shining, and there's a bench to sit on, and you know the Sunday papers are always fat and interesting. But you don't happen to have one with you."

"OK," I said. "I'm imagining."

"Have you noticed how a used newspaper kind of becomes community property? Seen what they do on a train, for instance? Or a subway? A guy reads his paper, leaves it on the seat when he gets out, another guy picks it up right away? He'd rather die than pick up half a candy bar, but he'll pick up a used newspaper with no problem at all?"

"OK," I said.

"Our guy is about forty," she said. "Tall, maybe six-one, trim, maybe one-ninety, short black hair going gray, fairly upmarket. He wears good clothes, chinos, golf shirts, and he kind of saunters through the lot to the can."

"Saunters?"

"It's a word," she said. "Like he's strolling, lost in thought, not a care in the world. Like maybe he's coming back from Sunday brunch. Then he notices the newspaper sitting in the top of the can, and he picks it up and checks the headlines for a moment, and he kind of tilts his head a little and he puts the paper under his arm like he'll read some more of it later and he strolls on."

"Saunters on," I said.

"It's incredibly natural," she said. "I was right there

watching it happen and I almost discounted it. It's almost subliminal."

I thought about it. She was right. She was a good student of human behavior. Which made her a good cop. If I ever did actually get around to a performance review, she was going to score off the charts.

"Something else you speculated about," she said. "He saunters on out to the marina and gets on a boat."

"He lives on it?"

"I don't think so," she said. "I mean, it's got bunks and all, but I think it's a hobby boat."

"How do you know it's got bunks?"

"I've been aboard," she said.

"When?"

"The second Sunday," she said. "Don't forget, all I'd seen up to that point was the business with the newspaper. I still hadn't positively identified the document. But he went out on another boat with some other guys, so I checked it out."

"How?"

"Exemplary application of relevant skills," she said. "I wore a bikini."

"Wearing a bikini is a skill?" I said. Then I looked away. In her case, it would be more like world-class performance art.

"It was still hot then," she said. "I blended in with the other yacht bunnies. I strolled out, walked up his little gangplank. Nobody noticed. I picked the lock on the hatch and searched for an hour."

I had to ask.

"How did you conceal lock picks in a bikini?" I said.

"I was wearing shoes," she said.

"Did you find the blueprint?"

"I found all of them."

"Did the boat have a name?"

She nodded. "I traced it. There's a yacht registry for all that stuff."

"So who's the guy?"

"This is the part you're going to hate," she said. "He's a senior Military Intelligence officer. A lieutenant colonel, a Middle East specialist. They just gave him a medal for something he did in the Gulf."

"Shit," I said. "But there might be an innocent explanation."

"There might," she said. "But I doubt it. I just met with Gorowski an hour ago."

"OK," I said. That explained the dress greens. Much more intimidating than wearing a bikini, I guessed. "And?"

"And I made him explain his end of the deal. His little girls are twelve months and two. The two-year-old disappeared for a day, two months ago. She won't talk about what happened to her while she was gone. She just cries a lot. A week later our friend from Military Intelligence showed up. Suggested that the kid's absence could last a lot longer than a day, if daddy didn't play ball. I don't see any innocent explanation for that kind of stuff."

"No," I said. "Nor do I. Who is the guy?"

"His name is Francis Xavier Quinn," she said.

THE COOK BROUGHT THE NEXT COURSE, WHICH was some kind of a rib roast, but I didn't really notice it because I was still thinking about Francis Xavier Quinn. Clearly he had come out of the California hospital and left the *Quinn* part of his name behind him in the trash with his used gowns and his surgical dressings and his *John Doe* wrist bands. He had just walked away and stepped straight into a new identity, ready made. An identity that he felt comfortable with, one that he would always remember deep down at the primeval level he knew hidden people had to operate on. No longer United States Army Lieutenant Colonel Quinn, F.X., Military Intelligence. From that point on, he was just plain Frank Xavier, anonymous citizen.

"Rare or well?" Beck asked me.

He was carving the roast with one of the black-handled knives from the kitchen. They had been stored in a knife block and I had thought about using one of them to kill him with. The one he was using right then would have been a good choice. It was about ten inches long, and it was razor sharp, judging by how well the meat was slicing. Unless the meat happened to be unbelievably tender.

"Rare," I said. "Thank you."

He carved me two slices and I regretted it instantly. My mind flashed back seven hours to the body bag. I had pulled the zipper down and seen another knife's work. The image was so vivid I could still feel the cold metal tag between my fingers. Then I flashed back ten whole years, right back to the beginning with Quinn, and the loop was complete.

"Horseradish?" Elizabeth said.

I paused. Then I took a spoonful. The old army rule was *Eat every time you can, sleep every time you can,* because you didn't know when you were going to get another chance to do either. So I shut Quinn out of my mind and helped myself to vegetables and started eating. Restarted thinking. *Everything I'd heard, everything I'd seen.* I kept coming back to the Baltimore marina in the bright sunlight, and to the envelope and the newspaper. *Not this, but that.* And to the thing Duffy had said to me: *You haven't found anything useful. Not a thing. No evidence at all.*

"Have you read Pasternak?" Elizabeth asked me.

"What do you think of Edward Hopper?" Richard asked.

"You think the M16 should be replaced?" Beck said.

I surfaced again. They were all looking at me. It was like they were starved for conversation. Like they were all lonely. I listened to the waves crashing around three sides of the house and understood how they could feel that way. They were very isolated. But that was their choice. I like isolation. I can go three weeks without saying a word.

"I saw *Doctor Zhivago* at the movies," I said. "I like the Hopper painting with the people in the diner at night."

"Nighthawks," Richard said.

I nodded. "I like the guy on the left, all alone."

"Remember the name of the diner?"

"Phillies," I said. "And I think the M16 is a fine assault rifle."

"Really?" Beck said.

"It does what an assault rifle is supposed to do," I said. "You can't ask for much more than that."

"Hopper was a genius," Richard said.

"Pasternak was a genius," Elizabeth said. "Unfortunately the movie trivialized him. And he hasn't been well translated. Solzhenitsyn is overrated by comparison."

"I guess the M16 is an *improved* rifle," Beck said.

"Edward Hopper is like Raymond Chandler," Richard said. "He captured a particular time and place. Of course, Chandler was a genius, too. Way better than Hammett."

"Like Pasternak is better than Solzhenitsyn?" his mother said.

They went on like that for a good long time. Day fourteen, a Friday, nearly over, eating a beef dinner with three doomed people, talking about books and pictures and rifles. *Not this, but that.* I tuned them out again and trawled back ten years and listened to Sergeant First Class Dominique Kohl instead.

"HE'S A REAL PENTAGON INSIDER," SHE SAID
to me, the seventh time we met. "Lives close by in Virginia. That's why he keeps his boat up in Baltimore, I guess."

"How old is he?" I asked.

"Forty," she said.

"Have you seen his full record?"

She shook her head. "Most of it is classified."

I nodded. Tried to put the chronology together. A forty-year-old would have been eligible for the last two years of the Vietnam draft, at the age of eighteen or nineteen. But a guy who wound up as an intel light colonel before the age of forty had almost certainly been a college graduate, maybe even a Ph.D., which would have gotten him a deferment. So he probably didn't go to Indochina, which in the normal way of things would have slowed his promotion. No bloody wars, no dread diseases. But his promotion hadn't been slow, because he was a light colonel before the age of forty.

"I know what you're thinking," Kohl said. "How come he's already two whole pay grades above you?"

"Actually I was thinking about you in a bikini."

She shook her head. "No you weren't."

"He's older than me."

"He went up like a bottle rocket."

"Maybe he's smarter than me," I said.

"Almost certainly," she said. "But even so, he's gone real far, real fast."

I nodded.

"Great," I said. "So now we're messing with a big star from the intel community."

"He's got lots of contact with foreigners," she said. "I've seen him with all kinds of people. Israelis, Lebanese, Iraqis, Syrians."

"He's supposed to," I said. "He's a Middle East specialist."

"He comes from California," she said. "His dad was a railroad worker. His mom stayed at home. They lived in a small house in the north of the state. He inherited it, and it's his only asset. And we can assume he's been on military pay since college."

"OK," I said.

"He's a poor boy, Reacher," she said. "So how come he rents a big house in MacLean, Virginia? How come he owns a yacht?"

"Is it a yacht?"

"It's a big sailboat with bedrooms. That's a yacht, right?"

"POV?"

"A brand-new Lexus."

I said nothing.

"Why don't his own people ask these kind of questions?" she said.

"They never do," I said. "Haven't you noticed that? Something can be plain as day and it passes them by."

"I really don't understand how that happens," she said.

I shrugged.

"They're human," I said. "We should cut them some slack. Preconceptions get in the way. They ask themselves how good he is, not how bad he is."

She nodded. "Like I spent two days watching the envelope, not the newspaper. Preconceptions."

"But they should know better."

"I guess."

"Military Intelligence," I said.

"The world's biggest oxymoron," she replied, in the familiar old ritual. "Like safe danger."

"Like dry water," I said.

"DID YOU ENJOY IT?" ELIZABETH BECK ASKED me, ten years later.

I didn't answer. *Preconceptions get in the way.*

"Did you enjoy it?" she asked again.

I looked straight at her. *Preconceptions.*

"Sorry?" I said. *Everything I had heard.*

"Dinner," she said. "Did you enjoy it?"

I looked down. My plate was completely empty.

"It was fabulous," I said. *Everything I had seen.*

"Really?"

"No question," I said. *You haven't found anything useful.*

"I'm glad," she said.

"Forget Hopper and Pasternak," I said. "And Raymond Chandler. Your cook is a genius."

"You feeling OK?" Beck said. He had left half his meat on his plate.

"Terrific," I said. *Not a thing.*

"You sure?"

I paused. *No evidence at all.*

"Yes, I really mean it," I said.

And I really did mean it. *Because I knew what was in the Saab.* I knew for sure. No doubt about it. So I felt terrific. But I felt a little ashamed, too. Because I had been very, very slow. Painfully slow. Disgracefully slow. It had taken me eighty-six hours. More than three and a half days. I had been every bit as dumb as Quinn's old unit. *Something can be plain as day and it passes them by.* I turned my head and looked straight at Beck like I was seeing him for the very first time.

CHAPTER 11

I KNEW, BUT I CALMED DOWN FAST DURING dessert and coffee. And I gave up on feeling terrific. Gave up on feeling ashamed, too. Those emotions were crowded out. I started to feel a little concerned instead. Because I started to see the exact dimensions of the tactical problem. And they were huge. They were going to force a whole new definition of working alone and undercover.

Dinner ended and everybody scraped their chairs back and stood up. I stayed in the dining room. I left the Saab's headliner undisturbed. I was in no hurry. I could get to it later. There was no point risking trouble to confirm something I already knew. I helped the cook clean up instead. It seemed polite. Maybe it was even expected. The Becks went off somewhere and I carried dishes through to the kitchen. The mechanic was in there, eating a bigger portion of beef than I had gotten. I looked at him and started to feel a little ashamed again. I hadn't paid him any attention at all. Hadn't thought much about him. I had never even asked myself what he was for. But now I knew.

I loaded the dishes into the machine. The cook did economical things with the leftovers and wiped off the counters and within about twenty minutes we had everything squared away. Then she told me she was headed for bed so I said good night to her and went out the back door and walked across the rocks. I wanted to look at the sea. Wanted to gauge the tide. I had no experience with the ocean. I knew the tides came in and out maybe twice a day. I didn't know when or why. Something to do with the moon's gravity, maybe. Possibly it turned the Atlantic into a giant bathtub sloshing east and west between Europe and America. Maybe when it was low tide in Portugal it was high tide in Maine, and vice versa. I had no idea. Right then the tide looked to be changing from high to low. From in to out. I watched the waves for five more minutes and then headed back to the kitchen. The mechanic had left. I used the bunch of keys Beck had given me to lock the inner door. I left the outer door open. Then I walked through the hallway and checked the front. I guessed I was supposed to do stuff like that now. It was locked and chained. The house was quiet. So I went upstairs to Duke's room and started planning the endgame.

THERE WAS A MESSAGE FROM DUFFY WAITING for me in my shoe. It said: *You OK?* I replied: *Sincere thanks for the phones. You saved my ass.*

She came back with: *Mine too. Equal element of self-interest.*

I didn't reply to that. I couldn't think of anything to say. I just sat there in the silence. She had won a minor postponement, but that was all. Her ass was toast, whatever happened next. Nothing I could do about that.

Then she sent: *Have searched all files and cannot repeat cannot find authorization for 2nd agent.*

I sent: *I know.*

She came back with just two characters: *??*

I sent: *We need to meet. I will either call or just show up. Stand by.*

Then I shut down the power and nailed the device back into my heel and wondered briefly whether I would ever take it out again. I checked my watch. It was nearly midnight. Day fourteen, a Friday, was nearly over. Day fifteen, a Saturday, was about to begin. Two weeks to the day since I had barged through the crowd outside Symphony Hall in Boston, on my way to a bar I never reached.

I LAY DOWN ON THE BED, FULLY DRESSED. I FIGured the next twenty-four or forty-eight hours were going to be crucial, and I wanted to spend five of the first six of them fast asleep. In my experience tiredness causes more foul-ups than carelessness or stupidity put together. Probably because tiredness itself creates carelessness and stupidity. So I got comfortable and closed my eyes. Set the alarm in my head for two o'clock in the morning. It worked, like it always does. I woke up after a two-hour nap, feeling OK.

I rolled off the bed and crept downstairs. Went through the hallway and the kitchen and unlocked the back door. I left all my metal stuff on the table. I didn't want the detector to make a noise. I stepped outside. It was very dark. There was no moon. No stars. The sea was loud. The air was cold. There was a breeze. It smelled of dampness. I walked around to the fourth garage and opened the doors. The Saab was still there, undisturbed. I eased the hatch open and pulled out my bundle. Carried it around and stowed it in its dip. Then I went back for the first bodyguard. He had been dead for several hours and the low temperature was bringing rigor on early. He was pretty stiff. I hauled him out and jacked him up on my shoulder. It was like carrying a two-hundred-pound tree trunk. His arms stuck out like branches.

I carried him to the V-shaped cleft that Harley had shown me. Laid him down next to it and started counting waves. Waited for the seventh. It rolled in and just before it got to me I nudged the body into the cleft. The water came in under it and pushed it right back up at me. It was like the guy was trying to grab me with his rigid arms and take me with him. Or like he wanted to kiss me good-bye. He floated there for a second quite lazily and then the wave receded and the cleft drained and he was gone.

It worked the same way for the second guy. The ocean took him away to join his buddy, and the maid. I squatted there for a moment, feeling the breeze on my face, listening to the tireless tide. Then I went back and closed up the Saab's hatch and slid into the driver's seat. Finished the job on the headliner and reached back and pulled out the maid's notes. There were eight legal-size pages of them. I read them all in the dim glow from the dome light. They were full of specifics. They had plenty of fine detail. But in general they didn't tell me anything I didn't already know. I checked them twice and when I was finished I butted them into a neat stack and carried them back to the tip of the point. Sat down on a rock and folded each page into a paper boat. Somebody had showed me how, when I was a kid. Maybe it had been my dad. I couldn't remember. Maybe it had been my brother. I launched the eight little boats on the receding tide one after the other and watched them sail and bob away into the pitch darkness in the east.

Then I went back and spent some time fixing the headliner. I got it looking pretty good. I closed up the garage. I figured I would be gone before anybody opened it up again and noticed the damage on the car. I headed back to the house. Reloaded my pockets and relocked the door and crept back upstairs. Stripped to my shorts and slid into bed. I wanted to get three more hours. So I reset the alarm in my head and hauled the sheet and the blanket up around me and pressed a dip into the pillow and closed my eyes again. Tried to sleep. But I couldn't. It wouldn't come. Dominique Kohl came instead. She came straight at me out of the darkness, like I knew she would.

The eighth time we met we had tactical problems to discuss. Taking down an intel officer was a can of worms. Obviously MPs deal exclusively with military people gone bad, so acting against one of our own was not a novelty. But the intel community was a case apart. Those guys were separate and secretive and they tried very hard to be accountable to nobody. They were tough to get at. Generally they closed ranks faster than the best drill squad you ever saw. So Kohl and I had a lot to talk about. I didn't want to have the meeting in my office. There was no visitor's chair. I didn't want her standing up the whole time. So we went back to the bar in town. It seemed like an appropriate location. The whole thing was getting so heavy we were ready to feel a little paranoid about it. Going off-base seemed like a smart thing to do. And I liked the idea of discussing intel matters like a couple of regular spies, in a dark little booth at the back of a tavern. I think Kohl did, too. She showed up in civilian clothes. Not a dress, but jeans and a white T-shirt with a leather jacket over it. I was in fatigues. I didn't have any civilian clothes. The weather was cold by then. I ordered coffee. She got tea. We wanted to keep our heads clear.

"I'm glad we used the real blueprints now," she said.

I nodded.

"Good instinct," I said. As far as evidence went we needed to slam-dunk the whole thing. For Quinn to be in possession of the real blueprints would go a long way. Anything less than that, he could start spinning stories about test procedures, war games, exercises, entrapment schemes of his own.

"It's the Syrians," she said. "And they're paying in advance. On an installment plan."

"How?"

"Briefcase exchange," she said. "He meets with an attaché from the Syrian Embassy. They go to a café in Georgetown. They both carry those fancy aluminum briefcases, identical."

"Halliburton," I said.

She nodded. "They put them side by side under the table and he picks up the Syrian guy's when he leaves."

"He's going to say the Syrian is a legit contact. He's going to say the guy is passing *him* stuff."

"So we say, OK, show us the stuff."

"He'll say he can't, because it's classified."

Kohl said nothing. I smiled.

"He'll give us a big song and dance," I said. "He'll put his hand on our shoulders and look into our eyes and say, *Hey, trust me on this, folks, national security is involved*."

"Have you dealt with these guys before?"

"Once," I said.

"Did you win?"

I nodded. "They're generally full of shit. My brother was MI for a time. Now he works for Treasury. But he told me all about them. They think they're smart, whereas they're really the same as anybody else."

"So what do we do?"

"We'll have to recruit the Syrian."

"Then we can't bust him."

"You wanted two-for-one?" I said. "Can't have it. The Syrian is only doing his job. Can't fault him for that. Quinn is the bad guy here."

She was quiet for a moment, a little disappointed. Then she shrugged.

"OK," she said. "But how do we do it? The Syrian will just walk away from us. He's an embassy attaché. He's got diplomatic immunity."

I smiled again. "Diplomatic immunity is just a sheet of paper from the State Department. The way I did it before was I got hold of the guy and told him to hold a sheet of paper up in front of his gut. Then I pulled my pistol out and asked him if he figured the paper was going to stop a bullet. He said I would get into trouble. I told him however much trouble I got into wasn't going to affect how slowly he bled to death."

"And he saw it your way?"

I nodded. "Played ball like Mickey Mantle."

She went quiet again. Then she asked me the first of two questions that much later I wished I had answered differently.

"Can we see each other socially?" she said.

It was a private booth in a dark bar. She was cute as hell, and she was sitting there right next to me. I was a young man back then, and I thought I had all the time in the world.

"You asking me on a date?" I said.

"Yes," she said.

I said nothing.

"We've come a long way, baby," she said. Then she added, "Women, I mean," just in case I wasn't up-to-date with current cigarette advertising.

I said nothing.

"I know what I want," she said.

I nodded. I believed her. And I believed in equality. I believed in it big time. Not long before that I had met a woman Air Force colonel who captained a B52 bomber and cruised the night skies with more explosive power aboard her single plane than all the bombs ever dropped in the whole of human history put together. I figured if she could be trusted with enough power to explode the planet, then Sergeant First Class Dominique Kohl could be trusted to figure out who she wanted to date.

"So?" she said.

Questions I wished I had answered differently.

"No," I said.

"Why not?"

"Unprofessional," I said. "You shouldn't do it."

"Why not?"

"Because it'll put an asterisk next to your career," I said. "Because you're a talented person who can't get any higher than sergeant major without going to officer candidate school, so you'll go there, and you'll ace it, and you'll be a lieutenant colonel within ten years, because you deserve it, but everybody will be saying that you got it because you dated your captain way back when."

She said nothing. Just called the waitress over and ordered us two beers. The room was getting hotter as it got more crowded. I took my jacket off, she took her jacket off. I was wearing an olive-drab T-shirt that had gotten small and thin and faded from being washed a thousand times. Her T-shirt was a boutique item. It was scooped a little lower at the neck than most T-shirts, and the sleeves were cut away at an angle so they rode up on the small deltoid muscles at the top of her arms. The fabric was snow white against her skin. And it was slightly translucent. I could see that she was wearing nothing underneath it.

"Military life is full of sacrifices," I said, more to myself than to her.

"I'll get over it," she said.

Then she asked me the second question I wish I had answered differently.

"Will you let me make the arrest?" she said.

TEN YEARS LATER I WOKE UP ALONE IN DUKE'S bed at six o'clock in the morning. His room was at the front of the house, so I had no view of the sea. I was looking west, at America. There was no morning sun. No long dawn shadows. Just dull gray light on the driveway, and the wall, and the granite landscape beyond. The wind was blowing in off the sea. I could see trees moving. I imagined black storm clouds behind me, way out over the Atlantic, moving fast toward the shore. I imagined sea birds fighting the turbulent air with their feathers whipped and ruffled by the gale. Day fifteen, starting out gray and cold and inhospitable, and likely to get worse.

I showered, but I didn't shave. I dressed in more of Duke's black denim and laced my shoes and carried my jacket and my coat over my arm. Walked quietly down to the kitchen. The cook had already made coffee. She gave me a cup and I took it and sat at the table. She lifted a loaf of bread out of the freezer and put it in the microwave. I figured I would need to evacuate her, at some point before things turned unpleasant. And Elizabeth, and Richard. The mechanic and Beck himself could stay to face the music.

I could hear the sea from the kitchen, loud and clear. The waves crashed in and the relentless undertow sucked back out. Pools filled and drained, the gravel rattled across the rocks. The wind moaned softly through the cracks in the outer porch door. I heard frantic cries from the gulls. I listened to them and sipped my coffee and waited.

Richard came down ten minutes after me. His hair was all over the place and I could see his missing ear. He took coffee and sat down across from me. His ambivalence was back. I could see him facing up to no more college and the rest of his life hidden away with his folks. I figured if his mother got away without an indictment they could start over somewhere else. Depending on how resilient he was, he could get back to school without missing much more than a week of the semester. If he wanted to. Unless it was an expensive school, which I guessed it was. They were going to have money problems. They were going to walk away with nothing more than they stood up in. If they walked away at all.

The cook went out to set the dining room up for breakfast. Richard watched her go and I watched him and saw his ear again and a piece of the puzzle clicked into place.

"Five years ago," I said. "The kidnap."

He kept his composure. Just looked down at the table and then looked up at me and combed his hair over his scar with his fingers.

"Do you know what your dad is really into?" I asked.

He nodded. Said nothing.

"Not just rugs, right?" I said.

"No," he said. "Not just rugs."

"How do you feel about that?"

"There are worse things," he said.

"Want to tell me what happened five years ago?" I said.

He shook his head. Looked away.

"No," he said. "I don't."

"I knew a guy called Gorowski," I said. "His two-year-old daughter was abducted. Just for a day. How long were you gone for?"

"Eight days," he said.

"Gorowski fell right into line," I said. "One day was enough for him."

Richard said nothing.

"Your dad isn't the boss here," I said, like a statement.

Richard said nothing.

"He fell into line five years ago," I said. "After you had been gone eight days. That's the way I figure it."

Richard was silent. I thought about Gorowski's daughter. She was twelve years old now. She probably had the Internet and a CD player and a phone in her room. Posters on her walls. And a tiny dim ache in her mind about something that had happened way in the past. Like the itch you get from a long-healed bone.

"I don't need details," I said. "I just want you to say his name."

"Whose name?"

"The guy who took you away for eight days."

Richard just shook his head.

"I heard the name *Xavier*," I said. "Someone mentioned it."

Richard looked away and his left hand went straight to the side of his head, which was all the confirmation I needed.

"I was raped," he said.

I listened to the sea, pounding on the rocks.

"By Xavier?"

He shook his head again.

"By Paulie," he said. "He was just out of prison. He still had a taste for that kind of thing."

I was quiet for a long moment.

"Does your father know?"

"No," he said.

"Your mother?"

"No."

I didn't know what to say. Richard said nothing more. We sat there in silence. Then the cook came back and fired up the stove. She put fat in a skillet and started heating it. The smell made me sick to my stomach.

"Let's go for a walk," I said.

Richard followed me outside to the rocks. The air was

salty and fresh and bitter cold. The light was gray. The wind was strong. It was blowing straight in our faces. Richard's hair strung way out behind him, almost horizontal. The spray was smashing twenty feet in the air and foamy drops of water were whipping toward us like bullets.

"Every silver lining has a cloud," I said. I had to talk loud, just to be heard over the wind and the surf. "Maybe one day Xavier and Paulie will get what's coming to them, but your dad will go to prison in the process."

Richard nodded. There were tears in his eyes. Maybe they were from the cold wind. Maybe they weren't.

"He deserves to," he said.

Very loyal, his father had said. *Best buddies.*

"I was gone eight days," Richard said. "One should have been enough. Like with the other guy you mentioned."

"Gorowski?"

"Whoever. With the two-year-old girl. You think she was raped?"

"I sincerely hope not."

"Me too."

"Can you drive?" I said.

"Yes," he said.

"You might need to get out of here," I said. "Soon. You and your mother and the cook. So you need to be ready. For if and when I tell you to go."

"Who are you?"

"I'm a guy paid to protect your father. From his so-called friends, as much as his enemies."

"Paulie won't let us through the gate."

"He'll be gone soon."

He shook his head.

"Paulie will kill you," he said. "You have no idea. You can't deal with Paulie, whoever you are. Nobody can."

"I dealt with those guys outside the college."

He shook his head again. His hair streamed in the wind. It reminded me of the maid's hair, under the water.

"That was phony," he said. "My mom and I discussed it. It was a setup."

I was quiet for a second. *Did I trust him yet?*

"No, it was for real," I said. *No, I didn't trust him yet.*

"It's a small community," he said. "They have about five cops. I never saw that guy before in my life."

I said nothing.

"I never saw those college cops either," he said. "And I was there nearly three full years."

I said nothing. *Mistakes, coming back to haunt me.*

"So why did you quit school?" I said. "If it was a setup?"

He didn't answer.

"And how come Duke and I were ambushed?"

He didn't answer.

"So what was it?" I said. "A setup or for real?"

He shrugged. "I don't know."

"You saw me shoot them all," I said.

He said nothing. I looked away. The seventh wave came rolling in. It crested forty yards out and hit the rocks faster than a man can run. The ground shuddered and spray burst upward like a star shell.

"Did either of you discuss this with your father?" I said.

"I didn't," he said. "And I'm not going to. I don't know about my mom."

And I don't know about you, I thought. Ambivalence works both ways. You blow hot, then you blow cold. The thought of his father in a prison cell might look pretty good to him right now. Later, it might look different. When push came to shove, this guy was capable of swinging either way.

"I saved your ass," I said. "I don't like it that you're pretending I didn't."

"Whatever," he said. "There's nothing you can do anyway. This is going to be a busy weekend. You've got the shipment to deal with. And after that you'll be one of them anyway."

"So help me out," I said.

"I won't double-cross my dad," he said.

Very loyal. Best buddies.

"You don't have to," I said.

"So how can I help you?"

"Just tell him you want me here. Tell him you shouldn't be alone right now. He listens to you, about stuff like that."

He didn't reply. Just walked away from me and headed back to the kitchen. He went straight through to the hallway. I guessed he was going to eat breakfast in the dining room. I stayed in the kitchen. The cook had set my place at the deal table. I wasn't hungry, but I forced myself to eat. Tiredness and hunger are bad enemies. I had slept, and now I was going to eat. I didn't want to wind up weak and light-headed at the wrong moment. I had toast, and another cup of coffee. Then I got more into it and had eggs and bacon. I was on my third cup of coffee when Beck came in to find me. He was wearing Saturday clothes. Blue jeans and a red flannel shirt.

"We're going to Portland," he said. "To the warehouse. Right now."

He went back out to the hallway. I guessed he would wait at the front. And I guessed Richard hadn't talked to him. Either he hadn't gotten a chance, or he hadn't wanted to. I wiped my mouth with the back of my hand. Checked my pockets to make sure the Beretta was safely stowed and the keys were there. Then I walked out and fetched the car. Drove it around to the front. Beck was waiting there for me. He had put a canvas jacket over his shirt. He looked like a regular Maine guy heading out to split logs or tap his maple trees for syrup. But he wasn't.

Paulie was about ready with the gate so I had to slow but I didn't have to stop. I glanced at him as I passed. I figured he would die today. Or tomorrow. Or I would. I left him behind and gunned the big car along the familiar road. After a mile I passed the spot where Villanueva had parked. Four miles after that I rounded the narrow curve where I had trapped the bodyguards. Beck didn't speak. He had his knees apart with his hands held down between them. He was leaning forward in his seat. His head was down, but his eyes were up. He was staring straight ahead through the windshield. He was nervous.

"We never had our talk," I said. "About the background information."

"Later," he said.

I passed Route One and used I-95 instead. Headed north for the city. The sky stayed gray. The wind was strong enough to push the car a little off line. I turned onto I-295 and passed by the airport. It was on my left, beyond the tongue of water. On my right was the back of the strip mall where the maid had been captured, and the back of the new business park where I figured she had died. I kept on going straight and threaded my way into the harbor area. I passed the lot where Beck parked his trucks. One minute later we arrived at his warehouse.

It was surrounded by vehicles. There were five of them parked head-in against the walls, like airplanes at a terminal. Like animals at a trough. Like suckerfish on a corpse. There were two black Lincoln Town Cars and two blue Chevy Suburbans and a gray Mercury Grand Marquis. One of the Lincolns was the car I had been in when Harley drove me out to pick up the Saab. After we put the maid into the sea. I looked for enough space to park the Cadillac.

"Just let me out here," Beck said.

I eased to a stop. "And?"

"Head back to the house," he said. "Take care of my family."

I nodded. So maybe Richard had talked to him, after all. Maybe his ambivalence was swinging my way, just temporarily.

"OK," I said. "Whatever you need. You want me to pick you up again later?"

He shook his head.

"I'm sure I'll get a ride back," he said.

He slid out and headed for the weathered gray door. I took my foot off the brake and looped around the warehouse and rolled back south.

I USED ROUTE ONE INSTEAD OF I-295 AND DROVE straight to the new business park. Pulled in and cruised through the network of brand-new roads. There were maybe three dozen identical metal buildings. They were very plain. It wasn't the kind of place that depends on attracting casual passersby. Foot-traffic wasn't important. There were no retail places. No gaudy come-ons. No big billboards. Just discreet unit numbers with business names printed small next to them. There were lock-and-key people, ceramic tile merchants, a couple of print shops. There was a beauty products wholesaler. Unit 26 was an electric wheelchair distributor. And next to it was Unit 27: *Xavier eXport Company*. The *X*s were much larger than the other letters. There was a main office address on the sign that didn't match the business park's location. I figured it referred to someplace in downtown

Portland. So I rolled north again and recrossed the river and did some city driving.

I came in on Route One with a park on my left. Made a right onto a street full of office buildings. They were the wrong buildings. It was the wrong street. So I quartered the business district for five long minutes until I spotted a street sign with the right name on it. Then I watched the numbers and pulled up on a fireplug outside a tower that had stainless steel letters stretched across the whole of the frontage, spelling out a name: *Missionary House.* There was a parking garage under it. I looked at the vehicle entrance and was pretty sure Susan Duffy had walked through it eleven weeks earlier, with a camera in her hand. Then I recalled a high school history lesson, somewhere hot, somewhere Spanish, a quarter-century in the past, some old guy telling us about a Spanish Jesuit called Francisco Javier. I could even remember his dates: 1506 to 1552. Francisco Javier, Spanish missionary. Francis Xavier, Missionary House. Back in Boston at the start Eliot had accused Beck of making jokes. He had been wrong. It was Quinn with the twisted sense of humor.

I MOVED OFF THE FIREPLUG AND FOUND ROUTE One again and headed south on it. I drove fast but it took me thirty whole minutes to reach the Kennebunk River. There were three Ford Tauruses parked outside the motel, all plain and identical apart from color, and even then there wasn't much variation between them. They were gray, gray blue, and blue. I put the Cadillac where I had put it before, behind the propane store. Walked back through the cold and knocked on Duffy's door. I saw the peephole black out for a second and then she opened up. We didn't hug. I saw Eliot and Villanueva in the room behind her.

"Why can't I find the second agent?" she said.

"Where did you look?"

"Everywhere," she said.

She was wearing jeans and a white Oxford shirt. Different jeans, different shirt. She must have had a large supply. She was wearing boat shoes over bare feet. She looked good, but there was worry in her eyes.

"Can I come in?" I said.

She paused a second, preoccupied. Then she moved out of the way and I followed her inside. Villanueva was in the desk chair. He had it tilted backward. I hoped the legs were strong. He wasn't a small guy. Eliot was on the end of the bed, like he had been in my room in Boston. Duffy had been sitting at the head of the bed. That was clear. The pillows were stacked vertically and the shape of her back was pressed into them.

"Where did you look?" I asked her again.

"The whole system," she said. "The whole Justice Department, front to back, which means FBI as well as DEA. And she's not there."

"Conclusion?"

"She was off the books too."

"Which begs a question," Eliot said. "Like, what the hell is going on?"

Duffy sat down at the head of the bed again and I sat down next to her. There was no other place for me to go. She wrestled a pillow out from behind her and shoved it in behind me. It was warm from her body.

"Nothing much is going on," I said. "Except all three of us started out two weeks ago just like the Keystone Cops."

"How?" Eliot said.

I made a face. "I was obsessed with Quinn, you guys were obsessed with Teresa Daniel. We were all so obsessed we went right ahead and built a house of cards."

"How?" he said again.

"My fault more than yours," I said. "Think about it from the very beginning, eleven weeks ago."

"Eleven weeks ago was nothing to do with you. You weren't involved yet."

"Tell me exactly what happened."

He shrugged. Rehearsed it in his mind. "We got word from LA that a top boy just bought himself a first-class ticket to Portland, Maine."

I nodded. "So you tracked him to his rendezvous with Beck. And took pictures of him doing what?"

"Checking samples," Duffy said. "Doing a deal."

"In a private parking garage," I said. "And as an aside, if it was private enough to get you in trouble with the Fourth Amendment, maybe you should have wondered how Beck got himself in there."

She said nothing.

"Then what?" I said.

"We looked at Beck," Eliot said. "Concluded he was a major importer and a major distributor."

"Which he most definitely is," I said. "And you put Teresa in to nail him."

"Off the books," Eliot said.

"That's a minor detail," I said.

"So what went wrong?"

"It was a house of cards," I said. "You made one tiny error of judgment at the outset. It invalidated everything that came after it."

"What was it?"

"Something that I should have seen a hell of a lot earlier than I did."

"What?"

"Just ask yourself why you can't find a computer trail for the maid."

"She was off the books. That's the only explanation."

I shook my head. "She was as legal as can be. She

was all over the damn books. I found some notes she made. There's no doubt about it."

Duffy looked straight at me. "Reacher, what exactly is going on?"

"Beck has a mechanic," I said. "Some kind of a technician. For what?"

"I don't know," she said.

"I never even asked myself," I said. "I should have. I shouldn't have needed to, actually, because I should have known before I even met the damn mechanic. But I was locked in a groove, just like you were."

"What groove?"

"Beck knew the retail on a Colt Anaconda," I said. "He knew how much it weighed. Duke had a Steyr SPP, which is a weird Austrian gun. Angel Doll had a PSM, which is a weird Russian gun. Paulie's got an NSV, probably the only one inside the United States. Beck was obsessed with the fact that we attacked with Uzis, not H and Ks. He knew enough to spec out a Beretta 92FS so it looked just like a regular military M9."

"So?"

"He's not what we thought he was."

"So what is he? You just agreed he's definitely a major importer and distributor."

"He is."

"So?"

"You looked in the wrong computer," I said. "The maid didn't work for the Justice Department. She worked for Treasury."

"Secret Service?"

I shook my head.

"ATF," I said. "The Bureau of Alcohol, Tobacco and Firearms."

The room went quiet.

"Beck isn't a drug dealer," I said. "He's a gunrunner."

THE ROOM STAYED QUIET FOR A VERY LONG time. Duffy looked at Eliot. Eliot looked back at her. Then they both looked at Villanueva. Villanueva looked at me. Then he looked out the window. I waited for the tactical problem to dawn on them. But it didn't. Not right away.

"So what was the LA guy doing?" Duffy said.

"Looking at samples," I said. "In the Cadillac's trunk. Exactly like you thought. But they were samples of the weapons Beck was dealing. He as good as told me. He said dope dealers were driven by fashion. They like new and fancy things. They change weapons all the time, always looking for the latest thing."

"He told you?"

"I wasn't really listening," I said. "I was tired. And it was all mixed in with stuff about sneakers and cars and coats and watches."

"Duke went to Treasury," she said. "After he was a cop."

I nodded. "Beck probably met him on the job. Probably bought him off."

"Where does Quinn fit in?"

"I figure he was running a rival operation," I said. "He probably always was, ever since he got out of the hospital in California. He had six months to make his plans. And guns are a much better fit with a guy like Quinn than narcotics. I figure at some point he identified Beck's operation as a takeover target. Maybe he liked the way Beck was mining the dope dealer market. Or maybe he just liked the rug side of the business. It's great cover. So he moved in. He kidnapped Richard five years ago, to get Beck's signature on the dotted line."

"Beck told you the Hartford guys were his customers," Eliot said.

"They were," I said. "But for their guns, not for their dope. That's why he was puzzled about the Uzis. He'd probably just gotten through selling them a whole bunch of H and Ks, and now they're using Uzis? He couldn't understand it. He must have thought they had switched suppliers."

"We were pretty dumb," Villanueva said.

"I was dumber than you," I said. "I was amazingly dumb. There was evidence all over the place. Beck isn't rich enough to be a dope dealer. He makes good money, for sure, but he doesn't make millions a week. He noticed the marks I scratched on the Colt cylinders. He knew the price and the weight of a laser sight to use on the Beretta he gave me. He put a couple of mint H&Ks in a bag when he needed to take care of some business down in Connecticut. Probably pulled them right out of stock. He's got a private collection of Thompson grease guns."

"What's the mechanic for?"

"He gets the guns ready for sale," I said. "That's my guess. He tweaks them, adjusts them, checks them out. Some of Beck's customers wouldn't react well to substandard merchandise."

"Not the ones we know," Duffy said.

"Beck talked about the M16 at dinner," I said. "He was conversing about an assault rifle, for God's sake. And he wanted to hear my opinion about Uzis versus H&Ks, like he was really fascinated. I thought he was just a gun nerd, you know, but it was actually professional interest. He has computer access to the Glock factory in Deutsch-Wagram in Austria."

Nobody spoke. I closed my eyes, then I opened them again.

"There was a smell in a basement room," I said. "I should have recognized it. It was the smell of gun oil on cardboard. It's what you get when you stack boxes of new weapons and leave them there for a week or so."

Nobody spoke.

"And the prices in the Bizarre Bazaar books," I said. "Low, medium, high. Low for ammunition, medium for handguns, high for long guns and exotics."

Duffy was looking at the wall. She was thinking hard.

"OK," Villanueva said. "I guess we were all a little dumb."

Duffy looked at him. Then she stared at me. The tactical problem was finally dawning on her.

"We have no jurisdiction," she said.

Nobody spoke.

"This is ATF business," she said. "Not DEA."

"It was an honest mistake," Eliot said.

She shook her head. "I don't mean *then*. I mean *now*. We can't be in there. We have to butt out, right now, immediately."

"I'm not butting out," I said.

"You have to. Because *we* have to. We have to fold our tents and leave. And you can't be in there on your own and unsupported."

A whole new definition of alone and undercover.

"I'm staying," I said.

I SEARCHED MY SOUL FOR A WHOLE YEAR AFter it happened and concluded I wouldn't have answered any differently even if she hadn't been fragrant and naked under a thin T-shirt and sitting next to me in a bar when she asked the fateful question. *Will you let me make the arrest?* I would have said yes, whatever the circumstances. For sure. Even if she had been a big ugly guy from Texas or Minnesota standing at attention in my office, I would have said yes. She had done the work. She deserved the credit. I was vaguely interested in getting ahead back then, maybe a little less so than most people, but any structure that has a ranking system tempts you to try to climb it. So I was vaguely interested. But I wasn't a guy who hijacked subordinates' achievements in order to make myself look good. I never did that. If somebody performed well, did a good job, I was always happy to stand back and let them reap the rewards. It was a principle I adhered to throughout my career. I could always console myself by basking in their reflected glow. It was my company, after all. There was a certain amount of collective recognition. Sometimes.

But anyway, I really liked the idea of an MP noncom busting an intel light colonel. Because I knew a guy like Quinn would absolutely hate it. He would see it as the ultimate indignity. A guy who bought Lexuses and sailboats and wore golf shirts didn't want to be taken down by a damn *sergeant*.

"Will you let me make the arrest?" she asked again.

"I want you to," I said.

"IT'S A PURELY LEGAL ISSUE," DUFFY SAID.

"Not to me," I said.

"We have no authority."

"I don't work for you."

"It's suicide," Eliot said.

"I survived so far."

"Only because she cut the phones."

"The phones are history," I said. "The bodyguard problem resolved itself. So I don't need backup anymore."

"Everybody needs backup. You can't go undercover without it."

"ATF backup did the maid a whole lot of good," I said.

"We lent you a car. We helped you every step of the way."

"I don't need cars anymore. Beck gave me my own set of keys. And a gun. And bullets. I'm his new right-hand man. He trusts me to protect his family."

They said nothing.

"I'm an inch away from nailing Quinn," I said. "I'm not butting out now."

They said nothing.

"And I can get Teresa Daniel back," I said.

"ATF can get Teresa Daniel back," Eliot said. "We go to ATF now, we're off the hook with our own people. The maid was theirs, not ours. No harm, no foul."

"ATF isn't up to speed," I said. "Teresa will be caught in the crossfire."

There was a long silence.

"Monday," Villanueva said. "We'll sit on it until Monday. We'll have to tell ATF by Monday at the latest."

"We should tell them right now," Eliot said.

Villanueva nodded. "But we won't. And if necessary I'll make sure that we don't. I say we give Reacher until Monday."

Eliot said nothing more. He just looked away. Duffy laid her head back on the pillow and stared up at the ceiling.

"Shit," she said.

"It'll be over by Monday," I said. "I'll bring Teresa back to you here and then you can head home and make all the calls you want."

She was quiet for a whole minute. Then she spoke.

"OK," she said. "You can go back. And you should probably go back right now. You've been gone a long time. That's suspicious in itself."

"OK," I said.

"But think first," she said. "Are you absolutely sure?"

"I'm not your responsibility," I said.

"I don't care," she said. "Just answer the question. Are you sure?"

"Yes," I said.

"Now think again. Still sure?"

"Yes," I said again.

"We'll be here," she said. "Call us if you need us."

"OK," I said.

"Still sure?"

"Yes," I said.

"So go."

She didn't get up. None of them did. I just eased myself off the bed and walked out through the silent room. I was halfway back to the Cadillac when Terry Villanueva came out after me. He waved me to wait and walked across to me. He moved stiff and slow, like the old guy he was.

"Bring me in," he said. "Any chance you get, I want to be there."

I said nothing.

"I could help you out," he said.

"You already did."

"I need to do more. For the kid."

"Duffy?"

He shook his head. "No, Teresa."

"You got a connection?"

"I got a responsibility," he said.

"How?"

"I was her mentor," he said. "It worked out that way. You know how that is?"

I nodded. I knew exactly, totally, and completely how that was.

"Teresa worked for me for a spell," he said. "I trained her. I broke her in, basically. Then she moved up. But ten weeks ago she came back to me and asked if I thought she should accept this mission. She had doubts."

"But you said yes."

He nodded. "Like a damn fool."

"Could you really have stopped her?"

"Probably. She would have listened to me if I had made a case why she shouldn't do it. She'd have made up her own mind, but she'd have listened."

"I understand," I said.

And I did, no question about it. I left him standing there in the motel lot and slid into the car and watched him watch me drive away.

I STAYED ON ROUTE ONE ALL THE WAY THROUGH Biddeford and Saco and Old Orchard Beach and then struck out east on the long lonely road out to the house. I checked my watch as I got close and figured I had been away two whole hours, of which only forty minutes were legitimate. Twenty minutes to the warehouse, twenty back. But I didn't expect to have to explain myself to anybody. Beck would never know I hadn't come straight home and the others would never know I had been supposed to. I figured I was right there in the endgame, freewheeling toward victory.

But I was wrong.

I knew it before Paulie got halfway through opening the gate. He came out of his house and stepped across to the latch. He was wearing his suit. No coat. He lifted the latch by butting it upward with his clenched fist. Everything was still normal. I had seen him open the gate a dozen times and he was doing nothing he hadn't done before. He wrapped his fists around the bars. Pulled the gate. But before he got halfway through opening it he stopped it dead. He just made enough space to squeeze his giant frame through. Then he stepped out to meet me. He walked around toward my window and when he got six feet from the car he stopped and smiled and took two guns out of his pockets. It happened in less than a second. Two pockets, two hands, two guns. They were my Colt Anacondas. The steel looked dull in the gray light. I could see they were both loaded. There were bright snub-nose copper jackets winking at me from every chamber I could see. Remington .44 Magnums, without a doubt. Full metal jacket. Eighteen bucks for a box of twenty. Plus tax. Ninety-five cents each. Twelve of them. Eleven dollars and forty cents' worth of precision ammunition, ready to go, five dollars and seventy cents in each hand. And he was holding those hands very steady. They were like rocks. The left was aimed a little ahead of the Cadillac's front tire. The right was aimed directly at my head. His fingers were tight on the triggers. The muzzles weren't moving at all. Not even a fraction. He was like a statue.

I did all the usual things. I ran all the numbers. The Cadillac was a big car with long doors but he had put himself just far enough away that I couldn't jerk my door open and hit him with it. And the car was stationary. If I hit the gas he would fire both guns instantly. The bullet from the one in his right hand might well pass behind my head but the car's front tire would roll straight into the path of the one from his left. Then I would hit the gates hard and lose momentum and with a blown front tire and maybe with damaged steering I would be a sitting duck. He would fire ten more times and even if I wasn't killed outright I would be badly wounded and the car would be crippled. He could just step over and watch me bleed while he reloaded.

I could sneak it into reverse and howl away backward but reverse gear is pretty low on most cars and therefore I would be moving slowly. And I would be moving directly away from him in a perfectly straight line. No lateral displacement. None of the usual benefits of a moving target.

And a Remington .44 Magnum leaves a gun barrel at more than eight hundred miles an hour. No easy way to outrun one.

I could try my Beretta. It would have to be a very fast snap shot through the window glass. But the window glass on a Cadillac is pretty thick. They make it that way to keep the interior quiet. Even if I got the gun out and fired before he did, it would be pure chance if I hit him. The glass would shatter for sure, but unless I took all the time I needed to make absolutely certain the trajectory was exactly perpendicular to the window the bullet would deflect. Perhaps radically. It could miss him altogether. And even if it hit him it would be pure chance if it hurt him. I remembered kicking him in the kidney. Unless I happened to hit him in the eye or straight through the heart he would think he had been stung by a bee.

I could buzz the window down. But it was very slow. And I could predict exactly what would happen. He would straighten his arm while the glass was moving and bring the right-hand Colt within three feet of my head. Even if I got the Beretta out real fast he would still have a hell of a jump on me. The odds were not good. Not good at all. *Stay alive,* Leon Garber used to say. *Stay alive and see what the next minute brings.*

Paulie dictated the next minute.

"Put it in Park," he yelled.

I heard him clearly, even through the thick glass. I moved the gearshift into Park.

"Right hand where I can see it," he yelled.

I put my right palm up against the window, fingers extended, just like when I signaled *I see five people* to Duke.

"Open the door with your left," he yelled.

I scrabbled blindly with my left hand and pulled the door release. Pushed on the glass with my right. The door swung open. Cold air came in. I felt it around my knees.

"Both hands where I can see them," he said. He spoke quieter, now the glass wasn't between us. He brought the left-hand Colt around on me, now the car was out of gear. I looked at the twin muzzles. It was like sitting on the foredeck of a battleship looking up at a pair of naval guns. I put both hands where he could see them.

"Feet out of the car," he said.

I swiveled on my butt, slowly on the leather. Got my feet out onto the blacktop. I felt like Terry Villanueva outside the college gate, early in the morning of day eleven.

"Stand up," he said. "Step away from the car."

I levered myself upright. Stepped away from the car. He pointed both guns directly at my chest. He was four feet away from me.

"Stand very still," he said.

I stood very still.

"Richard," he called.

Richard Beck came out of the gatehouse door. He was pale. I saw Elizabeth Beck behind him in the shadows. Her blouse was open at the front. She was clutching it tight around herself. Paulie grinned at me. A sudden, lunatic grin. But the guns didn't waver. Not even a fraction. They stayed rock steady.

"You came back a little too soon," he said. "I was about to make him have sex with his mother."

"Are you out of your mind?" I said. "What the hell is going on?"

"I got a call," he said. "That's what's going on."

I should have been back an hour and twenty minutes ago.

"Beck called you?"

"Not Beck," he said. "My boss."

"Xavier?" I said.

"*Mr.* Xavier," he said.

He stared at me, like a challenge. The guns didn't move.

"I went shopping," I said. *Stay alive. See what the next minute brings.*

"I don't care what you did."

"I couldn't find what I wanted. That's why I'm late."

"We expected you to be late."

"Why?"

"We got new information."

I said nothing to that.

"Walk backward," he said. "Through the gate."

He kept both guns four feet from my chest and walked forward while I walked backward through the gate. He matched me pace for pace. I stopped twenty feet inside, in the middle of the driveway. He stepped to one side and half-turned so he could cover me on his left and Richard and Elizabeth on his right.

"Richard," he called. "Close the gate."

He kept the left-hand Colt aimed at me and swung the right-hand Colt toward Richard. Richard saw it coming around at him and stepped up and grabbed the gate and pushed it shut. It clanged into place, loud and metallic.

"Chain it."

Richard fumbled with the chain. I heard it ringing and rattling against the iron. I heard the Cadillac, idling quietly and obediently forty feet away on the wrong side of the gate. I heard the waves pounding on the shore behind me, slow and regular and distant. I saw Elizabeth Beck in the gatehouse doorway. She was ten feet away from the big machine gun hanging on its chain. It had no safety catch. But Paulie was in the blind spot. The back window couldn't see him.

"Lock it," Paulie called.

Richard snapped the padlock shut.

"Now you and your mom go stand behind Reacher."

They met near the gatehouse door. Walked toward me. Passed right by me. They were both white and trembling. Richard's hair was blowing. I saw his scar. Elizabeth had her arms crossed tight against her chest. I heard them both stop behind me. Heard their shoes on the blacktop as they shuffled around to face my back. Paulie stepped over to the center of the driveway. He was ten feet away. Both barrels were aimed at my chest, one to the left side, one to the right. Jacketed .44 Magnums would go straight through me and probably straight through Richard and Elizabeth, too. They might make it all the way to the house. Might break a couple of first-floor windows.

"Now Reacher holds his arms out by his sides," Paulie called.

I held them out, away from my body, stiff and straight, angled down.

"Now Richard takes Reacher's coat off," Paulie called. "He pulls it down, from the collar."

I felt Richard's hands on my neck. They were cold. They grasped my collar and peeled the coat down. It slid off my shoulders and came down my arms. It pulled past one wrist, then past the other.

"Ball it up," Paulie called.

I heard Richard balling it up.

"Bring it here," Paulie called.

Richard came out from behind me carrying the balled coat. He got within five feet of Paulie and stopped.

"Throw it over the gate," Paulie said. "Real far."

Richard threw it over the gate. Real far. The arms flapped in the air and it sailed up and then down and I heard the dull padded thump of the Beretta in the pocket landing hard on the Cadillac's hood.

"Same thing with the jacket," Paulie said.

My jacket landed next to the coat on the Cadillac's hood and slid down the shiny paint and ended up on the road in a crumpled heap. I was cold. The wind was blowing and my shirt was thin. I could hear Elizabeth breathing behind me, fast and shallow. Richard was just standing there, five feet from Paulie, waiting for his next instruction.

"Now you and your mom walk fifty paces," Paulie said to him. "Back toward the house."

Richard turned and walked back and passed by me again. I heard his mother get in step with him. Heard them walk away together. I turned my head and saw them stop about forty yards back and turn around and face front again. Paulie tracked backward toward the gate, one pace, two, three. He stopped five feet from it. His back was to it. He had me fifteen feet in front of him and I guessed he could see Richard and Elizabeth over my shoulder, maybe a hundred feet farther on in the distance. We were all in a perfect straight line on the driveway, Paulie near the gate and facing the house, Richard and Elizabeth halfway to the house and facing back at him, me in the middle, trying to stay alive to see what the next minute would bring, facing Paulie, looking him square in the eye.

He smiled.

"OK," he said. "Now watch carefully."

He stayed facing me the whole time. He maintained eye contact. He crouched down and placed both guns on the blacktop by his feet and then flipped them backward toward the base of the gate. I heard their steel frames scraping on the rough surface. Saw them come to rest a yard behind him. Saw his hands come back, empty. He stood up again and showed me his palms.

"No guns," he said. "I'm going to beat you to death."

CHAPTER 12

I COULD STILL HEAR THE CADILLAC. I COULD hear its lumpy V-8 whisper and the faint liquid burble from its tailpipes. I could hear drive belts turning slowly under the hood. I could hear the muffler ticking as it adjusted to a new temperature.

"Rules," Paulie called. "You get past me, you get the guns."

I said nothing.

"You get to them, you can use them," he called.

I said nothing. He kept smiling.

"You understand?" he called.

I nodded. Watched his eyes.

"OK," he said. "I won't touch the guns unless you run away. You do that, I'll pick them up and shoot you in the back. That's fair, right? You got to stand and fight now."

I said nothing.

"Like a man," he called.

Still I said nothing. I was cold. No coat, no jacket.

"Like an officer and a gentleman," he said.

I watched his eyes.

"We clear on the rules?" he said.

I said nothing. The wind was on my back.

"We clear on the rules?" he said again.

"Crystal," I said.

"You going to run?" he said.

I said nothing.

"I think you will," he said. "Because you're a pussy."

I didn't react.

"Officer pussy," he said. "Rear-echelon whore. Coward."

I just stood there. *Sticks and stones may break my bones, but words will never hurt me.* And I doubted he knew any words I hadn't heard a hundred thousand times before. Military cops are never very popular. I tuned his voice out. Watched his eyes and his hands and his feet instead. Thought hard. I knew a lot about him. None of it was good. He was big and he was crazy and he was fast.

"Damn ATF spy," he called.

Not exactly, I thought.

"Here I come," he called.

He didn't move. I didn't, either. I just stood my ground. He was full of meth and steroids. His eyes were blazing.

"Coming to get you," he sang.

He didn't move. He was heavy. Heavy, and strong. Very strong. If he hit me, I would go down. And if I went down, I would never get up again. I watched him. He came up on the balls of his feet. Moved, fast. Feinted left, and stopped. I stood still. Held my ground. Watched him. Thought hard. He was heavier than nature intended, maybe by a hundred or a hundred and fifty pounds. Maybe by more. So he was fast, but he wouldn't be fast forever.

I took a breath.

"Elizabeth tells me you can't get it up," I said.

He stared in at me. I could still hear the Cadillac. I

could still hear the waves. They were crashing in, way behind the house.

"Big guy," I said. "But not big everywhere."

No reaction.

"I bet my left-hand pinkie is bigger," I said.

I held it out, halfway curled into my palm.

"And stiffer," I said.

His face darkened. He seemed to swell up. He exploded at me. Just launched himself forward with his right arm scything around in a giant roundhouse strike. I sidestepped his body and ducked under his arm and bounced up again and spun around. He stopped short on stiff legs and whipped back toward me. We had changed places. Now I was nearer the guns than he was. He panicked and came at me again. Same move. His right arm swung. I sidestepped and ducked and we were back where we started. But he was breathing a little heavier than I was.

"You're a big girl's blouse," I said.

It was a term of abuse I had picked up somewhere. England, maybe. I had no idea what it meant. But it worked real well, with a certain type of guy. It worked real well with Paulie. He came at me again, no hesitation. Same exact move. This time I crashed an elbow into his side as I spun under his arm. He bounced straight off of locked knees and came right back at me. I dodged away again and felt the breeze as his giant fist passed an inch above my head.

He stood there, panting. I was warming up nicely. I was beginning to feel I had some kind of a chance. He was a very poor fighter. Lots of very big guys are. Either their sheer size is so intimidating it stops fights from ever starting in the first place, or else it lets them win every one directly after their first punch lands. Either way, they don't get much practice. They don't develop much finesse. And they get out of shape. Weight machines and treadmills are no substitute for the kind of urgent, anxious, breathless tight-throat high-speed high-adrenaline fitness you need to fight on the street. I figured Paulie was a prime example. I figured he had weight-lifted himself right out of the frame.

I blew him a kiss.

He swarmed through the air at me. Came on like a pile driver. I dodged left and put an elbow in his face and he connected with his left hand and knocked me sideways like I weighed nothing at all. I went down on one knee and got back up just in time to arch around his next crazy lunge. His fist missed my gut by a quarter-inch and its wild momentum pulled him past me and downward a little which put the side of his head right in line for a left hook. I let it go with everything I had from my toes on up. My fist crashed into his ear and he staggered back and I followed up with a colossal right to his jaw. Then I danced back and took a breather and tried to see what damage I'd done.

No damage.

I had hit him four times and it was like I hadn't hit him at all. The two elbows had been solid smashes and the two punches had been as hard as anything I had ever thrown in my life. There was blood on his upper lip from the second elbow, but there was absolutely nothing else wrong with him. Theoretically he should have been unconscious. Or in a coma. It was probably thirty years since I ever had to hit a guy more than four times. But he showed no pain. No concern. He wasn't unconscious. He wasn't in a coma. He was dancing around and smiling again. He was relaxed. Moving easy. Huge. Impregnable. *There was no way to hurt him.* I looked at him and knew for sure I had no chance at all. And he looked at me and knew exactly what I was thinking. He smiled wider. Got balanced on the balls of both feet and hunched his shoulders down low and held his hands out in front of him like claws. He stamped his feet, left, right, left, right. It was like he was pawing the ground. Like he was going to come and get me and tear me apart. The smile distorted into a terrible wide grin of pleasure.

He came straight at me and I dodged left. But he was ready for that maneuver and he landed a right hook in the center of my chest. It felt exactly like being hit by a four-hundred-pound weight-lifter moving at six miles an hour. My sternum seemed to crack and I thought my heart would stop from the shock. I came up off my feet and went down on my back. Then it was about choosing to live or choosing to die. I chose to live. Rolled over twice and pushed with my hands and levered myself upright. Jumped back and sideways and dodged a straight drive that would have killed me.

After that it was about staying alive and seeing what the next half-second would bring. My chest hurt badly and my mobility was below a hundred percent but I dodged whatever he threw for about a minute. He was fast, but he wasn't talented. I got an elbow in his face. It cracked his nose. It should have punched it out the back of his head. But at least it started bleeding. He opened his mouth to breathe. I dodged and danced and waited. Caught a huge roundhouse punch on the left shoulder that nearly paralyzed my arm. Then he near-missed with a right and for a fraction of a split second his stance was wide open. His mouth was open because of the blood in his nose. I wound up and let go with a cigarette punch. It's a bar fight trick I learned long ago. You offer your guy a cigarette and he takes it and lifts it to his lips and opens his mouth maybe three-quarters of an inch. Whereupon you time it just right and land a huge uppercut under his chin. It slams his mouth shut and breaks his jaw and busts his teeth and maybe he bites his tongue off. *Thank you and good night.* I didn't need to offer Paulie a cigarette because his mouth was already hanging open. So I just let go with the uppercut. Gave it everything I had. It was a perfect blow. I was still thinking and still steady on my feet and although I was small compared with him I'm really a very big guy with a lot of training and experience. I landed the punch right where his jaw narrowed under his chin. Solid bone-to-bone contact. I came up on my toes and followed through a whole yard. It should have broken his neck as well as his jaw. His head should have come right off and rolled away in the dirt. But the blow did nothing at all. Absolutely nothing. Just rocked him back an inch. He shook his head once and hit me in the face. I saw it coming and did all the right things. I whipped my head back and opened my mouth wide so I wouldn't lose teeth from both parts of my jaw. Because my head was moving backward I took some momentum out of the blow but it was still a tremendous impact. Like being hit by a train. Like a car wreck. My lights went out and I went down hard and lost track of where I was so the blacktop came up at me like a second huge punch in the back. Air thumped out of my lungs and I saw a spray of blood from my mouth. The back of my skull hit the driveway. The sky dimmed above me.

I tried to move but it was like a car that doesn't start with the first turn of the key. *Click . . . nothing.* I lost half a second. My left arm was weak so I used my right. Got halfway off the floor. Folded my feet under me and heaved myself upright. I was dizzy. I was all over the place. But Paulie was just standing still and watching me. And smiling.

I realized he was going to take his time with me. I realized he was going to really enjoy himself.

I looked for the guns. They were still behind him. I couldn't get to them. I had hit him six times and he was laughing at me. He had hit me three times and I was a mess. I was badly shaken up. I was going to die. I knew it with sudden clarity. I was going to die in Abbot, Maine, on a dull Saturday morning in late April. And half of me was saying *Hey, we've all got to die. What does it matter exactly where or when?* But the other half was blazing with the kind of fury and arrogance that has powered so much of my life: *You going to let this particular guy take you down?* I followed the silent argument intently and made my choice and spat blood and breathed hard and shaped up one last time. My mouth hurt. My head hurt. My shoulder hurt. My chest hurt. I was sick and dizzy. I spat again. Traced my teeth with my tongue. It made me feel like I was smiling. *So look on the bright side.* I had no fatal injuries. Yet. I hadn't been shot. So I smiled for real and spat for the third time and said to myself *OK, let's die fighting.*

Paulie was still smiling, too. He had blood on his face but other than that he looked completely normal. His tie was still neat. He still had his suit coat on. He still looked like he had basketballs stuffed up into the shoulders. He watched me shape up and he smiled wider and got down into the crouch again and did the claw-hands thing again and started pawing the ground again. I figured I could dodge one more time, maybe twice, maybe three times if I was really lucky, and then it would be all over. Dead, in Maine. On an April Saturday. I pictured Dominique Kohl in my mind and I said *I tried, Dom, I really did.* I faced front. I saw Paulie take a breath. Then I saw him move. He turned away. Walked ten feet. Turned back. Then he came straight at me, fast. I dodged away. His coat slapped at me as he went past. In the corner of my eye I saw Richard and Elizabeth, far in the distance, watching. Their mouths were open, like they were saying *Those who are about to die, we salute you.* Paulie switched direction fast and came toward me at a dead run.

But then he got fancy, and I saw I was going to win, after all.

He tried to kick me martial-arts style, which is about the stupidest thing you can do in a face-to-face street fight. As soon as you have one foot off the floor you're off balance and you're vulnerable. You're just begging to lose. He came at me fast with his body turned sideways like some kung-fu idiot on the television. His foot was way up in the air and he led with it, heel first, with his giant shoe held parallel with the ground. If he had connected, he would have killed me, no question. But he didn't connect. I rocked backward and caught his foot in both hands and just heaved it upward. *Can I bench-press four hundred pounds? Well, let's find out, asshole.* I put every ounce of my strength into it and jerked him right off the ground and got his foot way up in the air and then I dropped him on his head. He sprawled in a stunned heap with his face turned toward me. The first rule of street fighting is when you get your guy on the ground you finish him, no hesitation, no pause, no inhibition, no gentlemanly conduct. You *finish* him. Paulie had ignored that rule. I didn't. I kicked him as hard as I could in the face. Blood spurted and he rolled away from me and I stamped on his right hand with my heel and shattered all the carpals and metacarpals and phalanges that he had in there. Then I did it again, two hundred fifty pounds of dead weight stamping down on broken bones. Then I stamped again and bust his wrist. Then his forearm.

He was superhuman. He rolled away and pushed himself upright with his left hand. He got on his feet and stepped away. I danced in and he swung a huge left hook and I knocked it aside and landed a short left on his broken nose. He rocked back and I kneed him in the groin.

His head snapped forward and I hit him with the cigarette punch again, right-handed. His head snapped back and I put my left elbow in his throat. Stamped on his instep, once, twice, and then stabbed my thumbs in his eyes. He wheeled away and I kicked his right knee from behind and his leg folded up and he went down again. I got my left foot on his left wrist. His right arm was completely useless. It was just flopping around. He was pinned, unless he could backhand two hundred fifty pounds vertically with his left arm alone. And he couldn't. I guessed steroids only got you so far. So I stamped on his left hand with my right foot until I could see the shattered bones coming out through the skin. Then I spun and jumped and landed square on his solar plexus. Stepped off him and kicked him hard in the top of his head, once, twice, three times. Then again a fourth time, so hard my shoe fell apart and the e-mail device came out and skittered away across the blacktop. It landed exactly where Elizabeth Beck's pager had landed when I had thrown it from the Cadillac. Paulie followed it with his eyes and stared at it. I kicked him in the head again.

He sat up. Just levered himself upright with the strength in his massive abs. Both arms hung uselessly by his sides. I grabbed his left wrist and turned his elbow inside out until the joint dislocated and then broke. He flapped his broken right wrist at me and slapped me with his bloody hand. I grabbed it in my left and squeezed the broken knuckles. Just stared into his eyes and crushed the shattered bones. He didn't make a sound. I kept hold of his slimy hand and turned his right elbow inside out and fell on it with my knees and heard it break. Then I wiped my palms on his hair and walked away. Made it to the gate and picked up the Colts.

He stood up. It was a clumsy move. His arms were useless. He slid his feet in toward his butt and jerked his weight forward onto them and levered himself upright. His nose was crushed and pouring with blood. His eyes were red and angry.

"Walk," I said. I was out of breath. "To the rocks."

He stood there like a stunned ox. There was blood in my mouth. Loose teeth. I felt no satisfaction. None at all. I hadn't beaten him. He had beaten himself. With the kung-fu nonsense. If he had come at me swinging, I would have been dead inside a minute, and we both knew it.

"Walk," I said. "Or I'll shoot you."

His chin came up, like a question.

"You're going in the water," I said.

He just stood there. I didn't want to shoot him. I didn't want to have to move a four-hundred-pound carcass a hundred yards to the sea. He stood still and my mind started working on the problem. Maybe I could wrap the gate chain around his ankles. Did Cadillacs have tow hooks? I wasn't sure.

"Walk," I said again.

I saw Richard and Elizabeth coming toward me. They were looping around in a wide circle. They wanted to get behind me without coming too close to Paulie. It was like he was a mythic figure. Like he was capable of anything. I knew how they felt. He had two broken arms, but I was watching him like my life depended on it. Which it did. If he ran at me and knocked me over he could crush me to death with his knees. I began to doubt that the Colts would do anything to him. I imagined him swarming at me, and emptying twelve bullets into him and watching them hit without slowing him down at all.

"Walk," I said.

He walked. He turned away and started up the driveway. I followed, ten paces behind. Richard and Elizabeth moved farther onto the grass. We passed them and they fell in behind me. At first I thought of telling them to stay where they were. But then I figured they had earned the right to watch, each in their own separate ways.

He followed the carriage circle around. He seemed to know where I wanted him. And he didn't seem to care. He passed by the garage block and headed behind the house and out onto the rocks. I followed, ten paces back. I was limping, because the heel had come off my right shoe. The wind was in my face. The sea was loud around us. It was rough and raging. He walked all the way to the head of Harley's cleft. He stopped there and stood still and then turned back to face me.

"I can't swim," he said. He slurred his words. I had broken some of his teeth, and hit him hard in the throat. The wind howled around him. It lifted his hair and added another inch to his height. Spray blew past him, right at me.

"No swimming involved," I replied.

I shot him twelve times in the chest. All twelve bullets passed straight through him. Big chunks of flesh and muscle followed them out over the ocean. One guy, two guns, twelve loud explosions, eleven dollars and forty cents in ammunition. He went down backward into the water. Made a hell of a splash. The sea was rough, but the tide was wrong. It wasn't pulling. He just settled in the roiling water and floated. The ocean turned pink around him. He floated, static. Then he started drifting. He drifted out, very slowly, bucking up and down violently on the swell. He floated for a whole minute. Then two. He drifted ten feet. Then twenty. He rolled over on his front with a loud sucking sound and pinwheeled slowly in the current. Then faster. He was trapped just underneath the surface of the water. His jacket was soaked and air was ballooned under it and leaking out of twelve separate bullet holes. The ocean was tossing him up and down like he weighed nothing at all. I put both empty guns on the rocks and squatted down and threw up into the ocean. Stayed down, breathing hard, watching him float. Watching him spin. Watching him drift away. Richard and Elizabeth kept themselves twenty feet from me. I cupped my hand and rinsed my face with cold salt water. Closed my eyes. Kept them closed for a long, long time. When I opened them again I looked out over the rough surface of the sea and saw that he wasn't there anymore. He had finally gone under.

I stayed down. Breathed out. Checked my watch. It was only eleven o'clock. I watched the ocean for a spell. It rose and fell. Waves broke and spray showered me. I saw the Arctic tern again. It was back, looking for a place to nest. My mind was blank. Then I started thinking. Started scoping things out. Started assessing the changed circumstances. I thought for five whole minutes and eventually got around to feeling pretty optimistic. With Paulie gone so early I figured the endgame had just gotten a whole lot faster and easier.

I was wrong about that, too.

THE FIRST THING THAT WENT WRONG WAS THAT Elizabeth Beck wouldn't leave. I told her to take Richard and the Cadillac and get the hell out. But she wouldn't go. She just stood there on the rocks with her hair streaming and her clothes flapping in the wind.

"This is my home," she said.

"Pretty soon it's going to be a war zone," I said.

"I'm staying."

"I can't let you stay."

"I'm not leaving," she said. "Not without my husband."

I didn't know what to tell her. I just stood there, getting

colder. Richard came up behind me and circled around and looked out at the sea, and then back at me.

"That was cool," he said. "You beat him."

"No, he beat himself," I said.

There were noisy seagulls in the air. They were fighting the wind, circling a spot in the ocean maybe forty yards away. They were dipping down and pecking at the crests of the waves. They were eating floating fragments of Paulie. Richard was watching them with blank eyes.

"Talk to your mother," I said to him. "You need to convince her to get away."

"I'm not leaving," Elizabeth said again.

"Me either," Richard said. "This is where we live. We're a family."

They were in some kind of shock. I couldn't argue with them. So I tried to put them to work instead. We walked up the driveway, slow and quiet. The wind tore at our clothes. I was limping, because of my shoe. I stopped where the bloodstains started and retrieved the e-mail device. It was broken. The plastic screen was cracked and it wouldn't turn on. I dropped it in my pocket. Then I found the heel rubber and sat cross-legged on the ground and put it back in place. Walking was easier after that. We reached the gate and unchained it and opened it and I got my jacket and my coat back and put them on. I buttoned the coat and turned the collar up. Then I drove the Cadillac in through the gate and parked it near the gatehouse door. Richard chained the gate again. I went inside and opened the big Russian machine gun's breech and freed the ammunition belt. Then I lifted the gun off its chain. Carried it outside into the wind and put it sideways across the Cadillac's rear seat. I went back in and rolled the belt back into its box and took the chain off its ceiling hook and unscrewed the hook from the joist. Carried the box and the chain and the hook outside and put them in the Cadillac's trunk.

"Can I help with anything?" Elizabeth asked.

"There are twenty more ammunition boxes," I said. "I want them all."

"I'm not going in there," she said. "Never again."

"Then I guess you can't help with anything."

I carried two boxes at a time, so it took me ten trips. I was still cold and I was aching all over. I could still taste blood in my mouth. I stacked the boxes in the trunk and all over the floor in back and in the front passenger footwell. Then I slid into the driver's seat and tilted the mirror. My lips were split and my gums were rimed with blood. My front teeth at the top were loose. I was upset about that. They had always been misaligned and they had been a little chipped for years, but I got them when I was eight and I was used to them and they were the only ones I had.

"Are you OK?" Elizabeth asked.

I felt the back of my head. There was a tender spot where I had hit the driveway. There was a serious bruise on the side of my left shoulder. My chest hurt and breathing wasn't entirely painless. But overall I was OK. I was in better shape than Paulie, which was all that mattered. I thumbed my teeth up into my gums and held them there.

"Never felt better," I said.

"Your lip is all swollen."

"I'll live."

"We should celebrate."

I slid out of the car.

"We should talk about getting you out of here," I said.

She said nothing to that. The phone inside the gatehouse started ringing. It had an old-fashioned bell in it, low and slow and relaxing. It sounded faint and far away, muffled by the noise of the wind and the sea. It rang once, then twice. I walked around the Cadillac's hood and went inside and picked it up. Said Paulie's name and waited a beat and heard a voice I hadn't heard in ten years.

"Did he show up yet?" it said.

I paused.

"Ten minutes ago," I said. I kept my hand halfway over the mouthpiece and made my voice high and light.

"Is he dead yet?"

"Five minutes ago," I said.

"OK, stay ready. This is going to be a long day."

You got that right, I thought. Then the phone clicked off and I put it down and stepped back outside.

"Who was it?" Elizabeth asked.

"Quinn," I said.

THE FIRST TIME I HEARD QUINN'S VOICE WAS ten years previously on a cassette tape. Kohl had a telephone tap going. It was unauthorized, but back then military law was a lot more generous than civilian procedure. The cassette was a clear plastic thing that showed the little spools of tape inside. Kohl had a player the size of a shoe box with her and she clicked the cassette into it and pressed a button. My office filled with Quinn's voice. He was talking to an offshore bank, making financial arrangements. He sounded relaxed. He spoke clearly and slowly with the neutral homogenized accent you get from a lifetime in the army. He read out account numbers and gave passwords and issued instructions concerning a total of half a million dollars. He wanted most of it moved to the Bahamas.

"He mails the cash," Kohl said. "To Grand Cayman, first."

"Is that safe?" I said.

She nodded. "Safe enough. The only risk would be

postal workers stealing it. But the destination address is a PO box and he sends it book rate, and nobody steals books out of the mail. So he gets away with it."

"Half a million dollars is a lot of money."

"It's a valuable weapon."

"Is it? *That* valuable?"

"Don't you think so?"

I shrugged. "Seems like a lot to me. For a lawn dart?"

She pointed at the tape player. Pointed at Quinn's voice filling the air. "Well, that's what they're paying, obviously. I mean, how else did he get half a million dollars? He didn't save it out of his salary, that's for sure."

"When will you make your move?"

"Tomorrow," she said. "We'll have to. He's got the final blueprint. Gorowski says it's the key to the whole thing."

"How will it go down?"

"Frasconi is dealing with the Syrian. He's going to mark the cash, with a judge advocate watching. Then we'll all observe the exchange. We'll open the briefcase that Quinn gives to the Syrian, immediately, in front of the same judge. We'll document the contents, which will be the key blueprint. Then we'll go pick Quinn up. We'll arrest him and impound the briefcase that the Syrian gave to *him*. The judge can watch us open it later. We'll find the marked cash inside, and therefore we'll have a witnessed and documented transaction, and therefore Quinn will go down, and he'll stay down."

"Watertight," I said. "Good work."

"Thank you," she said.

"Will Frasconi be OK?"

"He'll have to be. I can't deal with the Syrian myself. Those guys are weird with women. They can't touch us, can't look at us, sometimes they can't even talk to us. So Frasconi will have to do it."

"Want me to hold his hand?"

"His part is all offstage," she said. "There's nothing much he can screw up."

"I think I'll hold his hand anyway."

"Thank you," she said again.

"And he'll go with you to make the arrest."

She said nothing.

"I can't send you one-on-one," I said. "You know that."

She nodded.

"But I'll tell him you're the lead investigator," I said. "I'll make sure he understands it's your case."

"OK," she said.

She pressed the *stop* button on her tape player. Quinn's voice died, halfway through a word. The word was going to be *dollars,* as in *two hundred thousand.* But it came out as *doll.* He sounded bright and happy and alert, like a guy at the top of his game, fully aware he was busy playing and winning. Kohl ejected the cassette. Slipped it into her pocket. Then she winked at me and walked out of my office.

"WHO'S QUINN?" ELIZABETH BECK ASKED ME, ten years later.

"Frank Xavier," I said. "He used to be called Quinn. His full name is Francis Xavier Quinn."

"You *know* him?"

"Why else would I be here?"

"Who are you?"

"I'm a guy who knew Frank Xavier back when he was called Francis Xavier Quinn."

"You work for the government."

I shook my head. "This is strictly personal."

"What will happen to my husband?"

"No idea," I said. "And I don't really care either way."

I went back inside Paulie's little house and locked the front door. Came out again and locked the back door behind me. Then I checked the chain on the gate. It was tight. I figured we could keep intruders out for a minute, maybe a minute and a half, which might be good enough. I put the padlock key in my pants pocket.

"Back to the big house now," I said. "You'll have to walk, I'm afraid."

I drove the Cadillac down the driveway, with the ammunition boxes stacked behind and beside me. I saw Elizabeth and Richard in the mirror, hurrying side by side. They didn't want to get out of town, but they weren't too keen on being left alone. I stopped the car by the front door and backed it up ready to unload. I opened the trunk and took the ceiling hook and the chain and ran upstairs to Duke's room. His window looked out along the whole length of the driveway. It would make an ideal gunport. I took the Beretta out of my coat pocket and snicked the safety off and fired it once into the ceiling. I saw Elizabeth and Richard fifty yards away stop dead and then start running toward the house. Maybe they thought I had shot the cook. Or myself. I stood on a chair and punched through the bullet hole and raked the plaster back until I found a wooden joist. Then I aimed carefully and fired again and drilled a neat nine-millimeter hole in the wood. I screwed the hook into it and slipped the chain onto it and tested it with my weight. It held.

I went back down and opened the Cadillac's rear doors. Elizabeth and Richard arrived and I told them to carry the ammunition boxes. I carried the big machine gun. The metal detector on the front door squealed at it, loud and urgent. I carried it upstairs. Hung it on the chain and fed the end of the first belt into it. Swung the muzzle to the wall and opened the lower sash of the window.

Swung the muzzle back and traversed it side to side and ranged it up and down. It covered the whole width of the distant wall and the whole length of the driveway down to the carriage circle. Richard stood and watched me.

"Keep stacking the boxes," I said.

Then I stepped over to the nightstand and picked up the outside phone. Called Duffy at the motel.

"You still want to help?" I asked her.

"Yes," she said.

"Then I need all three of you at the house," I said. "Quick as you can."

After that there was nothing more to be done until they arrived. I waited by the window and pressed my teeth into my gums with my thumb and watched the road. Watched Richard and Elizabeth struggling with the heavy boxes. Watched the sky. It was noon, but it was darkening. The weather was getting even worse. The wind was freshening. The North Atlantic coast, in late April. Unpredictable. Elizabeth Beck came in and stacked a box. Breathed hard. Stood still.

"What's going to happen?" she asked.

"No way of telling," I said.

"What's this gun for?"

"It's a precaution."

"Against what?"

"Quinn's people," I said. "We've got our backs to the sea. We might need to stop them on the driveway."

"You're going to shoot at them?"

"If necessary."

"What about my husband?" she asked.

"Do you care?"

She nodded. "Yes, I do."

"I'm going to shoot at him, too."

She said nothing.

"He's a criminal," I said. "He can take his chances."

"The laws that make him a criminal are unconstitutional."

"You think?"

She nodded again. "The Second Amendment is clear."

"Take it to the Supreme Court," I said. "Don't bother me with it."

"People have the right to bear arms."

"Drug dealers don't," I said. "I never saw an amendment that says it's OK to fire automatic weapons in the middle of a crowded neighborhood. Using bullets that go through brick walls, one after the other. And through innocent bystanders, one after the other. Babies and children."

She said nothing.

"You ever seen a bullet hit a baby?" I said. "It doesn't slide right in, like a hypodermic needle. It *crushes* its way through, like a bludgeon. Crushing and tearing."

She said nothing.

"Never tell a soldier that guns are fun," I said.

"The law is clear," she said.

"So join the NRA," I said. "I'm happy right here in the real world."

"He's my husband."

"You said he deserved to go to prison."

"Yes," she said. "But he doesn't deserve to die."

"You think?"

"He's my husband," she said again.

"How does he make the sales?" I asked.

"He uses I-95," she said. "He cuts the centers out of the cheap rugs and rolls the guns in them. Like tubes, or cylinders. Drives them to Boston or New Haven. People meet him there."

I nodded. Remembered the stray carpet fibers I had seen around.

"He's my husband," Elizabeth said.

I nodded again. "If he's got the sense not to stand right next to Quinn he might be OK."

"Promise me he'll be OK. Then I'll leave. With Richard."

"I can't promise," I said.

"Then we're staying."

I said nothing.

"It was never a voluntary association, you know," she said. "With Xavier, I mean. You really need to understand that."

She moved to the window and gazed down at Richard. He was heaving the last ammunition case out of the Cadillac.

"There was coercion," she said.

"Yes, I figured that out," I said.

"He kidnapped my son."

"I know," I said.

Then she moved again and looked straight at me.

"What did he do to you?" she asked.

I SAW KOHL TWICE MORE THAT DAY AS SHE PRE-pared her end of the mission. She was doing everything right. She was like a chess player. She never did anything without looking two moves ahead. She knew the judge advocate she asked to monitor the transaction would have to recuse himself from the subsequent court-martial, so she picked one she knew the prosecutors hated. It would be one less obstacle later. She had a photographer standing by to make a visual record. She had timed the drive out to Quinn's Virginia house. The file I had given her at the start now filled two cardboard boxes. The second time I saw her she was carrying them. They were stacked one on top of the other and her biceps were straining against their weight.

"How is Gorowski holding up?" I asked her.

"Not good," she said. "But he'll be out of the woods tomorrow."

"You're going to be famous."

"I hope not," she said. "This should stay classified forever."

"Famous in the classified world," I said. "Plenty of people see that stuff."

"So I guess I should ask for my performance review," she said. "Day after tomorrow, maybe."

"We should have dinner tonight," I said. "We should go out. Like a celebration. Best place we can find. I'll buy."

"I thought you were on food stamps."

"I've been saving up."

"You've had plenty of opportunity. It's been a long case."

"Slow as molasses," I said. "That's your only problem, Kohl. You're thorough, but you're slow."

She smiled again and hitched the boxes higher.

"You should have agreed to date me," she said. "Then I could have shown you how slow can be better than fast."

She carried the boxes away and I met her two hours later at a restaurant in town. It was an upmarket place so I had showered and put a clean uniform on. She showed up wearing a black dress. Not the same one as before. No dots on it. Just sheer black. It was very flattering, not that she needed the help. She looked about eighteen.

"Great," I said. "They're going to think you're dining with your dad."

"My uncle, maybe," she said. "My dad's younger brother."

It was one of those meals where the food wasn't important. I can remember everything else about the evening, but I can't remember what I ordered. Steak, maybe. Or ravioli. Something. I know we ate. We talked a lot, about the kind of stuff we probably wouldn't share with just anybody. I came very close to breaking down and asking her if she wanted to find a motel. But I didn't. We had a glass of wine each and then switched to water. There was an unspoken agreement we needed to stay sharp for the next day. I paid the check and we left at midnight, separately. She was bright, even though it was late. She was full of life and energy and focus. She was bubbling with anticipation. Her eyes were shining. I stood on the street and watched her drive away.

"SOMEONE'S COMING," ELIZABETH BECK SAID, ten years later.

I glanced out the window and saw a gray Taurus far in the distance. The color blended with the rock and the weather and made it hard to see. It was maybe two miles away, coming around a curve in the road, moving fast. Villanueva's car. I told Elizabeth to stay put and keep an eye on Richard and I went downstairs and out the back door. I retrieved Angel Doll's keys from my hidden bundle. Put them in my jacket pocket. I took Duffy's Glock and her spare magazines, too. I wanted her to get them back intact. It was important to me. She was already in enough trouble. I stashed them in my coat pocket with my Beretta and walked around to the front of the house and got in the Cadillac. Drove it up to the gate and slid out and waited out of sight. The Taurus stopped outside the gate and I saw Villanueva at the wheel with Duffy next to him and Eliot in the back. I stepped out of hiding and took the chain off the gate and swung it open. Villanueva eased through and stopped nose to nose with the Cadillac. Then three doors opened and they all climbed out into the cold and stared at me.

"What the hell happened to you?" Villanueva said.

I touched my mouth. It felt swollen and tender.

"Walked into a door," I said.

Villanueva glanced at the gatehouse.

"Or a door*man*," he said. "Am I right?"

"You OK?" Duffy asked.

"I'm in better shape than the doorman," I said.

"Why are we here?"

"Plan B," I said. "We're going to Portland, but if we don't find what we need up there we're going to have to come back here and wait. So two of you are coming out with me right now and the other one is staying here to hold the fort." I turned around and pointed at the house. "The center second-floor window has got a big machine gun mounted in it to cover the approach. I need one of you in there manning it."

Nobody volunteered. I looked straight at Villanueva. He was old enough to have been drafted, way back. He might have spent time around big machine guns.

"You do it, Terry," I said.

"Not me," he said. "I'm coming out with you to find Teresa."

He said it like there was going to be no way to argue with him.

"OK, I'll do it," Eliot said.

"Thanks," I said. "You ever seen a Vietnam movie? Seen the door gunner on a Huey? That's you. If they come, they won't try to get through the gate. They'll go in the front window of the gatehouse and out the back door or the back window. So you be ready to hose them down as they come out."

"What if it's dark?"

"We'll be back before dark."

"OK. Who's in the house?"

"Beck's family. And the cook. They're noncombatants, but they won't leave."

"What about Beck himself?"

"He'll come back with the others. If he got away again in the confusion it wouldn't break my heart. But if he got hit in the confusion it wouldn't break my heart either."

"OK."

"They probably won't show up," I said. "They're busy. This all is just a precaution."

"OK," he said again.

"You keep the Cadillac," I said. "We'll take the Taurus."

Villanueva got back in the Ford and reversed it out through the gate again. I walked out with Duffy and closed the gate from the outside and chained it and locked it and tossed the padlock key over to Eliot.

"See you later," I said.

He turned the Cadillac around and I watched him drive it down toward the house. Then I got in the Taurus with Duffy and Villanueva. She took the front seat. I took the back. I got her Glock and her spare magazines out of my pocket and passed them forward to her, like a little ceremony.

"Thanks for the loan," I said.

She put the Glock in her shoulder holster and the magazines in her purse.

"You're very welcome," she said.

"Teresa first," Villanueva said. "Quinn second. OK?"

"Agreed," I said.

He K-turned on the road and took off west.

"So where do we look?" he said.

"Choice of three locations," I said. "There's the warehouse, there's a city-center office, and there's a business park near the airport. Can't keep a prisoner in a city-center office building over the weekend. And the warehouse is too busy. They just had a big shipment. So my vote goes with the business park."

"I-95 or Route One?"

"Route One," I said.

We drove in silence, fifteen miles inland, and turned north on Route One toward Portland.

CHAPTER 13

IT WAS EARLY AFTERNOON ON A SATURDAY, SO the business park was quiet. It was rinsed clean by rain and it looked fresh and new. The metal buildings glowed like dull pewter under the gray of the sky. We cruised through the network of streets at maybe twenty miles an hour. Saw nobody. Quinn's building looked locked up tight. I turned my head as we drove by and studied the sign again: *Xavier eXport Company.* The words were professionally etched on thick stainless steel, but the oversized *X*s looked like an amateur's idea of graphic design.

"Why does it say *export*?" Duffy asked. "He's importing stuff, surely."

"How do we get in?" Villanueva asked.

"We break in," I said. "Through the rear, I guess."

The buildings were laid out back-to-back, with neat parking lots in front of each of them. Everything else in the park was either a road or new lawn bounded by neat poured-concrete curbs. There were no fences anywhere. The building directly behind Quinn's was labeled *Paul Keast & Chris Maden Professional Catering Services.* It was closed up and deserted. I could see past it all the way to Quinn's back door, which was a plain metal rectangle painted dull red.

"Nobody around," Duffy said.

There was a window on Quinn's back wall near the red door. It was made from pebbled glass. Probably a bathroom window. It had iron bars over it.

"Security system?" Villanueva said.

"On a new place like this?" I said. "Almost certainly."

"Wired direct to the cops?"

"I doubt it," I said. "That wouldn't be smart, for a guy like Quinn. He doesn't want the cops snooping around every time some kid busts his windows."

"Private company?"

"That's my guess. Or his own people."

"So how do we do it?"

"We do it real fast. Get in and out before anybody reacts. We can risk five or ten minutes, probably."

"One at the front and two at the back?"

"You got it," I said. "You take the front."

I told him to pop the trunk and then Duffy and I slid out of the car. The air was cold and damp and the wind was blowing. I took the tire iron out from under the spare wheel and closed the trunk lid and watched the car drive away. Duffy and I walked down the side of the catering place and across the dividing lawn to Quinn's bathroom window. I put my ear against the cold metal siding and listened. Heard nothing. Then I looked at the window bars. They were made up from a shallow one-piece rectangular iron basket that was secured by eight machine screws, two on each of the four sides of the rectangle. The screws went through welded flanges the size of quarters. The screw heads themselves were the size of nickels. Duffy pulled the Glock out of her shoulder holster. I heard it scrape on the leather. I checked the Beretta in my coat pocket. Held the tire iron two-handed. Put my ear back on the siding. Heard Villanueva's car pull up at the front of the building. I could hear the beat of the engine coming through the metal. I heard his door open and close. He left the engine running. I heard his feet on the front walkway.

"Stand by," I said.

I felt Duffy move behind me. Heard Villanueva knocking loudly on the front door. I stabbed the tire iron end-on into the siding next to one of the screws. Made a shallow dent in the metal. Shoved the iron sideways into it and under the bars and hauled on it. The screw held. Clearly it went through the siding all the way into the steel framing. So I reseated the iron and jerked harder, once, twice. The screw head broke off and the bars moved a little.

I had to break six screw heads in total. Took me nearly thirty seconds. Villanueva was still knocking. Nobody was answering. When the sixth screw broke I grabbed the bars themselves and hauled them open ninety degrees like a door. The two remaining screws screeched in protest. I picked up the tire iron again and smashed the pebbled glass. Reached in with my hand and found the catch and pulled the window open. Took out the Beretta and went headfirst into the bathroom.

It was a small cubicle, maybe six-by-four. There was a toilet and a sink with a small frameless mirror. A trash can and a shelf with spare toilet rolls and paper towels on it. A bucket and a mop propped in a corner. Clean linoleum on the floor. A strong smell of disinfectant. I turned around and checked the window. There was a small alarm pad screwed to the sill. But the building was still quiet. No siren. A silent alarm. Now a phone would be ringing somewhere. Or an alert would be flashing on a computer screen.

I stepped out of the bathroom into a back hallway. Nobody there. It was dark. I faced front and backed away to the rear door. Fumbled behind me without looking and unlocked it. Pulled it open. Heard Duffy step inside.

She had probably done six weeks at Quantico during her basic training and she still remembered the moves. She held the Glock two-handed and slid past me and took up station by a door that was going to lead out of the hallway into the rest of the building. She leaned her shoulder on the jamb and crooked her elbows to pull the gun up out of my way. I stepped forward and kicked the door and went through it and dodged left and she spun after me and went to the right. We were in another hallway. It was narrow. It ran the whole length of the building, all the way to the front. There were rooms off it, left and right. Six rooms, three on either side. Six doors, all of them closed.

"Front," I whispered. "Villanueva."

We crabbed our way along, back-to-back, covering each door in turn. They stayed closed. We made it to the front door and I unlocked it and opened it up. Villanueva stepped through and closed it again behind him. He had a Glock 17 in his gnarled old hand. It looked right at home there.

"Alarm?" he whispered.

"Silent," I whispered back.

"So let's be quick."

"Room by room," I whispered.

It wasn't a good feeling. We had made so much noise that nobody in the building could have any doubt we were there. And the fact that they hadn't blundered out to confront us meant they were smart enough to sit tight with their hammers back and their sights trained chest-high at the inside of their doors. And the center hallway was only about three feet wide. It didn't give us much room to maneuver. Not a good feeling. The doors were all hinged on the left, so I put Duffy on my left facing out to cover the doors opposite. I didn't want us all facing the same way. I didn't want to get shot in the back. Then I put Villanueva on my right. His job was to kick in the doors, one by one. I took the center. My job was to go in first, room by room.

We started with the front room on the left. Villanueva kicked the door, hard. The lock broke and the frame splintered and the door crashed open. I went straight in. The room was empty. It was a ten-by-ten square with a window and a desk and a wall of file cabinets. I came straight out and we all spun around and hit the room opposite, immediately. Duffy covered our backs and Villanueva kicked the door and I went in. It was empty, too. But it was a bonus. The partition wall between it and the next room had been removed. It was ten-by-twenty. It had two doors to the hallway. There were three desks in the room. There were computers and phones. There was a coat rack in the corner with a woman's raincoat hanging on it.

We crossed the hallway to the fourth door. The third room. Villanueva kicked the door and I rolled around the jamb. Empty. Another ten-by-ten square. No window. A desk, with a big cork notice board behind it. Lists pinned to the cork. An Oriental carpet covering most of the linoleum.

Four down. Two to go. We chose the back room on the right. Villanueva hit the door. I went in. It was empty. Ten-by-ten, white paint, gray linoleum. Completely bare. Nothing in it at all. Except bloodstains. They had been cleaned up, but not well. There were brown swirls on the floor, where an overloaded mop had pushed them around. There was splatter on the walls. Some of it had been wiped. Some of it had been missed altogether. There were lacy trails up to waist height. The angles between the baseboards and the linoleum were rimed with brown and black.

"The maid," I said.

Nobody replied. We stood still for a long silent moment. Then we backed out and turned around and hit the last door, hard. I went in, gun-first. And stopped dead.

It was a prison. And it was empty.

It was ten-by-ten. It had white walls and a low ceiling. No windows. Gray linoleum on the floor. A mattress on the linoleum. Wrinkled sheets on the mattress. Dozens of Chinese food cartons all over the place. Empty plastic bottles that had held spring water.

"She was here," Duffy said.

I nodded. "Just like in the basement up at the house."

I stepped all the way inside and lifted up the mattress. The word *JUSTICE* was smeared on the floor, big and obvious, painted with a finger. Underneath it was today's date, six numbers, month, day, year, fading and then strengthening as she had reloaded her fingertip with something black and brown.

"She's hoping we'll track her," Villanueva said. "Day by day, place by place. Smart kid."

"Is that written in blood?" Duffy said.

I could smell stale food and stale breath, all through the room. I could smell fear and desperation. She had heard the maid die. Two thin doors wouldn't have blocked much sound.

"Hoisin sauce," I said. "I hope."

"How long since they moved her?"

I looked inside the closest cartons. "Two hours, maybe."

"Shit."

"So let's go," Villanueva said. "Let's go find her."

"Five minutes," Duffy said. "I need to get something I can give to ATF. To make this whole thing right."

"We haven't got five minutes," Villanueva said.

"Two minutes," I said. "Grab what you can and look at it later."

We backed out of the cell. Nobody looked at the charnel house opposite. Duffy led us back to the room with the Oriental carpet. *Smart choice,* I thought. It was probably Quinn's office. He was the kind of guy who would give himself a rug. She took a thick file marked *Pending* from a desk drawer and pulled all the lists off the cork board.

"Let's go," Villanueva said again.

We came out through the front door exactly four minutes after I had gone in through the bathroom window. It felt more like four hours. We piled into the gray Taurus and were back on Route One a minute after that.

"Stay north," I said. "Head for the city center."

WE WERE QUIET AT FIRST. NOBODY LOOKED AT anybody. Nobody spoke. We were thinking about the maid. I was in the back and Duffy was in the front with Quinn's paperwork spread over her knees. Traffic across the bridge was slow. There were shoppers heading into the city. The roadway was slick with rain and salt spray. Duffy shuffled papers, glancing at one after another. Then she broke the silence. It was a relief.

"This all is pretty cryptic," she said. "We've got an *XX* and a *BB*."

"Xavier Export Company and Bizarre Bazaar," I said.

"BB is importing," she said. "XX is exporting. But they're obviously linked. They're like two halves of the same operation."

"I don't care," I said. "I just want Quinn."

"And Teresa," Villanueva said.

"First-quarter spreadsheet," Duffy said. "They're on track to turn over twenty-two million dollars this year. That's a lot of guns, I guess."

"Quarter-million Saturday Night Specials," I said. "Or four Abrams tanks."

"Mossberg," Duffy said. "You heard that name?"

"Why?" I said.

"XX just received a shipment from them."

"O.F. Mossberg and Sons," I said. "From New Haven, Connecticut. Shotgun manufacturer."

"What's a Persuader?"

"A shotgun," I said. "The Mossberg M500 Persuader. It's a paramilitary weapon."

"XX is sending Persuaders someplace. Two hundred of them. Total invoice value sixty thousand dollars. Basically in exchange for something BB is receiving."

"Import-export," I said. "That's how it works."

"But the prices don't add up," she said. "BB's incoming shipment is invoiced at seventy thousand. So XX is coming out ten thousand dollars ahead."

"The magic of capitalism," I said.

"No, wait, there's another item. Now it balances. Two hundred Mossberg Persuaders plus a ten-thousand-dollar bonus item to make the values match."

"What's the bonus item?" I said.

"It doesn't say. What would be worth ten grand?"

"I don't care," I said again.

She shuffled more paper.

"Keast and Maden," she said. "Where did we see those names?"

"The building behind Quinn's," I said. "The caterers."

"He hired them," she said. "They're delivering something today."

"Where?"

"Doesn't say."

"What kind of something?"

"Doesn't say. Eighteen items at fifty-five dollars each. Almost a thousand dollars' worth of something."

"Where to now?" Villanueva said.

We were off the bridge and looping north and west, with the park on our left.

"Make the second right," I said.

WE PULLED STRAIGHT INTO MISSIONARY HOUSE'S underground garage. There was a rent-a-cop in a fancy uniform in a booth. He logged us in without paying a whole lot of attention. Then Villanueva showed him his DEA badge and told him to sit tight and keep quiet. Told him not to call anybody. Behind him the garage was quiet. There were maybe eighty spaces and fewer than a dozen cars in them. But one of them was the gray Grand Marquis I had seen outside Beck's warehouse that morning.

"This is where I took the photographs," Duffy said.

We drove to the back of the garage and parked in a corner. Got out and took the elevator up one floor to the lobby. There was some tired marble decor and a building directory. The Xavier Export Company shared the fourth floor with a law firm called *Lewis, Strange & Greville*. We were happy about that. It meant there would be an interior hallway up there. We wouldn't be stepping straight out of the elevator into Quinn's offices.

We got back in the elevator and pressed *4*. Faced front. The doors closed and the motor whined. We stopped on four. We heard voices. The elevator bell pinged. The doors opened. The hallway was full of lawyers. There was a mahogany door on the left with a brass plate marked *Lewis, Strange & Greville, Attorneys at Law.* It was open and three people had come out through it and were standing around waiting for one of them to close it. Two men, one woman. They were in casual clothes. They were all carrying briefcases. They all looked happy. They all turned and looked at us. We stepped out of the elevator. They smiled and nodded at us, like you do with strangers in a small hallway. Or maybe they thought we had come to consult with them on a legal matter. Villanueva smiled back and nodded toward Xavier Export's door. *It's not you we're looking for. It's them.* The woman lawyer looked away and squeezed past us into the elevator. Her partners locked up their office and joined her. The elevator doors closed on them and we heard the car whining down.

"Witnesses," Duffy whispered. "Shit."

Villanueva pointed at Xavier Export's door. "And there's someone in there. Those lawyers didn't seem surprised that we should be up here at this time on a Saturday. So they must *know* there's someone in there. Maybe they thought we've got an appointment or something."

I nodded. "One of the cars in the garage was at Beck's warehouse this morning."

"Quinn?" Duffy said.

"I sincerely hope so."

"We agreed, Teresa first," Villanueva said. "Then Quinn."

"I'm changing the plan," I said. "I'm not walking away. Not if he's in there. Not if he's a target of opportunity."

"But we can't go in anyway," Duffy said. "We've been seen."

"*You* can't go in," I said. "I can."

"What, alone?"

"That's the way I want it. Him and me."

"We left a trail."

"So roll it up. Go back to the garage and drive away. The guard will log you out. Then call this office five minutes later. Between the garage log and the phone log it'll be on record that nothing happened while you were here."

"But what about you? It'll be on record that we left you in here."

"I doubt it," I said. "I don't think the garage guy paid that much attention. I don't think he counted heads or anything. He just wrote down the plate number."

She said nothing.

"I don't care anyway," I said. "I'm a hard person to find. And I plan to get harder."

She looked at the law firm's door. Then at Xavier Export's. Then at the elevator. Then at me.

"OK," she said. "We'll leave you to it. I really don't want to, but I really have to, you understand?"

"Completely," I said.

"Teresa might be in there with him," Villanueva whispered.

I nodded. "If she is, I'll bring her to you. Meet me at the end of the street. Ten minutes after you make the phone call."

They both hesitated and then Duffy put her finger on the elevator call button. We heard noises in the shaft as the machinery started.

"Take care," she said.

The bell pinged and the doors opened. They stepped in. Villanueva glanced out at me and hit the button for the lobby and the doors closed on them like theater curtains and they were gone. I stepped away and leaned on the wall on the far side of Quinn's door. It felt good to be alone. I put my hand around the Beretta's grip in my pocket and waited. I imagined Duffy and Villanueva stepping out of the elevator and walking to their car. Driving it out of the garage. Getting noticed by the guard. Parking around the corner and calling information. Getting Quinn's number. I turned and stared at the door. Imagined Quinn on the other side of it, at his desk, with a phone in front of him. I stared at the door like I could see him right through it.

THE FIRST TIME I EVER SAW HIM WAS ON THE AC-
tual day of the bust. Frasconi had done well with the Syrian. The guy was all squared away. Frasconi was very
adequate in a situation like that. Give him time and a clear
objective and he could deliver. The Syrian brought cash
money with him from inside his embassy and we all sat
down together in front of the judge advocate and counted
it. There was fifty thousand dollars. We figured it was the
final installment of many. We marked each bill separately.
We even marked the briefcase. We put the judge advocate's initials on it with clear nail varnish, near one of the
hinges. The judge advocate wrote up an affidavit for the
file and Frasconi held on to the Syrian, and Kohl and I
moved into position ready for the surveillance itself. Her
photographer was already standing by in a second-floor
window in a building across the street from the café and
twenty yards south. The judge advocate joined us ten minutes later. We were using a utility truck parked at the curb.
It had portholes with one-way glass. Kohl had borrowed it
from the FBI. She had drafted three grunts to complete
the illusion. They were wearing power company overalls
and actually digging up the street.

We waited. There was no conversation. There wasn't
much air in the truck. The weather was warm again. Frasconi released the Syrian after forty minutes. He came
strolling into view from the north. He had been warned
what would happen if he gave us away. Kohl had written
the script and Frasconi had delivered it. They were threats
we probably wouldn't have carried out. But he didn't
know that. I guess they were plausible, based on what
happened to people in Syria.

He sat down at a sidewalk table. He was ten feet from
us. He put his briefcase on the floor, level with the side of
the table. It was like a second guest. The waiter came and
took his order. Came back after a minute with an espresso.

The Syrian lit a cigarette. Smoked it halfway down and crushed it out in the ashtray.

"The Syrian is waiting," Kohl said, quietly. She had a tape recorder running. Her idea was to have a real-time audio record as a backup. She was wearing her dress greens, ready for the arrest. She looked real good in them.

"Check," the judge said. "The Syrian is waiting."

The Syrian finished his coffee and waved to the waiter for another. He lit another cigarette.

"Does he always smoke so much?" I asked.

"Why?" Kohl said.

"Is he warning Quinn off?"

"No, he always smokes," Kohl said.

"OK," I said. "But they're bound to have an abort sign."

"He won't use it. Frasconi really put a fright in him."

We waited. The Syrian finished his second cigarette. He put his hands flat on the table. He drummed his fingers. He looked OK. He looked like a guy waiting for another guy who was maybe a little overdue. He lit another cigarette.

"I don't like all this smoking," I said.

"Relax, he's always like this," Kohl said.

"Makes him look nervous. Quinn could pick up on it."

"It's normal. He's from the Middle East."

We waited. I watched the crowd build up. It was close to lunch time.

"Now Quinn is approaching," Kohl said.

"Check," the judge replied. "Quinn is approaching now."

I looked to the south. Saw a tidy-looking guy, neat and trim, maybe six feet one and a little under two hundred pounds. He looked a little younger than forty. He had black hair with a little gray in it in front of his ears. He was wearing a blue suit with a white shirt and a dull red tie. He looked just like everybody else in D.C. He moved fast, but he made it look slow. He was neat in his movements. Clearly fit and athletic. Almost certainly a jogger. He was carrying a Halliburton briefcase. It was the exact twin of the Syrian's. It flashed slightly gold in the sunlight.

The Syrian laid his cigarette in the ashtray and sketched a wave. He looked a little uneasy, but I guessed that was appropriate. Big-time espionage in the heart of your enemy's capital is not a game. Quinn saw him and moved toward him. The Syrian stood up and they shook hands across the table. I smiled. They had a smart system going. It was a tableau so familiar in Georgetown that it was almost invisible. An American in a suit shaking hands with a foreigner across a table loaded with coffee cups and ashtrays. They both sat down. Quinn shuffled on his chair and got comfortable and placed his briefcase tight alongside the one that was already there. At a casual glance the two cases looked like one in a larger size.

"Briefcases are adjacent," Kohl said, into the microphone.

"Check," the judge said. "The briefcases are adjacent."

The waiter came back with the Syrian's second espresso. Quinn said something to the waiter and he left again. The Syrian said something to Quinn. Quinn smiled. It was a smile of pure control. Pure satisfaction. The Syrian said something else. He was playing his part. He thought he was saving his life. Quinn craned his neck and looked for the waiter. The Syrian picked up his cigarette again and turned his head the other way and blew smoke directly at us. Then he put the cigarette out in the ashtray. The waiter came back with Quinn's drink. A large cup. Probably white coffee. The Syrian sipped his espresso. Quinn drank his coffee. They didn't talk.

"They're nervous," Kohl said.

"Excited," I said. "They're nearly through. This is the last meeting. The end is in sight. For both of them. They just want to get it done."

"Watch the briefcases," Kohl said.

"Watching them," the judge replied.

Quinn put his cup down on the saucer. Scraped his chair back. Reached forward with his right hand. Picked up the Syrian's case.

"Quinn has the Syrian's case," the judge said.

Quinn stood up. Said one last thing and turned around and walked away. There was a spring in his step. We watched him until he was out of sight. The Syrian was left with the check. He paid it and walked away north, until Frasconi stepped out of a doorway and took his arm and led him right back toward us. Kohl opened up the truck's rear door and Frasconi pushed the guy inside. We didn't have much space, with five people in the truck.

"Open the case," the judge said.

Up close the Syrian looked a lot more nervous than he had through the glass. He was sweating and he didn't smell too good. He laid the case flat on the floor and squatted in front of it. Glanced at each of us in turn and clicked the catches and lifted the lid.

The case was empty.

I HEARD THE PHONE RING INSIDE THE XAVIER Export Company's office. The door was thick and heavy and the sound was muffled and far away. But it was a phone, and it was ringing exactly five minutes after Duffy and Villanueva must have left the garage. It rang twice and was answered. I didn't hear any conversation. I guessed Duffy would make up some kind of a wrong-number story. I guessed she would keep it going just long enough to look significant in a phone log. I gave it a minute. Nobody keeps a bogus call going longer than sixty seconds.

I took the Beretta out of my pocket and pulled open the door. Stepped inside into a wide-open reception area. There was dark wood and carpet. An office to the left, closed up. An office to the right, closed up. A reception desk in front of me. A person at the desk, in the act of hanging up a phone. Not Quinn. It was a woman. She was maybe thirty years old. She had fair hair. Blue eyes. In front of her was an acetate plaque in a wooden holder. It said: *Emily Smith*. Behind her was a coat rack. There was a raincoat on it. And a black cocktail dress sheathed in dry-cleaner's plastic hanging on a wire hanger. I fumbled behind my back left-handed and locked the hallway door. Watched Emily Smith's eyes. They were staring straight at me. They didn't move. They didn't turn left or right toward either office door. So she was probably alone. And they didn't drop toward a purse or a desk drawer. So she was probably unarmed.

"You're supposed to be dead," she said.

"Am I?"

She nodded, vaguely, like she couldn't process what she was seeing.

"You're Reacher," she said. "Paulie told us he took you out."

I nodded. "OK, I'm a ghost. Don't touch the phone."

I stepped forward and looked at her desk. No weapons on it. The phone was a complicated multi-line console. It was all covered in buttons. I leaned down left-handed and ripped its cord out of its socket.

"Stand up," I said.

She stood up. Just pushed her chair back and levered herself upright.

"Let's check the other rooms," I said.

"There's nobody here," she said. There was fear in her voice, so she was probably telling me the truth.

"Let's check anyway," I said.

She came out from behind her desk. She was a foot shorter than me. She was wearing a dark skirt and a dark shirt. Smart shoes, which I figured would go equally well later with her cocktail dress. I put the Beretta's muzzle against her spine and bunched the back of her shirt collar in my left hand and moved her forward. She felt small and fragile. Her hair fell over my hand. It smelled clean. We checked the left-hand office first. She opened the door for me and I pushed her all the way inside and stepped sideways and moved out of the doorway. I didn't want to get shot in the back from across the reception area.

It was just an office. A decent-sized space. Nobody in it. There was an Oriental carpet, and a desk. There was a bathroom. Just a small cubicle with a toilet and a sink. Nobody in it. So I spun her around and moved her all the way across the reception area and into the right-hand office. Same decor. Same type of carpet, same type of desk. It was unoccupied. Nobody in it. No bathroom. I kept tight hold of her collar and pushed her back to the center of the reception area. Stopped her right next to her desk.

"Nobody here," I said.

"I told you," she said.

"So where is everybody?"

She didn't answer. And I felt her stiffen, like she was going to make a big point out of not answering.

"Specifically, where is Teresa Daniel?" I said.

No reply.

"Where's Xavier?" I said.

No reply.

"How do you know my name?"

"Beck told Xavier. He asked his permission to employ you."

"Xavier checked me out?"

"As far as he could."

"And he gave Beck his OK?"

"Obviously."

"So why did he set Paulie on me this morning?"

She stiffened again. "The situation changed."

"This morning? Why?"

"He got new information."

"What information?"

"I don't know exactly," she said. "Something about a car."

The Saab? The maid's missing notes?

"He made certain deductions," Emily Smith said. "Now he knows all about you."

"Figure of speech," I said. "Nobody knows all about me."

"He knows you were talking to ATF."

"Like I said, nobody really knows anything."

"He knows what you've been doing here."

"Does he? Do you?"

"He didn't tell me."

"Where do you fit in?"

"I'm his operations manager."

I wrapped her shirt collar tighter in my left fist and moved the Beretta's muzzle and used it to itch my cheek where the bruising was tightening the skin. I thought about Angel Doll, and John Chapman Duke, and two bodyguards whose names I didn't even know, and Paulie. I figured adding Emily Smith to the casualty list wasn't going to cost me much, in a cosmic sense. I put the gun to her head. I heard a plane in the distance, leaving from the airport. It roared through the sky, less than a mile away. I figured I could just wait for the next one and pull the trigger. Nobody would hear a thing. And she probably deserved it.

Or, maybe she didn't.

"Where is he?" I said.

"I don't know."

"You know what he did ten years ago?"

Live or die, Emily. If she knew, she would say so. For sure. Out of pride, or inclusion, or self-importance. She wouldn't be able to keep it in. And if she knew, she deserved to die. Because to know and to still work with the guy made it that way.

"No, he never told me," she said. "I didn't know him ten years ago."

"You sure?"

"Yes."

I believed her.

"You know what happened to Beck's maid?" I said.

A truthful person is perfectly capable of saying no, but generally they stop and think about it first. Maybe they come out with some questions of their own. It's human nature.

"Who?" she said. "No, what?"

I breathed out.

"OK," I said.

I put the Beretta back in my pocket and let go of her collar and turned her around and trapped both her wrists together in my left hand. Picked up the electrical cord from the phone with my right. Then I straight-armed her into the left-hand office and all the way through to the bathroom. Shoved her inside.

"The lawyers next door have gone home," I said. "There won't be anybody in the building until Monday morning. So go ahead and shout and scream all you want, but nobody will hear you."

She said nothing. I closed the door on her. Tied the phone cord tight around the knob. Opened the office door as wide as it would go and tied the other end of the cord to its handle. She could haul on the inside of the bathroom door all weekend long without getting anywhere. Nobody can break electrical wire by pulling on it lengthwise. I figured she'd give up after an hour and sit tight and drink water from the sink faucet and use the toilet and try to pass the time.

I sat down at her desk. I figured an operations manager should have some interesting paperwork. But she didn't. The best thing I found was a copy of the Keast and Maden order. The caterers. *18 @ $55.* Somebody had penciled a note on the bottom. A woman's handwriting. Probably Emily Smith's own. The note said: *lamb, not pork!* I swiveled her chair around and looked at the wrapped dress on the coat rack. Then I swiveled it back and checked my watch. My ten minutes were up.

I RODE THE ELEVATOR TO THE GARAGE AND LEFT by a fire exit in the rear. The rent-a-cop didn't see me. I walked around the block and came up on Duffy and Villanueva from behind. Their car was parked on the corner and they were together in the front, staring forward through the windshield. I guessed they were hoping to see two people walking down the street toward them. I opened the door and slid into the back seat and they spun around and looked disappointed. I shook my head.

"Neither of them," I said.

"Somebody answered the phone," Duffy said.

"A woman called Emily Smith," I said. "His operations manager. She wouldn't tell me anything."

"What did you do with her?"

"Locked her in the bathroom. She's out of the picture until Monday."

"You should have sweated her," Villanueva said. "You should have pulled her fingernails out."

"Not my style," I said. "But you can go right ahead, if you want. Feel free. She's still up there. She's not going anywhere."

He just shook his head and sat still.

"So what now?" Duffy asked.

"SO WHAT NOW?" KOHL ASKED.

We were still inside the utility truck. Kohl, the judge advocate, and me. Frasconi had taken the Syrian away. Kohl and I were thinking hard and the judge was in the process of washing his hands of the whole thing.

"I was only here to observe," he said. "I can't give you legal advice. It wouldn't be appropriate. And frankly I wouldn't know what to tell you anyway."

He glared at us and let himself out the rear door and just walked away. He didn't look back. I guess that was the downside of picking out a royal pain in the ass for an observer. *Unintended consequences.*

"I mean, what happened?" Kohl said. "What exactly did we see?"

"Only two possibilities," I said. "One, he was ripping the guy off, plain and simple. Classic confidence trick. You drip, drip, drip the unimportant stuff, and then you hold back on the final installment. Or two, he was working as a legitimate intelligence officer. On an official operation. Proving that Gorowski was leaky, proving that the Syrians were willing to pay big bucks for stuff."

"He kidnapped Gorowski's daughter," she said. "No way was that officially sanctioned."

"Worse things have happened," I said.

"He was ripping them off."

I nodded. "I agree with you. He was ripping them off."

"So what can we do about it?"

"Nothing," I said. "Because if we go ahead and accuse him of scamming them for personal profit, he'll just automatically say no, I wasn't doing that, actually I was running a sting, and I invite you to try to prove otherwise. And then he'll not very politely remind us to keep our big noses out of intelligence business."

She said nothing.

"And you know what?" I said. "Even if he *was* ripping them off, I wouldn't know what to charge him with. Does the Uniform Code stop you taking money from foreign idiots in exchange for briefcases full of fresh air?"

"I don't know."

"Neither do I."

"But whatever, the Syrians will go ape," she said. "I mean, won't they? They paid him half a million bucks. They'll have to react. Their pride is at stake. Even if he *was* legit, he took a hell of a big risk. Half a million big risks. They'll be coming after him. And he can't just disappear. He'll have to stay on-post. He'll be a sitting target."

I paused a beat. Looked at her. "If he's not going to disappear, why was he moving all his money?"

She said nothing. I looked at my watch. Thought: *This, not that.* Or, just perhaps, just for once, this *and* that.

"Half a million is too much money," I said.

"For what?"

"For the Syrians to pay. It's just not worth it. There'll be a prototype soon. Then there'll be a preproduction batch. There'll be a hundred finished weapons down at the quartermaster level within a matter of months. They could buy one of those for ten thousand dollars, probably. Some bent corporal would sell them one. They could even steal one for free. Then they could just reverse-engineer it."

"OK, so they're dumb businessmen," Kohl said. "But

we heard Quinn on the tape. He put half a million in the bank."

I looked at my watch again. "I know. That's a definite fact."

"So?"

"It's still too much. The Syrians are no dumber than anybody else. Nobody would value a fancy lawn dart at half a million bucks."

"But we know that's what they paid. You just agreed it's a definite fact."

"No," I said. "We know Quinn's got half a million in the bank. That's the fact. It doesn't prove the Syrians paid him half a million. That part is speculation."

"What?"

"Quinn's a Middle East specialist. He's a smart guy, and he's a bad guy. I think you stopped looking too soon."

"Looking at what?"

"At him. Where he goes, who he meets. How many dubious regimes are there in the Middle East? Four or five, minimum. Suppose he's in bed with two or three of them at once? Or all of them? With each one thinking it's the only one? Suppose he's leveraging the same scam three or four times over? That would explain why he's got half a million in the bank for something that isn't worth half a million to any one individual."

"And he's ripping them *all* off?"

I checked my watch again.

"Maybe," I said. "Or maybe he's playing for real with one of them. Maybe that's how it got started. Maybe he intended it to be for real all along, with one favored client. But he couldn't get the kind of big money he wanted from them. So he decided to multiply the yield."

"I should have watched more cafés," she said. "I shouldn't have stopped with the Syrian guy."

"He's probably got a fixed route," I said. "Lots of

separate meetings, one after another. Like a damn mail carrier."

She checked her watch.

"OK," she said. "So right now he's taking the Syrian's cash home."

I nodded. "And then he's heading out again right away to meet with the next guy. So you need to get Frasconi and get some more surveillance going. Find Quinn on his way back into town. Haul in anybody he swaps a briefcase with. Maybe you'll just end up with a bunch of empty briefcases, but maybe one of them won't be empty, in which case we're back in business."

She glanced around the inside of the truck. Glanced down at her tape recorder.

"Forget it," I said. "No time for the clever stuff. It'll have to be just you and Frasconi, out there on the street."

"THE WAREHOUSE," I SAID. "WE'RE GOING TO have to check it out."

"We'll need support," Duffy said. "They'll all be there."

"I hope they are."

"Too dangerous. There are only three of us."

"Actually I think they're all on their way to someplace else. It's possible they've left already."

"Where are they going?"

"Later," I said. "Let's take it one step at a time."

Villanueva moved the Taurus off the curb.

"Wait," I said. "Make the next right. Something else I want to check first."

I directed him two blocks over and one up and we came to the parking garage where I had left Angel Doll in the trunk of his car. Villanueva waited on a hydrant and I slipped out. I walked down the vehicle entrance and let my eyes adjust to the gloom. Walked on until I came to the space I had used. There was a car in it. But it wasn't Angel Doll's black Lincoln. It was a metallic green Subaru Legacy. It was the Outback version, with the roof rails and the big tires. It had a Stars and Stripes sticker in the back window. A patriotic driver. But not quite patriotic enough to buy an American automobile.

I walked the two adjacent aisles, just to make sure, although I already was. Not the Saab, but the Lincoln. Not the maid's missing notes, but Angel Doll's missing heartbeat. *Now he knows all about you.* I nodded to myself in the dark. Nobody knows all about anybody. But I guessed now he knew more about me than I was totally comfortable with. I walked back the way I had come. Up the entrance ramp and out into the daylight. It was cloudy and gray and dim and shadowed by tall buildings but it felt like a searchlight beam had hit me. I slid back into the Taurus and closed the door quietly.

"OK?" Duffy asked.

I didn't answer. She turned around in her seat and faced me.

"OK?" she said again.

"We need to get Eliot out of there," I said.

"Why?"

"They found Angel Doll."

"Who did?"

"Quinn's people."

"How?"

"I don't know."

"Are you sure?" she said. "It could have been the Portland PD. A suspicious vehicle, parked too long?"

I shook my head. "They'd have opened the trunk. So now they'd be treating the whole garage as a crime scene. They'd have it taped off. There'd be cops all over the place."

She said nothing.

"It's completely out of control now," I said. "So call Eliot. On his cell. Order him out of there. Tell him to take the Becks and the cook with him. In the Cadillac. Tell him to arrest them all at gunpoint if necessary. Tell him to find a different motel and hide out."

She dug in her purse for her Nokia. Hit a speed dial button. Waited. I timed it out in my head. One ring. Two rings. Three rings. Four rings. Duffy glanced at me, anxious. Then Eliot answered. Duffy breathed out and gave him the instructions, loud and clear and urgent. Then she clicked off.

"OK?" I said.

She nodded. "He sounded very relieved."

I nodded back. He would be. No fun in crouching over the butt end of a machine gun, your back to the sea, staring out at the gray landscape, not knowing what's coming at you, or when.

"So let's go," I said. "To the warehouse."

Villanueva moved off the curb again. He knew the way. He had watched the warehouse twice, with Eliot. Two long days. He threaded southeast through the city and approached the port from the northwest. We all sat quiet. There was no conversation. I tried to assess the damage. It was total. A disaster. But it was also a liberation. It clarified everything. No more pretending. The scam had dissolved away to nothing. Now I was their enemy, plain and simple. And they were mine. It was a release.

Villanueva was a smart operator. He did everything right. He worked his way around the warehouse on a three-block radius. Covered all four sides. We were limited to brief glimpses down alleys and through gaps between buildings. Four passes, four glimpses. There were no cars there. The roller door was closed tight. No lights in the windows.

"Where are they all?" Duffy said. "This was supposed to be a big weekend."

"It is," I said. "I think it's very big. And I think what they're doing makes perfect sense."

"What *are* they doing?"

"Later," I said. "Let's go take a look at the Persuaders. And let's see what they're getting in exchange."

Villanueva parked two buildings north and east, outside a door marked *Brian's Fine Imported Taxidermy*. He locked the Taurus and we walked south and west and then looped around to come up on Beck's place from the blind side where there were no windows. The personnel door into the warehouse office was locked. I looked in through the back office window and saw nobody. Rounded the corner and looked in at the secretarial area. Nobody there. We arrived at the unpainted gray door and stopped. It was locked.

"How do we get in?" Villanueva asked.

"With these," I said.

I pulled out Angel Doll's keys and unlocked the door. Opened it. The burglar alarm started beeping. I stepped in and flipped through the papers on the notice board and found the code and entered it. The red light changed to green and the beeping stopped and the building went silent.

"They're not here," Duffy said. "We don't have time to explore. We need to go find Teresa."

I could already smell gun oil. It was floating right there on top of the smell of the raw wool from the rugs.

"Five minutes," I said. "And then ATF will give you a medal."

———

"THEY SHOULD GIVE YOU A MEDAL," KOHL SAID.

She was calling me from a pay phone on the Georgetown University campus.

"Should they?"

"We've got him. We can stick a fork in him. The guy is totally done."

"So who was it?"

"The Iraqis," she said. "Can you believe that?"

"Makes sense, I guess," I said. "They just got their asses kicked and they want to be ready for the next time."

"Talk about audacious."

"How did it go down?"

"The same as we saw before. But with Samsonites, not Halliburtons. We got empty cases from a Lebanese guy and an Iranian. Then we hit the motherlode with the Iraqi guy. The actual blueprint."

"You sure?"

"Totally certain," she said. "I called Gorowski and he authenticated it by the drafting number in the bottom corner."

"Who witnessed the transfer?"

"Both of us. Me and Frasconi. Plus some students and faculty. They did it in a university coffee shop."

"What faculty?"

"We got a law professor."

"What did he see?"

"The whole thing. But he can't swear to the actual transfer. They were real slick, like a shell game. The briefcases were identical. Is it enough?"

Questions I wish I had answered differently. It was possible Quinn could claim the Iraqi already had the blueprint, from sources unknown. Possible he could suggest the guy just liked to carry it around with him. Possible he could deny there was any exchange at all. But then I thought about the Syrian, and the Lebanese guy, and the

Iranian. And all the money in Quinn's bank. The rip-off victims would be smarting. They might be willing to testify in closed session. The State Department might be able to offer them some kind of a quid pro quo. And Quinn's fingerprints would be on the briefcase in the Iraqi's possession. He wouldn't have worn gloves to the rendezvous. Too suspicious. Altogether I thought we had enough. We had a clear pattern, we had inexplicable dollars in Quinn's bank account, we had a top-secret U.S. Army blueprint in an Iraqi agent's possession, and we had two MPs and a law professor to say how it got there, and we had fingerprints on a briefcase handle.

"It's plenty," I said. "Go make the arrest."

"WHERE DO I GO?" DUFFY SAID.

"I'll show you," I said.

I moved past her through the open area. Into the back office. Through the door into the warehouse cubicle. Angel Doll's computer was still there on the desk. His chair was still leaking its stuffing all over the place. I found the right switch and lit up the warehouse floor. I could see everything through the glass partition. The racks of carpets were still there. The forklift was still there. But in the middle of the floor were five head-high stacks of crates. They were piled into two groups. Farthest from the roller door were three piles of battered wooden boxes all stenciled with markings in unfamiliar foreign alphabets, mostly Cyrillic, overlaid with right-to-left scrawls in some kind of Arabic language. I guessed those were Bizarre Bazaar's imports. Nearer the door were two piles of new crates printed in English: *Mossberg Connecticut*. Those would be the Xavier Export Company's outgoing shipment. Import-export, barter at its purest. *Fair exchange is no robbery,* as Leon Garber might have said.

"It's not huge, is it?" Duffy said. "I mean, five stacks of boxes? A hundred and forty thousand dollars? I thought it was supposed to be a big deal."

"I think it is big," I said. "In importance, maybe, rather than quantity."

"Let's take a look," Villanueva said.

We moved out onto the warehouse floor. He and I lifted the top Mossberg crate down. It was heavy. My left arm was still a little weak. And the center of my chest still hurt. It made my smashed mouth feel like nothing at all.

Villanueva found a claw hammer on a table. Used it to pull the nails out of the crate's lid. Then he lifted the lid off and laid it on the floor. The crate was full of foam peanuts. I plunged my hands in and came out with a long gun wrapped in waxed paper. I tore the paper off. It was an M500 Persuader. It was the Cruiser model. No shoulder stock. Just a pistol grip. 12-gauge, eighteen-and-a-half-inch barrel, three-inch chamber, six shot capacity, blued metal, black synthetic front grip, no sights. It was a nasty, brutal, close-up street weapon. I pumped the action, *crunch crunch*. It moved like silk on skin. I pulled the trigger. It clicked like a Nikon.

"See any ammunition?" I said.

"Here," Villanueva called. He had a box of Brenneke Magnum slugs in his hand. Behind him was an open carton full of dozens of identical packages. I broke open two boxes and loaded six shells and jacked one into the chamber and loaded a seventh. Then I clicked the safety, because the Brennekes were not birdshot. They were one-ounce solid copper slugs that would leave the Persuader at nearly eleven hundred miles an hour. They would punch a hole in a cinder block wall big enough to crawl through. I put the weapon on the table and unwrapped another one. Loaded it and clicked the safety and laid it next to the first one. Caught Duffy looking right at me.

"It's what they're for," I said. "An empty gun is no good to anybody."

I put the empty Brenneke boxes back in the carton and closed the lid. Villanueva was looking at Bizarre Bazaar's crates. He had paperwork in his hands.

"These look like carpets to you?" he said.

"Not a whole lot," I said.

"U.S. Customs thinks they do. Guy called Taylor signed off on them as handwoven rugs from Libya."

"That'll help," I said. "You can give this Taylor guy to ATF. They can check his bank accounts. Might make you more popular."

"So what's really in them?" Duffy said. "What do they make in Libya?"

"Nothing," I said. "They grow dates."

"This all is Russian stuff," Villanueva said. "It's been through Odessa twice. Imported to Libya, turned right around, and exported here. In exchange for two hundred Persuaders. Just because somebody wants to look tough on the streets of Tripoli."

"And they make a lot of stuff in Russia," Duffy said.

I nodded. "Let's see what, exactly."

There were nine crates in three stacks. I lifted the top crate off the nearest stack and Villanueva got busy with his claw hammer. He pulled the lid off and I saw a bunch of AK-74s nested in wood shavings. Standard Kalashnikov assault rifles, well used. Boring as hell, street value maybe two hundred bucks each, depending on where you were selling them. They weren't fashion items. I couldn't see any guys in North Face jackets trading in their beautiful matte-black H&Ks for them.

The second crate was smaller. It was full of wood shavings and AKSU-74 submachine guns. They're AK-74 derivatives. Efficient, but clunky. They were used too, but well maintained. Not exciting. No better than a half-dozen

Western equivalents. NATO hadn't lain awake at night worrying about them.

The third crate was full of nine-millimeter Makarov pistols. Most of them were scratched and old. It's a crude and lazy design, ripped off from the ancient Walther PP. The Soviet military was never much of a handgun culture. They thought using sidearms was right down there with throwing stones.

"This is all crap," I said. "Best thing to do with this stuff would be melt it down and use it for boat anchors."

We started on the second stack, and found something much more interesting in the very first crate. It was full of VAL Silent Sniper rifles. They were secret until 1994, when the Pentagon captured one. They're all black, all metal, with a skeleton stock. They fire special heavy nine-millimeter subsonic rounds. Tests showed they penetrated any body armor you chose to wear at a range of five hundred yards. I remember a fair amount of consternation at the time. There were twelve of them. The next crate held another twelve. They were quality weapons. And they looked good. They would go really well with the North Face jackets. Especially the black ones with the silver linings.

"Are they expensive?" Villanueva asked.

I shrugged. "Hard to say. Depends on what a person is willing to pay, I guess. But an equivalent Vaime or SIG bought new in the U.S. could cost over five grand."

"Then that's the whole invoice value right there."

I nodded. "They're serious weapons. But not a lot of use in south-central LA. So their street value might be much less."

"We should go," Duffy said.

I stepped back to line up the view through the glass and out the back office window. It was mid-afternoon. Gloomy, but still light.

"Soon," I said.

Villanueva opened the last crate in the second stack.

"What the hell is this?" he said.

I stepped over. Saw a nest of wood shavings. And a slim black tube with a short wooden section to act as a shoulder rest. A bulbous missile loaded ready in the muzzle. I had to look twice before I was sure.

"It's an RPG-7," I said. "It's an anti-tank rocket launcher. An infantry weapon, shoulder-fired."

"RPG means rocket propelled grenade," he said.

"In English," I said. "In Russian it means Reaktivniy Protivotankovyi Granatomet, rocket anti-tank grenade launcher. But it uses a missile, not a grenade."

"Like the long-rod penetrator?" Duffy said.

"Sort of," I said. "But it's explosive."

"It blows up tanks?"

"That's the plan."

"So who's going to buy it from Beck?"

"I don't know."

"Drug dealers?"

"Conceivably. It would be very effective against a house. Or an armored limousine. If your rival bought a bulletproof BMW, you'd need one of these."

"Or terrorists," she said.

I nodded. "Or militia whackos."

"This is very serious."

"They're hard to aim," I said. "The missile is big and slow. Nine times out of ten even a slight crosswind will make you miss. But that's no consolation to whoever else gets hit by mistake."

Villanueva wrenched the next lid off.

"Another one," he said. "The same."

"We need to call ATF," Duffy said. "FBI too, probably. Right now."

"Soon," I said.

Villanueva opened the last two crates. Nails squealed and wood split.

"More weird stuff," he said.

I looked. Saw thick metal tubes painted bright yellow. Electronic modules bolted underneath. I looked away.

"Grails," I said. "SA-7 Grails. Russian surface-to-air missiles."

"Heat seekers?"

"You got it."

"For shooting down planes?" Duffy said.

I nodded. "And really good against helicopters."

"What kind of range?" Villanueva asked.

"Good up to nearly ten thousand feet," I said.

"That could take down an airliner."

I nodded.

"Near an airport," I said. "Soon after takeoff. You could use it from a boat in the East River. Imagine hitting a plane coming out of La Guardia. Imagine it crashing in Manhattan. It would be September 11 all over again."

Duffy stared at the yellow tubes.

"Unbelievable," she said.

"This is not about drug dealers anymore," I said. "They've expanded their market. This is about terrorism. It has to be. This one shipment alone would equip a whole terrorist cell. They could do practically anything with it."

"We need to know who's lining up to buy it. And why they want it."

Then I heard the sound of feet on the floor in the doorway. And the *snick* of a round seating itself in an automatic pistol's chamber. And a voice.

"We don't ask why they want it," it said. "We never do. We just take their damn money."

CHAPTER 14

IT WAS HARLEY. HIS MOUTH WAS A RAGGED hole above his goatee. I could see his yellow teeth. He was holding a Para Ordnance P14 in his right hand. The P14 is a solid Canadian-made copy of the Colt 1911 and it was way too heavy for him. His wrists were thin and weak. He would have been better off with a Glock 19, like Duffy's.

"Saw the lights were on," he said. "Thought I'd come in and check."

Then he looked straight at me.

"I guess Paulie screwed up," he said. "And I guess you faked his voice when Mr. Xavier called you on the phone."

I looked at his trigger finger. It was in position. I spent half a second mad at myself for letting him walk in unannounced. Then I moved on to working out how to take him down. Thought: *Villanueva is going to yell at me if I take him down before we ask about Teresa.*

"You going to introduce me around?" he said.

"This is Harley," I said.

Nobody spoke.

"Who are these other people?" Harley asked me.

I said nothing.

"We're federal agents," Duffy said.

"So what are you all doing in here?" Harley asked.

He asked the question like he was genuinely interested. He was wearing a different suit. It was shiny black. He had a silver tie under it. He had showered and washed his hair. His pony tail was secured by a regular brown rubber band.

"We're working in here," Duffy said.

He nodded. "Reacher has seen what we do to government women. He's seen it with his own eyes."

"You should jump ship, Harley," I said. "It's all coming apart now."

"You think?"

"I know."

"See, we don't get that feeling from the computers. Your friend and mine in the body bag, she didn't tell them nothing yet. They're still waiting on her first report. Matter of fact, most days it seems like they've forgotten about her altogether."

"We've nothing to do with computers."

"Even better," he said. "You're freelance operators, nobody knows you're here, and I got you all covered."

"Paulie had me covered," I said.

"With a gun?"

"With two."

His eyes flicked down for a second. Then back up.

"I'm smarter than Paulie," he said. "Put your hands on your heads."

We put our hands on our heads.

"Reacher's got a Beretta," he said. "I know that for sure. I'm guessing there are two Glocks in the room as well. Most likely a 17 and a 19. I want to see them all on the floor, nice and slow, one at a time."

Nobody moved. Harley shaded the P14 toward Duffy.

"The woman first," he said. "Finger and thumb."

Duffy slid her left hand under her jacket and dragged her Glock out, pinched between her finger and thumb. She dropped it on the floor. I moved my arm and started my hand toward my pocket.

"Wait," Harley said. "You're not a trustworthy character."

He stepped forward and reached up and pressed the P14's muzzle into my lower lip, right where Paulie had hit me. Then he reached down with his left hand and burrowed in my pocket. Came out with the Beretta. Dropped it next to Duffy's Glock.

"You next," he said to Villanueva. He kept the P14 where it was. It was cold and hard. I could feel the muzzle's pressure on my loose teeth. Villanueva dropped his Glock on the floor. Harley raked all three guns behind him with his foot. Then he stepped backward.

"OK," he said. "Now get over here by the wall."

He wheeled us around until he was next to the crates and we were lined up against the back wall.

"There's one more of us," Villanueva said. "He isn't here."

Mistake, I thought. Harley just smiled.

"So call him," he said. "Tell him to come on down."

Villanueva said nothing. It felt like a dead end. Then it turned into a trap.

"Call him," Harley said again. "Right now, or I'll start shooting."

Nobody moved.

"Call him, or the woman gets a bullet in the thigh."

"She's got the phone," Villanueva said.

"In my purse," Duffy said.

"And where's your purse?"

"In the car."

Good answer, I thought.

"Where's the car?" Harley asked.

"Close by," Duffy said.

"The Taurus next to the stuffed animal place?"

Duffy nodded. Harley hesitated.

"You can use the phone in the office," he said. "Call the guy."

"I don't know his number," Duffy said.

Harley just looked at her.

"It's on my speed dial," she said. "I don't have it memorized."

"Where's Teresa Daniel?" I asked.

Harley just smiled. *Asked and answered,* I thought.

"Is she OK?" Villanueva said. "Because she better be."

"She's fine," Harley said. "Mint condition."

"You want me to go get the phone?" Duffy asked.

"We'll all go," Harley said. "After you put these crates back in order. You messed them up. You shouldn't have done that."

He stepped up next to Duffy and put the muzzle of his gun to her temple.

"I'll wait right here," he said. "And the woman can wait here with me. Like my own personal life insurance policy."

Villanueva glanced at me. I shrugged. I figured we were nominated to do the quartermaster work. I stepped forward and picked up the hammer from the floor. Villanueva picked up the lid from the first Grail crate. Glanced at me again. I shook my head just enough for him to see. I would have loved to bury the hammer in Harley's head. Or his mouth. I could have solved his dental problems permanently. But a hammer was no good against a guy with a gun to a hostage's head. And anyway, I had a better idea. And it would depend on a show of compliance. So I just held the hammer and waited politely until Villanueva had the lid in place over the fat yellow missile tube. I butted it with the heel of my hand until the nails found their original holes. Then I hammered them in and stood back and waited again.

We did the second Grail crate the same way. Lifted it up and piled it back on top of the first one. Then we did the RPG-7s. Nailed down the lids and stacked them exactly like we had found them. Then we did the VAL Silent Snipers. Harley watched us carefully. But he was relaxing a little. We were compliant. Villanueva seemed to understand what we were aiming for. He had caught on fast. He found the lid for the Makarov crate. Paused with it halfway into position.

"People buy these things?" he said.

Perfect, I thought. His tone was conversational, and a little puzzled. And professionally interested, just like a real ATF guy might be.

"Why wouldn't they buy them?" Harley said.

"Because they're junk," I said. "You ever tried one?"

Harley shook his head.

"Let me show you something," I said. "OK?"

Harley kept the gun pressed hard against Duffy's temple. "Show me what?"

I put my hand in the crate and came out with one of the pistols. Blew wood shavings off it and held it up. It was old and scratched. Well used.

"Very crude mechanism," I said. "They simplified the original Walther design. Ruined it, really. Double-action, like the original, but the pull is a nightmare."

I pointed the gun at the ceiling and put my finger on the trigger and used just my thumb on the back of the butt to exaggerate the effect. Pincered my hand and pulled the trigger. The mechanism grated like a balky stick shift in an old car and the gun twisted awkwardly in my grip.

"Piece of junk," I said.

I did it again, listening to the bad sound and letting the gun twist and rock between my finger and thumb.

"Hopeless," I said. "No chance of hitting anything unless it's right next to you."

I tossed the gun back into the crate. Villanueva slid the lid into position.

"You should be worried, Harley," he said. "Your reputation won't be worth shit if you put junk like this on the street."

"Not my problem," Harley said. "Not my reputation. I just work here."

I hammered the nails back in, slowly, like I was tired. Then we started on the AKSU-74 crate. The old submachine guns. Then we did the AK-74s.

"You could sell these to the movies," Villanueva said. "For historical dramas. That's about all they're good for."

I hammered the nails into position and we stacked the crate with the others until we had all of Bizarre Bazaar's imports back into a neat separate pile, just like we had found them. Harley was still watching us. He still had his gun at Duffy's head. But his wrist was tired and his finger wasn't hard on the trigger anymore. He had let it slide upward to the underside of the frame, where it was helping take the weight. Villanueva shoved the Mossberg crate across the floor toward me. Found the lid. We had only opened one.

"Nearly done," I said.

Villanueva slid the lid into position.

"Wait up," I said. "We left two of them on the table."

I stepped across and picked up the first Persuader. Stared at it.

"See this?" I said to Harley. I pointed at the safety catch. "They shipped it with the safety on. Shouldn't do that. It could damage the firing pin."

I snicked the safety to *fire* and wrapped the gun in its waxed paper and burrowed it deep down into the foam peanuts. Stepped back for the second one.

"This one's exactly the same," I said.

"You guys are going out of business for sure," Villanueva said. "Your quality control is all over the place."

I set the safety to *fire* and stepped back toward the crate. Pivoted off my right foot like a second baseman lining up a double play and pulled the trigger and shot Harley through the gut. The Brenneke round sounded like a bomb going off and the giant slug cut Harley in half, literally. He was there, and then suddenly he wasn't. He was in two large pieces on the floor and the warehouse was full of acrid smoke and the air was full of the hot stink of Harley's blood and his digestive system and Duffy was screaming because the man she had been standing next to had just exploded. My ears were ringing. Duffy kept on screaming and danced away from the spreading pool at her feet. Villanueva caught her and held on tight and I racked the Persuader's slide and watched the door in case there were any more surprises coming at us. But there weren't. The warehouse structure stopped resonating and my hearing came back and then there was nothing except silence and Duffy's fast loud breathing.

"I was standing right next to him," she said.

"You aren't standing right next to him now," I said. "That's the bottom line."

Villanueva let go of her and stepped over and bent down and picked up our handguns from where Harley had kicked them. I took the second loaded Persuader out of the crate and unwrapped it again and clicked the safety on.

"I really like these," I said.

"They seem to work," Villanueva said.

I held both shotguns in one hand and put my Beretta in my pocket.

"Get the car, Terry," I said. "Somebody's probably calling the cops right now."

He left by the front door and I looked at the sky

through the window. There was plenty of cloud, but there was still plenty of daylight, too.

"What now?" Duffy said.

"Now we go somewhere and wait," I said.

I WAITED MORE THAN AN HOUR, SITTING AT MY desk, looking at my telephone, expecting Kohl to call me. She had timed the drive out to MacLean at thirty-five minutes. Starting from the Georgetown University campus might have added five or ten, depending on traffic. Assessing the situation at Quinn's house could have added another ten. Taking him down should have taken less than one. Cuffing him and putting him in the car should have taken another three. Fifty-nine minutes, beginning to end. But a whole hour passed and she didn't call.

I started to worry after seventy minutes. Started to worry badly after eighty. Dead on ninety minutes I scared up a pool car and hit the road myself.

TERRY VILLANUEVA PARKED THE TAURUS ON THE patch of broken blacktop outside the office door and left the engine running.

"Let's call Eliot," I said. "Find out where he went. We'll go wait with him."

"What are we waiting for?" Duffy said.

"Dark," I said.

She went out to the idling car and got her bag. Brought it back. Dug out her phone and hit the number. I timed it out in my head. One ring. Two. Three. Four. Five. Six.

"No answer," Duffy said.

Then her face brightened. Then it fell again.

"Gone to voice mail," she said. "Something's wrong."

"Let's go," I said.

"Where to?"

I looked at my watch. Looked out the window at the sky. *Too early*.

"The coast road," I said.

We left the warehouse with the lights off and the doors locked. There was too much good stuff in it to leave it open and accessible. Villanueva drove. Duffy sat next to him in the front. I sat in the back with the Persuaders on the seat beside me. We threaded our way out of the harbor area. Past the lot where Beck parked his blue trucks. Onto the highway, past the airport, and south, away from the city.

WE CAME OFF THE HIGHWAY AND STRUCK OUT east on the familiar coast road. There was no other traffic. The sky was low and gray and the wind off the sea was strong enough to set up a howling around the Taurus's windshield pillars. There were drops of water in the air. Maybe they were raindrops. Maybe it was sea spray, lashed miles inland by the gale. It was still way too light. *Too early*.

"Try Eliot again," I said.

Duffy took her phone out. Speed-dialed the number. Put the phone to her ear. I heard six faint rings and the whisper of the voice mail announcement. She shook her head. Clicked the phone off again.

"OK," I said.

She twisted around in her seat.

"You sure they're all out at the house?" she said.

"Did you notice Harley's suit?" I said.

"Black," she said. "Cheap."

"It was as close as he could get to a tux. It was his

idea of evening wear. And Emily Smith had a black cocktail dress ready in her office. She was going to change. She already had her smart shoes on. I think there's going to be a banquet."

"Keast and Maden," Villanueva said. "The caterers."

"Exactly," I said. "Banquet food. Eighteen people at fifty-five dollars a head. Tonight. And Emily Smith made a note on the order. Lamb, not pork. Who eats lamb and not pork?"

"People who keep kosher."

"And Arabs," I said. "Libyans, maybe."

"Their suppliers."

"Exactly," I said again. "I think they're about to cement their commercial relationship. I think all the Russian stuff in the crates was some kind of a token shipment. It was a gesture. Same with the Persuaders. They've demonstrated to each other that both sides can deliver. Now they're going to break bread together and go into business for real."

"At the house?"

I nodded. "It's an impressive location. Isolated, very dramatic. And it's got a big dining table."

He turned the windshield wipers on. The glass streaked and smeared. It was sea spray, whipping horizontally off the Atlantic. Full of salt.

"Something else," I said.

"What?"

"I think Teresa Daniel is part of the deal," I said.

"What?"

"I think they're selling her along with the shotguns. A cute blond American girl. I think she's the ten-thousand-dollar bonus item."

Nobody spoke.

"Did you notice what Harley said about her? Mint condition."

Nobody spoke.

"I think they've kept her fed and alive and un-touched." I thought: *Paulie wouldn't have bothered with Elizabeth Beck if Teresa had been available to him. With all due respect to Elizabeth.*

Nobody spoke.

"They're probably cleaning her up right now," I said.

Nobody spoke.

"I think she's headed for Tripoli," I said. "Part of the deal. Like a sweetener."

Villanueva accelerated hard. The wind howled louder around the windshield pillars and the door mirrors. Two minutes later we reached the spot where we had ambushed the bodyguards and he slowed again. We were five miles from the house. Theoretically we were already visible from the upper floor windows. We came to a stop in the center of the road and we all craned forward and stared into the east.

I USED AN OLIVE-GREEN CHEVROLET AND MADE it out to MacLean in twenty-nine minutes. Stopped in the center of the road two hundred yards shy of Quinn's residence. It was in an established subdivision. The whole place was quiet and green and watered and was baking lazily in the sun. The houses were on acre lots and were half-hidden behind thick evergreen foundation plantings. Their driveways were jet black. I could hear birds singing and a far-off sprinkler turning slowly and hissing against a soaked sidewalk through sixty degrees of its rotation. I could see fat dragonflies in the air.

I took my foot off the brake and crawled forward a hundred yards. Quinn's house was sided with dark cedar boards. It had a stone walk and knee-high stone walls boxing in earth beds full of low spruces and rhododen-drons. It had small windows and the way the eaves of the roof met the tops of the walls made it feel like the house was crouched down with its back to me.

Frasconi's car was parked in the driveway. It was an olive-green Chevrolet identical to my own. It was empty. Its front bumper was tight against Quinn's garage door. The garage was a long low triple. It was closed up. There was no sound anywhere, except the birds and the sprinkler and the hum of insects.

I parked behind Frasconi's car. My tires sounded wet on the hot blacktop. I slid out and eased my Beretta out of its holster. Clicked the safety to *fire* and started up the stone walk. The front door was locked. The house was silent. I peered in through a hallway window. Saw noth-ing, except the kind of solid neutral furniture that goes into an expensive rental.

I walked around to the rear. There was a flagstone pa-tio with a barbecue grill on it. A square teak table going gray in the weather and four chairs. An off-white canvas sun umbrella on a pole. A lawn, and plenty of low-mainte-nance evergreen bushes. A cedar fence stained the same dark color as the house siding closed off the neighbors' view.

I tried the kitchen door. It was locked. I looked in the window. Saw nothing. I moved around the rear perimeter. Came to the next window and saw nothing. Moved to the next window and saw Frasconi lying on his back.

He was in the middle of the living room floor. There was a sofa and two armchairs all covered in durable mud-colored fabric. The floor was done in wall-to-wall carpet and it matched the olive of his uniform. He had been shot once through the forehead. Nine millimeter. Fatal. Even through the window I could see the single crusted hole and the dull ivory color of his skull under his skin. There was a lake of blood under his head. It had soaked into the carpet and was already drying and turning dark.

I didn't want to go in on the first floor. If Quinn was still in there he would be waiting upstairs where he had the tactical advantage. So I dragged the patio table over to the back of the garage and used it to climb onto the roof. Used the roof to get me next to an upstairs window. Used my elbow to get me through the glass. Then I went feet-first into a guest bedroom. It smelled musty and unused. I walked through it and came out in an upstairs hallway. Stood still and listened. Heard nothing. The house sounded completely empty. There was a deadness. A total absence of sound. No human vibrations.

But I could smell blood.

I crossed the upstairs hallway and found Dominique Kohl in the master bedroom. She was on her back on the bed. She was completely naked. Her clothes had been torn off. She had been hit in the face enough times to make her groggy and then she had been butchered. Her breasts had been removed with a large knife. I could see the knife. It had been thrust upward through the soft flesh under her chin and through the roof of her mouth and into her brain.

By that point in my life I had seen a lot of things. I had once woken up after a terrorist attack with part of another man's jawbone buried in my gut. I had had to wipe his flesh out of my eyes before I could see well enough to crawl away. I had crawled twenty yards through severed legs and arms and butted my knees against severed heads with my hands pressed hard into my abdomen to stop my own intestines falling out. I had seen homicides and accidents and men machine-gunned in feuds and people reduced to pink paste in explosions and blackened twisted lumps in fires. But I had never seen anything as bad as Dominique Kohl's butchered body. I threw up on the floor and then for the first time in more than twenty years I cried.

"SO WHAT NOW?" VILLANUEVA SAID, TEN YEARS later.

"I'm going in alone," I said.

"I'm coming with you."

"Don't argue," I said. "Just get me a little closer. And drive real slow."

It was a gray car on a gray day and slow-moving objects are less perceptible than fast-moving objects. He took his foot off the brake and touched the gas and got it rolling at about ten miles an hour. I checked the Beretta and its spare magazines. Forty-five rounds, less two fired into Duke's ceiling. I checked the Persuaders. Fourteen rounds, less one fired through Harley's gut. Total of fifty-six rounds, against less than eighteen people. I didn't know who was on the guest list, but Emily Smith and Harley himself were going to be no-shows for sure.

"Stupid to do it alone," Villanueva said.

"Stupid to do it together," I said back. "The approach is going to be suicidal."

He didn't answer.

"Better that you guys stand by out here," I said.

He made no reply to that. He wanted my back and he wanted Teresa but he was smart enough to see that walking toward a fortified and isolated house in the last of the daylight was going to be no kind of fun. He just kept the car rolling slowly. Then he took his foot off the gas and put the transmission in neutral and let it coast to a stop. He didn't want to risk the flare of brake lights in the mist. We were maybe a quarter-mile short of the house.

"You guys wait here," I said. "For the duration."

Villanueva looked away.

"Give me one hour," I said.

I waited until they both nodded.

"Then call ATF," I said. "After an hour, if I'm not back."

"Maybe we should do that now," Duffy said.

"No," I said. "I want the hour first."

"ATF will get Quinn," she said. "It's not like they're going to let him walk."

I thought back to what I had seen and just shook my head.

I BROKE EVERY REGULATION AND IGNORED EVERY procedure in the book. I walked away from a crime scene and failed to report it. I obstructed justice left and right. I left Kohl in the bedroom and Frasconi in the living room. Left their car on the driveway. Just drove myself back to the office and took a silenced Ruger Standard .22 from the company armory and went to find Kohl's boxed-up files. My gut told me Quinn would make one stop before he headed for the Bahamas. He would have an emergency stash somewhere. Maybe phony ID, maybe a wad of cash, maybe a packed bag, maybe all three. He wouldn't hide the stash on-post. Nor in his rented house. He was too professional for that. Too cautious. He would want it safe and far away. I was gambling it would be in the place he had inherited in northern California. From his parents, the railroad worker and the stay-at-home mom. So I needed that address.

Kohl's handwriting was neat. The two cartons were filled with her notes. They were comprehensive. They were meticulous. They broke my heart. I found the California address in an eight-page bio she had prepared. It was a five-digit house number on a road that came under the Eureka post office. Probably a lonely place, far out of town. I went to my company clerk's desk and signed a stack of travel warrants for myself. Put my service Beretta and the silenced Ruger in a canvas bag and drove to the airport. They gave me papers to sign before they let me carry loaded firearms inside the cabin. I wasn't about to check them. I figured there was a good chance Quinn might take the same flight. I figured if I saw him at the gate or on the plane I would waste him right there and then.

But I didn't see him. I got on a plane for Sacramento and walked the aisle after takeoff and scanned every face and he wasn't there. So I sat tight for the duration of the flight. Just stared into space. The stewardesses stayed well away from me.

I rented a car at the Sacramento airport. Drove it north on I-5 and then northwest on Route 299. It was a designated scenic road. It wound through the mountains. I looked at nothing except the yellow line ahead of me. I had picked up three hours because of flying across three time zones but even so it was gathering dark when I hit the Eureka limit. I found Quinn's road. It was a meandering strip that ran north-south high in the hills above U.S. 101. The highway was laid out far below me. I could see headlights streaming north. Taillights heading south. I guessed there was a rail line down there somewhere. Maybe a station or a depot nearby, convenient for Quinn's old man back when he was working.

I found the house. Drove past it without slowing. It was a rough one-story cabin. It used an old milk churn instead of a mailbox post. The front yard had gone to seed a decade ago. I K-turned five hundred yards south of it and drove two hundred yards back toward it with my lights off. Parked behind an abandoned diner with a caved-in roof. Got out and climbed a hundred feet into the hills.

Walked north three hundred yards and came on his place from the rear.

In the dusk I could see a narrow back porch and a scuffed area next to it where cars could be parked. Clearly it was the sort of place where you use the back door, not the front. There were no lights on inside. I could see dusty sun-faded drapes half-closed in the windows. The whole place looked empty and unused. I could see a couple of miles north and south and there were no cars on the road.

I came down the hill slowly on foot. Circled the house. Listened at every window. There was nobody inside. I figured Quinn would park in back and come in through the rear, so I broke in through the front. The door was thin and old and I just pushed hard on it until the inner jamb started to give and then I smacked it once above the lock with the heel of my hand. Wood splintered and the door swung open and I stepped inside and closed it again and wedged it shut with a chair. It would look OK from the outside.

It was musty inside and easily ten degrees colder than outside. It was dark and dim. I could hear a refrigerator running in the kitchen, so I knew there was electricity. The walls were covered in ancient wallpaper. It was faded and yellow. There were only four rooms. There was an eat-in kitchen, and a living room. There were two bedrooms. One was small and the other was smaller. I figured the smaller one had been Quinn's, as a kid. There was a lone bathroom between the bedrooms. White fixtures, stained with rust.

Four rooms plus a bath is an easier search than most. I found what I was looking for almost immediately. I lifted a rag rug off of the living room floor and found a square hatch let into the boards. If it had been in the hallway I would have figured it for an inspection cover above the crawl space. But it was in the living room. I took a fork from the kitchen and levered it open. Under it was a shallow wooden tray built between the floor joists. On the tray was a shoe box wrapped in milky plastic sheeting. Inside the shoe box were three thousand dollars and two keys. I figured the keys were for safety-deposit boxes or left-luggage lockers. I took the cash and left the keys where they were. Then I put the hatch lid back and replaced the rug and chose a chair and sat down to wait with my Beretta in my pocket and the Ruger laid across my lap.

"TAKE CARE," DUFFY SAID.

I nodded. "Sure."

Villanueva said nothing. I slid out of the Taurus with the Beretta in my pocket and the Persuaders held one in each hand. Crossed straight to the shoulder of the road and got as far down on the rocks as I could and started picking my way east. There was still daylight behind the clouds but I was dressed in black and I was carrying black guns and I wasn't exactly on the road itself and I thought I might have a chance. The wind was blowing hard toward me and there was water in the air. I could see the ocean ahead. It was raging. The tide was on the way out. I could hear the distant waves pounding and the long suck of the undertow ripping through sand and gravel.

I came around a shallow curve and saw that the wall lights were on. They blazed blue-white against the dim sky. The contrast between the electric light and the late-afternoon darkness beyond it would mean they would see me less and less well the closer I got. So I climbed back onto the roadway and started to jog. I got as close as I dared and then slipped back down the rocks and hugged the shore. The ocean was right at my feet. I could smell salt and seaweed. The rocks were slippery. Waves pounded and spray burst up at me and the water swirled angrily.

I stood still. Took a breath. Realized I couldn't swim around the wall. Not this time. It would be madness. The sea was way too rough. I would have no chance. No chance at all. I would be tossed around like a cork and smashed against the rocks and battered to death. Unless the undertow got me first and pulled me out and swallowed me into the depths and drowned me.

Can't go around it, can't go over it. Got to go through it.

I climbed up the rocks again and stepped into the bar of light as far from the gate as I could get. I was all the way over where the foundations canted down toward the water. Then I kept very close to the wall and walked along its length. I was bathed in light. But nobody east of the wall could see me because it was between me and the house and it was taller than me. And anybody west of me was a friend. All I had to worry about was tripping the sensors buried in the ground. I stepped as lightly as I could and hoped they hadn't buried any this close in.

And I guess they hadn't, because I made it to the gatehouse OK. I risked a glance inside through the gap in the drapes in the front window and saw the brightly-lit living room and Paulie's replacement busy relaxing on the collapsed sofa. He was a guy I hadn't seen before. He was about Duke's age and size. Maybe approaching forty, maybe a little slighter than me. I spent some time figuring his exact height. That was going to be important. He was possibly two inches shorter than me. He was dressed in jeans and a white T-shirt and a denim jacket. Clearly he wasn't going to the ball. He was Cinderella, tasked to watch the gate while the others partied. I hoped he was the only one. I hoped they were working a skeleton crew. But I wasn't about to bet on it. Any kind of minimal caution would put a second guy on the front door of the house, and maybe a third up there in Duke's window. Because they knew Paulie hadn't gotten the job done. They knew I was still out there somewhere.

I couldn't afford the noise involved in shooting the new guy. The waves were loud and the wind was howling but neither sound would mask the Beretta. And nothing on earth would mask a Persuader firing a Brenneke Magnum. So I retreated a couple of yards and put the Persuaders down on the ground and took my coat and my jacket off. Then I took my shirt off and wrapped it tight around my left fist. Put my bare back against the wall and sidestepped my way to the edge of the window. Used the nails on my right hand to tap softly on the bottom corner of the glass, where it was draped, on and off, faint little paradiddles like a mouse makes when he runs across above a ceiling. I did it four times and was about to try a fifth when I saw in the corner of my eye the light in the window suddenly go dim. That meant the new guy had gotten off his sofa and pressed his face up against the glass to try to see what kind of little creature was out there bothering him. So I concentrated on getting the height exactly right and spun one-eighty and threw a huge roundhouse left with my padded fist and bust the window first and the new guy's nose a millisecond later. He went down in a heap below the inside sill and I reached in through the hole I had made and unlatched the casement and swung it open and climbed inside. The guy was sitting on his butt on the floor. He was bleeding from his nose and the glass cuts in his face. He was groggy. There was a handgun on the sofa. He was eight feet away from it. He was twelve feet from the phones. He shook his head to clear it and looked up at me.

"You're Reacher," he said. There was blood in his mouth.

"Correct," I said back.

"You've got no chance," he said.

"You think?"

He nodded. "We've got shoot-to-kill orders."

"On me?"

He nodded again.

"Who has?"

"Everybody."

"Xavier's orders?"

He nodded again. Put the back of his hand up under his nose.

"People going to obey those orders?" I asked.

"For sure."

"Are you?"

"I guess not."

"Promise?"

"I guess so."

"OK," I said.

I paused for a moment and thought about asking him some more questions. He might be reluctant. But I figured I could slap him around some and get all the answers he had to give. But in the end I figured those answers didn't matter very much. Made no practical difference to me if there were ten or twelve or fifteen hostiles in the house, or what they were armed with. *Shoot to kill. Them or me.* So I just stepped away and was trying to decide what to do with the guy when he made my mind up for me by reneging on his promise. He came up off the floor and made a dive for the handgun on the sofa. I caught him with a wild left in the throat. It was a solid punch, and a lucky one. But not for him. It crushed his larynx. He went down on the floor again and suffocated. It was reasonably quick. About a minute and a half. There was nothing I could do for him. I'm not a doctor.

I stood completely still for a minute. Then I put my shirt back on and climbed back out of the window and retrieved the shotguns and my jacket and my coat and climbed back in and crossed the room and looked out of the back window at the house.

"Shit," I said, and looked away.

The Cadillac was parked on the carriage circle. Eliot hadn't gotten away. Nor had Elizabeth, or Richard, or the cook. That put three noncombatants into the mix. And the presence of noncombatants makes any assault a hundred times harder. And this one was hard enough to begin with.

I looked again. Next to the Cadillac was a black Lincoln Town Car. Next to the Town Car were two dark blue Suburbans. There was no catering truck. Maybe it was around the side, next to the kitchen door. Maybe it was coming later. Or maybe it wasn't coming at all. Maybe there was no banquet. Maybe I had screwed up completely and misinterpreted the whole situation.

I stared through the harsh lights on the wall into the gloom around the house. I couldn't see a guard on the front door. But then, it was cold and wet and anybody with any sense would be inside the hallway looking out through the glass. I couldn't see anybody in Duke's window, either. But it was standing open, exactly the way I had left it. Presumably the NSV was still hanging there on its chain.

I looked at the vehicles again. The Town Car could have brought four people in. The Suburbans could have brought seven each. Eighteen people, maximum. Maybe fifteen or sixteen principals and two or three guards. Alternatively, maybe only three drivers came. Maybe I was completely wrong.

Only one way to find out.

And this was the hardest part. I had to get through the lights. I debated finding the switch and turning them off. But that would be an instant early warning to the people in the house. Five seconds after they went off they would be on the phone asking the gate guard what had happened. And the gate guard couldn't answer, because the gate guard was dead. Whereupon I would have fifteen or more people swarming straight at me in the gloom. Easy enough to avoid most of them. But the trick would be to know who to avoid, and who to grab. Because I was pretty sure if I let Quinn get behind me tonight I would never see him again.

So I had to do it with the lights blazing. Two possibilities. One was to run straight toward the house. That would minimize the time I spent actually illuminated. But it would involve rapid motion, and rapid motion catches the eye. The other possibility would be to traverse the wall all the way to the ocean. Sixty yards, slowly. It would be agony. But it was probably the better option.

Because the lights were mounted on the wall, trained away from it. There would be a dark tunnel between the wall itself and the rear edge of the beams. It would be a slim triangle. I could crawl along it, right down at the base of the structure. Slowly. Through the NSV's field of fire.

I eased the rear door open. There were no lights on the gatehouse itself. They started twenty feet to my right, where the gatehouse wall became the perimeter wall. I stepped halfway out and crouched down. Turned ninety degrees right and looked for my tunnel. It was there. It was less than three feet deep at ground level. It narrowed to nothing at head height. And it wasn't very dark. There was scatter coming back off the ground and there were occasional misaligned beams and there was glow coming out of the rear of the lamps themselves. My tunnel was maybe halfway between pitch dark and brilliantly lit.

I shuffled forward on my knees and reached back and closed the door behind me. Put a Persuader in each hand and dropped to my stomach and pressed my right shoulder hard against the base of the wall. Then I waited. Just long enough for anybody who thought they'd seen the door move to lose interest. Then I started crawling. Slowly.

I got maybe ten feet. Then I stopped again. Fast. I heard a vehicle out on the road. Not a sedan. Something bigger than that. Maybe another Suburban. I reversed direction. Dug my toes in and crawled backward to the doorway. Knelt up and opened the door and slid inside the gatehouse and stood up. Put the Persuaders on a chair and took the Beretta out of my pocket. I could hear a big-inch V-8 idling on the other side of the gate.

Decisions. Whoever was out there was expecting the gate guard's services. And a buck got ten whoever was out there would know I wasn't the real gate guard. So I figured I would have to give up on the crawling. I figured I would have to go noisy. Shoot them, take their vehicle, make it down to the house real fast before the NSV gunner could draw a bead. Then take my chances in the ensuing chaos.

I stepped to the back door again. Clicked the Beretta's safety off and took a breath. I had the initial advantage. I already knew exactly what I was going to do. Everybody else would have to react first. And that would take them a second too long.

Then I remembered the camera on the gatepost. The video monitor. I could see exactly what I was faced with. I could count heads. *Forewarned is forearmed.* I stepped across to check. The picture was gray and milky. It showed a white panel van. Writing on the side. *Keast & Maden Catering.* I breathed out. No reason why they should know the gate man. I put the Beretta back in my pocket. Stripped off my coat and jacket. Pulled the denim thing off the gate man's body and slipped it on. It was tight, and there was blood on it. But it was reasonably convincing. I stepped out the door. Kept my back to the house and tried to make myself look two inches shorter. Walked to the gate. Butted the latch upward with my fist, the same way Paulie used to. Hauled it open. The white truck drove up level with me. The passenger buzzed his window down. He was wearing a tux. The guy at the wheel was in a tux. *More noncombatants.*

"Where to?" the passenger asked.

"Around the house to the right," I said. "Kitchen door's all the way at the back."

The window went back up. The truck drove past me. I waved. Closed the gate again. Stepped back into the lodge and watched the truck from the window. It headed straight for the house and then swung right at the carriage circle. Its headlight beams washed over the Cadillac and the Town Car and the two Suburbans and I caught a flare from its brake lights and then it disappeared from view.

I waited two minutes. Willed it to get darker. Then I changed back into my own coat and jacket and retrieved the Persuaders from the chair. Eased the door open and crawled out and closed it behind me and dropped to my stomach. Pressed my shoulder to the base of the wall and started the slow crawl all over again. I kept my face turned away from the house. There was grit underneath me and I could feel small stones sharp against my elbows and my knees. But mostly I could feel a tingle in my back. It was facing a weapon that could fire twelve half-inch bullets every second. There was probably some tough guy right behind it with his hands resting lightly on the handles. I was hoping he would miss with the first burst. I figured he probably would. I figured he would fire the first burst way low or way high. Whereupon I would be up and running zigzags into the darkness before he lined up for a better try.

I inched forward. Ten yards. Fifteen. Twenty. I kept it really slow. Kept my face turned to the wall. Hoped I looked like a vague indistinct shadow in the penumbra. It was completely counterintuitive. I was fighting a powerful desire to jump up and run. My heart was pounding. I was sweating, even though it was cold. The wind was battering me. It was coming off the sea and hitting the wall and streaming down it like a tide and trying to roll me out to where the lights were brightest.

I kept going. Made it about halfway. About thirty yards covered, about thirty yards to go. My elbows were sore. I was keeping the Persuaders up off the ground and my arms were taking the toll. I stopped to rest. Just pressed myself into the dirt. Tried to look like a rock. I turned my head and risked a glance toward the house. It was quiet. I glanced ahead. Glanced behind. *The point of no return.* I crawled on. Had to force myself to keep the speed slow. The farther I got, the worse my back tingled. I was breathing hard. Getting close to panic. Adrenaline was boiling through me, screaming *run, run.* I gasped and panted and forced my arms and legs to stay coordinated. To stay *slow.* Then I got within ten yards of the end and started to believe I could make it. I stopped. Took a breath. And another. Started again. Then the ground tilted down and I followed it headfirst. I reached the water. Felt wet slime underneath me. Small rough waves came at me and spray hit me. I turned a ninety-degree left and paused. I was way on the edge of anybody's field of view, but I had to get through thirty feet of bright light. I gave up on keeping it slow. I ducked my head and half-stood and just ran for it.

I spent maybe four seconds lit up brighter than I had ever been before. It felt like four lifetimes. I was blinded. Then I crashed back into darkness and crouched down and listened. Heard nothing except the wild sea. Saw nothing except purple spots in my eyes. I stumbled on another ten paces over the rocks and then stood still. Looked back. *I was in.* I smiled in the dark. *Quinn, I'm coming to get you now.*

CHAPTER 15

TEN YEARS AGO I WAITED EIGHTEEN HOURS FOR him. I never doubted he was coming. I just sat in his arm-chair with the Ruger on my lap and waited. I didn't sleep. I barely even blinked. Just sat. All through the night. Through the dawn. All through the next morning. Midday came and went. I just sat and waited for him.

He came at two o'clock in the afternoon. I heard a car slowing on the road and stood up and kept well back from the window and watched as he turned in. He was in a rental, similar to mine. It was a red Pontiac. I saw him clearly through the windshield. He was neat and clean. His hair was combed. He was wearing a blue shirt with the collar open. He was smiling. The car swept past the side of the house and I heard it crunch to a stop on the dirt outside the kitchen. I stepped through to the hallway. Pressed myself against the wall next to the kitchen door.

I heard his key in the lock. Heard the door swing open. The hinges squealed in protest. He left it open. I heard his car idling outside. He hadn't switched it off. He wasn't planning on staying long. I heard his feet on the kitchen linoleum. A fast, light, confident tread. A man who thought he was playing and winning. He came through the door. I hit him in the side of the head with my elbow.

He went down on the floor on his back and I spanned my hand and pinned him by the throat. Laid the Ruger aside and patted him down. He was unarmed. I let go of his neck and his head came up and I smashed it back down with the heel of my hand under his chin. The back of his head hit the floor and his eyes rolled up in his head. I walked through the kitchen and closed the door. Stepped back and dragged him into the living room by the wrists. Dropped him on the floor and slapped him twice. Aimed the Ruger at the center of his face and waited for his eyes to open.

They opened and focused first on the gun and then on me. I was in uniform and all covered in badges of rank and unit designations so it didn't take him long to work out who I was and why I was there.

"Wait," he said.

"For what?"

"You're making a mistake."

"Am I?"

"You've got it wrong."

"Have I?"

He nodded. "They were on the take."

"Who were?"

"Frasconi and Kohl."

"Were they?"

He nodded again. "And then he tried to cheat her."

"How?"

"Can I sit up?"

I shook my head. Kept the gun where it was.

"No," I said.

"I was running a sting," he said. "I was working with the State Department. Against hostile embassies. I was trawling."

"What about Gorowski's kid?"

He shook his head, impatiently. "Nothing happened with the damn kid, you idiot. Gorowski had a script to follow, that's all. It was a setup. In case the hostiles checked on him. We play these things deep. There has to be a chain to follow, in case anyone is suspicious. We were doing proper dead drops and everything. In case we were being watched."

"What about Frasconi and Kohl?"

"They were good. They picked up on me real early. Assumed I wasn't legit. Which pleased me. Meant I was playing my part just right. Then they went bad. They came to me and said they'd slow the investigation if I paid them. They said they'd give me time to leave the country. They thought I wanted to do that. So I figured, hey, why not play along? Because who knows in advance what bad guys a trawl will find? And the more the merrier, right? So I played them out."

I said nothing.

"The investigation was slow, wasn't it?" he said. "You must have noticed that. Weeks and weeks. It was real slow."

Slow as molasses.

"Then yesterday happened," he said. "I got the Syrians and the Lebanese and the Iranians in the bag. Then the Iraqis, who were the big fish. So I figured it was time to put your guys in the bag too. They came over for their final payoff. It was a lot of money. But Frasconi wanted it all. He hit me over the head. I came around and found he had sliced Kohl up. He was a crazy man, believe me. I got to a gun in a drawer and shot him."

"So why did you run?"

"Because I was freaked. I'm a Pentagon guy. I never saw blood before. And I didn't know who else might be in it with your guys. There could have been more."

Frasconi and Kohl.

"You're very good," he said to me. "You came right here."

I nodded. Thought back to his eight-page bio, in Kohl's tidy handwriting. *Parents' occupations, childhood home.*

"Whose idea was it?" I said.

"Originally?" he said. "Frasconi's, of course. He outranked her."

"What was her name?"

I saw a flicker in his eyes.

"Kohl," he said.

I nodded again. She had gone out to make the arrest in dress greens. A black acetate nameplate above her right breast. *Kohl.* Gender-neutral. *Uniform, female enlisted, the nameplate is adjusted to individual figure differences and centered horizontally on the right side between one and two inches above the top button of the coat.* He would have seen it as soon as she walked in the door.

"First name?"

He paused.

"Don't recall," he said.

"Frasconi's first name?"

Uniform, male officer, the nameplate is centered on the right-side breast pocket flap equidistant between the seam and the button.

"I don't recall."

"Try," I said.

"I can't recall it," he said. "It's only a detail."

"Three out of ten," I said. "Call it an E."

"What?"

"Your performance," I said. "A failing grade."

"What?"

"Your dad was a railroad worker," I said. "Your mom was a homemaker. Your full name is Francis Xavier Quinn."

"So?"

"Investigations are like that," I said. "You plan to put somebody in the bag, you find out all about them first. You were playing those two for weeks and weeks and never found out their first names? Never looked at their service records? Never made any notes? Never filed any reports?"

He said nothing.

"And Frasconi never had an idea in his life," I said. "Never even took a dump unless somebody told him to. Nobody connected to those two would ever say *Frasconi and Kohl*. They'd say *Kohl and Frasconi*. You were dirty all the way and you never saw my guys in your life before the exact minute they showed up at your house to arrest you. And you killed them both."

He proved I was right by trying to fight me. I was ready for him. He started to scramble up. I knocked him back down, a lot harder than I really needed to. He was still unconscious when I put him in the trunk of his car. Still unconscious when I transferred him to the trunk of mine, behind the abandoned diner. I drove a little way south on U.S. 101 and took a right that led toward the Pacific. I stopped on a gravel turnout. There was a fabulous view. It was three o'clock in the afternoon and the sun was shining and the ocean was blue. The turnout had a knee-high metal barrier and then there was another half-yard of gravel and then there was a long vertical drop into the surf. Traffic was very light. Maybe a car every couple of minutes. The road was just an arbitrary loop off the highway.

I opened the trunk and then slammed it again just in case he was awake and planning to jump out at me. But he wasn't. He was starved of air and barely conscious. I dragged him out and propped him up on rubbery legs and made him walk. Let him look at the ocean for a minute while I checked for potential witnesses. There were none. So I turned him around. Stepped away five paces.

"Her name was Dominique," I said.

Then I shot him. Twice in the head, once in the chest. I expected him to go straight down on the gravel, whereupon I was planning to step in close and put a fourth up through his eye socket before throwing him into the ocean. But he didn't go straight down on the gravel. He staggered backward and tripped on the rail and went over it and hit the last half-yard of America with his shoulder and rolled straight over the cliff. I grabbed the barrier with one hand and leaned over and looked down. Saw him hit the rocks. The surf closed over him. I didn't see him again. I stayed there for a full minute. Thought: *Two in the head, one in the heart, a hundred-twenty-foot fall into the ocean, no way to survive that.*

I picked up my shell cases. "Ten-eighteen, Dom," I said to myself, and walked back to my car.

TEN YEARS LATER IT WAS GOING DARK VERY fast and I was picking my way over the rocks behind the garage block. The sea was heaving and thrashing on my right. The wind was in my face. I didn't expect to see anybody out and about. Especially not at the sides or the back of the house. So I was moving fast, head up, alert, a Persuader in each hand. *I'm coming to get you, Quinn.*

When I cleared the rear of the garage block I could see the catering company's truck parked at the back corner of the building. It was exactly where Harley had put the Lincoln to unload Beck's maid from the trunk. The truck's rear doors were open and the driver and the passenger were shuttling back and forth unpacking it. The metal detector on the kitchen door was beeping at every foil dish they carried. I was hungry. I could smell hot food on the wind. Both guys were in tuxedos. Their heads were ducked down because of the weather. They weren't paying attention to anything except their jobs. But I gave them a wide berth anyway. I stayed all the way on the edge of the rocks and skirted around in a loop. Jumped over Harley's cleft and kept on going.

When I was as far from the caterers as I could get I cut in and headed for the opposite back corner of the house. I felt real good. I felt silent and invisible. Like some kind of a primeval force, howling in from the sea. I stood still and worked out which would be the dining room windows. I found them. The lights were on in the room. I stepped in close and risked a look through the glass.

First person I saw was Quinn. He was standing up straight in a dark suit. He had a drink in his hand. His hair was pure gray. The scars on his forehead were small and pink and shiny. He was a little stooped. A little heavier than he had been. He was ten years older.

Next to him was Beck. He was in a dark suit, too. He had a drink. He was shoulder to shoulder with his boss. Together they were facing three Arab guys. The Arabs were short, with black oiled hair. They were in American clothes. Sharkskin suits, light grays and blues. They had drinks, too.

Behind them Richard and Elizabeth Beck were standing close together, talking. The whole thing was like a free-form cocktail party crammed around the edges of the giant dining table. The table was set with eighteen places. It was very formal. Each setting had three glasses and enough flatware to last a week. The cook was bustling about the room with a tray of drinks. I could see champagne flutes and whiskey tumblers. She was in a dark skirt and a white blouse. She was relegated to cocktail waitress.

Maybe her expertise didn't stretch to Middle Eastern cuisine.

I couldn't see Teresa Daniel. Maybe they planned to make her jump out of a cake, later. The other occupants of the room were all men. Three of them. Quinn's best boys, presumably. They were a random trio. A mixture. Hard faces, but probably no more dangerous than Angel Doll or Harley had been.

So, eighteen settings, but only ten diners. Eight absentees. Duke, Angel Doll, Harley, and Emily Smith made four of them. The guy they had sent to the gatehouse to replace Paulie was presumably the fifth. That left three unaccounted for. One on the front door, one in Duke's window, and one with Teresa Daniel, probably.

I stayed on the outside, looking in. I had been to cocktail parties and formal dinners plenty of times. Depending on where you served they played a big part in base life. I figured these people would be in there four hours, minimum. They wouldn't come out except for bathroom breaks. Quinn was talking. He was sharing eye contact scrupulously among the three Arabs. He was holding forth. Smiling, gesturing, laughing. He looked like a guy who was playing and winning. But he wasn't. His plans had been disrupted. A banquet for eighteen had become dinner for ten, because I was still around.

I ducked under the window and crawled toward the kitchen. Stayed on my knees and slipped out of my coat and left the Persuaders wrapped in it where I could find them again. Then I stood up and walked straight into the kitchen. The metal detector beeped at the Beretta in my pocket. The catering guys were in there. They were doing something with aluminum foil. I nodded at them like I lived there and walked straight into the hallway. My feet were quiet on the thick rugs. I could hear the loud buzz of cocktail conversation from the dining room. I could see a guy at the front door. He had his back to me and he was staring out the window. He had his shoulder leaning on the edge of the window recess. His hair was haloed blue by the wall lights in the distance. I walked straight up behind him. *Shoot to kill. Them or me.* I paused for one second. Reached around and cupped my right hand under his chin. Put my left knuckles against the base of his neck. Jerked up and back with my right and down and forward with my left and snapped his neck at the fourth vertebra. He sagged back against me and I caught him under the arms and walked him into Elizabeth Beck's parlor and dumped him on the sofa. *Doctor Zhivago* was still there on a side table.

One down.

I closed the parlor door on him and headed for the stairs. Went up, quick and quiet. Stopped outside Duke's room. Eliot was sprawled just inside the doorway. Dead. He was on his back. His jacket was thrown open and his shirt was stiff with blood and full of holes. The rugs under him were crusty. I stepped over him and kept behind the door and glanced into the room. Saw why he had died. The NSV had jammed. He must have taken Duffy's call and been on his way out of the room when he looked up and saw a convoy coming toward him on the road. He must have darted toward the big gun. Squeezed the trigger and felt it jam. It was a piece of junk. The mechanic had it field-stripped on the floor and was crouched over it trying to repair the belt feed mechanism. He was intent on his task. Didn't see me coming. Didn't hear me.

Shoot to kill. Them or me.

Two down.

I left him lying on top of the machine gun. The barrel stuck out from under him and looked like a third arm. I checked the view from the window. The wall lights were still blazing. I checked my watch. I was exactly thirty minutes into my hour.

I went back downstairs. Through the hallway. Like a ghost. To the basement door. The lights were on down there. I went down the stairs. Through the gymnasium. Past the washing machine. I pulled the Beretta out of my pocket. Clicked the safety. Held it out in front of me and turned the corner and walked straight toward the two rooms. One of them was empty and had its door standing open. The other was closed up and had a young thin guy sitting on a chair in front of it. He had the chair tilted back against it. He looked straight at me. His eyes went wide. His mouth came open. No sound came out. He didn't seem like much of a threat. He was wearing a T-shirt with *Dell* on it. Maybe this was Troy, the computer geek.

"Keep quiet if you want to live," I said.

He kept quiet.

"Are you Troy?"

He stayed quiet and nodded *yes.*

"OK, Troy," I said.

I figured we were right underneath the dining room. I couldn't risk firing a gun in a stone cellar right under everybody's feet. So I put the Beretta back in my pocket and caught him around the neck and banged his head on the wall, twice, and put him to sleep. Maybe I cracked his skull, maybe I didn't. I didn't really care either way. His keyboard work had killed the maid.

Three down.

I found the key in his pocket. Used it in the lock and swung open the door and found Teresa Daniel sitting on her mattress. She turned and looked straight at me. She looked exactly like the photographs Duffy had shown me in my motel room early in the morning on day eleven. She looked in perfect health. Her hair was washed and brushed. She was wearing a virginal white dress. White panty hose and white shoes. Her skin was pale and her eyes were blue. She looked like a human sacrifice.

I paused a moment, unsure. I couldn't predict her reaction. She must have figured out what they wanted from her. And she didn't know me. As far as she knew, I was one of them, ready to lead her right to the altar. And she was a trained federal agent. If I asked her to come with me, she might start fighting. She might be storing it up, waiting for her chance. And I didn't want things to get noisy. Not yet.

But then I looked again at her eyes. One pupil was enormous. The other was tiny. She was very still. Very quiet. Slack and dazed. She was all doped up. Maybe with some kind of a fancy substance. What was it? The date rape drug? Rohypnol? Rophynol? I couldn't remember its name. Not my area of expertise. Eliot would have known. Duffy or Villanueva would still know. It made people passive and obedient and acquiescent. Made them lie back and take anything they were told to take.

"Teresa?" I whispered.

She didn't answer.

"You OK?" I whispered.

She nodded.

"I'm fine," she said.

"Can you walk?"

"Yes," she said.

"Walk with me."

She stood up. She was unsteady on her feet. Muscle weakness, I guessed. She had been caged for nine weeks.

"This way," I said.

She didn't move. She just stood there. I put out my hand. She reached out and took it. Her skin was warm and dry.

"Let's go," I said. "Don't look at the man on the floor."

I stopped her again just outside the door. Let her hand go and dragged Troy into the room and closed the door on him and locked it. Took Teresa's hand again and walked away. She was very suggestible. Very obedient. She just fixed her gaze out in front of her and walked with me. We turned the corner and passed by the washing machine. We walked through the gymnasium. Her dress was silky and lacy. She was holding my hand like a date. I felt like I was going to the prom. We walked up the stairs, side by side. Reached the top.

"Wait here," I said. "Don't go anywhere without me, OK?"

"OK," she whispered.

"Don't make any noise at all, OK?"

"I won't."

I closed the door on her and left her on the top step, with her hand resting lightly on the rail and a bare light-bulb burning behind her. I checked the hallway carefully and headed back to the kitchen. The food guys were still busy in there.

"You guys called Keast and Maden?" I said.

The one nearer me nodded.

"Paul Keast," he said.

"Chris Maden," his partner said.

"I need to move your truck, Paul," I said.

"Why?"

"Because it's in the way."

The guy just looked at me. "You told me to put it there."

"I didn't tell you to leave it there."

He shrugged and rooted around on a counter and came up with his keys.

"Whatever," he said.

I took the keys and went outside and checked the back of the truck. It was fitted out with metal racks on either side. For trays of food. There was a narrow aisle running down the center. No windows. It would do. I left the rear doors open and slid into the driver's seat and fired it up. Backed it out to the carriage circle and turned it around and reversed it back to the kitchen door. Now it was facing the right way. I killed the motor but left the keys in it. Went back inside the kitchen. The metal detector beeped.

"What are they eating?" I asked.

"Lamb kebabs," Maden said. "With rice and couscous and hummus. Stuffed grape leaves to start. Baklava for dessert. With coffee."

"That's Libyan?"

"It's generic," he said. "They eat it everywhere."

"I used to get that for a dollar," I said. "You're charging fifty-five."

"Where? In *Portland*?"

"In Beirut," I said.

I stepped out and checked the hallway. All quiet. I opened the basement door. Teresa Daniel was waiting right there, like an automaton. I held out my hand.

"Let's go," I said.

She stepped out. I closed the door behind her. Walked her into the kitchen. Keast and Maden stared at her. I ignored them and walked her through. Out through the door. Over to the truck. She shivered in the cold. I helped her climb into the back.

"Wait there for me now," I said. "Very quiet, OK?"

She nodded and said nothing.

"I'm going to close the doors on you," I said.

She nodded again.

"I'll get you out of there soon," I said.

"Thank you," she said.

I closed the doors on her and went back to the kitchen. Stood still and listened. I could hear talking from the dining room. It all sounded reasonably social.

"When do they eat?" I said.

"Twenty minutes," Maden said. "When they're through with the drinks. There was champagne included in the fifty-five dollars, you know."

"OK," I said. "Don't take offense."

I checked my watch. Forty-five minutes gone. Fifteen minutes to go.

Show time.

I went back outside into the cold. Slipped into the food truck and fired it up. Eased it forward, slowly around the corner of the house, slowly around the carriage circle, slowly down the driveway. Away from the house. Through the gate. Onto the road. I hit the gas. Took the curves fast. Jammed to a stop level with Villanueva's Taurus. Jumped out. Villanueva and Duffy were instantly out to meet me.

"Teresa's in the back," I said. "She's OK but she's all doped up."

Duffy pumped her fists and jumped on me and hugged me hard and Villanueva wrenched open the doors. Teresa fell into his arms. He lifted her down like a child. Then Duffy grabbed her away from him and he took a turn hugging me.

"You should take her to the hospital," I said.

"We'll take her to the motel," Duffy said. "We're still off the books."

"You sure?"

"She'll be OK," Villanueva said. "Looks like they gave her roofies. Probably from their dope-dealer pals. But they don't last long. They flush out fast."

Duffy was hugging Teresa like a sister. Villanueva was still hugging me.

"Eliot's dead," I said.

That put a real damper on the mood.

"Call ATF from the motel," I said. "If I don't call you first."

They just looked at me.

"I'm going back now," I said.

I TURNED THE TRUCK AROUND AND HEADED back. I could see the house ahead of me. The windows were lit up yellow. The wall lights flared blue in the mist. The truck fought the wind. *Plan B,* I decided. Quinn was mine, but the others could be ATF's headache.

I stopped on the far side of the carriage circle and reversed down the side of the house. Stopped outside the kitchen. Got out and walked around the back of the house and found my coat. Unwrapped the Persuaders. Put my coat on. I needed it. It was a cold night and I would be on the road again in about five minutes.

I stepped across to the dining room windows to check inside. They had closed the drapes. *Makes sense,* I thought. It was a wild blustery night. The dining room would look better with closed drapes. Cozier. Oriental rugs on the floor, wood paneling, silver on the linen tablecloth.

I picked up the Persuaders and walked back to the kitchen. The metal detector squealed. The food guys had ten plates with stuffed grape leaves all lined up on a counter. The leaves looked dark and oily and tough. I was hungry but I couldn't have eaten one. The way my teeth were right then would have made it impossible. I figured I would be eating ice cream for a week, thanks to Paulie.

"Hold off with the food for five minutes, OK?" I said.

Keast and Maden stared at the shotguns.

"Your keys," I said.

I dropped them next to the grape leaves. I didn't need them anymore. I had the keys Beck had given me. I figured I would leave by the front door and use the Cadillac. Faster. More comfortable. I took a knife from the wooden block. Used it to put a slit in the inside of my right-hand coat pocket, just wide enough to allow a Persuader's barrel down into the lining. I picked the gun I had killed Harley with and holstered it there. I held the other one two-handed. Took a breath. Stepped into the hallway. Keast and Maden watched me go. First thing I did was check the powder room. No point in getting all dramatic if Quinn wasn't even in the dining room. But the powder room was empty. Nobody on bathroom break.

The dining room door was closed. I took another breath. Then another. Then I kicked it in and stepped inside and fired two Brennekes into the ceiling. They were like stun grenades. The twin explosions were colossal. Plaster and wood rained down. Dust and smoke filled the air. Everybody froze like statues. I leveled the gun at Quinn's chest. Echoes died away.

"Remember me?" I said.

Elizabeth Beck screamed in the sudden silence.

I moved another step into the room and kept the muzzle on Quinn.

"Remember me?" I said again.

One second. Two. His mouth started moving.

"I saw you in Boston," he said. "On the street. A Saturday night. Maybe two weeks ago."

"Try again," I said.

His face was completely blank. He didn't remember me. *They diagnosed amnesia,* Duffy had said. *Certainly about the trauma, because that's almost inevitable. They figured he might be genuinely blank about the incident and the previous day or two.*

"I'm Reacher," I said. "I need you to remember me."

He glanced helplessly at Beck.

"Her name was Dominique," I said.

He turned back to me. Stared at me. Eyes wide. Now he knew who I was. His face changed. Blood drained out and fury swarmed in. And fear. The .22 scars went pure white. I thought about aiming right between them. It would be a difficult shot.

"You really thought I wouldn't find you?" I said.

"Can we talk?" he said. Sounded like his mouth was dry.

"No," I said. "You've already been talking ten extra years."

"We're all armed here," Beck said. He sounded afraid. The three Arabs were staring at me. They had plaster dust stuck to the oil in their hair.

"So tell everybody to hold their fire," I said. "No reason for more than one casualty here."

People eased away from me. Dust settled on the table. A slab of falling ceiling had broken a glass. I moved with the crowd and turned and adjusted the geometry to herd the bad guys together at one end of the room. At the same time I tried to force Elizabeth and Richard and the cook together at the other. Where they would be safe, by the window. Pure body language. I turned my shoulder and inched forward and even though the table was between me and most of them they went where I wanted them. The little gathering parted obediently into two groups, eight and three.

"Everybody should step away from Mr. Xavier now," I said.

Everybody did, except Beck. Beck stayed right at his shoulder. I stared at him. Then I realized Quinn had a grip on his arm. He was holding it tight just above the elbow. Pulling on it. Pulling on it hard. Looking for a human shield.

"These slugs are an inch wide," I said to him. "As long as I can see an inch of you, that won't work very well."

He said nothing back. Just kept on pulling. Beck was resisting. There was fear in his eyes, too. It was a static

little slow-motion contest. But I guessed Quinn was winning it. Inside ten seconds Beck's left shoulder was over-
lapping Quinn's right. Both of them were quivering with
effort. Even though the Persuader had a pistol grip instead
of a stock I raised it high to my shoulder and sighted carefully down the barrel.

"I can still see you," I said.

"Don't shoot," Richard Beck said, behind me.

Something in his voice.

I glanced back at him. Just a brief turn of my head.
Just a flash. There and back. He had a Beretta in his hand.
It was identical to the one in my pocket. It was pointed at
my head. The electric light was harsh on it. It was high-
lighted. Even though I had only looked for a fraction of a
second I had seen the elegant engraving on the slide.
Pietro Beretta. I had seen the dew of new oil. I had seen
the little red dot that is revealed when the safety is pushed
to *fire.*

"Put it away, Richard," I said.

"Not while my father is there," he said.

"Let go of him, Quinn," I said.

"Don't shoot, Reacher," Richard said. "I'll shoot you
first."

By then Quinn had Beck almost all the way in front of
him.

"Don't shoot," Richard said again.

"Put it down, Richard," I said.

"No."

"Put it down."

"No."

I listened carefully to his voice. He wasn't moving.
He was standing still. I knew exactly where he was. I
knew the angle I would have to turn through. I rehearsed it
in my head. *Turn. Fire. Pump. Turn. Fire.* I could get them

both within a second and a quarter. Too fast for Quinn to react. I took a breath.

Then I pictured Richard in my mind. The silly hair, the missing ear. The long fingers. I pictured the big Brenneke slug blasting through him, crushing, bludgeoning, the immense kinetic energy blowing him apart. I couldn't do it.

"Put it away," I said.

"No."

"Please."

"No."

"You're helping them."

"I'm helping my dad."

"I won't hit your dad."

"I can't take that risk. He's my dad."

"Elizabeth, tell him."

"No," she said. "He's my husband."

Stalemate.

Worse than stalemate. Because there was absolutely nothing I could do. I couldn't fire on Richard. Because I wouldn't let myself. Therefore I couldn't fire on Quinn. And I couldn't *say* I wasn't going to fire on Quinn because then eight guys would immediately pull guns on me. I might get a few of them, but sooner or later one of them would get me. And I couldn't separate Quinn from Beck. No way was Quinn going to let go of Beck and walk out of the room alone with me. *Stalemate.*

Plan C.

"Put it away, Richard," I said.

Listen.

"No."

He hadn't moved. I rehearsed it again. *Turn. Fire.* I took a breath. Spun and fired. A foot to Richard's right, at the window. The slug smashed through the drapes and caught the casement frame and blew it away. I ran three paces and went headfirst through the hole. Rolled twice wrapped in a torn velvet curtain and scrambled up on my feet and ran. Straight out on the rocks.

I turned back after twenty yards and stood still. The remaining curtain was billowing in the wind. It was flapping in and out of the hole. I could hear the fabric snapping and beating. Yellow light shone behind it. I could see backlit figures crowding together behind the shattered glass. Everything was moving. The curtain, the people. The light was fading and blazing as the curtain flapped in and out. Then shots started coming at me. Handguns were firing. First two, then four, then five. Then more. Rounds were buzzing through the air all around me. Hitting the rocks and sparking and ricocheting. Chips of stone flew everywhere. The shots sounded quiet. They sounded like dull insignificant pops. Their sound was lost in the howl of the wind and the crash of the waves. I dropped to my knees. Raised the Persuader. Then the shooting stopped. I held my fire. The curtain disappeared. Somebody had torn it down. Light flooded out at me. I saw Richard and Elizabeth forced to the front of the crowd at the window. Their arms were twisted up behind them. I saw Quinn's face behind Richard's shoulder. He was aiming a gun straight at me.

"Shoot me now," he screamed.

His voice was nearly lost in the wind. I heard the seventh wave crash in behind me. Spray burst upward and the wind caught it and it hit me hard in the back of the head. I saw one of Quinn's guys behind Elizabeth. Her face was twisted in pain. His right wrist was resting on her shoulder. His head was behind her head. He had a gun in his hand. I saw another gun butt come forward and knock shards of glass out of the frame. It raked it clean. Then Richard was jerked forward. His knee came up on the sill.

Quinn pushed him all the way outside. Came out after him, still holding him close.

"Shoot me now," he screamed again.

Behind him Elizabeth was lifted out through the window. There was a thick arm around her waist. Her legs kicked desperately. She was planted on the ground and pulled backward to cover the guy holding her. I could see her face, pale in the darkness. Twisted in pain. I shuffled backward. More people climbed out. They swarmed. They formed up together. They made a wedge. Richard and Elizabeth were held shoulder to shoulder at the front like a blunt point. The wedge started lurching toward me. It was uncoordinated. I could see five guns. I shuffled backward. The wedge kept coming. The guns started firing again.

They were aiming to miss. They were aiming to corral me. I moved backward. Counted rounds. Five guns, full mags, they had at least seventy-five shells between them. Maybe more. And they had fired maybe twenty. They were a long way from empty. And their fire was controlled. They weren't just blasting away. They were aiming left and right of me, into the rocks, regular spaced shots every couple of seconds. Coming on like a machine. Like a tank armored with humans. I stood up. Moved backward. The wedge kept coming at me.

Richard was on the right and Elizabeth was on the left. I picked a guy behind Richard and to his right and aimed. The guy saw me do it and crowded in tight. The wedge jammed together. Now it was a narrow column. It kept on coming. I had no shot. I walked backward, step by step.

My left heel found the edge of Harley's cleft.

Water boiled in and covered my shoe. I heard the waves. Gravel rattled and sucked. I moved my right foot level with my left. Balanced on the edge. I saw Quinn smiling at me. Just the gleam of his teeth in the dark.

"Say good night now," he screamed.

Stay alive. See what the next minute brings.

The column grew arms. Six or seven of them, reaching out, turning forward with their guns. Aiming. They were waiting for a command. I heard the seventh wave crash in at my feet. It came up over my ankles and flooded ten feet in front of me. It paused there for a second and then it drained back, indifferent, like a metronome. I looked at Elizabeth and Richard. Looked at their faces. Took a deep breath. Thought: *Them or me.* I dropped the Persuader and threw myself backward into the water.

FIRST WAS THE SHOCK OF THE COLD, AND THEN it was like falling off a building. Except it wasn't a free fall. It was like landing in a freezing lubricated tube and being sucked down it at a steep and controlled angle. With acceleration. I was upside down. I was traveling headfirst. I had landed on my back and for a split second I had felt nothing. Just the freezing water in my ears and my eyes and my nose. It stung my lip. I was about a foot under the surface. I wasn't going anywhere. I was worried about floating back up. I would bob to the surface right in front of them. They would be crowding around the lip of the cleft with their guns aimed down at the water.

But then I felt my hair stand up. It was a gentle sensation. Like somebody was combing it upright and pulling on it. Then I felt a grip on my head. Like a strong man with big hands was clamping my face between his palms and pulling, very gently at first, and then a little harder. And harder. I felt it in my neck. It was like I was getting taller. Then I felt it in my chest and my shoulders. My arms were floating free and suddenly they were wrenched up above my head. Then I fell off the building. It was like a perfect swallow dive, on my back. I just arched downward. But I accelerated. Much faster than a free fall through the air. It was like I was being reeled in by a gigantic elastic cord.

I couldn't see anything. I didn't know if my eyes were open or shut. The cold was so stunning and the pressure on my body was so uniform that I didn't really feel anything, either. No physical force. It was completely fluid. It was like some kind of science fiction transportation. Like I was being beamed down. Like I was liquid. Like I had been elongated. Like I was suddenly thirty feet tall and an inch wide. There was blackness and coldness everywhere. I held my breath. All the tension went out of me and I leaned my head back to feel the water on my scalp. Pointed my toes. Arched my spine. Stretched my arms far up ahead of me. Opened my fingers to feel the water flow between them. It felt very peaceful. I was a bullet. I liked it.

Then I felt a panicked thump all through my chest and knew I was drowning. So I started to fight. I tumbled myself over and my coat came up around my head. I tore it off, spinning and somersaulting in the freezing tube. The coat whipped across my face and hurtled away. I slid out of my jacket. It disappeared. I suddenly felt the bitter cold. I was still going down fast. My ears were hissing. I was tumbling in slow motion. Whipping down and down faster than I had ever traveled and rolling and tumbling like I was mired in treacle.

How wide was the tube? I didn't know. I kicked desperately and clawed at the water around me. It felt like quicksand. *Don't swim down.* I kicked and fought and tried to find the edge. Bargained with myself. *Concentrate. Find the edge. Make progress. Stay calm. Let it take you down fifty feet for every foot you move sideways.* I stopped for a second and regrouped and started swimming properly. And hard. Like the tube was the flat surface of a pool and I was in a race. Like there was a girl and a drink and a chair on the patio for the winner.

How long had I been down? I didn't know. Maybe fifteen seconds. I could hold my breath for maybe a minute. *So relax. Swim hard. Find the edge.* There had to be an edge. The whole ocean wasn't moving like this. It couldn't be, otherwise Portugal was going to be under water. And half of Spain. Pressure roared in my ears.

Which way was I facing? Didn't matter. I just had to get out of the current. I swam onward. Felt the tide fighting me. It was incredibly powerful. It had been gentle before. Now it tore at me. Like it resented my decision to fight back. I clamped my teeth and kicked on. It was like crawling across a floor with a thousand tons of bricks on my back. My lungs swelled and burned. I trickled air out between my lips. Kicked on and on. Clawed the water ahead of me.

Thirty seconds. I was drowning. I knew it. I was weakening. My lungs were empty. My chest was crushed. I had a billion tons of water on top of me. I could feel my face twisting in pain. My ears were roaring. My stomach was knotted. My left shoulder was burning where Paulie had hit it. I heard Harley's voice in my head: *We never had one come back.* I kicked on.

Forty seconds. I was making no progress. I was being hurled down into the depths. I was going to hit the seabed. I kicked on. Clawed at the tide. *Fifty seconds.* My ears were hissing. My head was bursting. My lips were clamped against my teeth. I was very angry. Quinn had made it out of the ocean. *Why couldn't I?*

I kicked on desperately. *A whole minute.* My fingers were frozen and cramped. My eyes were scoured. *More than a minute.* I flailed and lashed. I battered my way through the water. Kicked and fought. Then I felt a change in the tide. *I found the edge.* It was like grabbing a telegraph pole from a speeding train. I punched through the skin of the tube and a new tide seized my hands and hit me in the head and turbulence battered me and I was suddenly cartwheeling head over feet and floating free in water that felt still and clear and freezing.

Now think. Which way is up? I used every ounce of self-control I had and stopped fighting. Just floated. Tried to gauge my direction. I went nowhere. *My lungs were empty.* My lips were clamped tight. *I couldn't breathe.* I had neutral buoyancy. I wasn't moving. I was dead in the water. In a cubic mile of black ocean. I opened my eyes. Stared all around me. Above me, below me, to the sides. I twisted and turned. Saw nothing. It was like outer space. Everything was pitch dark. No light at all. *We never had one come back.*

I felt slight pressure on my chest. Less on my back. I was hanging facedown in the water. Suspended. I was floating upward, very slowly, back-first. I concentrated hard. Fixed the sensation clearly in my mind. Fixed my position. Arched my spine. Scrabbled with my hands. Kicked my legs down. Stretched my arms toward the surface. *Now go. Don't breathe.*

I kicked furiously. Scooped huge strokes with my arms. Clamped my lips. *I had no air.* I held my face up at an angle so that the first thing to break the surface would be my mouth. *How far?* It was black above me. There was nothing there. I was a mile down. *I had no air.* I was going to die. I opened my lips. Water flooded my mouth. I spat and swallowed. Kicked onward. I could see purple colors in my eyes. My head hummed. I felt feverish. Like I was burning. Then like I was freezing. Then like I was wrapped in thick feather quilts. They were soft. I could feel nothing at all.

I stopped kicking then, because I was pretty sure I had died. So I opened my mouth to breathe. Sucked in seawater. My chest spasmed and coughed it out. In and out, twice more. I was breathing pure water. I kicked once more. It was all I could manage. One last kick. I made it a big one. Then I just closed my eyes and floated and breathed the cold water.

I hit the surface half a second later. I felt the air on my face like a lover's caress. I opened my mouth and my chest heaved and a high spout of water shot up and I gulped air even before it came back down on me. Then I fought like a madman to keep my face up in the cold sweet oxygen. Just kicked and panted and breathed, sucking and blowing and coughing and retching.

I spread my arms wide and let my legs float up and tilted my head back with my mouth wide open. Watched my chest rise and fall, rise and fall, fill and empty. It moved incredibly fast. I felt tired. And peaceful. And vague. I had no oxygen in my brain. I tossed around in the water for a full minute, just breathing. My vision cleared. I saw dull clouds above me. My head cleared. I breathed some more. *In, out, in, out,* with my lips pursed, blowing like a locomotive. My head starting aching. I trod water and looked for the horizon. Couldn't find it. I was pitching and falling on fast urgent waves, up and down, up and down, maybe ten or fifteen feet at a time. I kicked a little and timed it so the next wave carried me up to its peak. Stared ahead. Saw nothing at all before I fell back into its trough.

I had no idea where I was. I turned ninety degrees and rode the next peak and looked again. To my right. Maybe there would be a boat out there somewhere. There wasn't. There was nothing. I was alone in the middle of the Atlantic. Drifting. *We never had one come back.*

I turned one-eighty and rode a peak and looked to my

left. Nothing there. I fell back into the trough and rode the next peak and looked behind me.

I was a hundred yards from shore.

I could see the big house. I could see lit windows. I could see the wall. I could see the blue haze of its lights. I hauled my shirt up on my shoulders. It was soaked and heavy. I took a breath. Rolled onto my front and started swimming.

ONE HUNDRED YARDS. ANY KIND OF A HALFWAY decent Olympic competitor could swim a hundred yards in about forty-five seconds. And any kind of a halfway decent high school swimmer could do it in less than a minute. It took me nearly fifteen. The tide was going out. I felt like I was going backward. I felt like I was still drowning. But eventually I touched the shore and got my arms around a smooth rock that was coated with freezing slime and held on tight. The sea was still rough. Big waves thumped in on me and smashed my cheek against the granite, regular as clockwork. I didn't care. I savored the impacts. Each and every one of them. I loved that rock.

I rested on it for a minute more and then crawled my way around behind the garage block, sloshing along half in and half out of the water, crouched low. Then I crawled out on my hands and knees. Rolled over on my back. Stared up at the sky. *Now you had one come back, Harley.*

The waves came in and reached my waist. I shuffled on my back until they reached only my knees. Rolled onto my front again. Lay with my face pressed down on the rock. I was cold. Chilled to the bone. My coat was gone. My jacket was gone. The Persuaders were gone. The Beretta was gone.

I stood up. Water sluiced off me. I staggered a couple of steps. Heard Leon Garber in my head: *What doesn't kill you only makes you stronger.* He thought JFK had said it. I thought it was actually Friedrich Nietzsche, and he said *destroy,* not *kill. What doesn't destroy us makes us stronger.* I staggered two more steps and leaned up against the back of the courtyard wall and threw up about a gallon of salt water. That made me feel a little better. I jerked my arms around and kicked each leg in turn to try to get some circulation going and some water out of my clothes. Then I plastered my soaking hair back on my head and tried a couple of long slow breaths. I was worried about coughing. My throat was raw and aching from the cold and the salt.

Then I walked along the back wall and turned at the corner. Found my little dip and visited my hidden bundle one last time. *I'm coming to get you, Quinn.*

MY WATCH WAS STILL WORKING AND IT SHOWED me my hour was long gone. Duffy would have called ATF twenty minutes ago. But their response would be slow. I doubted if they had a field office in Portland. Boston was probably the closest. Where the maid had been sent out from. So I still had enough time.

The food truck was gone. Evidently dinner had been canceled. But the other vehicles were still there. The Cadillac, the Town Car, the two Suburbans. Eight hostiles still in the house. Plus Elizabeth and the cook. I didn't know which category to put Richard in.

I kept tight against the house wall and looked in every window. The cook was in the kitchen. She was cleaning up. Keast and Maden had left all their stuff there. I ducked under the sill and moved on. The dining room was a ruin. The wind blowing in through the shattered window had caught the linen tablecloth and thrown plates and glasses everywhere. There were dunes of plaster dust in the corners where the wind had piled them. There were two big holes in the ceiling. Probably in the ceiling of the room above, and the room above that, too. The Brennekes had probably made it all the way out through the roof, like moon shots.

The square room where I had played Russian roulette had the three Libyans and Quinn's three guys in it. They were all sitting around the oak table, doing nothing. They looked blank and shocked. But they looked settled. They weren't going anywhere. I ducked under the sill and moved on. Came all the way around to Elizabeth Beck's parlor. She was in there. With Richard. Somebody had taken the dead guy out. She was on her sofa, talking fast. I couldn't hear what she was saying, but Richard was listening hard. I ducked under the sill and moved on.

Beck and Quinn were in Beck's little room. Quinn was in the red armchair and Beck was standing in front of the cabinet with the machine gun display. Beck looked pale and grim and hostile and Quinn looked full of himself. He had a fat unlit cigar in his hand. He was rolling it between his fingers and thumb and lining up a silver cutter at the business end.

I made it back to the kitchen after completing a whole circle. Stepped inside. I didn't make a sound. The metal detector stayed quiet. The cook didn't hear me coming. I caught her from behind. Clamped a hand over her mouth and dragged her over to a counter. I wasn't taking any chances after what Richard had done to me. I found a linen towel in a drawer and used it as a gag. Found another to tie her wrists. Found another to tie her ankles. I left her sitting uncomfortably on the floor next to the sink. I found a fourth towel and put it in my pocket. Then I stepped out into the hallway.

It was quiet. I could hear Elizabeth Beck's voice,

faintly. Her parlor door was standing open. I couldn't hear anything else. I went straight to the door of Beck's den. Opened it. Stepped inside. Closed it again.

I was met by a haze of cigar smoke. Quinn had just lit up. I got the feeling he had been laughing about something. Now he was frozen with shock. Beck was the same. Pale, and frozen. They were just staring at me.

"I'm back," I said.

Beck had his mouth open. I hit him with a cigarette punch. His mouth slammed shut and his head snapped back and his eyes rolled up and he went straight down on the three-deep rugs on the floor. It was a decent blow, but not my best. His son had saved his life after all. If I hadn't been so tired from swimming, a better punch would have killed him.

Quinn came straight at me. Straight out of the chair. He dropped his cigar. Went for his pocket. I hit him in the stomach. Air punched out of him and he folded forward and dropped to his knees. I hit him in the head and pushed him down on his stomach. Knelt on his back, with my knees high up between his shoulder blades.

"No," he said. He had no air. "Please."

I put the flat of one hand on the back of his head. Took my chisel out of my shoe and slid it in behind his ear and up into his brain, slowly, inch by inch. He was dead before it was halfway in, but I kept it going until it was buried all the way to the hilt. I left it there. I wiped the handle with the towel from my pocket and then I spread the towel over his head and stood up, wearily.

"Ten-eighteen, Dom," I said to myself.

I stepped on Quinn's burning cigar. Took Beck's car keys out of his pocket and slipped back into the hallway. Walked through the kitchen. The cook followed me with her eyes. I stumbled around to the front of the house. Slid into the Cadillac. Fired it up and took off west.

IT TOOK ME THIRTY MINUTES TO GET TO DUFFY'S motel. She and Villanueva were together in his room with Teresa Justice. She wasn't Teresa Daniel anymore. She wasn't dressed like a doll anymore, either. They had her in a motel robe. She had showered. She was coming around fast. She looked weak and wan, but she looked like a person. Like a federal agent. She stared at me in horror. At first I thought she was confused about who I was. She had seen me in the cellar. Maybe she thought I was one of them.

But then I saw myself in the mirror on the closet door and I saw her problem. I was wet from head to toe. I was shaking and shivering. My skin was dead white. The cut on my lip had opened and turned blue on the edges. I had fresh bruises where the waves had butted me against the rock. I had seaweed in my hair and slime on my shirt.

"I fell in the sea," I said.

Nobody spoke.

"I'll take a shower," I said. "In a minute. Did you call ATF?"

Duffy nodded. "They're on their way. Portland PD has already secured the warehouse. They're going to seal the coast road, too. You got out just in time."

"Was I ever there?"

Villanueva shook his head. "You don't exist. Certainly we never met you."

"Thank you," I said.

"Old school," he said.

I felt better after the shower. Looked better, too. But I had no clothes. Villanueva lent me a set of his. They were a little short and wide. I used his old raincoat to hide them. I wrapped it tight around me, because I was still cold. We had pizza delivered. We were all starving. I was very thirsty, from the salt water. We ate and we drank. I couldn't bite on the pizza crust. I just sucked the topping off. After an hour, Teresa Justice went to bed. She shook my hand. Said good night, very politely. She had no idea who I was.

"Roofies wipe out their short-term memory," Villanueva told me.

Then we talked business. Duffy was very down. She was living a nightmare. She had lost three agents in an illegal operation. And getting Teresa out was no kind of upside. Because Teresa shouldn't have been in there in the first place.

"So quit," I said. "Join ATF instead. You just handed them a big result on a plate. You'll be flavor of the month."

"I'm going to retire," Villanueva said. "I'm old enough and I've had enough."

"I can't retire," Duffy said.

IN THE RESTAURANT THE NIGHT BEFORE THE ARrest, Dominique Kohl had asked me, "Why are you doing this?"

I wasn't sure what she meant. "Having dinner with you?"

"No, working as an MP. You could be anything. You could be Special Forces, Intelligence, Air Cavalry, Armored, anything you wanted."

"So could you."

"I know. And I know why *I'm* doing this. I want to know why you're doing it."

It was the first time anybody had ever asked me.

"Because I always wanted to be a cop," I said. "But I was predestined for the military. Family background, no choice at all. So I became a military cop."

"That's not really an answer. Why did you want to be a cop in the first place?"

I shrugged. "It's just the way I am. Cops put things right."

"What things?"

"They look after people. They make sure the little guy is OK."

"That's it? The little guy?"

I shook my head.

"No," I said. "Not really. I don't really care about the little guy. I just hate the big guy. I hate big smug people who think they can get away with things."

"You produce the right results for the wrong reasons, then."

I nodded. "But I try to do the right thing. I think the reasons don't really matter. Whatever, I like to see the right thing done."

"Me too," she said. "I try to do the right thing. Even though everybody hates us and nobody helps us and nobody thanks us afterward. I think doing the right thing is an end in itself. It has to be, really, doesn't it?"

"DID YOU DO THE RIGHT THING?" I ASKED, TEN years later.

Duffy nodded.

"Yes," she said.

"No doubt at all?"

"No," she said.

"You sure?"

"Totally."

"So relax," I said. "That's the best you can ever hope for. Nobody helps and nobody says thanks afterward."

She was quiet for a spell.

"Did *you* do the right thing?" she said.

"No question," I said.

We left it at that. Duffy had put Teresa Justice in Eliot's old room. That left Villanueva in his, and me in Duffy's. She seemed a little awkward about what she had said before. About our lack of professionalism. I wasn't sure if she was trying to reinforce it or trying to withdraw it.

"Don't panic," I said. "I'm way too tired."

And this time, I proved I was. Not for lack of trying. We started. She made it clear she wanted to withdraw her earlier objection. Made it clear she agreed that saying *yes* was better than saying *no*. I was very happy about that, because I liked her a lot. So we started. We got naked and got in bed together and I remember kissing her so hard it made my mouth hurt. But that's all I remember. I fell asleep. I slept the sleep of the dead. Eleven hours straight. They were all gone when I woke up. Gone to face whatever their futures held for them. I was alone in the room, with a bunch of memories. It was late morning. Sunlight was coming in through the shades. Motes of dust were dancing in the air. Villanueva's spare outfit was gone from the back of the chair. There was a shopping bag there instead. It was full of cheap clothes. They looked like they would fit me very well. Susan Duffy was a good judge of sizes. There were two complete sets. One was for cold weather. One was for hot. She didn't know where I was headed. So she had catered for both possibilities. She was a very practical woman. I figured I would miss her. For a time.

I dressed in the hot weather stuff. Left the cold weather stuff right there in the room. I figured I could drive Beck's Cadillac out to I-95. To the Kennebunk rest area. I figured I could abandon it there. Figured I could catch a ride south without any problem. And I-95 goes to all kinds of places, all the way down to Miami.

If

mis

And rea

NOTHING TO LOSE

LEE CHILD

NOTHING
TO LOSE

NOTHING TO LOSE
On Sale Now

Despair's downtown area began with a vacant lot where something had been planned maybe twenty years before but never built. Then came an old motor court, closed, shuttered, maybe permanently abandoned. Across the street and fifty yards west was a gas station. Two pumps, both of them old. Not the kind of upright rural antiques Reacher had seen in Edward Hopper's paintings, but still a couple of generations off the pace. There was a small hut in back with a grimy window full of quarts of oil arrayed in a pyramid. Reacher crossed the apron and stuck his head in the door. It was dark inside the hut and the air smelled of creosote and hot raw wood. There was a guy behind a counter, in worn blue overalls stained black with dirt. He was about thirty, and lean.

"Got coffee?" Reacher asked him.

"This is a gas station," the guy said.

"Gas stations sell coffee," Reacher said. "And water, and soda."

"Not this one," the guy said. "We sell gas."

"And oil."

"If you want it."

"Is there a coffee shop in town?"

"There's a restaurant."

"Just one?"

"One is all we need."

Reacher ducked back out to the daylight and kept on walking. A hundred yards farther west the road grew sidewalks and according to a sign on a pole changed its name to Main Street. Thirty feet later came the first developed block. It was occupied by a dour brick cube, three stories high, on the left side of the street, to the south. It might once have been a dry goods emporium. It was still some kind of a retail enterprise. Reacher could see three customers and bolts of cloth and plastic household items through its dusty ground floor windows. Next to it was an identical three-story brick cube, and then another, and another. The downtown area seemed to be about twelve blocks square, bulked mostly to the south of Main Street. Reacher was no kind of an architectural expert, and he knew he was way west of the Mississippi, but the whole place gave him the feel of an old Connecticut factory town, or the Cincinnati riverfront. It was plain, and severe, and unadorned, and out of date. He had seen movies about small-town America in which the sets had been artfully dressed to look a little more perfect and vibrant than reality. This place was the exact opposite. It looked like a designer and a whole team of grips had worked hard to make it dowdier and gloomier than it needed to be. Traffic on the streets was light. Sedans and pick-up trucks were moving slow and lazy. None of them was newer than three years old. There were few pedestrians on the sidewalks.

Reacher made a random left turn and set about finding the promised restaurant. He quartered a dozen blocks and passed a grocery store and a barbershop and a bar and a rooming house and a faded old hotel before he found the eatery. It took up the whole ground floor of another dull brick cube. The ceiling was high and the windows were floor-to-ceiling plate glass items filling most of the walls. The place might have been an automobile showroom in the past. The floor was tiled and the tables and chairs were plain brown wood and the air smelled of boiled vegetables. There was a register station inside the door with a *Please Wait to be Seated* sign on a short brass pole with a heavy base. Same sign he had seen everywhere, coast to coast. Same script, same colors, same shape. He figured there was a catering supply company somewhere turning them out by the millions. He had seen identical signs in Calais, Maine, and expected to see more in San Diego, California. He stood next to the register and waited.

And waited.

There were eleven customers eating. Three couples, a threesome, and two singletons. One waitress. No front of house staff. Nobody at the register. Not an unusual ratio. Reacher had eaten in a thousand similar places and he knew the rhythm, subliminally. The lone waitress would soon glance over at him and nod, as if to say *I'll be right with you*. Then she would take an order, deliver a plate, and scoot over, maybe blowing an errant strand of hair off her cheek in a gesture designed to be both an apology and an appeal for sympathy. She would collect a menu from a stack and lead him to a table and bustle away and then revisit him in strict sequence.

But she didn't do any of that.

She glanced over. Didn't nod. Just looked at him for a long second and then looked away. Carried on with what she was doing. Which by that point wasn't much. She had all her eleven customers pacified. She was just making work. She was stopping by tables and asking if everything was all right and refilling coffee cups that were less than an inch down from the rim. Reacher turned and checked the door glass to see if he had missed an opening-hours sign. To see if the place was about to close up. It wasn't. He checked his reflection, to see if he was committing a social outrage with the way he was dressed. He wasn't. He was wearing dark gray pants and a matching dark gray shirt, both bought two days before in a janitorial surplus store in Kansas. Janitorial supply stores were his latest discovery. Plain, strong, well-made clothing at reasonable prices. Perfect. His hair was short and tidy. He had shaved the previous morning. His fly was zipped.

He turned back to wait.

Customers turned to look at him, one after the other. They appraised him quite openly and then looked away. The waitress made another slow circuit of the room, looking everywhere except at him. He stood still, running the situation through a mental database and trying to understand it. Then he lost patience with it and stepped past the sign and moved into the room and sat down alone at a table for four. He scraped his chair in and made himself comfortable. The waitress watched him do it, and then she headed for the kitchen.

She didn't come out again.

Reacher sat and waited. The room was silent. No talking. No sounds at all, except for the quiet metallic clash of silverware on plates and the smack of people chewing and the ceramic click of cups being lowered carefully into saucers and the wooden creak of chair legs under shifting bodies. Those tiny noises rose up and echoed around the vast tiled space until they seemed overwhelmingly loud.

Nothing happened for close to ten minutes.

Then an old crew-cab pick-up truck slid to a stop on the curb outside the door. There was a second's pause and four guys climbed out and stood together on the sidewalk outside the restaurant's door. They grouped themselves into a tight little formation and paused another beat and came inside. They paused again and scanned the room and found their target. They headed straight for Reacher's table. Three of them sat down in the empty chairs and the fourth stood at the head of the table, blocking Reacher's exit.

The four guys were each a useful size. The shortest was probably an inch under six feet and the lightest was maybe an ounce over two hundred pounds. They all had walnut knuckles and thick wrists and knotted forearms. Two of them had broken noses and none of them had all their teeth. They all looked pale and vaguely unhealthy. They were all grimy, with ingrained gray dirt in the folds of their skin that glittered and shone like metal. They were all dressed in canvas work shirts with their sleeves rolled to their elbows. They were all somewhere between thirty and forty. And they all looked like trouble.

"I don't want company," Reacher said. "I prefer to eat alone."

The guy standing at the head of the table was the biggest of the four, by maybe an inch and ten pounds. He said, "You're not going to eat at all."

Reacher said, "I'm not?"

"Not here, anyway."

"I heard this was the only show in town."

"It is."

"Well, then."

"You need to get going."

"Going?"

"Out of here."

"Out of where?"

"Out of this restaurant."

"You want to tell me why?"

"We don't like strangers."

"Me either," Reacher said. "But I need to eat

somewhere. Otherwise I'll get all wasted and skinny like you four."

"Funny man."

"Just calling it like it is," Reacher said. He put his forearms on the table. He had thirty pounds and three inches on the big guy, and more than that on the other three. And he was willing to bet he had a little more experience and a little less inhibition than any one of them. Or than all of them put together. But ultimately, if it came to it, it was going to be his two hundred and fifty pounds against their cumulative nine hundred. Not great odds. But Reacher hated turning back.

The guy who was standing said, "We don't want you here."

Reacher said, "You're confusing me with someone who gives a shit what you want."

"You won't get served in here."

"Won't I?"

"Not a hope."

"You could order for me."

"And then what?"

"Then I could eat your lunch."

"Funny man," the guy said again. "You need to leave now."

"Why?"

"Just leave now."

Reacher asked, "You guys got names?"

"Not for you to know. And you need to leave."

"You want me to leave, I'll need to hear it from the owner. Not from you."

"We can arrange that." The guy who was standing nodded to one of the guys in the seats, who scraped his chair back on the tile and got up and headed for the kitchen. A long minute later he came back out with a man in a stained apron. The man in the apron was wiping his hands on a dish towel and didn't look particularly worried or perturbed. He walked up to Reacher's table and said, "I want you to leave my restaurant."

"Why?" Reacher asked.

"I don't need to explain myself."

"You the owner?"

"Yes, I am."

Reacher said, "I'll leave when I've had a cup of coffee."

"You'll leave now."

"Black, no sugar."

"I don't want trouble."

"You already got trouble. If I get a cup of coffee, I'll walk out of here. If I don't get a cup of coffee, these guys can try to throw me out, and you'll spend the rest of the day cleaning blood off the floor and all day tomorrow shopping for new chairs and tables."

The guy in the apron said nothing.

Reacher said, "Black, no sugar."

The guy in the apron stood still for a long moment and then headed back to the kitchen. A minute later the waitress came out with a single cup balanced on a saucer. She carried it across the room and set it down in front of Reacher, hard enough to slop some of the contents out of the cup and into the saucer.

"Enjoy," she said.

Reacher lifted the cup and wiped the base on his

sleeve. Set the cup down on the table and emptied the saucer into it. Set the cup back on the saucer and squared it in front of him. Then he raised it again and took a sip.

Not bad, he thought. A little weak, a little stewed, but at heart it was a decent commercial product. Better than most diners, worse than most franchise places. Right in the middle of the curve. The cup was a porcelain monstrosity with a lip about three-eighths of an inch thick. It was cooling the drink too fast. Too wide, too shallow, too much mass. Reacher was no big fan of fine china, but he believed a receptacle ought to serve its contents.

The four guys were still clustered all around. Two sitting, two standing now. Reacher ignored them and drank, slowly at first, and then faster as the coffee grew cold. He drained the cup and set it back on the saucer. Pushed it away, slowly and care-fully, until it was exactly centered on the table. Then he moved his left arm fast and went for his pocket. The four guys jumped. Reacher came out with a dollar bill and flattened it and trapped it under the saucer.

"So let's go," he said.

The guy standing at the head of the table moved out of the way. Reacher scraped his chair back and stood up. Eleven customers watched him do it. He pushed his chair in neatly and stepped around the head of the table and headed for the door. He sensed the four guys behind him. Heard their boots on the tile. They were forming up in single file, threading between tables, stepping past the sign and the regis-ter. The room was silent.

Reacher pushed the door and stepped outside to the street. The air was cool, but the sun was out. The sidewalk was concrete, cast in five-by-five squares. The squares were separated by inch-wide expansion joints. The joints were filled with black compound.

Reacher turned left and took four steps until he was clear of the parked pick-up and then he stopped and turned back, with the afternoon sun behind him. The four guys formed up in front of him, with the sun in their eyes. The guy who had stood at the head of the table said, "Now you need to get out."

Reacher said, "I am out."

"Out of town."

Reacher said nothing.

The guy said, "Make a left, and then Main Street is four blocks up. When you get there, turn either left or right, west or east. We don't care which. Just keep on walking."

Reacher asked, "You still do that here?"

"Do what?"

"Run people out of town."

"You bet we do."

"You want to tell me why you do?"

"We don't have to tell you why we do."

Reacher said, "I just got here."

"So?"

"So I'm staying."

The guy on the end of the line pushed his rolled cuffs above his elbows and took a step forward. Broken nose, missing teeth. Reacher glanced at the guy's wrists. The width of a person's wrists was the only failsafe indicator of a person's raw strength. This guy's were wider than a long-stemmed rose, narrower than a two-by-four. Closer to the two-by-four than the rose.

Reacher said, "You're picking on the wrong man."

The guy who had been doing all the talking said, "You think?"

Reacher nodded. "I have to warn you. I promised my mother, a long time ago. She said I had to give folks a chance to walk away."

"You a momma's boy?"

"She liked to see fair play."

"There are four of us. One of you."

Reacher's hands were down by his sides, relaxed, gently curled. His feet were apart, securely planted. He could feel the hard concrete through the soles of his shoes. It was textured. It had been brushed with a yard broom just before it dried, ten years earlier. He folded the fingers of his left hand flat against his palm. Raised the hand, very slowly. Brought it level with his shoulder, palm out. The four guys stared at it. The way his fingers were folded made them think he was hiding something. *But what?* He snapped his fingers open. *Nothing there.* In the same split second he moved sideways and heaved his right fist up like a convulsion and caught the guy who had stepped forward with a colossal uppercut to the jaw. The guy had been breathing through his mouth because of his broken nose and the massive impact snapped his jaw shut and lifted him up off the ground and dumped him back down in a vertical heap on the sidewalk. Like a puppet with the strings cut. Unconscious before he got halfway there.

"Now there are only three of you," Reacher said. "Still one of me."

They weren't total amateurs. They reacted pretty well and pretty fast. They sprang back and apart into a wide defensive semicircle and crouched, fists ready.

Reacher said, "You can still walk away."

The guy that had been doing the talking said, "I don't think so."

"You're not good enough."

"You got lucky."

"Only suckers get sucker punched."

"Won't happen twice."

Reacher said nothing.

The guy said, "Get out of town. You can't take us three on one."

"Try me."

"Can't be done. Not now."

Reacher nodded. "Maybe you're right. Maybe one of you will stay on your feet long enough to get to me."

"You can count on it."

"But the question you need to ask is, which one of you will it be? Right now you've got no way of knowing. One of you will be driving the other three to the hospital for a six-month stay. You want me out of town bad enough to take those odds?"

Nobody spoke. Stalemate. Reacher rehearsed his next moves. A right-footed kick to the groin of the guy on his left, spin back with an elbow to the head for the guy in the middle, duck under the inevitable roundhouse swing incoming from the guy on the right, let him follow through, put an elbow in his kidney. One, two, three, no fundamental problem. Maybe a little clean-up afterward, more feet and elbows. Main difficulty would be limiting the damage. Careful restraint would be required. It was always wiser to stay on the right side of the line, closer to brawling than homicide.

The tableau stayed frozen. Reacher upright and relaxed, three guys in a crouch, one sprawled face down on the floor, breathing but bleeding and not moving. In the distance beyond the three guys Reacher could see people going about their lawful business on the sidewalks. He could see cars and trucks driving slow on the streets, pausing at four-way stops, moving on.

Then he saw one particular car blow straight through a four-way and head in his direction. A Crown Victoria, white and gold, black push bars on the front, a light bar on the roof, antennas on the trunk lid. A shield on the door, with *DPD* scrolled across it. *Despair Police Department*. A heavyset cop in a tan jacket visible behind the glass.

"Behind you," Reacher said. "The cavalry is here." But he didn't move. And he kept his eyes on the three guys. The cop's arrival didn't necessarily guarantee anything. Not yet. The three guys looked mad enough to move straight from a verbal warning to an actual assault charge. Maybe they already had so many they figured one more wouldn't make any difference. *Small towns*. In Reacher's experience they all had a lunatic fringe.

The Crown Vic braked hard in the gutter. The

door swung open. The driver took a riot gun from a holster between the seats. Climbed out. Pumped the gun and held it diagonally across his chest. He was a big guy. White, maybe forty. Black hair. Wide neck. Tan jacket, brown pants, black shoes, a groove in his forehead from a Smokey the Bear hat that was presumably now resting on his passenger seat. He stood behind the three guys and looked around. Surveyed the scene. *Not exactly rocket science,* Reacher thought. *Three guys surrounding a fourth? We're not discussing the weather here.*

The cop said, "Back off now." Deep voice. Authoritative. The three guys stepped backward. The cop stepped forward. They swapped their relative positions. Now the three guys were behind the cop. The cop moved his gun. Pointed it straight at Reacher's chest.

"You're under arrest," he said.